Special thanks to the following people for helping breathe life into the Godsverse:

Amba Nevell, Andrea Johnson, Anij Fallows, Ashley, Beth Barany, Brad Com, Burnel Smith, C, Caledonia, Cat Fleming (MadCatter), Catherine Leja, Chad Bowden, Chris Call, Christina Lopez, Christine Chandra, Christopher Stillwell, Cristian Dinu, Daniel Groves, Dave Baxter, David Irgang, Dr.Salt, Earl Weiss, EconKelly, Elizabeth Noel Bennett, Emerson Kasak, Emily, Emily, Eric Williamson, Erica, Erica Hecker, Erica Jordan, Eva Jayet, Garry James Watts, Gavran, Genevieve Perosa, Gerald P. McDaniel, GMarkC, goodmancoming, Greywolfe, Isaac "Will It Work" Dansicker, James Kralik, Jason Crase, Jason 'XenoPhage' Frisvold, Jeff Frisone, Jeff Lewis, Jeremy Reppy, John "AcesofDeath7" Mullens, John Idlor, JohnDoe, Joshua Bowers, Joshua McGinnis, Juanita Nesbitt, Katrina Kunstmann, Kenny Endlich, Laura Ann Moylan, Lia, maileguy, Manic, Martin Nehmiz, Matthew Johnson, Maxi Organ, Melissa Showers, Michael Di Salvo, Nathaniel Adams Jr, Nick Smith, Paul Nygard, Paul Rose Jr., Pavlos Chatzipantelidis, Peter Anders, Peter Tarasewich, Randy Graham, Rebecca Carter, Rebecca M. Senese, Rhel ná DecVandé, Robert Brown, Robinflight,Rowan Stone, Ryan Scott James, Scantrontb, Scott Chisholm, Scott Kilburn, Shannon Carlin, Sil, Snir Kolodni, Stephan Szabo, Stephen Ballentine, Sunny Side Up, Venron, Victoria Nohelty, Walter Weiss, Winter, and Xavier Hugonet.

GODSVERSE PLANETS

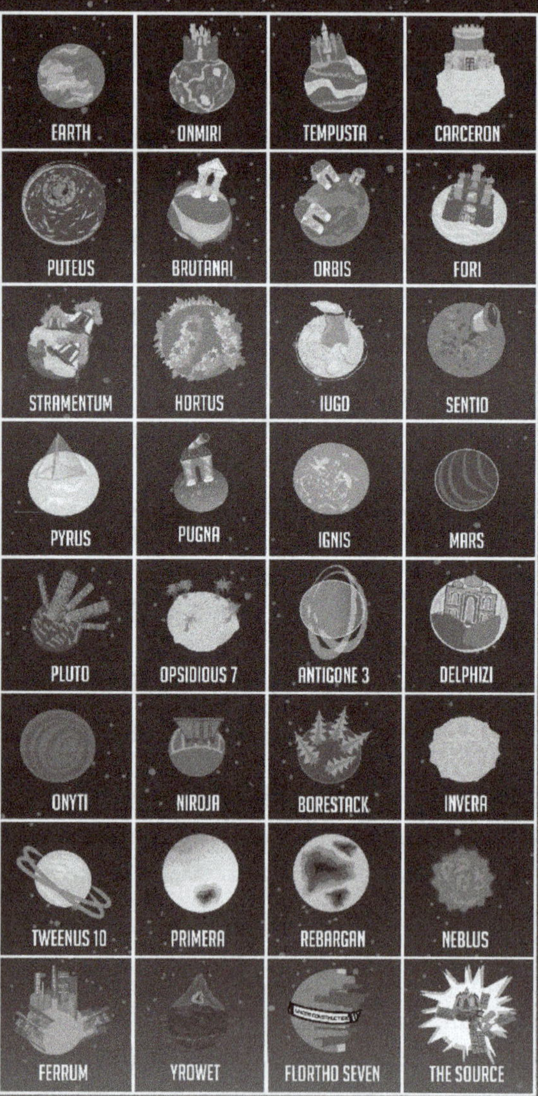

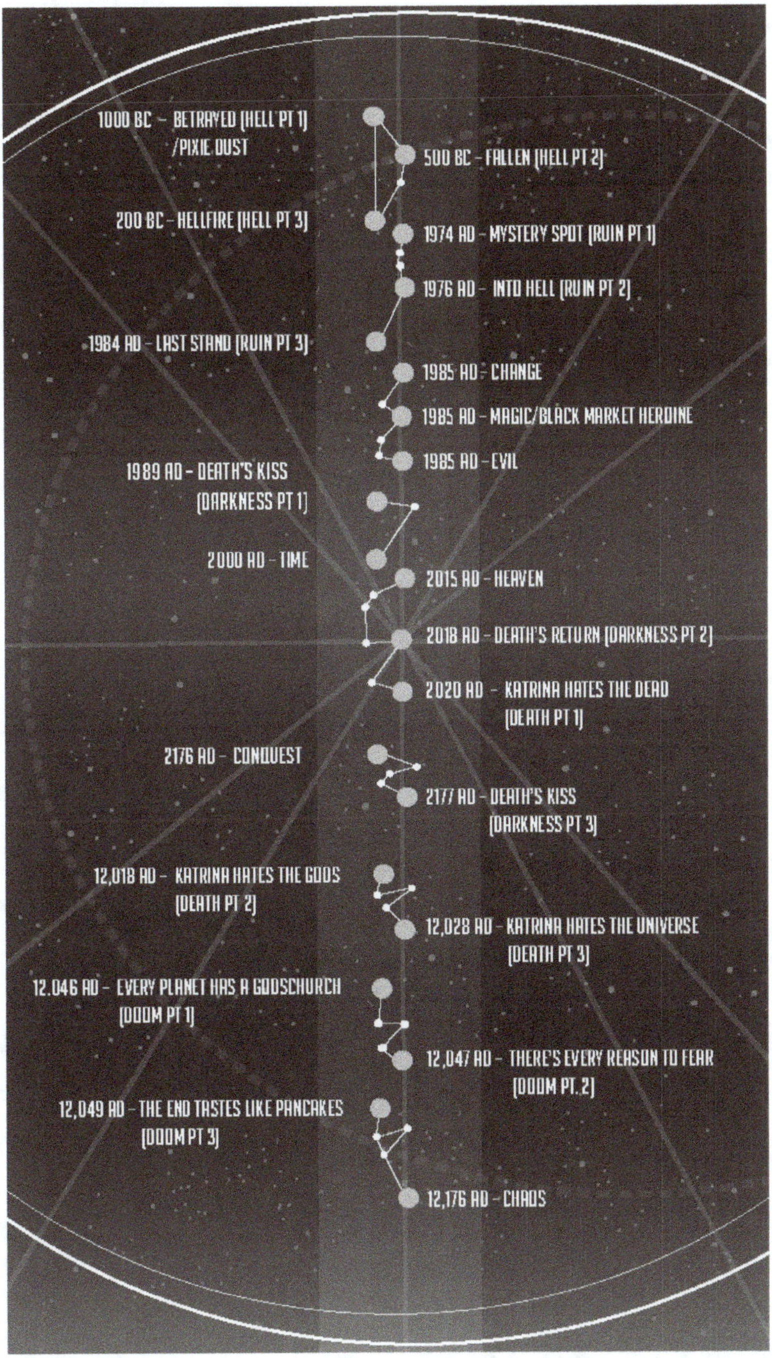

1000 BC – BETRAYED (HELL PT 1)
/PIXIE DUST
500 BC – FALLEN (HELL PT 2)
200 BC – HELLFIRE (HELL PT 3)
1974 AD – MYSTERY SPOT (RUIN PT 1)
1976 AD – INTO HELL (RUIN PT 2)
1984 AD – LAST STAND (RUIN PT 3)
1985 AD – CHANGE
1985 AD – MAGIC/BLACK MARKET HEROINE
1985 AD – EVIL
1989 AD – DEATH'S KISS
(DARKNESS PT 1)
2000 AD – TIME
2015 AD – HEAVEN
2018 AD – DEATH'S RETURN (DARKNESS PT 2)
2020 AD – KATRINA HATES THE DEAD
(DEATH PT 1)
2176 AD – CONQUEST
2177 AD – DEATH'S KISS
(DARKNESS PT 3)
12,018 AD – KATRINA HATES THE GODS
(DEATH PT 2)
12,028 AD – KATRINA HATES THE UNIVERSE
(DEATH PT 3)
12,046 AD – EVERY PLANET HAS A GODSCHURCH
(DOOM PT 1)
12,047 AD – THERE'S EVERY REASON TO FEAR
(DOOM PT 2)
12,049 AD – THE END TASTES LIKE PANCAKES
(DOOM PT 3)
12,176 AD – CHAOS

ALSO BY RUSSELL NOHELTY

NOVELS
My Father Didn't Kill Himself
Sorry for Existing
Gumshoes: The Case of Madison's Father
Invasion
The Vessel
The Void Calls Us Home
Worst Thing in the Universe
Anna and the Dark Place
The Marked Ones
The Dragon Scourge
The Dragon Champion
The Dragon Goddess
The Obsidian Spindle Saga

COMICS and OTHER ILLUSTRATED WORK
The Little Bird and the Little Worm
Ichabod Jones: Monster Hunter
Gherkin Boy
How NOT to Invade Earth

www.russellnohelty.com

EVIL

Book 2 of The Godsverse Chronicles

By:
Russell Nohelty

Edited by:
Leah Lederman

Proofread by:
Katrina Roets & Toni Cox

Cover by:
Psycat Covers

Planet chart and timeline design by:
Andrea Rosales

BOOK 1

CHAPTER 1

Bronard, Missouri wasn't on my list of top 10,000 cities in the world to visit, and yet that was where I found myself, sitting across from a magical pixie, a mere twenty-four hours after a crazy monster had tried to use my blood to start the Apocalypse…all because I was a demon.

No, I wasn't just a demon. I was the antichrist. Actually, that's not right, either. I'm *an* antichrist. One of dozens, hundreds, thousands. I had no idea how many little demon babies were growing up around the world waiting to explode and cause the Apocalypse, just that I wasn't the only one. According to Kimberly, whatever crazy potion I drank last night had diffused the part of my blood that was capable of ending the world…but that only neutralized the antichrist part of me.

I was still a demon and would be for the rest of my hopefully rather long life. On top of that, demons and other evil creatures would continue to pop out of the woodwork and cause trouble for me if I stayed in Los Angeles.

Which meant I was a danger to myself and my mother until I figured out how to control my powers and could defend myself at least, and that fact brought me to Bronard, Missouri, a small town in the middle of nowhere, hours outside of St. Louis, where cows outnumbered people ten to one—according to a proud sign outside of town.

"You're not eating," Kimberly said to me with a small smile. "This isn't going to suck any less with an empty stomach."

How was she my age? She wasn't big, but she commanded a room with confidence and poise. Even with half the diner staring daggers at her, she didn't cower or fold to them. Bronard wasn't the kind of place that welcomed dark-skinned teenagers. Or maybe they were wary of her because there was a very good chance she could kill everybody in this restaurant all at one time with both hands tied behind her back and not break a sweat.

"I'm not hungry." That was strange in and of itself. I was always hungry.

Kimberly reached over and pulled a fry from my plate. "That's too bad. If there's one thing Bronard does well, it's diner food. This town runs on pancakes and ribs." She popped the whole fry in her mouth and smiled at me. After a few seconds, her face fell. "They're nice people. You'll see."

She was talking about my new "parents," Carl and Junebug. "I'm sure they are, but like, I just wanna go home."

"If you go home, you're putting everyone in danger, including your mother. I can't protect you in Los Angeles. I can protect you here."

"But you really aren't protecting me, are you?" My eyes narrowed. "You're dumping me here and leaving so that Junebug and Carl can protect me."

Kimberly leaned forward. "There's a lot of fairy-folk in this town, and they look out for each other. I'm leaving you in the best hands I can, given the circumstances."

After I'd said goodbye to my savior Ollie and left the coast of Hawaii with Kimberly, I was filled with excited adrenaline, ready for a new challenge, thrilled to start a fresh adventure. However, in the hours that followed, that excitement drained from me, and I realized the ramifications of my decision. I was relegated to a small-town life, cut off from everything I ever knew, and I would have to build from nothing again.

"I don't want to seem ungrateful," I started. "But—"

"You can stop there. Nobody has ever looked good after they started a sentence like that." She shook her head. "Listen, this is your decision. I can tell Junebug you had a change of heart and take you back to Los Angeles right now, let you fend for yourself. We both know how well that worked last time."

"Hey!" I said. "I survived."

"You survived because you lucked into finding Ollie, and that somehow Ollie knew Phil, and Phil contacted me. If any of those things didn't happen, you would be dead, and you know it."

I started to argue but stopped. She was right, of course, and any argument I formulated seemed stupid in comparison. "I do appreciate it."

Kimberly yawned. We had been up for over a day now, and it was wearing on both of us. "You could do a better job showing it, but like I said, I know this sucks."

I popped a fry in my mouth. I had to admit, they were really good. Just the right amount of salt. I thought for a second, chewing slowly before I finally looked at her again. "Why did it have to happen to me?"

"I don't know," Kimberly said as if she expected the question. "Life sucks. Did I ever tell you how I was kidnapped by a banshee when I was eight?"

I shook my head. "No, I would have remembered that kind of story."

"Well, it happened," she said. "It brought me to Hell, like real-life Hell, and I was rescued by my mentor, Julia, who I watched die in front of me some years later."

"That sucks."

"Yeah, and I go to bed most nights wondering why all this happened to me. I just want to play soccer, graduate, and go to college. Here I am, helping you instead. Do you know I have an exam today? Like, a hard one, too. I am woefully underprepared."

"Why are you doing it then?" I asked.

"Because we all gotta deal with our lot in life. We can't run from it. Destiny doesn't care what we want."

"Sure you could, you could run away."

"Then you would be dead," she replied. "I can't have that on my conscience. I have these powers for a reason, and it's my responsibility to use them to help people. Especially because everything else in the world is working to hurt them."

"Crud," I replied. "When you put it like that, I guess I should just shut my mouth."

Kimberly took another fry. "That was my polite way of saying as much. Now, if you're done having a pity party, finish eating so I can introduce you to your adopted parents."

I swallowed my sadness and dug into the food. The salty, deep-fried chicken sandwich made me feel better. It really was some amazing diner food. Kimberly was right about that, even if I had my doubts about everything else.

***

After stuffing ourselves with a second helping of fries, Kimberly and I left the diner and began walking down the street. It was mid-morning, and the sun beat down, protecting us from the winter cold.

"Why don't we just flash directly to the house? I mean, you can literally teleport from one place to another at will."

"I can," she replied. "As long as I know exactly where I'm going. Otherwise, I'll get lost in the ether, and I absolutely do not want that."

"No, I imagine you wouldn't." The rocky ground crunched under our feet as we walked. "Doesn't walking seem boring by comparison, though?"

She kicked a rock through the white fence next to us, and we watched it skid into a thatch of corn stalks. "Honestly, no. When you can flash anywhere you want, walking is a luxury. Besides, another reason we're walking is for you to get a sense of the town—your town." She pointed to a big silo painted to look like Big Bird. "That's the Henson Silo. Aside from the water tower, it's the highest place in town, so you get your bearings if you need it. Sun sets right over the silo from your house." She pointed over to the other side of the road, where a big blue water tower loomed over everything else. "That's the Bronard water tower, tallest structure in town. Sun rises behind it, directly east."

"A silo and a water tower are my two biggest landmarks. Jesus Christ, what did I sign up for?"

"It's not like Los Angeles has a lot of big buildings, either."

"No, but it has more than here."

"Fair enough." She laughed. "Small-town life takes getting used to, but there's a calmness to it. You're not going to get a lot of high-profile celebrities rolling through, but everyone will know your name. For our purposes, that's important." We reached a stop sign, and she pointed to the right. "This way."

"What if I hate it?" I said, following her. "This is a big change for me."

She thought for a moment. "Did you like Los Angeles?"

I nodded. "Of course. What's not to like?"

"So much stuff." Kimberly kicked another rock off the side of the road. "I mean, it's dirty. The people…suck. Plus, everything costs a ton of money. It smells like smoke everywhere you go…did I mention the people suck?"

"I'm from Los Angeles. So is Ollie. Do we suck?"

"Ollie most definitely sucks," she said playfully. "But you're okay, I guess. I'm just saying, this place has its charm if you let yourself see it. It's not as progressive as the big city, but it's beautiful country. You can actually smell the freshness in the air."

That I couldn't deny. As we walked, the sun glimmered in gold, orange, and yellow over the wheat fields, rippling from the wind. There was a tranquility to it that I never had in Los Angeles. I loved LA, but the city felt slapped together in a hurry. Even "new" roads felt a hundred years old and taking a stroll without a destination just didn't happen there, not unless you had a death wish.

After a twenty-minute walk, with the water tower behind us in the distance, we turned down a dirt road. "Here we are."

A rusted shed sat offset to the right of the driveway. An old tractor rested inside, covered by a dirty, rusted, metal overhang. Some farm equipment stood against the wall of the shed. I recognized a hoe and a shovel, but the rest were foreign to me. Wild grass grew in thick patches and several large trees arched over the road. At the end of it was a big white house with a pick-up out front. Two rocking chairs sat on the porch, and on them, a Black man and white woman sat, drinking from coffee cups.

When Kimberly saw them, she smiled. "Hi, Carl! Junebug!"

"There she is," Carl said, standing. "We thought you had a change of heart, girl. Where you been?"

"Took her to Cheryl's for breakfast."

"Last supper," Junebug said with a smile. "Just kidding, kid. Cheryl's is pretty good for an out-of-towner. You must be Anjelica."

I nodded. "Yes, ma'am."

"Good manners," Carl said. "Better than the last one you brought 'round."

"The last one?" I asked, confused.

June set her cup down and walked toward me. I placed my hand out to shake hers, but she wasn't interested in my hand. Instead, she wrapped me in a big hug. "Don't you worry about that none. All you gotta know is that you're safe here."

I wanted to protest, but something about her energy made me collapse into her bosom, and suddenly all the pain of the last day, everything that I had been through, burst out of me. I fell into her, crying.

"It's okay, child," Junebug said. "You let it all out. There's no shame in crying. None at all."

"Kimberly," Carl said, waving her forward. "Why don't you come inside for some coffee. Leave those two outside for a moment."

Kimberly patted me on the back as she walked past. The weight of my legs became too heavy a burden to carry, and I slid to the ground. Junebug came with me, settling onto her knees. I collapsed into her lap and cried, and cried, and cried, for my mother, for myself, and for the life that I left behind.

CHAPTER 2

I laid on the dirt road in front of Junebug and Carl's house until all my tears dried up and my back stopped heaving.

"You feel better?" Junebug asked when my whimpers fell silent.

"I don't think I'm ever going to feel better again."

She sighed. "You will. Someday you'll wake up, and you'll barely feel the pain at all."

"How?" I asked hopefully. "How do you know?"

"I'm quite a bit older than you, and I've lost a lot in my years. Most people have a lifetime to get comfortable with that much sadness. You just got too much thrown on you too soon. You left your mom, right?"

I nodded, wiping my face. "Uh-huh."

"I lost my mom to cancer about a decade ago. Lost my dad, too, and my brother. It's awful every time. You have any siblings?"

I shook my head. "No, I was an only child. My mom called me a spoiled…brat…" When I said that last word, the tears came again. "Brat…because of…because of it," I sputtered out through my tears.

Junebug rubbed her hand through my hair. "It's going to come in waves like that. Over time, those crashing waves recede and finally just leave a little wake behind them. That's when it gets survivable, though none of us get out of this life alive."

I looked up at her. For the first time, I saw June's bright green eyes and her soft skin. Age hadn't hit her hard, and she barely had any wrinkles on her face, though there was great wisdom in it all the same. "Thank you." I took a deep breath. "When did you find out you were different?"

"Different?"

"You're a fairy, right?"

She laughed. "Oh yeah. Sorry, 'round here that doesn't make me very different from most of the people." She thought for a moment. "It was later in life when my mom was sick. I don't have much fairy blood, just a drop, so I can't do much. Not like Carl. He's more like Kimberly. He can move through the ether at will. Very handy for vacations."

I wiped my nose on my sleeve. "I think I'm ready to go inside now."

"Oh good," she said. "This road was not meant for sitting."

Junebug stood up with a small groan and brushed the dirt off her flower dress, then held out her arm to help me up. I wiped myself off and followed her inside. The wooden steps up to the porch creaked as my weight pressed down upon them, and I made sure to note that for later in case I needed to leave unnoticed.

She pulled the storm door open and held it open for me. The hardwood foyer was cluttered with shoes and coats. A mirror hung over a little table filled with keys, and I had my first look at myself since before I was kidnapped.

I was a wreck. My freckled face was blotchy and red, and my red hair frayed like wild thatch. It hadn't been combed in two days. My green eyes were cracked with red veins from crying, and my nose was as puffy as the bags under my eyes.

"I look terrible."

"No," Junebug said, pulling a hair tie from her wrist. "Well, yes, but we can fix that."

She handed it to me, and I pulled my hair back into a ponytail. "Thank you." I still looked terrible, but slightly less so now. "I feel like I'm just going to keep saying that forever now."

"Well, don't thank me until I show you around." She pointed me to a room set off the main foyer. Ruddy old couches were arranged in front of a TV at the far end. "This is the TV room." She turned to the left, where Kimberly and Carl waved from a long table. "That's the dining room." She pointed to another door. "Behind there is the kitchen. That's where I spend a lot of time."

"You a cook?"

"I have a little bakery in the middle of town, sells everything from bread to pies. Pretty popular, too, if I do say so. Most of the ingredients I use come right from this farm or from trading our produce for whatever we need."

"Sounds nice," I said. "Quaint even."

"There isn't much around here, but we like it. You'll get used to it in a while. Or you won't, and then it's good you only have a couple of years before you're off on your own." In front of us, the wooden staircase matched the grain of the foyer.

She beckoned me to followed her up the stairs, which led to another short hallway with four doors. She pointed to the one on the far left. "There at the end is our room." She moved her attention to the door next to it. "That's the office. Carl likes to putz around in there when he's not out in the fields." She walked to the furthest door on the right and knocked. "Lizzie, open up!"

"Coming!" The door opened, and a light-skinned girl opened it. She was every bit the mix of Carl and Junebug, with June's green eyes and Carl's stern jaw. Her hair was buzzed short, and she wore a bullring in her nose.

"Take that out," June said, pulling on the bullring. I gasped, thinking it might rip her septum out, but instead, it slid off like nothing. June glanced in my direction. "It's just a clip-on. She's twelve and just getting to that rebellious stage."

I chuckled. "I remember it well."

"Who's this?" Lizzie asked, studying me.

"Lizzie, meet Anjelica."

"Hi," I said with a little wave.

"She's staying with us for a while," Junebug replied.

"Another one?" Lizzie rolled her eyes. "Nice to meet you, I guess. Can I go now?"

"Yes, but next time I see you, I expect a better attitude, yes? Otherwise, don't bother coming out 'til school tomorrow."

"Fine," Lizzie said over her shoulder as she shut the door.

"She's nice," I said.

"Usually, at least," Junebug turned back to me. "I wish I could beg my mother's forgiveness for how I treated her at that age. I guess this is my punishment."

"I heard that!" Lizzie called from behind her door.

"Good!" Junebug said, the smile never leaving her face. She pointed to the room next door. "This is your room."

She held the door for me, and I walked through. At home, the walls of my room were painted a dark green and covered in posters. This room had boring, plain, white walls that were bare, save for a single flower painting near the window. On the wall closest to Lizzie was a long closet with double doors. The furniture was plain. A writing desk, a dresser, and a mirror. Near the window on the other side was a small curio. Along the far wall was a queen size bed, covered in a similar floral pattern as Junebug's dress, along with a small, whitewashed vanity.

"We'll go to the store and get you some proper clothes later today, but I'll leave you to settle for now."

"Actually," I said. "Could I have some coffee?"

"You sure you don't want to sleep?"

"I know I should, but…can I have some anyway?"

***

There was a simple reason why I wanted coffee. Kimberly was downstairs, and once she left, I had no idea when I would see her again. She was the only anchor to my past life. When she left, I would have nothing left and no choice but to literally start from scratch.

I sat at the dining room table listening to Kimberly and Carl swap stories, each more fantastical than the last, until my second cup of coffee was gone.

"And then," Carl clapped his hands together, "just like that, I was gone, and the chonchon was left flying toward an empty space in the forest." He laughed. "I would have paid to see its face when I just vanished in thin air."

"You say that now," Junebug said. "But I was there when you tumbled home—you were shook."

"It's basically a human face with bat wings." He looked directly at me when he said that. Kimberly must have told him I didn't know anything about magical life. Either that or my confusion was etched deep on my face. "And I don't want to meet the person who isn't scared of something like that. Ugly little buggers."

Kimberly took a final sip of coffee and then leaned back in her chair, stretching. "I could stay here all day swapping stories, but as I've told Anjelica, I have an exam today, and my mom is going to freak out that I was gone all night without calling."

"You're gonna get so grounded," I said, smiling.

She stood. "You laugh, but I will."

It sounded nice to have a mother that cared about you enough to ground you, even when you were a powerful pixie who could slaughter demons. I would be lucky if my mom even noticed I was gone before next weekend when she finally got a day off, and even then, it's not like we kept the same schedule. She might literally go weeks before realizing I was gone.

"I'll walk you out," Carl said.

I pushed my chair out. "Mind if I do it?"

Carl shrugged. "Fine with me. I need to go feed the hogs anyway."

"Don't take too long, dear," Junebug said, catching my eye. "If you're not going to sleep, you can help me bring some food to the bakery and we'll get you those clothes."

"Well, I didn't say I wasn't going to sle—" I looked over at Kimberly, and she shook her head. "I mean, that sounds great."

Kimberly led me outside and gave me an apologetic smile. "This is your life now." She dropped her head. "Don't get me wrong, it's a good life. They're nice people, but I know it's not what you signed up for." She leaped forward and hugged me tightly. "I'm glad you aren't dead."

"Me too." I patted her on the back. "And I have you to thank for it, for all of this."

"I don't think you understand how lucky you are." She pulled back from me. "You will, though. In time."

"I hope so."

She squeezed my arms before turning from me. "You saved the world, Anjelica."

"All I did was not die."

Kimberly raised her eyebrows slightly. "Sometimes, that's all it takes." She reached into her pocket and pulled out a black opal pendant on a silver necklace. "Don't ever take this off, no matter what. Understand?"

I put on the necklace. "I won't."

"Good." With that, she dropped a pinch of the pink pixie dust she kept in a pouch on her belt, vanishing in a puff of pink smoke.

The dust tickled my nose. When it had settled, I turned back to the house. Junebug was already bringing a plate of donuts down the steps toward the pick-up truck.

"You ride in the back, love. The wind will wake you right up."

That couldn't be a safe way to travel, but I hadn't been making very safe choices lately. I shrugged and hopped into the bed of the pick-up, ready for a new adventure.

CHAPTER 3

"How you doin' back there, hon?" Junebug asked from the front of the cab as we rattled down the street. "It's not much further."

"I'm fine!" I screamed back. I was not fine. I was struggling not to slide around the back of the cab, clinging tight to a tray of muffins June asked me to hold after she stuffed the cab full of trays. It was freezing, and the wind whipping over the hood made it worse.

I did my best to focus on the route from June's house. We made a right from the main road, away from the water tower, and across two train tracks until we arrived at a crossroad, where we took two lefts and a right before I lost the thread. The roads were winding and undulating, and I cheered inwardly when we finally reached the center of town, and Junebug slowed to a crawl after having gunned it irresponsibly fast on the country roads.

"This is Main Street," Junebug said. "You'll get to know it well."

Junebug pulled up to a small strip mall on the main drag. The town was out in full force, even though it was a workday, and dozens of people scurried down the sidewalks on either side of the street. I had seen quaint little towns in movies, but I had never been in one. The colorful vinyl siding alternated between every building, from forest green to powder blue to burgundy. All of the buildings had adorable white shutters on their windows.

"Can you help me?" Junebug said, pulling a tray out of the front seat after lowering the bed so I could scoot out of the truck. I centered the tray of muffins, and she placed another into my hands before I could answer. "It's over there. Dessertation."

She pointed to a powder blue shop across the street with *Dessertation* scrawled on the window in pretty cursive. "That's funny. Like dissertation?"

"What?" Junebug said, kicking the door closed after filling her hands with trays. "No, like dessert vacation, hon. The heck is a dissertation?"

"Like a PhD? You're kind of like a doctor of baking."

She looked at me, deadpan. "I like you, but that was a real dumb thing you said."

"Sorry," I replied, hanging my head.

"Don't drop yer head, kiddo," she said, crossing the street. "You need your head on a swivel at this intersection. People drive like maniacs through it. Come on, then."

Junebug scooted the door to the bakery open with her butt, and the bell atop the entrance rang to welcome us. She placed the trays on a glass counter filled with bakery goodness and walked around it to give a middle-aged woman in a white apron a hug. "Sorry, Betty. We had a busy morning."

"Oh, it's okay," Betty said. "Hasn't been busy yet, but Earl's going to come in for another two dozen glazed in about fifteen minutes."

Junebug pointed to a set of trays. She had made exactly two dozen glazed donuts. "I had a feeling."

"How do you always know?" Betty said.

"Intuition." Junebug winked at me.

I had a feeling that one of the gifts she had been given as a pixie was some sort of magical perception or something like that.

"Who's your friend?" Betty said. "And why is she standing in the doorway like a fool?"

"This is Anjelica. She's…staying with me for a while."

"Ah, another one of your strays." Betty raised her hand. "Well, nice to meet you. Anybody ever tell ya that you make a better door than a window?"

"Huh?" I said.

"Come in out of the doorway, sweetie," Junebug said softly.

I took a few steps into the shop and was overwhelmed by the smell of bread. I loved that smell. There was a bakery not far from my house, Randy's, and every time I passed it, I literally wanted to eat everything inside after one whiff…and that paled in comparison to the heavenly scents here at June's place.

"It smells great in here," I said, setting down the trays.

"It better," Betty said. "I've been baking since four."

"In the morning!" I breathed, incredulous. I was pretty sure I had been fighting demons at that time. The thought that people were going about their lives while mine was about to end left me shook for a moment.

"Every morning," Betty said with a smile that said she truly loved it.

"We've grown a little too big for this space, so every morning, I have to supplement our supply with some of my own." Junebug covered her mouth with a finger. "We're not supposed to, but what the health inspectors don't know won't hurt them."

I had to admit, Junebug was more fun than I expected. I worried that her rustic, down-home charm was going to wear on me quickly, but she was spunky, and she made cookies, which, in a mom, were two things that I highly valued.

Junebug must have seen me eyeing the eclairs because she pulled a pair of tongs and handed me one. "Take one."

"Oh no, I couldn't," I said.

"Girlie, you had a night. You could probably eat this whole place down to the floorboards and still deserve another one. Now, eat. I insist."

"Don't insult her," Betty said. "Trust me, denying food from a Campbell is an insult."

"Darn tootin' it is," Junebug said as I took the éclair.

"It's my favorite," I said, taking a bite. It was unlike anything I had eaten before. I thought I'd had delicious eclairs before, but this one set a new standard for everything else in my life. "Oh my god."

Junebug watched me with a knowing smile. "Kind of makes all that crap you dealt with worth it, eh?"

A bit of gooey vanilla cream slid down my throat. "Not even a little bit, but this is pretty amazing."

"Go wait outside for me. I'll be done in a second, and then we'll go shopping."

I didn't argue. I couldn't. Junebug's food had driven me to complacency. I would have done anything she asked me to as long as she kept feeding me her delicious goodies.

***

Dana's Dress Barn was not Melrose or Beverly Hills, but it was…a woman's clothing shop…and the things she stocked technically counted as clothes. I wasn't trying to be picky, especially since Junebug was paying the bill, but not many items spoke to me. After over an hour of searching through the racks, I pulled out four blouses, two pairs of jeans, a jacket, and three dresses that I wouldn't be mortified to wear. Mostly, I just enjoyed talking to Junebug.

"That one makes your butt look big," she said with a scrunched-up nose after I came out of the dressing room one last time. "I guess we'll just go with what we have and hope we can go to the mall this weekend."

"You guys have a mall?"

She grabbed the clothes we chose from a chair where she stashed them. "Well, it's an hour away, but it's a nice drive. We do a lot of driving out here, that's for sure. Not much is close."

"So did I, back in LA."

I never had a mother to do girlie things with, and my mom was an only child, which meant I didn't have aunts or cousins, or really anybody to hang out with that was family. Besides, it's not like she was going to have two demon-spawn babies. I'm sure I was enough of a handful in that department. I didn't blame her, of course, at least not much, for being an absentee parent. Mom worked as a nurse, and she was pretty much always on call. When she wasn't, the odd hours she worked always made her tired.

"So, can I ask why Lizzie is home today? I mean, I know it's a school day and all." I set down the clothes on the counter. The over-makeuped teller started ringing us up.

A curt smile from Junebug told me it was a sore subject. "That girl," she muttered. "She skipped school, so they suspended her…which is letting her miss another day of school. I swear they are idiots at that school. Why would you keep a kid home from school as punishment for them not wanting to go to school?"

"I gotta say, I agree with them," the woman behind the counter said. "Being in your house is the worst punishment I could imagine."

"Good for you, Dana." Junebug threw a credit card onto the counter. "Just ring us up, already. I don't need your lip." She turned to me. "Where was I?"

"You were complaining about the school and suspensions."

"Right." She pressed her finger to the bridge of her nose. "They are idiots, all of them. But you'll find that out soon enough. You start there next week, assuming all your paperwork is in order."

Oh yeah. School. That would be…fun? No. That wasn't the right word, was it?

CHAPTER 4

In the darkness, a hand crept toward me as I tossed and turned, fighting against the caffeine and an overactive mind. Its knobby knuckles latched onto the foot of my bed and then inched up onto my mattress. It crept along my leg, and my eyes popped open at its touch. I tried to kick it off, but suddenly, I couldn't move, except to let out a small whimper. I watched in horror as it skittered up my calf toward my thigh and hopped onto my stomach.

The wind left me as the hand continued up my chest until it reached my neck. It ringed my throat gently, gingerly caressing it with a finger. I shuddered at the touch of this foreign beast, but when I tried to jerk free, my body wouldn't listen.

After a moment of stillness, every muscle on the beast tensed. It leaped into the air and shot forward, palm open, grasping at my arm and trying to wrench me off the bed. I fought against it with all the strength I could muster. It yanked me harder, and my arm popped out of its socket at the shoulder. I called out in pain, but nobody came to help. Latching on to the post at the foot of my bed with my good arm, I tried to pull back. With one more pull, the post buckled and snapped. I fell into the darkness and disa—

My eyes snapped open, and instinctively, I grabbed at my shoulder. The light from morning fell into my eyes while I sat up and took great gasps of air. It was all a dream. A horrible dream. Then, the door to my room swung open, and Lizzie stood at the entrance, dressed like Robert Smith from the Cure down to the dark eyeliner and floopy hair, armed with a skateboard in her hand.

"Rise and shine, girl," she said.

I took another moment to calm my breath. It had felt so real. When my heart stopped racing, I looked at her. "Anjelica. My name is Anjelica."

"And I already forgot again." She looked down the hall. "The shower's free. Hurry up, though. You don't want to miss the bus. It's a long walk to school."

I nodded, and she shuffled down the stairs. I grabbed the bathroom essentials I kept on my dresser. The floor was cold beneath my feet as I stepped out of the room and shuffled across the hallway to the office and the bathroom situated inside of it. There was another one downstairs and in the master bedroom, but I valued my privacy, and it was the only one with a lock.

My mother wasn't perfect, but she brought me up independent, often to my own detriment. It would have been nice for her to tell me I shouldn't bleach my hair or get a nose ring, but I learned by doing, and I guess that was something. Carl and Junebug were already stifling me a bit, but their kindness—*I shouldn't complain.*

The office was small and crowded, with a new computer sitting on a makeshift desk made from loose wood and stone blocks, and bookshelves along the other walls, filled with manuals and books of all types from self-help to sci-fi. When the book collection ended, the records began. They had the greatest collection of old records I had ever seen and a record player on the shelf.

A small door to my left was cracked to reveal a bathroom behind it. I luxuriated under the hot water, smoothing the knots in my tangled hair until the water ran cold. The pain of the last two days fell away from me as I stood in the steam.

"Breakfast is ready!" Junebug hollered up to me. I was toweling off, and when I was done drying, I wrapped my hair. I usually used two towels, but Junebug only gave me the one.

I pulled on a black flowing blouse I'd gotten from Dana's the previous day along with a pair of jeans, then headed downstairs to breakfast. I was lucky if Mom threw cereal into a bowl for me, so seeing the dining room table covered in pancakes, bacon, eggs, and biscuits left me agog. It was more than ten people could eat.

"Hurry up," Lizzie said. "We've only got about five minutes before the bus gets here. It's never late."

Junebug set a plate down in front of an empty seat. "I made you a plate." She looked at my hair. "You are gonna catch your death of cold going out like that. Lizzie, go up and get her one of your little hats."

"They're beanies, Mom." Lizzie rolled her eyes before disappearing up the stairs. "God."

"Well, go on, sit," Junebug said, and I did, digging into the pancakes on instinct. "This isn't an everyday thing, but I wanted your first day here to be special. Should've gotten you up earlier, but, well, figured you needed the sleep."

"I did. Thank you."

I had barely finished my plate before Lizzie hopped down the stairs and tossed me a black beanie with a skull on the brow. "Here. I don't like this one anymore."

"Thanks."

Junebug walked past me while I was busy shoveling eggs into my face and pulled a puffy pink coat off the rack. "I know it's not fashionable, but it's warm enough. We'll get you something nicer as soon as we can get to the mall."

"It's fine," I said. "Better than freezing to death. Thank you."

I pulled the towel off my head and stuffed my hair inside the beanie. Then, I put on the coat and threw on my shoes. When I was done, Carl came over, holding a purple bookbag.

"This was Lizzie's before she went through her—" He circled her with his finger. "Whatever this is." He handed it to me. "Still works fine. I filled it with some pens, pencils, notebooks, and the like. We already set everything up with the principal based on the documents Kimberly gave us for you." He reached into his back pocket and pulled out a license. "Your name is Anjelica Arnold—no, wait. Now it's Anjelica Campbell, cuz we're the Campbells. We adopted you out of a foster program in Los Angeles. Your mom was a junkie who died when you were ten." He handed me the license. "Anything else, you just say you're too upset to talk about it. Got it?"

I nodded. "I got it. Seriously, I can't tha—"

Lizzie tapped me on the shoulder. "Come on, I see the bus. We gotta get out there."

"Thank you," I said, looking from Carl to Junebug before Lizzie dragged me out of the house.

***

"Welcome back, Ms. Campbell," a tall, bald, white man in a gray suit said as Lizzie hopped off the bus. *How could he not have a hat on in this blistering cold?*

"Morning, Principal Shaw." She nodded her head toward me. "This is my new sister, I guess. Anjelica, this is the principal."

Principal Shaw smiled, never revealing his teeth, which caused the fat rolls under his chin to tighten unnaturally. "Nice to meet you, Anjelica. We have sorted everything for you. Your arrival is a real treat." He pointed toward the kids funneling into the school. "Go on inside and to your right, and Vicki will have your schedule printed out."

"Thanks…um…I'm happy to be here, I guess." I nodded once, then a second time, more fervently. I was determined to make the best of this situation. "No, yeah. I'm happy to be here. Thank you very much for accommodating me."

The bell rang, and Principal Shaw looked back toward the school. "Hurry up, ladies. It's time to learn." He clapped his hands together. "How exciting."

I made it through the current of students toward the large, frosted glass door with the word OFFICE written across it. The woman who greeted me was straight out of the 1950s, complete with poodle skirt and pointed glasses, a golden chain connecting the sides together in the back of her feathered, black hair.

"Good morning," she said, smiling at me as she made her way to her desk. "I'm Ms. Vicki. You must be Anjelica."

"How can you tell?"

"I know every student in this school, and I've never seen you before. Two and two make four, and all that." She picked up a postcard with two dainty fingers and handed it to me. "This is your class schedule. I think you're gonna like it here."

"Well, you are all very nice, which is an interesting change of pace from Los Angeles."

"City of angels." She slid into her seat and put her head in her hands, whimsically. "What's it like there? I would love to visit."

"It's all right. Kind of gross, but it's home."

"Who's the most famous person you've ever met?"

"Umm…that's not really how it—" I saw her face falter. "I mean, I once saw Lou Ferrigno pumping gas, and we went on a studio tour for school once and met Johnny Carson."

"*The* Johnny Carson?" she said, giddy with excitement. "Wow, that is the wildest story I have ever heard."

"Yup. It was pretty wild." I looked down at my paper. "So, where is Mrs. Cooper's room?"

The second bell rang, jolting Ms. Vicki back to reality. "Oh, yes…of course." She stood up and pointed down the hall. "Room 123. Head down the hall and take the first right, then it's the third down on the left."

"Thanks." On my way out, I turned back to her. "I hope you do get out to LA someday. I really loved it there."

I bit my lip to avoid crying as I walked toward my first class of my new life. *The first day of the rest of my life.*

CHAPTER 5

"All right, students," Mrs. Cooper said from her spot at the front of the room. Even over a thousand miles away, classrooms were pretty much the same. I was used to having the school open to the elements, and this one was closed off, which made sense since it was negative a million degrees outside. The room itself, though, was still the same ugly box with a chalkboard at the front of it. Twenty or so desks spread out around it that resembled the ones I'd sat in since I was five. "Take out your workbooks to page 137."

When I walked in, all eyes turned to me. Aside from a distinct lack of diversity, even the students looked similar to those I remembered. The jocks wore sports hoodies, and a few preppy kids had on khakis and bright sweaters. There were a few goths with dark eyeliner and black shirts mixed among the huddled masses that would best be described as generic high school kids.

Mrs. Cooper smiled at me, her head cocked to one side. She wore a long, blue dress with a white cardigan draped around her shoulders. Her hair was short and pulled back with a headband.

"You must be Ms. Campbell," she asked.

For a moment, I forgot the part I was playing, but soon enough, I nodded. "Yes, that's me."

She waved me toward her. "Well, come up here and tell us about yourself."

"Must I?" I asked. I was perfectly happy to be social, but I didn't like being the center of attention.

"Yes, of course! I'm sorry, but none of us know even a little bit about you, and you simply must introduce yourself to the class." As I walked to the chalkboard, resigned to my fate, Mrs. Cooper cleared her throat. "Class, this is Anjelica Campbell. She's from Los Angeles. Fancy, eh?" When I got up to the front of the class, she shimmied out of the way. "Take it away, Anjelica."

I sighed. "Okay, so I'm Anjelica. As Mrs. Cooper said, I'm from Los Angeles. I pretty much grew up there. I've never been to Missouri before yesterday." I realized I was in an ugly pink, puffy coat and black beanie with a skull on it. "I don't usually dress like this. Me coming here was kind of sudden and unexpected." My eyes dropped for a moment. "But I'm happy to be here. I mean, not here at this moment. This particular experience is awful, but I guess I look forward to getting to know you and stuff."

"What did you do in Los Angeles?" Mrs. Cooper asked as if I was on Johnny Carson.

"Um, I was a cheerleader. I know it doesn't seem like it, but I have spirit…yes, I do…" I pumped my fist halfheartedly. "Whoo, or whatever."

"Really?" She pointed to a blonde girl in the front row with a big smile and yellow shirt. "Chrissy is the captain of our team. You two should get to know each other."

Chrissy smiled. "We can never have too much spirit."

"Thanks," I said. "I'll think about it. This is all a bit overwhelming, you know." I turned to Mrs. Cooper. "Am I done yet?"

"If you want to be done," she said, craning her neck around the room. "You can take a seat right behind Dante in the back over there. And don't mind the eyeliner. He's harmless, I think." Suddenly, she popped up like she had an idea. "I almost forgot, here is your book. Have you studied the Civil War out there in Los Angeles?"

I took the thick book from her. "Yes, ma'am."

"Super-duper." She turned to the board. "Then take your seat, and let's dig in."

***

Lunch used to be my favorite part of the day, but that was back when I had friends, and I did have friends. Lots of them. I was a perky, preppy, and pretty cheerleader. I had plenty of boys buttering me up for dates and girls who wanted me to hang out with them.

A thought ticker went through my brain…we had a basketball game against Manhattan Beach Prep this weekend. I was supposed to be the top of the pyramid. Afterward, we would go out for pizza. I wouldn't eat any because I needed to maintain my figure, but I would sit and gossip with Anna and Regina for over an hour as the boys tried to impress us.

One had already impressed me, Bobby Sherwin. The tall, gorgeous starting point guard. We went together like ham and mustard. Even though he hadn't asked me out yet, I had it on good authority that he was building up the nerve.

I'll never see him again. I wouldn't see any of them again. I was stuck in this stupid school, halfway around the country.

"Are you crying?" somebody said to me, and I realized I was sitting down in the middle of the cafeteria, crying my eyes out, lost in my previous life.

"Maybe," I said, wiping my eyes on my sleeve. Lizzie stood with two other girls flanking her, looking at me with shocked faces.

"Could you not do that, though?" Lizzie said. "I'm enough of a freak already without having a basket case sister."

"Sorry," I replied. "It's just—" I looked up at her and could see she didn't care about anything coming out of my mouth. "Nothing. I'll try to keep it together. Do you want to sit?"

"Absolutely not."

I ate alone, in a new place, watching the cliques chatter away around me. I found a paper bag in my backpack when I got to school, filled with a peanut butter and jelly sandwich, chips, and an apple. When I was finished eating, I walked to the office to inquire about a locker. My bookbag was already weighing me down after three classes, and I didn't feel like lugging everything around for the rest of the day.

Ms. Vicki was behind the desk, listening as "Little Deuce Coupe" played on the radio. She tapped her feet and bobbed her head until she saw me and straightened up with a lurch.

"Anjelica!" She smiled. "How's it going, rock star?"

"Okay," I said. "I was wondering about a locker…"

"Of course!" Ms. Vicki said, knocking herself on the head. "Silly me. I completely forgot." She reached into her desk and pulled out a Post-It note. "I even have it written down. Locker 321. Far end of the hall. Little bit of a hike, sorry."

I grabbed the Post-It note. "It's fine."

The second half of the day went the same as the first, except I didn't have to give any more introductory speeches. Every time I entered class, all the students stared at me, though, some of them whispering to each other, probably making guesses about why I was really there—the same kind of crap I did with my friends when a new kid came in. I hadn't realized how rude it was until I was the butt of it.

Finally, mercifully, the bell rang, and we were done for the day. I stopped by my locker to drop off my new books before making my way outside with the gaggle of students who all walked to their buses…and I realized I had no idea which bus to take home.

I hadn't paid attention to the bus number when I got picked up, and I didn't see Lizzie anywhere. I walked up to the first bus, but the driver didn't look the same. My driver was an old woman, and he was a younger man with glasses. I went down the line until I saw what I thought was my driver and waved to her.

"'Scuse me? You're going to the water tower, right?" It was the biggest landmark around where Junebug and Carl lived.

"Sure am," she replied. "Hop on."

I stepped onto the bus and took a seat at the first seat I could find. I was completely physically and mentally drained. All I wanted to do was lie in bed until I had to go through it all again the next day. Tomorrow would be better, and the day after that easier still. Eventually, this would all be completely normal. I wouldn't be a stranger. Somebody might even take pity and befriend me.

I leaned my head against the cool window and saw Lizzie walking up to the bus. *Oh good, I chose right.* As I watched her stroll toward me, the lids of my eyes got very heavy, and I closed my eyes. *Lizzie would wake me up when we got home,* I thought, as I drifted off to sleep.

CHAPTER 6

I woke with a jolt as the bus lurched to a stop. "Last stop!" the bus driver shouted. I rubbed my eyes and looked around. There was nobody on the bus, not even Lizzie. When I gazed outside, I didn't recognize anything familiar.

"Excuse me?" I said, walking to the front. "I think I missed my stop. Can you take me back?"

She shook her head. "Can't do it, kid. Got a route, and I run it."

I looked outside. "Okay, I guess. The water tower. How do you get to it?"

She pointed. "You're looking at it."

The sun was setting across the street. I stepped out of the bus and looked up at the red tower that said "Maynard Water." *What is a Maynard?*

I turned around to ask the driver, but she had already closed the door and started to drive off. I chased after her, pounding on the side of the bus as it pulled away, but she did not stop. Watching the bus turn the corner, I realized just how cold it was. I pulled my jacket tight, but the setting sun meant that it would only get colder. I needed to find shelter soon and get to a phone.

I started down the desolate road. The corn and wheat fields, so beautiful in the light of day, felt ominous at dusk. The stalks cast long shadows and waved in the breeze like demon fingers trying to drag me down to Hell and—no, that's stupid, Anjelica. It's just your mind playing tricks on you.

Wind kicked the cold in my face as the last of the light left the horizon. A light clicked on in the distance, and I saw a small farmhouse, blue with red shutters, offset from the road, surrounded by fields of wheat.

I ran to it and pounded on the door, my hands nearly numb from the chill. "Please," I whispered, my teeth chattering. "Please, somebody be home."

"Who is it?" I finally heard from the other side of the door. The girl sounded young, maybe around my age. "What do you want?"

"I'm Anjelica," I said. "I just got off the bus and…well…I'm lost…I'm new to town, and I think I'm in the wrong place."

The door swung open, and a brown-haired girl with thick glasses stared at me from a wheelchair. "You go to Mark Twain?"

"Honestly, I have no idea. I think so. The name sounds familiar, but maybe that's because he was a famous writer."

"Well, you don't look like you're going to kill me. Do you wanna come in?"

I nodded, and she opened the door for me. I hopped inside, grateful to be in a heated house again. I couldn't even put it into words. "Thank you. I'm saying that so much recently, I think it's losing its value, but seriously, thank you. I don't know what I would have done if you weren't home."

She shrugged before turning her chair around. "There's a farm about a mile up the road. The Mulveys are kind of dicks, though, and the man is a perv." She wheeled down the cramped hallway, and I followed her. "I was making myself some tea. Do you want any?"

"That would be lovely," I said. "It's not Lipton, is it beca—never mind, whatever you have is great."

She smiled and opened a cabinet underneath the sink. "Nah, I got the good stuff. If you want caffeine, I have some black tea, but I was going with some raspberry chamomile."

"That sounds great," I replied and watched her pull out a carton of loose-leaf tea and pour it into two different filters. Then, she poured hot water into two mugs and left them to steep.

"Are you new here?" she asked. "Pardon for sounding like a bad movie sheriff, but you don't sound like you're from around these parts."

I laughed. I hadn't really laughed since I came to Missouri. "Los Angeles."

"The big city."

"Second biggest."

"I guess that depends on by what metric you're using. Second biggest in the US, but there are plenty bigger in the world."

"Yeah, I guess I'm an American prick like that, always thinking the good ole USA is the center of the universe."

She pulled the strainer from one of the cups and handed it to me. "Careful, it's hot."

I grabbed the tea from her and took a sip. It was heavenly. I liked coffee just fine, but I lived for tea. Back home, I had about thirty different types I'd found in little shops all over Los Angeles. It was one of my great joys in life.

"Mmm…" escaped my lips.

"Is there anything like good tea?" the girl asked.

"There is not…umm…what is your name?"

"Margaret," she replied, tapping her tea mug with mine. "Nice to meet you."

"I'm Anjelica." I nodded to her. "Do you go to Mark Twain, too? I didn't see you on the bus, and I think I would have noticed you, no offense."

"Why? Because I'm such a magnetic personality?" She flipped her hair playfully. "Just kidding. I know I'm in a wheelchair. I take no offense. My mom does, though, which is why she home schools me…I mean, she doesn't flat out say she's ashamed, but like, I haven't left this house in years at this point."

"I'm sorry. That sucks."

"It totally sucks." She sipped her tea. "Absolutely and totally."

I could see a sadness fall over her, so I decided to change the subject. "Oh, another topic. I assume this is Maynard, right?"

"What gave it away? The huge water tower?"

"Yeah, and I'm from Bronard, which has a different one. Blue, if I remember correctly."

"Well, crud. You really are far from home. Three towns from home, to be exact. You must've gotten on the wrong bus."

"I missed my stop."

"Yeah, Mark Twain services most of the county, and the county is pretty enormous. Do you have anyone you can call?"

"Um…yes…my…parents, I guess…but I don't have their number."

"How…do you not know your own parent's number?" Margaret asked, confused.

"I…kinda just met them." I didn't even remember Carl and Junebug's last name. Carmen? Carter? Chamomile? I thought for a moment, and then I realized that, while I didn't know the number…or the name…I'd been to her bakery. "Do you have a phone book?"

"Yeah, next to the fridge." Margaret pointed to it, and I rushed over.

What was it called? It was a pun. *Desaster?* No. *Cake—* Nope. *Dessertation!* That was it! I flipped through the book until I found the number for Dessertation.

"Can I use your phone?" I asked.

"Is it a local call?" Her voice was deadpan. After a second, she smiled. "Just kidding. Go ahead."

I walked over to the phone and began to punch in the numbers. There was a crash behind me, and when I looked back, Margaret was writhing on the floor, foam coming out of her mouth, shaking uncontrollably. Junebug would have to wait. I hung up the phone to cancel the call I'd been making and then picked it up again to call an ambulance.

"Hello, 911?" I asked when the operator picked up. "We have an emergency."

CHAPTER 7

I felt completely helpless watching Margaret thrash on the floor. Mom taught me that when somebody was seizing, you needed to make sure they were on their side so they didn't choke on the foam spewing from her mouth. I did that much, but then all I could think to do was rub her back and hope that help came soon. Luckily, within a few minutes, I heard the ambulance's siren blaring down the road.

"Just hold on, Margaret. Help is on the way."

I let the paramedics in, and they took over, barking questions at me that I couldn't answer.

"How long has she been like this?" a brunette woman with pocky skin yelled, sliding a gurney under Margaret's body and turning her over.

"I don't—I called when it started—five minutes, maybe."

"Margaret?" the male EMT said, looking down at the girl. "Can you hear me? She's not responding."

They filled a syringe and poked it into her arm, and then pulled up the gurney, pushing it past me before I could fully comprehend what was going on.

"Are you coming with us?" the woman asked.

I couldn't stay there. It wasn't my house. I wanted to leave a note, but there wasn't time. They were running to the ambulance, and I had no idea what was happening to Margaret. I twisted the lock on the door and closed it behind me. "Yes."

It wasn't a long ride to the hospital, but the whole way, the woman riding in the back next to me peppered me with questions that I mumbled and muttered through without success. She clearly thought I was Margaret's sister, and I didn't want to dissuade her from that notion lest they banish me from the ambulance. I tried to just act dumb or panicked, instead of telling them the truth, that I was a stranger who didn't know the patient from Adam—or I guess Eve. Luckily, before their suspicions could coalesce, they arrived at the emergency room and pushed the gurney behind a door where I couldn't follow. I peered through the window inset into the door until they turned left and disappeared, and then, I was alone.

The good news was that I thought I was closer to home now…but I couldn't just leave Margaret, could I?

"Are you the sister?" a nurse asked me, coming out from behind a long reception desk covered in tinsel and garland even though Christmas was months ago. The woman's curly, black hair was frizzy like she hadn't combed it in days. Her fair skin shone with a thin layer of sweat, and the bags under her eyes pulled down the whole of her face. It was a good bet she had been working a long shift. My mother wore the same face too often after pulling a double.

"I don't know how to answer that," I replied.

The woman studied me with her bloodshot eyes. "Either you are, or you aren't. It's one of those yes or no questions." When my mouth did little besides fall open, she pushed a metal clipboard in my direction. "Somebody has to fill this out."

I shook my head. "I'm not her sister. I'm just a— friend?" My voice went up on that last word because it wasn't quite true, was it? I had only known Margaret for fifteen minutes before—

"We need to call the mother, then. Do you have her number?"

"No, I don't."

"Well, you're about as helpful as a butthole on your elbow, ain't ya?" She walked back behind the counter.

"Should I—fill this out?" I said, trailing off as the woman flipped through a big notebook. I looked down at the form and realized that aside from Margaret's first name, I didn't know the first thing about her. I tossed the clipboard on the seat next to me and dropped down into the uncomfortable cushion.

I didn't know what Junebug would do if I called her. She might come and pick me up, dragging me out of the hospital before I knew if Margaret was all right. I couldn't let that happen. I had no idea why I was there, but I had saved her life…maybe, and that meant she was bound to me, in a way.

An hour later, a woman rushed into the hospital. She was well put together, minus her frantic attitude. She pounded her leather-gloved hands on the counter of the reception desk until the nurse looked up from her book.

"My daughter—you called—she had a seizure." Her voice crackled between worry and sadness. "Is she here?"

The nurse nodded. "You're the mother?"

"I am."

She pointed to me. "I gave that one the admittance paperwork. Fill it out and get it back to me as soon as possible."

"Is she—"

"She's fine," the nurse said. "You're lucky her friend was there."

The woman didn't seem thankful. She eyed me menacingly as she walked over to me. "Who are you?"

"I'm—sorry," I said.

"How do you know my daughter?"

"I don't. I got off the bus at the wrong stop. It was late. I knocked on your door. Your daughter—she gave me tea—and then—"

"You're an idiot, then?" the woman said briskly.

"No, I'm just new to town." Why was she being so mean? If I hadn't been there, her daughter might be dead right now. "I was trying to do the right thing."

"Lots of dumb things were done by people trying to do the right thing." She pointed to the paperwork. "Is that the paperwork?"

I handed it to her. "Yes, ma'am."

She swiped it angrily and looked down at it. "You only have her first name written here."

"That's all I know about her."

"So, you don't remember our address or anything else?" She asked, breathing a sigh of what I could only describe as relief.

"No, ma'am. Like I said, it was dark, and your daughter was kind."

She took a deep breath. "I'm sorry. Thank you for helping my daughter. I'm just very protective of her. There are not many good people left in this world."

I smiled. "It's okay. I'm really sorry for causing you worry."

"That's okay," she scribbled down some information on the sheet and then smiled at me. "I'm going in to see my daughter now."

"Can I come?" I said. "I don't think I could sleep if I didn't know she was okay."

She thought for a moment and then nodded slowly. "Yes, I think that can be arranged."

***

I had been inside a hospital bunches of times. My mother—my real mother—was a nurse after all. It never made it easier, though, to see somebody you knew lying in a hospital bed. All the color had drained out of Margaret's face when a nurse pulled open the curtain to her bed.

When she saw her mother rolling a wheelchair into her room, Margaret smiled, but then she saw me and looked down in shame. "Oh god. I'm so sorry. I didn't mean…"

"Hey, it's okay, dude," I replied. "You have nothing to be ashamed of."

She placed her hand to her head. "It's just—I don't meet many people, and shit—" She caught her mother's eye. "Sorry."

Her mother walked around to the other side of the bed. "Can you grab her other arm?"

"Um, why?"

"We're getting her out of here." She looked at Margaret. "Are you ready, sweetie?"

Margaret nodded. "Yes, ma'am."

"Lift," she said, and before I could fully process the weirdness of the situation, I had Margaret wrapped around my shoulder, pulling her up from the bed before dropping her gently onto the wheelchair.

"Be a dear," Margaret's mom said to me. "Look outside and see if there are any doctors looking over here?"

I had so many questions, but it was all happening so quickly that instinct kicked in, and I pulled open the curtain despite myself. Even the biggest hospitals were criminally understaffed, and this small one was even more so. Two nurses milled around on the far end of the room, talking to each other, while a doctor near them checked over a patient's vitals.

"Nope," I replied. "Coast is clear."

She pushed the wheelchair from behind the curtain down the hallway before any of them looked over at us. As we walked down the hall, an orderly pushed a large cart out of a room. For a moment, my heart pounded in my chest, but he didn't pay us any mind.

Margaret's mom pushed the wheelchair with confidence toward the front entrance. Before we got there, she turned the corner down a side hallway, muttering something to herself. A door at the end of the hallway said EMERGENCY EXIT in white letters on a red background. We were heading for it as fast as we could walk.

"Um, aren't we going to sound an alarm?"

Margaret's mom shook her head. "Don't be silly. Now, open the door."

Against my better judgment, I pushed open the door, expecting a loud alarm to sound. Instead, all I heard was the click of the door as the cold wind slapped me across the face.

"Thank you so much for your help," Margaret's mom said as we walked across the parking lot, not an ounce of warmth in her voice. She stopped in front of a white van. "Please don't come around anymore."

"Wait," I said.

She opened the cargo van and picked Margaret up into the back of it like they had done it a hundred times before. "My daughter is fragile, and if this incident has taught us nothing, it's that she's not ready for friends. So, I would ask that you follow my wishes. I know what's best for my daughter."

I looked over at Margaret, whose gaze fell to the ground. "It was nice to meet you."

"You, too."

Margaret slid toward the front of the van as her mom pushed away the wheelchair. Then, she looked down at her watch. "Good, good." She slammed the back of the van closed. "I'm sure you understand, but we will be going now."

"Wait," I replied, remembering that I was still woefully lost. "Do you think you could drop me off at my house first?"

"How far is it?" she said, looking down at her watch.

"Bronard, right by the water tower." I made the most pitiful face I could muster. "I would really prefer not to walk home."

She thought for a second, then growled. "Very well. We have just enough time for that."

Luckily, Bronard wasn't a big town, and once I saw the water tower in the distance, I was able to guide them back to the dirt road where Junebug and Carl lived.

"I'm sorry for ruining your night," I said to them, sliding out of the van.

"Hey!" Margaret said. "You saved my life. You have nothing to apologize for."

"I wouldn't go that far," her mother grumbled. "Please shut the door."

I did, and that was that. No goodbye, just the van driving off into the distance. Before I could get to the stairs, the door flew open, and Junebug rushed out. "Oh my god, you're okay!" She hugged me tightly. "I was about to call Kimberly. I thought they got you."

"I'm fine," I said. "I just got lost, and I didn't have your number."

She slid her arm around my shoulders. "Well, I'm sure you're hungry. I'll heat up dinner, and you can tell me all about it."

Nobody had ever taken such an interest in the machinations of my day, and I was very, very confused by it. However, I would never say no to more of Junebug's delicious food.

CHAPTER 8

Before I left for school the next day, Carl made sure I had both the home phone number and the one for Junebug's shop, and Lizzie made me memorize the bus number so I wouldn't be confused again.

"Hey," I said before I walked out the door, "do you think I can use the truck after school today?"

Carl narrowed his eyes. "Can you drive?"

"I'm from Los Angeles. It's a driving city. Even the babies can drive there."

"Do you have a license?" Junebug said. "A real one? Not one forged by Kimberly's friends?"

I nodded. "Yup, I passed the test and everything." I took a short pause. "I want to check in on that girl Margaret from last night. Please. I won't be able to calm down until I know she's really okay."

I had been thinking about it all night. When I did shut my eyes, the weirdness of it all kept running through my head, from the moment I got off the bus to the moment I slammed the door to Margaret's van. It was better than my dream about disembodied hands strangling me, but not by enough.

"Ask your mother," Carl said as if it wasn't super weird, but I just went with it. "She usually needs the car ever—"

"It's okay," Junebug said from the kitchen. "Patty's driving into town today, and then we're playing bridge later." She poked her head in. "You'll be home for dinner?"

"I promise," I replied. "Please."

"Guess I'll drive you out there, then," Carl said. "I'm not quite ready to give you the car, and I don't think it's right to reward you for skipping out at night when we punish Lizzie for it."

"I didn't skip out. I got lost."

"Same result. Different name."

I knew when to stop pushing. "All right. You're right. You barely know me. I don't want to cause you trouble."

"Girl," Carl said. "Causing trouble's exactly what you did by stepping through that door. I don't begrudge it, but it's trouble all the same."

He was right, and it bummed me out. I didn't want to keep talking about it, though, so I simply smiled and made my way to the bus with Lizzie. The early morning chill was nearly unbearable to somebody born on the coast with thin blood.

"He likes you, ya know," Lizzie said. "That's just his way."

"And how about you?" I said. "Do you like me?"

"You're a lot of trouble, that's for sure. Got in a heap of trouble for not making sure you got home yesterday, like a lost puppy."

"What did you think when I didn't show up on the bus?"

"Honestly?" she asked, looking over at me.

"I would prefer it to lying."

"I didn't think about it. That sounds crappy, but it's true. I completely forgot you existed."

"I wish I could forget I existed sometimes." I sighed. "I get it. You had a life before this."

"Got that right, and I didn't sign up to be a babysitter. I could call a friend, though, if you need one. I know some people."

"Was that…a joke?"

She smiled. "Only if it was funny."

"I think I liked it." The bus appeared in the distance. "I know this can't be easy."

"I'm used to it. Mama's brought in a bunch of strays before. Usually, it's only for a night or two." She eyed her old bookbag and coat that I'd inherited. "They usually don't go to school with me."

"I'll try real hard to stay out of your way. I just want you to know, though…I'm cool."

The bus stopped, and Lizzie walked toward it. "Nobody cool has ever had to say they are."

"Until now."

"Was that a joke?" Lizzie asked.

"Only if it was funny."

I kept my distance from her on the way to school. She deserved her space. No matter how much I desperately wanted an anchor to rely on, it wasn't fair to make it her. She was just a kid, after all, and frankly, having to hang on to my younger "sister" made me feel like a little too much of a loser. No, I had to forge my own friendships, somehow.

I was at my locker between second and third period, studying my schedule to bring the right books, when Chrissy walked up to me. She was in a knee-length skirt and long leggings, with a thick, white sweater stitched with a black cat.

"We had a meeting last night," she said. "The girls and I. We've been down a flier since Teagan broke her leg. You look the right size for it. Are you interested in being a Catgirl?"

I nodded. "I was totally a flier on my old team."

"Great. Then we set up a try-out for you at lunch if you're game."

"Oh, I'm totally game. Just one question. How did Teagan break her leg? It wasn't—"

"Car accident," Chrissy said. "We're very careful, Anjelica." She stepped forward, as menacingly as a little blonde girl can be. "You'll learn that about me." Then, she stepped back and waved at me. "Gym, at lunch. Be there or be square."

So lame, but I kind of loved it. I had pep in my step for the rest of the morning and walked into the gym at lunch with the first feeling of glee that I'd had in a long time. A long table was set up at the far end of the gym under a basketball hoop, with three girls seated behind it. Chrissy was in the center. On the left of her, a black-haired girl with her hair pulled back in a ponytail scanned me like she was looking for any sign of weakness. I didn't blame her. I did the same with new recruits. The girl on Chrissy's right was chubbier than the other two, with acne on her face and braces. She wore a bow in her hair. All three wore the same hideous cat sweaters, and looking up to the rafters, I saw that it was the school's mascot, the Black Cats. *Cute.*

"This is Ella," Chrissy said, pointing to the hard-faced girl. "This is Harriet." She pointed to the girl with braces. "We're the decision committee for the squad. If we like what we see today, we'll bring you into a practice with the whole team where you'll show us how you fly."

"Tell me," Ella said, her voice dry, "do you have spirit?"

I nodded. "Yes, I do. I have spirit. How about you?"

"I have spirit, yes I do!" Harriet clapped giddily. "Lovely. Can you show us a cheer from your old school?"

I hadn't done a cheer in a couple of weeks, and it felt like a couple of years, but I knew enough to rely on muscle memory and clasped both my hands together before doing the same with my heels.

"Ready? Okay!" I shouted. I clapped my hands together twice and extended them into a Y. "S-C-O-R-E!" I jumped my legs out until I looked like an X. "We want more!" I brought my legs and hands back together and then pumped my left hand over my head. "Let's score!"

Chrissy cocked her head to the left. "Good. A little simple, but I like it. How about you, Harriet?"

"Oh yes, very nice."

"Hrm," Ella said. "I agree with you, Chrissy. Adequately pedestrian."

"I can do another one," I offered. I was barely winded.

"Oh, goodie," Ella said. "How fun. Let's see it, then."

I clapped my hands together again, shimmying my hips. "Steal it, swipe it, take that ball." I leaped up into the air and landed in a K with my feet together, my left hand high in the air, and my right hand down by my waist. "All that way—" I spun to the other side, keeping the same position. "Down the floor!" I leaped again into the air, clapping my hands together. "Go, Black Cats, go!"

Chrissy smiled. "I liked that one, too. And it is basketball season."

"For us too, back home."

"Nicely done," Harriet said with a smile. *I liked her.* "You're going to make a great Catgirl."

Ella, on the other hand, looked at me with malice in her eyes. "It was fine."

"What do you want from me?" I asked, stepping forward.

Her eyes narrowed. "Wow me."

"How?" I asked.

"If I knew that, then it wouldn't be much of a wow factor, would it?"

I growled. As a flier, I was quite nimble and agile, and while I hadn't stretched in a couple of days, I was very sure that I could "wow" one catty, little jerk. I pulled my hands above my head and stretched from one side to the other. I looked back behind me and stepped forward to get more space between me and the bleachers.

"Okay." I smiled. "I can do that."

I crouched down and then flew into a back handspring. I continued backward for not one, not two, but three flips before leaping into the air for a double backward tuck, coming to a stop on my feet with my hands in the air. And I did it all without breaking my neck.

I saw a small smile rise on Ella's face, but I wanted her to flip out with excitement, so I ran forward and did three more front flips before tucking into a forward roll and sliding to the ground with my hand holding the left side of my head.

"How was that?" I asked.

Harriet was on her feet, and Chrissy clapped as well. "Just so good."

I knew I didn't need to impress those two. My eyes were trained on Ella. Her small smile grew into a big one, and she gave me two claps. "Slightly better than adequate. I think I've seen enough."

"Me too," Harriet said.

"Then, let's vote. All those in favor of giving Anjelica a try-out with the whole Catgirl squad, raise your hand?"

All three hands went up enthusiastically, and I smiled as I pushed up to my feet. Maybe this new school wouldn't be so bad.

CHAPTER 9

This time I checked the bus number three times before I stepped onto it, but that wasn't enough for me. The driver was a kindly, old man with a beard that hid his sunken cheeks and sagging jaw.

"Does this bus go to the Bronard water tower? The blue one in *Bronard*."

"Yup, don't worry your pretty little head about it. Just sit down, and I'll get you there in one piece."

"You're sure it's the blue one in Bronard, not the red one in *Maynard?*" I asked more emphatically.

"I think I know where the dang bus is going, girl. Now, you wanna sit down or what?"

"I'm sorry, I'm just—"

"This one'll get you home," Lizzie interrupted, hopping onto the bus. "Sorry, Frank. She's new and got lost yesterday. I'll take care of her."

Lizzie grabbed me under the elbow as Frank eyed me. "See that you do," he grunted.

The anticipation of seeing Margaret nearly got the better of me, and I leaped off the bus when I got home. Not only was I one step closer to getting on the cheerleading team, but I was about to see the only other human who actually talked to me. *I hope she's okay.*

Carl was tuning something under the hood of the tractor when we reached the house, and I hollered at him. "Are you almost ready to go…Dad?"

"Almost," he shot back with a smile on his face. "Go put your stuff away, and I'll be done by the time you get out."

I didn't know how he had the skin to stay outside wearing little more than overalls and a flannel shirt in negative a million degrees, but I didn't ask questions. I threw my bag down on my bed and rushed back outside. True to his word, Carl left the tractor hood open and walked over to the pick-up. He waved me in, and I sat in the front seat. I didn't have an exact address, but I knew it was down the street from the Maynard water tower, so I told him to drive there. God bless small towns because he knew exactly where I was talking about and put the truck in gear.

"How are you fitting in?" he asked as he turned onto the main road.

"Pretty okay, I think. I had a cheerleading try-out today." I smiled. "I think I made an impression."

"I have no doubt. You haven't been around for long, but I can tell you're a special girl."

My mom never gave me compliments, and it was an odd feeling, but odd in a good way.

"So, it was a good day?" he asked.

"I don't know if I can have good days yet, but it was the best I've had in a while."

He didn't say much more on the ride. Carl didn't speak often, and when he did, he always had something to say. His words were deliberate, thoughtful, like nobody I had ever met before, and there was a stillness to him. He wasn't ever in a rush, but he always seemed to have purpose.

We pulled up to the Maynard water tower after about twenty minutes of driving. Unlike Junebug, he kept the speed limit. If I were ever in a rush, I would need to remember never to ask Carl for a ride.

"All right, the bus let me off here, and then I walked for a while in the opposite direction. So, turn around."

He spun the car around, and we slowly crept down the street. When we were about a mile down the road, we reached the only house in sight. It wasn't the house I remembered from the night before. This one was red, like a barn, and instead of having a second floor, it extended further back than Margaret's house. A little red silo sat next to it, which I didn't remember, either, but this had to be the place.

"What are we looking at? That the house?"

"I don't—" I opened the door. "Just wait here a minute."

I stepped down from the truck and closed the door behind me. I took the wooden stairs to the porch—I could have sworn they were concrete last time—and knocked on the door. A little dog yipped from inside the house. A Black girl with a tight afro and thick glasses opened the door. Before I could open my mouth, her eyes lit up.

"Anjelica!" She covered her mouth. "What are you doing here?"

"Um…I'm looking for Margaret."

She looked down at her hands. "Oh right. Uhhh…"

"Regina!" A booming voice I recognized came from the back of the house. "Who is it?"

Margaret—Regina—whoever it was, rode her wheelchair forward. "You need to leave. If my mom finds out you can remember where we live, she'll make us move again."

"What are you talking about?"

"Nothing, Mom. I think it was the wind." Margaret-Regina rolled back inside. "Come back tomorrow after school. She'll be gone then. I really can't believe you remembered where we live." Then the door slammed behind me, and I had never been so confused, and this was coming from a person who had been perpetually confused for the past several days on repeat.

***

When we pulled into the driveway, Carl put the car in park. I had to test what Margaret-Regina said about remembering where she lived. "Hey, Carl. Where did we just go?"

"Don't be silly, Anjelica. You were there, right?"

"Just humor me."

"You are a weird girl. We just went—Well, it was— uhhhh—well, ain't that the damnedest? I have no blasted idea where we went. I know we were gone and that we're back now, but—" He thought for a second and then shook his head. "You know what, I'm not surprised."

I followed him out of the car. "Why aren't you surprised? That's really weird."

"Kimberly told you this place was full of magic, right?"

"I think she said something about fairy folk when we came."

"There's a lot of us here. In the grand scheme of things, our numbers are pretty weak, but we've got more than most places, and with fairy folk comes magic. And with magic, well—magic is the darnedest thing." He stepped inside the house. "The darnedest thing."

I kept pace with him. "So that's your answer: magic is weird. I swear the house we went to wasn't the same as the one I visited last night."

"And it probably won't be the same as it will be tomorrow."

I turned to see a familiar face to match the voice I recognized. "Kimberly!" I smiled.

She took a step toward me, her face downturned in a scowl. "I'm afraid this isn't a social call, kid. Junebug called and told me what happened, and I need to explain something to you."

"Oh." My head dropped. God forbid she made a social call. "You're here to what, scold me?"

"Not like that," she replied. "I didn't tell you everything because I was trying to protect you, or so I thought. But if I'm mature enough to hunt monsters, you're mature enough to know the truth."

"It would be a refreshing change of pace."

"The reason Junebug and Carl were so worried last night—well, aside from the fact that they are worried about you—is that this place is heavily warded to prevent bad people from finding it." She pointed to the black opal medallion on my necklace. "This necklace uses the magic from the house and takes it with you, but it's only got so much charge and recharges itself from being inside this house. If you stay out too long, it will lose all of its ability to protect you, and any bad monsters trying to track you down will be able to do so." She put a hand on one hip. "And you'd be putting all of us at risk, including Junebug, Carl, and Lizzie. Is that what you want?"

"Of course not," I said. "I would never want anyone to get hurt because of me."

"Good," Kimberly said. "I didn't think so."

"I don't understand, though. You said…you said that they weren't after me anymore. You said I was safe."

"I hope you are," she replied. "Maybe it's just a bad feeling in my gut. I'm still looking into it, making sure the coast is clear. I can protect you here, but if you get lost again…well, I don't know what will happen to you." She looked over at Junebug, who had her arms crossed, leaning against the doorjamb to the kitchen. "Maybe we should homeschool her for a time."

"No!" I pleaded. "Please. I'll be good, okay?" It was pretty insulting to have someone my own age dictating my life, but Kimberly was the one calling the shots. I didn't have any other options but to beg. "I promise."

She bit her lip and frowned. "Okay. I don't want to overreact. I want you to have a life. You deserve that after what you've been through. Just remember, never take that necklace off."

"I won't." I looked down at the necklace. "So, this thing, it does what, repel magic?"

"Something like that," she said.

"Is that how I knew where my friend was when nobody else could?"

"Maybe, but that's not your concern. If she's being protected, whoever's doing it has their reasons. It's best not to be mixed up with them."

"Unless they're keeping her captive."

"This isn't a fairy tale." Kimberly gripped me by the shoulders. "You are not a handsome prince. Don't go around saving anyone. Just worry about protecting yourself. Got it?"

I swallowed my pride. "Got it."

"Good."

"How are you—"

She didn't let me finish. "I have to go now. I'll see you soon."

"Will you, though?" I called after her.

She didn't answer; she simply waved at Junebug and Carl before vanishing into the abyss.

CHAPTER 10

I was a prisoner. No, I didn't have a cage, but I was a prisoner all the same. Carl and Junebug weren't my "parents." They were my wardens, and Kimberly was my jailer. I knew they were trying to protect me, but I'd been sold a bill of goods when I agreed to move to the middle of nowhere, and nowhere did it say I had a curfew.

I appreciated them. I did. Did I? I did—I think I did. The next day at breakfast, though, I couldn't help feeling contempt in every word Junebug and Carl said to me. In every smile, I felt malice, and in every kind gesture, I read sinister underpinnings.

As I walked toward the bus, the black opal amulet thwapped against my chest. Each time I felt it touch my skin, it was like my shackles tightened. I would be wearing this amulet forever. I would be stuck in the house, away from people, for the rest of my natural life.

When I pushed my way into school, Chrissy and Ella made a beeline toward me. Ella was smiling brighter than I had seen her previously, and the dread of my imprisonment caught up to me. Basketball games happened at night. Sometimes, on-road games, we wouldn't get home until nine or later. If we went out for food afterward, then it might be closer to midnight. *I couldn't join the team.*

"Ready, superstar?" Chrissy asked. "We told the girls about your performance, and they are so excited to meet you. If they like you, then you're in."

"See you after school?" Ella added expectantly. It was less a question and more of a statement.

I wanted to tell her no, but when I opened my mouth, what came out was, "Looking forward to it!"

Chrissy squealed with excitement, and it filled me with joy that somebody wanted to hang out with me. I wasn't going to let them down. I might be a prisoner, but I was not going gentle into that good night.

After I decided to go to my full team cheerleading tryouts, my mood drastically improved, even though my classes were weird. I was as far ahead in Biology as I was behind in History, for instance. The first two days, I was lucky to avoid homework, but I wasn't so fortunate on the third day, which made up for the other two and then some. Each teacher dumped, except for gym and lunch. By the time I got to the end of the day, my enthusiasm for practice had waned. When Harriet guided me there with a big smile and can-do attitude, my tank refilled a bit.

"There are nine girls on the team right now, which puts us one short of a full pyramid." Harriet grinned ear to ear, wide enough to make my mouth hurt watching it. "Well, we can do a little pyramid, and we do, but it's just not the same as having the whole squad up there, ya know?" She didn't wait for me to answer before continuing. "Of course you do. You're from Los Angeles. I bet they have monster pyramids out there. How many girls were on your team?"

"About forty," I replied. "Double that if you include JV."

"Wow," she replied, starry-eyed. "We don't even have a JV team here."

"It's not so great in Los Angeles," I said, not sure if I was trying to convince her or myself. "You're totally replaceable over there. Everybody is super talented, and they're always gunning for your spot."

We reached the gym, and Harriet held the door for me. "You won't get too much of that here, except for Ella, but she's not 'destroy your body and soul' mean. She's more like 'I will not accept anything less than perfection' mean."

"I don't mind that kind," I replied, thinking back to the Ginnifer, the captain of my team back in LA, who screamed when we landed anything wrong, even in practice. "Honestly, Harriet, I'm just here to have fun."

"Me too!" she squealed.

"Harriet!" Ella screamed. "Don't fraternize with the fresh meat!" Harriet wasn't wrong. Ella was a drill sergeant. "New girl. There's a locker room to change."

"Change. Right." The rest of the girls were wearing black shorts and gray shirts with a black cat on them. Junebug hadn't bought me workout clothes, but the gym teacher provided a set of clothes for his class. After changing and pulling back my hair into a messy bun, I was ready to rock and roll. I tied my shoelaces tight and took a deep breath, gazing into the mirror.

"You can do this, Anjelica. You're a winner. Don't you forget that, and don't you dare forget to smile."

I used to have no problem smiling, but now it strained the muscles on my face. I closed my eyes and took a deep breath. As my chest expanded, I felt the black opal necklace on my skin. When I opened my eyes, it sparkled gently in the fluorescent overhead light.

I badly wanted to pull it off and throw it away, to run away, to run home, but that wouldn't be helpful to anyone, least of all my mother. I was mostly doing this for her, after all…and so I didn't die…I definitely didn't want to die.

"Hey!" I heard as the locker room door squeaked open. Chrissy stared at me, irritated. "Come on. We don't have all day, recruit." Then, she smiled at me. "Sorry. Ella forced me to say that. You'll be great. We're ready for you."

All eyes were on me when I stepped out of the locker room. Their looks ranged from wanton indifference to irritation to wide-eyed fascination. I rolled my shoulders back and cracked my neck as Chrissy led me to a set of black mats stretching out across the hardwood floor.

"All right," she said. "First things first, show everyone that thing you did yesterday."

I nodded and stepped to the front of the mat. Somehow, I was less nervous doing it on hardwood, risking breaking my own neck, than on the mats with so many eyes on me. I reached down to the floor to stretch out, buying myself some time.

Then, I sprung back again and again before twirling into the air. When I finally landed, I leaped forward, spinning, and slid to a stop to stunned applause.

"What do you call that?" Chrissy said. "It's so cool."

"The 'like whatever', cuz you kind of end like, whatever. It's got that, 'Yeah, I'm hot, but who even cares?' vibe."

Even Ella smiled at that one, but it didn't last long before her stern face returned. "That's all well and good. Now we have to see how you integrate with a team. Celia and Gina will show you a cheer, and you have to follow them."

She snapped her fingers, and a gawky girl popped up, as did a girl even smaller than me. They stood on either side of me. They clapped their hands together in unison.

"We are the Black Cats. We can't be beat. We got the magic to knock you off your feet!" The first time they just yelled it before adding in steps during the second time. First a clap after Cats, then a punch after beat. Then, a flex after power, and finally a kick after feet. They repeated it two more times before stopping.

"That's great, girls!" Harriet said. "Got it, Anjelica?"

"I think so. Can we add our own flare to the end, or do you want it in complete formation?"

"Do what's in your heart," Harriet said.

"As long as it doesn't suck," Ella added.

"All right." The girls clapped us off, and I followed them in harmony and rhythm. Not much in life made sense to me, but dance and cheer did. I could learn choreography in a snap. "We are the Black Cats." *Big clap.* "We can't be beat." *Punch.* "We got the magic." *Flex.* "To knock you off your feet!" *Kick.* When we were done, I leaped into the air for a flying split. Admittedly, I was showing off a bit, but I wanted them to know what I could do.

"Nice," Chrissy said with a clap when it was over. "Okay, you said you were a flier on your old team, right?"

I nodded. "That's why they let me on the team. Not many people want to be thrown in the air, you know?"

"Tell me about it," Chrissy said. "Let's work a couple more cheers, then some throws, if you're comfortable with that, and we'll finish with a pyramid. Cool?"

"Very cool," I replied. "How am I doing so far?"

She smiled. "So, so good."

***

After working on a couple more cheers and helping the girls roll out several more mats, it was time for me to fly. I preferred having a group of male cheerleaders launch me through the air, simply because they could toss me higher than the same number of girls could, but at the end of the day, I enjoyed anybody tossing me in the air. It was like going on a roller coaster without having to buy a ticket.

Celia was the tallest girl on the team. She, Harriet, and Ella formed the base, and I stepped into their interlocked hands. My heart fluttered in my stomach as they collectively took a deep breath and, with all their force, flung me into the air. For my first attempt, I decided to simply fall back down to Earth without any fancy splits, kicks, or spins, all of which I could do, of course, but I didn't know what the team could handle. I was still a little bit nervous about why the previous flier had broken her leg, and I didn't trust them enough…yet, and that was the operative word.

I leaned back and crossed my arms across my chest. Flying was mostly about trusting in somebody to catch you. My old team had days of trust fall exercises getting us comfortable with your team, but there was none of that at Mark Twain. Just grip it and rip it.

I took a deep breath and pressed my eyes tightly closed as I felt myself descend, and a second later, six arms wrapped around me. I exhaled deeply and opened my eyes to see Ella glowering at me.

"That was horrible," she said. "You were like a dead noodle up there." Her lip curled into a sneer. "Also, you're heavier than I thought. You need to lose some weight if you're gonna fly with us."

I pushed to stand. "First, it's muscle. Thank you very much. Second, you'll forgive me if I don't want to give it all away on the first day."

"That's literally the point of this try-out," she said. "To show all the girls your best."

I stumbled away from the team. "I just let you hurl me into the air. I could've broken my dang neck, but you wanna see something." *Don't do it, Anjelica. Don't let your competitive streak get the better of you.* "Let's go again." And there it was. "Set it up for me."

The other girls looked around for what to do, but Ella chuckled. "All right, limp noodle, let's see what you got. Actually try this time, okay?"

"I haven't even begun trying," I replied, stepping to their interlocked hands. "Shoot me!"

The girls took a collective breath and flung me into the air. As they did, I kicked out my legs into midair splits before twisting back down to the ground into their arms.

"That was—"

"Again!" I shouted.

They reset and threw me into the air again. This time I twisted from the beginning of the lift, executing a perfect corkscrew before they caught me again. I rolled out of their embrace and rose next to them. "Is that enough, or do you want to see mo—"

Past them, Carl stomped into the gym. I looked down at my watch. It was already dark, and I hadn't come home yet. *Shit.* I was in a whole heap of trouble.

CHAPTER 11

"Are you out of your dang mind!" Carl shouted at me across the gym. "Do you have any idea what time it is?"

"Who is that?" Chrissy asked.

"It's my dad…I guess?"

"You guess?" Harriet said. "How can you guess?"

"I'm adopted?" I replied. "It's kind of complicated."

"Why is he pissed?" Ella said.

"I might not have told him I was trying out."

"That's not good," Harriet replied. "You should strive to be truthful at all times."

"I should probably go before he blows a gasket," I told the three of them. "Thanks for this. Really. I appreciate your consideration. I hope—" I stopped to gather myself. "I look forward to hearing what you have to say."

I gave Carl the universal signal for one minute and rushed into the locker room to change back into my clothes. I had no interest in running outside in the little booty shorts that the school provided for us. Bundled up again, I ran out toward Carl.

"I thought we talked about this," he said, walking me out to the car.

"I know," I replied. "Time got away from me." I took a deep breath. "Can you appreciate how hard this is on me? I have never had a dad, dude. My 'dad' is a demon. My mom worked all hours, odd hours. I'm used to my independence." I grabbed the pendant from my neck. "And now I have none of that. I have nothing. Everything's changed."

He opened the door to his truck. "Maybe Kimberly's right. Maybe we should home school you."

"What?" I shouted, sliding into the cab of the truck. "How do you get 'let's be even more Draconian' from me wanting more independence?"

He turned to me after starting the truck. "I do appreciate how hard this is for you. That's the only reason we agreed to take you in. Can you appreciate how hard this is for us, though? We just got another kid in our lives, double the responsibility, and if we don't take care of her right, she can put everyone at risk, including herself." He pointed to the school. "You ever think what would happen if a demon came to attack you during that little practice?"

"I'm sorry." I had said it a lot recently, and this was the first time I actually didn't believe it. *I had every right to have a bit of fun.*

"You can't join that team."

"I know that!" I shouted, tears streaming down my face. "I absolutely know that. You made it very clear. I just wanted one normal day, okay? Just one. I'm sorry…I am sorry I was late…I should have taken better track of my time, but I'm not sorry for doing it, for trying to have one second of normalcy in this life I'm being forced to lead." *For the rest of my life.* I left that part out. I wasn't looking for a fight, but I wasn't a doormat.

***

"I think you better go to your room," Carl said when I walked into the house. "I'll talk with Junebug and have her bring you up some dinner."

"Fine with me," I mumbled. "I have a lot of homework."

I ran up the stairs and poured my stack of books out on the bed. *Where to begin?*

Did it even matter? There was no way Carl and Junebug were gonna let me keep living here if I couldn't follow their rules. *Would that be such a bad thing?* Maybe Kimberly would have a different family, a better family. *Who was I kidding?* She's the one who put these stupid rules on me in the first place. If anything, the next place I went would have bars on the windows.

Maybe I should just run away, go back to Los Angeles, try to summon my father for help. *God, you are such a wimp, Anjelica.* Your grandparents didn't even have refrigerators. General Grant barely had indoor plumbing. He had to use an outhouse on the battlefield, and you're complaining because you have people trying to look out for you. *You suck.*

There was a knock on the door, but it sounded too soft to be Junebug.

"Come in," I said, and the door eked open to reveal Lizzie with a plate of chicken tenders and fries in her hand.

"Mom said I should bring this up to you."

I took it from her. "Thanks." I set the plate on top of my books. "She hates me, huh?"

Lizzie shook her head. "She—they're just getting used to you. It happened to all of us. I remember when I first came here, it took me forever to get adjusted." She sucked her teeth. "I'm still not adjusted."

"Wait, you aren't their biological kid?"

She shook her head. She snapped her fingers, and an ice crystal formed in her hand. "I'm a freak, just like you. They can't have kids, which is probably why they are so into collecting strays." She looked me in the eyes. "They're good people, though. They'll give you a lot of chances. You just have to make the best of them. They really are looking out for your best interests, the best way they know how, even if it's not the way you want."

"My mom never cared about where I was or who I was hanging out with."

"You had a mom? Nice."

"You?"

She shook her head. "Nah. I've been bouncing around for years in the system. Then, Kimberly found me." She pulled up the sleeve of her shirt to reveal a black opal pendant on a bracelet around her wrist. "She brought me here, and I just never left. Carl and June never tried to get rid of me, and eventually, we just fell into whatever this thing was between us and made it official."

"How did you cope with not being able to be out after dark?"

"Listening to metal music—I just got a Nintendo. It's pretty sweet." She tapped the top of my stack of books. "And I do homework. Lots of homework."

I grabbed a chicken tender and took a bite. "Noted. I guess I'll get back to it."

Lizzie nodded. "It's not the end of your life, just the end of one part of your life and the beginning of another. How you deal with that is up to you."

***

Later that night, I was doing homework in the wee hours when the house began to rumble. "Earthquake!" I shouted. But it couldn't be an earthquake; we weren't close enough to a fault line. In the distance, a horn began to blow.

A gigantic crash echoed through the air, and a moment later, the Bronard water tower tumbled, the black funnel of a tornado in its wake. I had never seen one before except in movies, and it was much scarier in person than when watching *The Wizard of Oz.*

The tornado ripped through the field across from our house and snaked its way toward me, ripping up roots and branches as it carved a path of destruction through the farmland. It tore through the shed in an instant as the rusted tractor and farm equipment spun high into the air, followed close behind by Carl's pick-up truck. I tripped, trying to pull my feet from the hardwood floor, but they wouldn't listen to my commands. I was locked to the ground, helpless, as the tornado made its way toward the house.

The tornado crashed through the wall of my room, tearing out the window and pulling the floorboards, snapping them like twigs, before it engulfed me in its cyclone…and then I woke up with a start, a piece of paper pressed against my forehead. I had fallen asleep doing homework.

I smacked the bad taste out of my mouth and stuffed the homework into my bag. I managed to get everything done, though it took until near daybreak. I was tired, but school waited for no woman. I managed to shower and eat a quick piece of toast before I left for the day without seeing either Carl or Junebug. The truck was already gone, and I heard the mower in the back. Everybody too busy for each other was the kind of household I was completely comfortable in.

"We made a decision," Chrissy said, walking up to my locker when I got into school. I looked over at her, but she didn't have a smile on her face. "In light of the fact that you lied to your father, I just don't think you're Catgirl material. We value honesty, Anjelica, and we can't abide by liars." She patted me gently on the wrist. "I hope you get the help you need."

"You too," I replied, smiling as sweetly as I could, given the circumstances. She frowned, confused at what I said, and then walked off scratching her head. I wasn't even that mad, honestly. I would have probably done the same thing in her position. You have to look out for the whole squad when you're a leader. I had probably voted against people like me in the past, but being able to sympathize didn't hurt the sting, and it remained with me all day.

It didn't abate until later in the afternoon when I got off the bus and saw a friend waiting for me on my porch. It was Margaret, sitting with a cup of cocoa and waiting for me. When she saw me, a very nerdy smile accompanied a dorky wave.

I loved it.

CHAPTER 12

"What are you doing here?" I asked, walking up the steps to Margaret-Regina. A wooden plank had been strewn across the left side of the steps as a ramp. I hopped up them to greet her.

Margaret-Regina shrugged, taking a sip of her hot chocolate. "You're not the only one who can sneak out."

The screen door opened, and Carl walked out. "Welcome home. I told your friend that if you didn't come home on time today, you'd never be able to leave the house again, so she decided to wait. Took some doing to get her up here, but we figured it out." He sat down on the rocker. "I told her she could go inside with June. She said she preferred it out here. A girl after my own heart."

"This cocoa is helping, Mr. Campbell," Margaret-Regina said. "And I generally run hot anyway."

"Me too," Junebug said from the screen. "Mine's from menopause, though. You all better get in here before you catch your death of cold."

"Actually." Margaret-Regina set down her cup. "I need to run some errands for my mother, and I was wondering if Anjelica wanted to come with me."

Carl groaned. "I don't think—"

"Pleeeeease," I said. "I finished all my homework on the bus."

Carl thought for a second, then looked at June, who shrugged and went back inside. "Have her back by 4:30?"

"Of course," Margaret-Regina said, wheeling down the makeshift ramp. "Shouldn't take more than an hour."

Carl looked down at his watch. "See that it doesn't. Anjelica's on a special kind of grounding right now."

"Apparently, the kind of grounding where we still let her out the house," Junebug said from behind the screen. "Have a good time, I guess."

"We will!" I shouted back, then turned to my friend. "So, before we go, can I ask what your real name is?"

Margaret-Regina laughed. "My mom's given me a lot of them over the years, but I guess I liked Margaret the best. Since that's how you met me, you can call me that."

"Cool, cool, cool."

I followed Margaret to the white van. She stopped. "Can you get this for me? It's easier to get out than in." I opened the back door and watched her slide in, and then pull the wheelchair inside before slipping into the driver's seat. "Coming?"

I jumped into the passenger's seat as Margaret put it in gear and started to drive. I sat next to her, amazed. "How can you—How are you driving with no legs?"

"I can use my legs, just not well." She looked over at me. "But the answer to that, and most things in life, is magic."

"Magic?" I asked breathlessly. "So you are a fairy."

She shook her head. "Not quite, at least I don't think so, but my mother is a powerful witch." She snapped her fingers, and a small flash of fire danced in her hands. "She thinks it skipped a generation. It didn't. I just can't do fancy stuff like her."

"That's frigging awesome!" I shouted. "I wish I had cool magic."

"You do! You're the only person who has ever been able to find me a second time. You must have some really powerful sorcery."

I looked down at my black opal necklace. "No, just a strong protection charm."

She slammed the steering wheel. "Of course. That would explain it. Mom said she moved here because it was a fount of magical energy, and now this." She shook her head. "Sorry, this is like the first time I've been out of my house aside from the hospital since I turned twelve, and—" She trailed off.

"And what?"

"Nothing." She thought for a second. "Hey, do you want to go to the mall?"

"I've heard about this mall," I said. "Is it any good?"

"Honestly, I've never been to one, but they're supposed to be real cool."

"Wow, you really are sheltered, huh?"

"Told you." Margaret shrugged. "Now, hold onto your butt cheeks. We're about to travel an hour in about ten seconds."

She snapped her fingers, and suddenly we were no longer on a country road, but driving through the blackness of—well, I wasn't sure where we were. She looked over at me and smiled, and then, with another snap of her fingers, we appeared inside a parking lot. "Oh, thank god. I'm so glad I didn't crash this thing."

My eyes went wide. "Was that a possibility?"

She nodded. "Anything's a possibility inside the ether, Anjelica. Can I call you Angie, by the way?"

"I wish you wouldn't."

"Then I won't." She slid off the seat toward the back. "Now, like I was saying, the ether lets you move from one place to another. For instance, we just moved about sixty miles in a couple of seconds." *Like Kimberly and Ollie.* "I can see by the look on your face that you know what I'm talking about. It's really not all that impressive. Low-level magic stuff, at least the way I do it." She pushed open the door. "Can you help me? This is so much easier with two people, and we don't have much time."

***

The North Crescent Mall was nice. It wasn't anything special, but not everything had to be special. There was this misperception about Los Angeles that everything was glitzy and perfect all the time. Really, most of Los Angeles was achingly normal. Yes, there were places in Los Angeles, like Rodeo Drive, that fell into the category of glitzy, but everyone I knew frequented small bodegas, rundown thrift stores, and back-alley dive restaurants, saving the "glamour" of the city for visiting tourists.

"Come on," Margaret said as I stopped to admire the single-story mall.

The main thoroughfare of the mall was end-capped by a JCPenney's on one side, and a Macy's on the other. Between them were all manner of stores, and right in front of us was an Orange Julius, a Los Angeles staple. The sight of it brought a tear to my eye, though it was much too cold to enjoy one.

"What are we looking for?" I asked as we turned onto the main strip of the mall. "You seem to be on a mission."

She looked back at me. "You were the only person who has been able to see me, really see me, in years. The confusion spell Mom has on our house forces everyone who comes to our door to forget about it once they lose sight of it." She narrowed her eyes. "I think it all goes back to that necklace. Can you tell me about it?"

I nodded. "Kimbe—a friend gave it to me. She said it would prevent me from be—You know, I am not sure that I should be telling you. It's like, no offense, or anything, but I barely know you."

"That's okay," Margaret said. "I get it. I'm very intimidating."

"I think the point is that you aren't, which might make you the most threatening person I've ever met. I don't know magic well, but I do know it's sneaky like that."

"Oh, you're not wrong about that," Margaret said, searching the storefronts for something she hadn't found yet. "Magic is bonkers, you don't have to tell me. It's enchanted, though, right—the necklace? You don't find a lot of teenagers wearing black opal. It's not super fashionable."

"It's enchanted," I replied. "I can tell you that much, I think."

She stopped. "I've been stuck inside for the past fifteen years, my only respite is when we move from town to town, and I'm kind of sick of it. Mom says I can't go out without risking—well, since you are being coy, perhaps I should be too, but suffice to say, I shouldn't be out right now, and I'm exposing a lot to do so, assuming I trust my mom, which I do—*aha*. There!"

She pointed to a jewelry store, Dan Beer's Jewelers, and rolled across the slick floor toward it. I followed behind her, still not sure why I was there but enjoying having a low-stakes adventure for a change.

"What are we looking for?" I asked.

"Black opal has several very interesting properties about it, not the least of which is that it absorbs magical energy around it. My theory is that whatever it is doing for you, including making you immune to my mother's charms, it could also do for me, and if that's true, I might be able to have a real-life—real friends." She looked over at me. "I haven't had a real friend since I was young—before the accident and…I really want to have a normal life, or as normal as I can, given—"

She trailed off as a pudgy store clerk with a shiny tonsured head stepped out from behind the jewelry cases and walked toward us, straightening his black tie.

"Good afternoon. Welcome to Dan Beer's. How can I help you?" He looked directly at me, and I pointed over to Margaret, who smiled at him. "We shopping for a special occasion today, little miss?"

Her lip twitched, trying not to internalize the insult of being called little. "Do you have any black opal?"

The man's forehead furrowed. "Don't get a lot of requests for that kind here. Let me check the back. I don't think we have anything on the floor."

The man hopped away, and Margaret turned to me. "There's no chance of them having black opal in the stores by us, which is why I had to come here."

"Why don't you just go to like Los Angeles, or Portland, or anywhere with a magic shop?"

"First off, if I'm seen in a magic shop, somebody's definitely gonna know I'm not supposed to be there, and second, I'm not very experienced as a witch. I can't zap too far away from my house. And doing it more than twice a day kills my energy. This is about the furthest part of my range right now. Maybe someday in the future… I can't wait until I can."

A few minutes later, the portly clerk came back toward us holding a small pendant. "This was a return that we were about to send back to corporate. It's the only black opal I've seen in these parts for a while."

Margaret took the pendant from the clerk's outstretched hand and examined it. Disappointment washed over her face. "You don't have anything bigger?"

He shook his head. "Nothing in store, sorry. I could special order something for you." He leaned down to Margaret and whispered to us. "There's another jeweler in this mall, but frankly, they are smaller than us, and I doubt they would have any, either."

"How much for this little pendant?" Margaret asked.

"Well, the good news is that this is a flawless black opal. We sell only the best here at Dan Beers, so you're getting top quality. The bad news is that it's quite rare, and so it'll set you back two hundred dollars."

Margaret thought for a second and then pulled a wallet out of her jacket pocket. She opened it and pulled out two crisp, hundred-dollar bills. "If you throw in a chain, then you have yourself a deal."

The clerk took the money with a smile. "I think I can make that work."

I looked down at my watch when we left the store. It had been about half an hour, which meant I had half an hour to get home. Maybe they had a coffee shop, because I could really use something warm to prepare me for the cold outside.

"Happy now?" I asked as we left the mall.

"Never," she replied, smiling. "But I am content. Thank—" Her voice changed, and I followed her gaze. Two men wearing black suits with sunglasses were marching toward us. Two more people, a man and a woman, dressed the same as the others, came at us from the other direction.

CHAPTER 13

No, no, no, no, no. This couldn't be happening. It was barely four o'clock. I had plenty of time to get home before the protection of my magic wards wore off.

"I can't believe my mother was right," Margaret grumbled as she wheeled forward. "Kneel."

"Excuse me?" I said to her.

She didn't speak again. Instead, she grabbed me by the collar and pulled me to her level. Then, she closed her eyes, and when she opened them a second later, they glowed with blue light. She clapped her hands together and then extended them as wide as she could.

"*Arcticum inspiratione!*" she shouted as a blue wave exploded from her body, sending the agents flipping over on the ground. The decorative glass around the entrance to the mall shattered along with the store windows and the kiosks showing the directory. After the blue wave dissipated, there wasn't a single piece of glass left standing within twenty feet of us.

I let out an audible shriek, but Margaret was cool as a cucumber. She rolled herself down the hallway as fast as I could run, and we rushed past the agents who were already making their way back to standing.

"This is bad," Margaret said. "This is so bad."

"What's happening?" I asked, panting. "Do you know those guys?"

"Not really." She looked back over her shoulder. "Only by reputation."

The agents rushed after us as the assorted store clerks hobbled out of their stores to make sense of what just happened. Two more agents appeared from a mall kiosk in front of us.

"I can't—I don't have enough power."

Out of the corner of my eye, I saw a white door hidden by the white paint around it.

"In there!" I slammed my shoulder against the door, and it snapped opened into a long corridor. I grabbed Margaret's wheelchair and spun her into the hallway. "How about some of that teleportation magic, huh? We could really use it right about now."

"I—can't—" she said. "I only have so much magical energy, and if I spend it now, we'll never get home before our parents kill us."

"Can't you do anything else?" I croaked, pushing her toward a door marked exit at the other end of the white hall.

"Nothing comes to mind," she replied. "I have one more good spell in me before I'm spent, and I'm not leaving my mom's car at this mall. She will super ground me."

The door behind us slammed open, and six agents poured through it just as we reached the door and exited the mall. Outside, a rush of cold air shot at me, nearly taking the wind out of my lungs. I hated the cold so much. If I survived this, I was going to hide out in Bali next.

"Left!" Margaret shouted, spinning the wheels of her chair so hard that I couldn't hang on to the handlebars. We turned another corner and up the ramp to a loading dock. I knocked hard on the door at the end of it.

"Please, please, please."

The door fell open, and I tumbled inside, then clicked it closed as I heard the agents ascend the ramp to the dock, muttering to themselves.

"What are you girls doing causing all that racket?" A tall, well-built man with a mustache said in a thick Wisconsin accent. "You're not supposed to be back here. That's why we lock the door."

"Please," I replied. "Some very bad men are after us." The door shuddered from violent men knocking against it. "That's them. Please, help us."

"Don't worry. I'll keep you safe. No one's gonna hurt you on my watch." The man nodded. "Get behind that stack of pallets."

We did as he asked, and he went to open the door for them. "Can I help you gentlemen—sorry, ma'am? Gentlepeople?"

A gruff voice spoke, sending shivers down my spine. "Has a girl in a wheelchair passed through here?"

"Not that I've seen," the Wisconsin man replied. "This door is pretty much always locked, at least after morning load-in. It would be pretty hard for somebody to get in this way."

"Come on," I said, whispering to Margaret.

"But he said—"

"He doesn't know what they are, all right?"

"Neither do we."

"They're bad guys, and bad guys don't listen to reason. Any second—"

Before I said another word, there was a bright flash, and a pitiful croak came from the man as his body collapsed to the cement floor.

"Split up," the gruff voice said, and six pairs of loafers clacked along the floor, inching closer.

I looked up to the top of the stack of pallets and had an idea. "Get ready to move." Margaret didn't say anything and only nodded. The group of agents worked methodically through the loading dock, and eventually, I heard one pair right next to me. I pushed the pallets as hard as I could, and the pile collapsed on the agents. When I heard them cry out, I turned toward the blue doors furthest from them and hoped they led back into the mall.

"Go!" I screamed and bolted to the door. It led us into a massive store. All the agents gave chase as we made our way to where the sounds of elevator music blasted. We had come out into the gardening department and pushed through the plows, backhoes, and mowers. The agents were quicker than we were, and one of them caught us before we could make it to housewares. He grabbed at me, and I felt a surge of energy course through my body. I reached back with a guttural growl and tipped over a shelving unit. It toppled down on him.

Oh yeah. *I am a demon.* That was probably good for something.

Two agents circled us from the front, trying to outflank us. We passed a pair of mops, and I grabbed them, handing one to Margaret. "Use this like a lance on the left one!"

She built up a head of steam and charged them like we were in a joust, holding the mop handle while I leaped onto the back of her chair and pointed to the one on the right. I don't think they knew what to expect, having a girl in a wheelchair and her demon friend rolling at them full speed because they didn't even bother to dodge. Instead, they took the full brunt of the force and stumbled back into the menswear department, leaving an opening for us to blow through them.

I leaped down from Margaret's chair and pushed her toward the exit. I recognized it as the one we came through, and I didn't even bother to look behind us to confirm that the agents were chasing us. I kept my legs thrusting at top speed.

A big black van sat outside. The door slid open, and another agent lunged for us. I turned Margaret's chair on a dime and swerved around it into the parking lot. Luckily, I had a good memory, and we found Margaret's car without issue.

"Open the trunk! Hurry!" Margaret said. I pulled open the truck, and she lurched into it. I didn't even bother to close the wheelchair before flinging it inside and slamming the door closed.

By the time I dropped into the passenger's seat, Margaret was buckling herself into the chair behind the steering wheel. The black van skidded to a stop behind us, and the agents surrounded our car, pointing something that resembled a gun but was like nothing I had ever seen before.

"I guess this as good a time as any," Margaret said, closing her eyes. She mumbled something under her breath as she turned the ignition, and we disappeared from the parking lot, reappearing inside the black ether of nothingness. "You're really not supposed to start from a dead stop in here. Let's just hope—"

She stopped mid-sentence. I turned to her, hands shaking with nerves. "Hope what?"

"Nothing, nothing. It will be fine. Just sit back and relax."

"Relax? I can't relax! What are you? Are you an antichrist? A demon? What the heck is happening?"

"Nothing like that," she said, taking a breath. "But since you almost got caught up in it, I guess you have a right to know." She gripped the handle tightly. "I'm a prophecy girl."

"Uhhh…is that as—"

"As stupid it sounds? Yes. A long time ago, when I was just a little kid, a seer told me that I would lead a ruined world back from the brink." She pinched the bridge of her nose. "That sounds so stupid, and I'm not getting it exactly right, but it sent my mom into a tailspin. She's had me barricaded in my room ever since." She looked back, even though there was only the darkness. "Now, I know why."

I reached over and grabbed her shoulder. "Hey, hey, it's going to be okay."

"How?" She moaned. "I've messed everything up."

"This is going to sound really weird, but I actually have some experience stopping the end of the world, and I think I know somebody that can help."

"Well…that's convenient," she said.

"None of this is convenient."

A pinprick of light blinked into existence in front of us and slowly grew until it washed over the car. Margaret skidded to a stop on a small country road, in front of a big, blue water tower that said Bronard on it.

Home.

I smiled because it was the first time I'd thought of this place as home since I arrived in Missouri. Margaret was sobbing on the steering wheel. I reached over and rubbed her back.

"It's going to be okay," I said. "I promise."

I didn't know if I could actually help, but it was a thing to say. If anybody could help her, it would be Kimberly. I just had to hope the pixie wouldn't be too mad at me. I reached behind my head and pulled off the necklace, laying it down in the cupholder.

"You need this more than I do. It needs to be recharged, and I don't know how to do that, but yeah. There should be enough juice to get you home."

Yup, Kimberly was gonna be so mad at me.

CHAPTER 14

"You did what?" Junebug said, arms crossed, pacing across the living room. Carl hadn't said a word since I started my story, and now that I was done, he just shook his head, eyes narrowed, disappointed as all get out.

"I gave my necklace to Margaret," I said. "She needed it more than me."

"It wasn't yours to give away! And now you're being chased by agents of some organization or another. That's exactly why you shouldn't leave this house."

"I didn't think she was going to get chased by—by whatever those agents were. I just wanted to get us home, but yeah, I gave the necklace away, and now you know everything." I turned to Carl. "She's not a bad girl. You met her. She's sweet, right?"

"Did you know about this, Carl?" Junebug asked. "Is what she's saying true? Did you drive her over to this girl's house?"

"I don't—I don't remember. I took her somewhere, but I can't—the details are fuzzy."

"Well, it goes without saying that you can't hang out with this girl anymore. It's too dangerous." Junebug sighed. "I can't believe you gave her your necklace."

"She needed it more than me, and also…you can't stop me from seeing anyone, June. This girl needs my help."

"No, she doesn't," Carl said. "You're not some fighter, or mage, or anything that can help her, except get her into more trouble."

"Kimberly does it—"

"Don't finish that statement, young lady," June said. "Kimberly had lots of training and has been doing this a long time. You two are not the same."

"Maybe not." I stood. "But have you forgotten that I'm a demon? I can stand up for myself."

"You've done a mighty fine job of doing that up until now," Carl said, standing to tower over me. "Go to your room until we figure out what to do with you."

"But I—"

"You heard your father," June added, backing up her husband.

"You're not my dad," I said as biting as possible. I don't know why I said it, except that I wanted to hurt him. I wanted to hurt them, and it worked because I watched Carl's face contort into something unnatural. It was mean, but at that moment, it felt good to be mean. "And you're not my mom," I added with finality before stomping up to my room.

A shadowy figure sat on my bed. Usually, I would have jumped at such an intrusion, but my blood burned red with anger, and I flipped the lights on, ready to gut whoever was trying to sneak up on me. When I saw it was Kimberly, my face dropped, but my anger didn't subside.

"You're having quite a day," she said.

"Don't you start with me, too."

"I'm not trying to start with you," Kimberly said. "I'm trying to protect you. We're all trying to protect you, but you keep doing stupider and stupider stuff."

"I was just going to the mall. How is any of this my fault?"

She pointed. "You're not wearing your pendant."

"I gave it away," I replied.

"I heard."

"Then you know I gave it away to a girl who's in a way worse spot than me."

"And did you happen to remember that it only works if your house is warded?"

"Oh…no. I didn't."

"Just a teeny tiny, little, insignificant detail."

"At least I'm trying to support her," I grumbled. "She claims she's a prophecy girl. She said she's supposed to help usher in a new world order. Please, can't you help me figure this out, so she doesn't have to be locked in her house for the next century?"

She shook her head. "No. That's not my job. My job is to protect fairy folk, and them alone. I already broke that dictum once with you, and you've caused me nothing but trouble. I am not taking on another charity case."

"Charity case? I didn't ask for any of this." I stepped toward her. "If you just turned your back on me, that would be a real dick move."

"Yeah, and being an ungrateful jerk to the people trying to help makes you one, too. Junebug and Carl didn't ask for this. They don't have to help you. They are doing it out of the goodness of their hearts." She sighed. "I can't believe we have to keep having this discussion. Maybe this isn't working. Maybe I should just…"

"Just what? Abandon me to the wolves?"

"No, that's not what I was going to say, but make no mistake, if Carl and Junebug kick you out, there are no second chances. I've been trying to—to find somewhere you might get along better, but nobody else is willing to take a demon." She looked at me. "Frankly, the way you're acting, I can see why."

"Ouch," I said. "Well, at least you're honest. I'll give you that."

"We didn't meet under the best circumstances, and it all keeps going downhill, but I am on your team, Anjelica."

"If you are, then help me. And help Margaret, like you helped me."

Kimberly reached into her pocket and pulled out another black opal stone. "I hesitate to give you this, after how you treated the first one…but you were trying to be noble, if a little misguided. Lord knows I've been there. Still, I'm getting real sick of treating you like a child."

She placed it in my hands, then closed my fingers around it.

"Then why are you?" I asked, looking at the stone in my hand.

"I'm giving this to you to prove this isn't a prison, and we aren't jailers." She sighed. "Maybe if I keep saying it, eventually you'll believe it."

I shook my head. "I believe in actions. Nothing you say can convince me." I placed the pendant around my neck. "This helps, though."

"Good." She walked toward the door. "I'm going to talk to your parents now and try to figure out what to do with you, try to convince them not to feed you to the wolves."

"Tell them I'm sorry."

"I will."

"Kimberly, please look into Margaret for me. I'm begging you."

She paused for a moment at the door before she opened it, then said, "No."

***

If Kimberly wasn't going to help me, then there was one other person I knew who was a badass with this kind of thing. Well, two, but Ollie made it pretty clear she didn't want to see me again when we said goodbye. That left Phil, if I could find him.

I couldn't just open the phone book and look him up, but I knew he was good with computers. I figured that if I could get onto a computer, then I might be able to contact him…even though I had no idea how that worked. It was just tubes and junk, right?

There was a computer in the library of our school. It was an ugly looking thing, but two days before, we'd taken a trip to the library in English class, and I saw the librarian behind the green monitor, typing away furiously on the keyboard.

Before school the next day, I stopped into the library to find Mrs. Sloop pushing a cart of books.

"Good morning," I said.

The noise startled her, and she jumped a bit before glaring at me. "Shhh."

"Sorry," I whispered. "I thought being quiet was just a during-school hours thing."

She shook her head. "It's an always thing. How can I help you, Miss…" Her mind churned behind her eyes, trying to find my name. She was coming up empty.

"Anjelica."

"And what do you need, Anjelica?"

"I need to send a message to my friend on the computer. Can you help me?"

She looked at me like I was an idiot. "Our computer can't do that. You need a networked computer to send something complicated like that."

I pointed to the computer. "That one...isn't...?"

She shook her head. "Certainly not. You would need a...something connection, or a driver, maybe? I don't know all the ins and outs. They told us what we needed when they set our system up...I wasn't interested. Regardless...I can assure you the computer we have can't do any of that fancy stuff." She looked over at the boxy thing. "It's pretty worthless if you ask me." She tapped her temple. "My brain can find books faster than that stupid thing."

"I'm sure it can." I thought for a second. "Do you know where I could find one of those networked thingies?"

She nodded. "I believe the college has a few. They are mainly meant for universities to communicate with each other anyway. I don't know why you would need to send a message to somebody else over it. Can't you pick up a phone?"

"I just do, I guess. I don't know. Isn't the future all about computers? That's what people are saying."

She snorted. "I don't want to live in a world like that."

I thanked her for her time and walked out of the library. To get to the college, I needed a car. I hadn't seen a college driving back and forth around town, which meant it was out of my walking distance, especially in the middle of winter.

The problem was that I didn't know anyone, with or without a car. I doubted Chrissy, Ella, or Harriet would help me. The minute they refused me entry to the team, they acted like I didn't exist anymore. I didn't want to risk

Margaret getting caught by going to her…which only left one other person who might take pity on me—Lizzie.

I found her after second period. Her classes were on the other side of the school from mine, and all the junior high students looked tiny in comparison to me, even if I was a shrimp in comparison to the rest of the kids in my grade.

When she saw me, she rolled her eyes. "What do you want?"

"I need your help."

"Sorry," she said, barreling past me. "If Mom and Dad aren't your parents, then I'm not your sister, and that would make us strangers, and I don't help strangers. They're dangerous."

I grumbled. "What do you want?"

"I don't know what you mean. I'm distraught about how you are treating my beloved parents." I didn't know much, but I knew sarcasm, and it was oozing off her. "I'll play along. Tell me what you need, and I'll see what it'll cost you."

"I need a ride to the college."

She narrowed her eyes. "You know I'm twelve, right? I can't drive."

"Yeah, but I remember when I was twelve, I had friends who had older brothers with cars." I smirked. "Not to toot my own horn, but I'm pretty good at getting boys to do things for me."

"That," she said, "that's my price."

"What? Manipulating boys?"

She looked down the hall for a moment, and I followed her eyes to a tall, black-haired boy with dark rings under his eyes. When she saw me looking, she blushed. "If you want my help, show me what you know, and then I'll do what I can."

My eyes narrowed. "If I do this, you aren't going to screw me, are you?"

"I haven't decided yet." She held out her hand. "Do we have a deal?"

"Do I have a choice?"

"You could not do your thing."

I sighed and shook her hand. "Fine. Tonight, your room. Be there or be square."

"Of course I'll be there. It's my room." She spun and walked away from me. "Ugh. I regret this already."

CHAPTER 15

Flirting with somebody was one thing but teaching somebody to flirt was a whole different matter. Still, a promise was a promise, and that evening I stood in Lizzie's room, ready to teach her how to flirt with boys, specifically one very gothy-looking kid in her grade named Pete.

"All right, before we start, you should show me what you already know. So, let's pretend I'm Pete and flirt with me like you would flirt with him."

Lizzie sat cross-legged on the bed, shaking her head fervently. "No way."

"Come on." I pulled her arm to drag her up. "There are no wrong answers here."

She stopped resisting and allowed me to pull her to stand. "Fine, but if you laugh, I'm going to punch you."

"Fair enough. Now, pretend I'm Pete." I straightened myself and pushed back my shoulders, trying to act as "manly" as possible. I dropped my voice when I spoke. "Sup?"

"Uhhh." She began to laugh. "This is really weird."

"Why?" I said, keeping my deeper voice. "Are you saying I'm weird?"

"Oh, I think you are very weird."

"Come on!" I replied, breaking character. "I'm taking this seriously and trying to help you. Do you want my help or not?"

"OKAY!" she shouted. "Fine." She took a deep breath. She waved her arm in a very awkward gesture. "Hey, Pete. What's up?"

"Nothin', just hanging out, hatin' the world."

She ran her finger through her hair and tucked her hair behind her ear. "Cool. Cool. Cool." She stood silent for a second and then threw her hands in the air. "And that's about all I've got." She fell back into the bed. "God, this is lame. I'm hopeless."

I knelt next to her. "No, that was good." She gave me a blank look. "All right, that was terrible, but that's why we're doing this, right?"

She pulled a pillow close and screamed into it. When she was done, she flopped onto her stomach. "I guess."

"Good. Now, having boys like you. You just have to be yourself and know you're the best."

"Uhh, that's the first problem. I don't think that…at all."

I smirked. "Me either, but guess what? That's what lying is for. We fake it until we make it. The more confident we are in our own skin, the sexier we are to other people. It's all about being the best version of yourself."

Her eyes narrowed. "That can't be right. I'm a complete weirdo. Nobody thinks that's sexy."

"Um, have you ever seen Ally Sheedy? She's a complete weirdo, too, and Emilio Estevez is totally into her by the end of *The Breakfast Club*!"

"That's a movie," Lizzie replied. "It's not real life."

I pulled her up. "No, in real life, you're way cooler than Ally Sheedy, and Pete would be a fool not to fall madly in love with you."

"Whoa," Lizzie said, pushing me away. "I don't know if I want all that. I'll settle for him coming over to hang out and listen to records." She looked at me. "I thought you were gonna show me how to like brush my arm against his in homeroom, purse my lips, or something easy like bat my eyes at him."

I shook my head. "None of that sounds like you, does it?"

"No, it doesn't. But just being myself? It can't be that easy."

"I didn't say 'be yourself,' I said be a more confident version of yourself."

"Still, that's not 'here's how to be sexy.' That's what I want. Being myself is easy. I am stuck being myself every day, and I hate it."

"Are you kidding me? Being yourself is the hardest thing in the whole world. Being yourself, putting yourself out there, means letting down your guard and being vulnerable. That is true bravery, sister. All this other stuff—" I looked over at her nightstand and saw copies of *Cosmopolitan* and *Tiger Beat* mixed in with copies of *Rolling Stone*. "—all those stupid magazines, they are set up to leave you broken, so you keep needing them. Once you learn how to be yourself," I touched her shoulder. "you'll be unstoppable."

"You promise?"

"I do," I said. "It's not a perfect solution. Lots of people are going to hate it, they might think you're a weirdo, but the right people? To them, you'll be the sexiest thing alive."

Lizzie thought for a moment. "And how do you…be yourself?"

"That's the hard part. I'm still trying to figure it out. I'm in a new place, at a new school, with new people, and I struggle with it every day because I want to be liked—I want to be loved…and it's scary to be myself because what if nobody likes me."

She smiled. "I like you…just don't let it go to your head."

"I won't, and thank you."

"Can you just…teach me like one thing, though? I mean, you are making a big ask of me, and I feel like you just gave me a pep talk."

I chuckled. "All right, stand up." When she did, I stepped back. "I call this one the pet and giggle." I walked up to her. "Hi, Pete." My voice rose half an octave, and I let some extra breath into my words. When Lizzie looked at me, I cocked my head to the left. "How was your night?" I bit the tip of my thumb gently.

"Good. I just…hung out, man."

I smirked as I took my hand and ran it along Lizzie's forearm. "Sounds fun. Maybe we can do it together some time." When I was done, I shook it off and smiled at Lizzie.

"Whoa," Lizzie said. "That was awesome."

"Yeah, I know. That's my patented move, so use it well. It combines confidence, smiling, a playful touch, complimenting him, showing interest in his life, and drawing attention to your lips. It's a super-advanced trick, but if you pull it off, there's zero chance he won't look at your butt when you walk away, and that's what you are after. You just walk away when you're done, so there's less chance you'll mess it up."

"You are a master," Lizzie said. "I bow to you."

***

True to her word, Lizzie came through for me. Dennis's car wasn't much to look at, probably the only Yugo still on the road whose engine hadn't exploded in a blaze of hellfire, but I wasn't picky. I was just happy for the ride.

"Why do you need to go to the college?" Dennis asked, his eyes on the road. He was considerably more attractive than his car, with shaggy brown hair and blue eyes, but his voice was nasal and grating. He didn't have much of a style sense, either, but Bronard wasn't the fashion capital of the world. However, he stood out even from his peers in his ineptness. Half the collar of his checkered shirt was flipped up, and his khaki pants were stained with foodstuffs I didn't care to imagine.

I didn't know enough about Dennis to tell him the truth, so I concocted a passable lie. "I'm graduating in a couple of years, and I want to get a feel for the colleges in the area."

"Most people from here can't wait to leave," he replied. "Still, some of us like it."

Dennis was a freshman at Middleditch Polytechnical College, which was why I hadn't seen him around school. He turned the corner, and an old Big Gulp cup rolled off the dashboard onto my lap.

"Dang!" Dennis said, trying and failing to catch it. A couple of drops dripped onto my jeans. "Sorry."

"It's okay," I replied. "These weren't my favorite jeans or anything. Besides, you're doing me a favor, and I appreciate it, even if that was totally disgusting."

"I was going to clean it all out nice for you, but then life happened, and I didn't—well, I didn't know you would be so pretty."

"Groan."

He looked at me. "Did you just say groan?"

"I did, because if my level of attraction factored into whether you treated me with respect and dignity, it's totally groan-inducing."

"It's not that it's—man, I'm really blowing this—I just—I'm sorry." He sighed. "You might have noticed, but I don't talk to a lot of girls."

"I'm not a girl," I replied. "I'm just a human who needed a favor, and you were nice enough to give it to me."

"Right," he said, then cleared his throat. "So, what are you most excited about seeing today?"

"The librarian at my school said you have some networked computers, and I'm really interested in seeing them."

"Really? But you're so pre—I just thought you would major in communications or English or teaching or something."

I stared daggers at him, trying hard not to chew him out. After all, he could leave me on the side of the road at any moment.

He continued. "I'm a computer science major, actually. Those computers are kind of a specialty of mine. I'd love to show them to you. I believe the internet is the next great revolution in human communication. Everyone able to talk to everyone else in a fraction of a second. A universe of data at your fingertips."

"That sounds terrible."

"No way! Think about it; you can be a thousand miles away and talk to your mother on the phone or look up a long-lost friend from grade school you lost touch with."

"Yeah, and they can find me, too. I hope I don't live to see the day."

"It's coming, Anjelica. By the turn of the century, every computer in the world will be networked together…and we're going to be at the forefront of it."

I didn't feel like arguing and blowing the fact that I really didn't care for computers or technology at all. I was perfectly fine staying anonymous, especially with demons potentially trying to track me down. I turned up the radio just as it clicked from "Midnight Rider" to "Clyde." The radios in our little part of Missouri seemed to only pick up Country-Western stations, which brought back thoughts of the Palomino and the night I almost died. I cut the radio off, and we sat in silence for the rest of the ride.

We didn't have to wait long to cross into campus. Within five minutes of me stopping the music, it crested over the horizon, and in ten minutes, Dennis pulled into the entrance to campus. The archway above the street spelled out *Middleditch Polytechnical Institute* in big, green, metal letters.

The campus wasn't anything special—several brick buildings connected with concrete paths. The only things that distinguished them were the chrome names of the buildings on the side. We passed buildings for English, History, and Biology before coming to a stop in front of a small building on the edge of campus that said *Computer Science* in shiny silver letters outside.

"Here we are. Home sweet home." He opened the car door. "I know we didn't get off on the right foot, but I would very much like to show you around."

I didn't have any other leads, and Dennis was offering to walk me into the belly of the beast. I nodded and followed him toward the entrance. The campus was sparsely populated, and the few students walking between the buildings stepped double time to get out of the cold.

Dennis pushed open the green metal door and led me down a set of stairs into a dark hallway filled with a foreign hum.

"What are those?" I asked.

"Servers," Dennis said. "That's how we can communicate with other computers around the world. Basically, it's the backbone of the internet. It's really neat if you want to see—"

"No," I said emphatically. "Hey, you said you specialized in communication on the internet. Is there any way you can show me how to send a message on the internet to somebody else?"

"Sure!" Excitement filled his voice, and he shuffled into a room with several computers and slouched down behind one of the few open ones. The others were occupied by people with similar hunched postures.

"So, it's not quite as easy as just sending a message, you know," he said, typing. "However, there are some forums set up that allow us to communicate with other institutions, post questions, and exchange information."

"Can you post something on there for me?"

"On where? You need to know where you want to go for any of this to work."

"I don't know," I replied. "I just need to post a message on the internet for somebody."

"And I'm saying it's not that easy." His eyes narrowed. "Are you sure you are interested in computers at all?"

I smirked at him. "No, I'm not, but I need to get a message to somebody, and I don't know how to do that. I need your help. Please."

He thought for a moment. "Well, there are a finite number of these forums. I suppose we could just flood every message board with them and hope that the right person picks it up."

I reached into my pocket. "Okay, can you post 'Phil, need help. Anjelica. 417-555-3214.'"

He shut his eyes and took a breath. "I just want you to know this isn't how the internet is supposed to work. It's not for hooking up."

I squeezed his shoulder. "Anything taken to its logical conclusion devolves into hooking up, and eventually pornography because people are perverts. Now, send the stupid message."

His voice fluttered at my touch, and I felt him tense under my hand. "I mean, you're the boss, I guess, so okay."

CHAPTER 16

It took Dennis a while to post my message in all the forums where he could think to do so, and when he was done, I bought him dinner at the questionable cafeteria in the student union. I chose not to eat the mystery meat or unappetizing wilted salad, but I was happy to watch him scarf down half an extra greasy pepperoni pizza.

"I don't suppose you'll tell me why we just did that, will you?" Dennis asked.

"If I told you, I would have to kill you," I replied. "And you seem like such a nice boy."

He sighed. "That's me, Mr. Niceboy."

"Do you mind?" I asked, reaching over to fix his collar that he hadn't noticed was askew for the whole time we were together. "It was really bugging me. Now, what's so bad about being a nice person?"

"They don't get the girl," he said.

"Yeah, cuz nice is like the bare minimum, man." I took one of his pepperonis, and when it touched my tongue, I was glad I hadn't invested in a full meal. "You don't get extra credit for being nice, and nobody owes you anything for being decent. That's the price of being in a society, dingus."

When we were done eating, he drove me home, and that was that. I said my goodbyes and left him in the driveway of Junebug and Carl's house. I waved as he drove away and walked inside. The phone rang in the kitchen as I took off my shoes, and Carl picked it up on the second ring.

"Yes, she's here," he said with confusion in his voice. "Hang on."

He poked his head out of the kitchen. "Hey, Anjelica. Phone for you."

"Really?" I rushed over, my hands jittery with excitement. I had not expected my pleas to work so fast. I put the receiver to my mouth. "Phil?"

"You must be the dumbest human I have ever met." His voice was sharp. It was Phil, but he was absolutely not happy to hear from me. "Do you know how much trouble is out there searching for you?"

"*Might* be searching for me," I said, feeling slightly ruffled. "They might be searching for me, and I highly doubt anybody searching for me is computer literate."

"They can subcontract out this kind of thing. Listen, if I'm smart enough to find you, I promise you somebody else could."

"Come on, Phil. You are easily the smartest being I've ever met. Do you really think anyone else is even close to as good as you?"

There was silence for a moment. "Okay, maybe not. But still, what you just did was very dangerous. Luckily, when I found your message, I scrubbed all the servers. Unless they have a tracking bot to search for any combination of my name, we might be safe."

"Do you think I'm stupid, Phil?"

"Well, I didn't! But now, I don't know."

"Can you for one moment allow for the possibility that maybe I had a good reason to reach out, one that was worth risking myself?"

"I—honestly, I hadn't thought of that."

"I need your help, please."

"Now I am intrigued. How can I help you?"

"I have a friend, a sweet friend, a girl I met. She says she's the subject of a prophecy. She doesn't know what it is, exactly, but it's dangerous. Last time I went out with her, a bunch of people in black suits tried to abduct us."

"And you're sure they weren't after you?"

"No, but also yes. My friend seemed very sure they were after her, and I believe her. Kimberly refused to help me. She said I should mind my own business, but this is my business. My friend is in danger, and I can't sit back and do nothing. Please, Phil."

"This isn't fair. You are using my insatiable hunger for intrigue against me. Okay, I will help you, as long as you promise not to do anything else stupid until I call you again."

"I can't promise that. I'm a teenager. We do stupid things all the time. Don't you watch TV?"

"Yes, all of it, and it's the only thing I want you doing for the next 24 hours. Those are my terms. Agreed?"

"I have school," I said.

"Get the flu, then. Don't leave that house."

"Fine, but whatever you do, don't tell Kimberly."

***

It didn't take much to fake being sick. For one, Carl wasn't super excited for me to leave the house, and he jumped at the chance to keep me home. For another, since finding out I was a demon, I realized that I always ran hot. Spiking a 102 fever didn't take much effort. Combine that with some heaving sounds in the shower and spraying myself down to look sweaty, and I was easily able to convince Junebug to let me stay home from school the next day.

I hadn't had a good night's sleep in a long time, so I spent the morning napping and then watched soap operas for most of the afternoon. The phone rang three times, and I swiftly picked up each time. They all ended up being unimportant, at least to my cause. One farmer had a message for Carl about grain prices, another wanted to place an order with Junebug, and the final was a wrong number that clicked dead when I answered.

By the time Junebug arrived home and started cooking dinner, I was nervous that Phil had forgotten about me or that he never intended to help me in the first place. We were halfway through dinner when the phone rang again, and I bolted into the kitchen without even taking the napkin off my lap.

"Hello? Phil? Hello?"

There was a sigh on the other end of the line. "I'm sorry, kiddo."

"Sorry, what are you sorry for?"

"After I found out what was happening, I had no choice."

"What happened? What is going on?"

"I just wanted to call and tell you I was sorry. She'll tell you everything else."

I dropped the phone when a flash of pink appeared in the hallway, and when it dissipated, Kimberly's sneering face was looking directly at me. "You couldn't leave well enough alone, could you?"

"Jesus Criminy, Kimberly!" Carl shouted, jumping out of his chair. "I nearly shot out of my skin. Warn somebody when you appear in their dining room next time."

"I'm sorry, Carl, Junebug, Lizzie." Kimberly stomped forward. "But your daughter did something very stupid, which is becoming her M-O, and it couldn't wait."

Junebug sighed. "What did she do this time?"

"I didn't do anything!" I shouted. "I swear!"

"Oh really?" Kimberly said. "So, I suppose some other half demon posted her phone number on every server in America yesterday?"

"Oh, that." I shook my head. "No, I did that."

"What are we going to do with you?" Junebug said, shaking her head.

Kimberly held up her hand. "Don't do anything to her yet, but when I get done with her, you have my permission to kill her."

"Aren't you trying to prevent demons from killing me? Like, isn't killing me the antithesis of the point here?"

"Yes!" Kimberly screamed, clenching her fists. "Which should tell you how angry I am right now. I have other things to do than protect you. Did you ever think of that? You are like one-thousandth of my worries and 100 percent of the pain in my ass." She stopped talking, even if it looked like she had a lot more to say, and breathed. "Tell me what happened."

"I already did." I stepped forward. "And you told me to ignore it, but I won't. You're my age, and you're off saving the world. Why can't I try to save my friend?"

"Because—"

"NO!" I screamed at her. "I am not a child, and I refuse to be treated like one. I appreciate everything you're doing for me, but my friend is in trouble, and I'm not turning my back on her any more than you can turn your back on me."

I threw my hands in the air. "God, listen to yourself. You literally can't stop yourself from helping people, and you expect me to be any different."

"She's got you there," Lizzie said, taking a sip of orange juice.

"Lizzie!" Junebug barked.

"Thank you, sis," I said, then turned back to Kimberly. "It must be really bad if you are here. Tell me what Phil found out."

Kimberly sighed. "Margaret is a conduit between worlds. We don't quite know exactly what that means, but—people are after her, on our side and theirs, and I can't let them find her. If I do, it could mean the destruction of our world."

"So…it sounds like I made a good call, then."

Kimberly growled in her throat, a frustrated sound. "Perhaps, but that doesn't matter right now. What matters is that I find this girl."

"Good luck," Carl said, taking a sip of his beer. "I tried to find that house again ten times, and I have no idea where it is."

I raised my eyebrows. "I can take you there."

"You have a good heart, but you're an idiot," Kimberly said.

"So are you, and if you can be an idiot, then so can I."

She shook her head. "I am sick of arguing with you. If you help me, then when this is over, you return to Plain Jane middle America, yes?"

I made an X over my chest. "Cross my heart and hope to die."

Kimberly glared. "Oh, you don't have to tell me you have a death wish." She pressed her hands on my temples. "Think of the place you wish to travel. Picture it in your mind's eye. Make it real, down to the blades of grass on the front yard and the smell in the air."

I closed my eyes and thought of Margaret's house. I remembered it as I last saw it, spread out across the yard, surrounded by swaying wheat fields, the smell of thistle on the air. I filled in the details until I could almost step through and touch it.

"Good," Kimberly said.

A crackle filled the air, and we were gone. The next instant, I felt the breeze on the air, and I opened my eyes to see Margaret's house. I stepped up to the door and knocked. The door creaked open. I looked in horror at the body of Margaret's mother lying dead on the floor, blood pooling under her.

CHAPTER 17

"Look for the girl!" Kimberly shouted. "I'll check on the woman in the kitchen!"

I rushed through the living room, offset from the foyer. "MARGARET!" Past the living room into what was probably a tasteful dining room before somebody flipped the table over. The scorch marks on the walls indicated there had been a battle.

"Any luck?" Kimberly said, running into the room.

"Not yet. What about the mom?"

"She's super dead," Kimberly said. "Looks like a couple of hours ago. Keep down this hall, and I'll go to the other side of the house."

I nodded and passed through the dining room. The pictures on the wall had been torn down, and the glass that encased them smashed on the ground. "Margaret!" I screamed as I pulled open the first door on my right, only to find a bathroom. Something massive was under a torn shower curtain, and I pulled it back to see a burly man with dead eyes bleeding from his mouth.

"Shit!" I shouted as I stepped back. I recognized the man as one of the agents who had chased us through the mall.

"Are you okay?" Kimberly asked, storming in, daggers drawn.

"Yeah, it's just—" I pointed to the man in the tub.

Kimberly smirked. "Well done, Margaret."

She took too much joy in eyeing the dead body. I pushed her back out the door and continued down the hall.

The next room was the mother's room, where there were two more dead men on the floor. The window was shattered, and the television had blown off a nightstand across from a singed bed.

"Over here!" Kimberly shouted. I followed her voice into an open door at the end of the hall. It was filled with bookcases and books strewn across the ground. I saw something that made my stomach churn: Margaret's wheelchair had been turned on its side.

"Margaret!" I screamed, unable to contain the terror rushing through my body. "Margaret!"

"She's not here," Kimberly said, matter of fact.

"How can you be so calm?" I replied. "How can—my friend—she's gone!"

Her face turned hard. "When you ask me why I don't think you're ready, why I try to protect you, think back to this moment. I don't want you to harden to this kind of thing, but this is what it takes to do the work I do. It takes ice in your veins and steel in your heart."

"I—I—I don't think—"

"Pull it together!" Kimberly shouted. "You're in it now, and while I would love to call in somebody else for support, there's no time." Kimberly knelt and examined the books strewn across the floor. "You have to be strong if you want your friend back. Whatever they are planning, it's happening right now." She stood. "Remember when I said you were lucky to survive your kidnapping? Remember when I said how most people don't?"

I nodded. "I do."

"This is what I mean. The only thing standing between your friend becoming a statistic, and maybe even the end of the world as we know it, is us. I need you to be strong. Can you do that?"

I fought back tears. "Yes, yes I can."

"Good," she said. "Now, I need something, something important to her. Look around for it." She turned to me. "I need it to be important to both of you."

What could be important to both of us? I barely knew her; all we did was drink tea and go to the mall—then I saw it. Strewn on the ground in the wreckage of the room, the black opal necklace. The chain was broken as if it had been ripped off her neck, but the pendant was intact.

"Here!" I shouted, reaching for it. "Will this work?"

"Was it important to you?"

I nodded. "It was. You gave it to me when you left me that first time with Junebug and Carl. I gave it to her that first time we hung out, after the mall."

Kimberly nodded. "Let's just hope it was important to her, too."

She reached up before I could protest and yanked two hairs from my head, then ran into the bathroom. When I found her, she was pulling hair from a brush in the bathroom as the dead man looked on. The sight of him made me jerk back.

"Come on." Kimberly pushed me into the kitchen. "This part is going to make you gag."

She dipped her finger into the pool of blood and drew a circle. Inside, she drew what looked to be a bunch of squiggly lines and wrapped the pendant with both my hair and Margaret's before placing it in the middle of the circle. "Give me your hand."

"Gross," I said, placing my hand into Kimberly's bloody one.

She held my hands, pulled me into the middle of the circle, and bowed her head. "*Sanguis sanguinem, vinculum ex corde, duce nos utu nus ex nobis.*"

The pendant rose into the air, shaking violently, and then exploded into a bright white light, covering us in its white glow. Kimberly pulled me close and hugged me so tightly I could barely breathe, and then, in a flash, we disappeared.

***

We reappeared in a room bathed in light. My eyes hurt, fighting their natural instinct to close at the sight of the brightness. A pulsating whirl echoed off the stone walls and concrete floor as I wobbled to my feet. I never much enjoyed the ether but combined with the sights and sounds of the room, I was more disoriented than I normally was when rematerializing.

Two shadows dotted the white light on the other end of the room, and I held my arm up to shade my eyes. As I stepped closer, the shadows molded into shapes that I recognized. One, a girl, my friend, Margaret. The other, a tall, bald man, one of the ones that tried to chase us down in the mall. Maybe the last one left.

"Margaret!" I screamed at her.

"Anjelica?" Margaret's voice was brittle and cracking. "You have to run!"

"I'm not going anywhere without you!" I shouted back, stout and resolute.

The man's shadow eclipsed the source of the light, and he towered over me, holding a serrated knife. He had a thick Australian accent, and his teeth were moldy from lack of brushing. "We'll see about that."

The man sliced at me, and I jumped back to dodge. He missed me once, but he was quick, and when he swiped again, he sliced me across the shoulder. I stumbled back. The cut didn't hurt much, at least not as much as I expected, for the size of it.

"You made a mistake coming here," the man said. "Last one you'll ever make."

"We'll see about that," a voice grumbled. I turned to see Kimberly leap toward the man, knocking him back with a kick to the sternum. Blue, ethereal wings fluttered behind her as she tapped her feet on the ground and readied her daggers.

The man shouted and rushed forward, but Kimberly ducked his attack like a matador taunting a bull. He sliced at her, and she slid out of the way. By his third attack, she was done playing games. She knocked the knife out of his hand with one swipe and stabbed him through the chest with another, sending him flying backward into the white light, where he disappeared.

"Margaret!" I shouted, rushing over. She was tied to the chair, blood from a cut in her stomach pooling on the ground.

"It's a summoning circle," Kimberly said, pointing down to the circle surrounding Margaret's chair. "This isn't good."

"Cut her free," I said.

"She's in the middle of the summons. If I do that, I could kill her."

"Keeping her in there will kill her." Tears flowed down my cheeks. The man's knife was on the ground, and I grabbed it. I started hacking away at Margaret's rope bonds. "I'll do it if you won't."

Kimberly grabbed my hand. "You don't understand. Magic this powerful could destabilize the whole world, and then she'll be dead, and you along with it." She knelt down. "I have to break the summon first, but this is more complicated—it's like nothing I've ever seen before."

Margaret's eyes rolled back in her head. She needed a hospital.

"You have fifteen seconds, and then I'm cutting her out. She's not dying today."

"That's not enough time," Kimberly replied.

"I don't care."

Kimberly cursed me under her breath, but I didn't care. I had made one friend since I came to Missouri, and she wasn't going to die. Not if I had anything to say about it.

"Last chance," I said.

Kimberly looked down. "You realize I could kill you right now and then—"

"Then do it!" I screamed. "Kill me or let me cut her free. Three, two, o—"

She took a deep breath. "I hope this works." She took her knives and cut through the summoning circle, breaking the line of blood. The light flickered, and the sound undulated unnaturally. Both pulsated faster and faster, faster and faster, until a thunderous explosion shot me backward. A torrent of wind sucked me forward, and I tumbled through the room until—it was over, and I fell on the ground.

My head slammed on the floor. Something was different. I wasn't lying on cold concrete but warm hardwood. I looked around and realized I was no longer in a shady basement, but a bright, airy coffee shop. All of the patrons eyed me and an unconscious, bleeding Margaret laid in front of me. Across the shop, somebody tended to a dead man with one of Kimberly's knives dug deep in his chest.

"Kimberly?" I whispered, groggy and concussed. She was nowhere to be found. I was alone, and I had no idea where I was. *Perfect.*

BOOK 2

CHAPTER 18

Moments ago, I was in a basement, trying to free my friend Margaret from her kidnapper. Kimberly had stabbed the man in the chest and sent him tumbling backward through the same white light that enveloped me soon after. I only knew that because he laid on a plush, peach couch behind me, dead, a gnarly knife sticking out of his chest, as he bled on two patrons of the quaint coffee shop in which I now found myself.

The writing on the walls was in English, or at least most of it was, and a vibrant sign read *Lambzen Coffee and Tea Shop*. A line of people wrapped around the store as patrons waited for their cup of java…or at least they had been before I materialized out of thin air, hands covered in blood. Now, the mundanity of their day had been interrupted by a dead man, myself, and a girl bleeding out in front of them.

"Margaret!" I screamed, crawling toward her on wobbly knees. My head throbbed with the aftermath of what was likely a concussion—I hit that floor hard. Still, I made it over to her and cradled her curly hair in my hands. "Margaret, are you okay?"

"No," she replied softly. "I'm not okay at all. I'm not sure if you saw, but I've been stabbed." She winced in pain. "Ow."

She had lost a lot of blood before I even found her and was still bleeding onto the floor.

"Somebody call an ambulance!" Everyone looked at me with blank eyes, except the barista, who was already on the phone. Her eyes didn't say concern, at least not to me. No, they looked at me with malice.

"Yes," the barista said. "The girl has blood on her hands, and there is a man who has been stabbed to death, and another one—well, I know because he has a knife sticking out of his chest and he's not breathing…yes, I agree. That would do it…the other girl is bleeding but looks to be alive. For the moment, at least. She was just talking." The woman looked at me. "I don't know if she— she just appeared…No, she doesn't look armed. Thank you." The barista peered over the counter at me. "I've called the police. They'll be here any minute. Stay put because I think you'll be totally under arrest pretty soon." She turned back to the people waiting in line. "We'll get this cleaned up ASAP. You'll all receive complimentary drinks and ten free Java bucks to use in the future for your trouble."

The masses seemed appeased by that, but they still eyed me suspiciously. I couldn't blame them. After all, I had just appeared out of thin air.

"And the ambulance?" I asked. "Are they sending one for my friend?"

"Some friend," an old woman grumbled.

"Why would you stab your friend?" A tiny shell of a man asked. The skin of his face folded inside itself so far that his eyes were barely visible. "Doesn't seem very friendly to me!"

"Stab?" It finally connected in my brain that they thought I had done all of this. "I didn't—I'm not a killer!"

"Could have fooled me," a younger man said.

"Why you got blood on your hands then?" a woman with blue hair shouted from the back of the line.

The group of people started to surround me, and they looked neither kind nor polite. I laid Margaret back on the floor and scooted away from them. In the distance, sirens blared, and I knew they were coming for me.

"I—I—I don't have to explain myself to you." I fell backward, practically crab-walking across the floor, leaving bloody handprints in my wake. The group enveloped Margaret, and through their legs, I saw two of them applying pressure to her wound.

They had no such concern for me, and with every step, their eyes grew more vicious. When I bumped against a black coffee table, one of them lunged at me. I rolled out of the way and pushed myself to stand.

"The king will have your head for what you've done, witch!"

"Witch?" I said, trying to process everything that had happened. It was hard to concentrate with the ringing in my ears. "I'm not a witch." *I'm a demon if anything*, but I kept that to myself.

"Well, you appeared out of nothing, didn't ya?" It was impossible to pick one voice out of the crowd at this point. "I'll bet ya was doing a blood ritual to a demon, wasn't ya?"

"No, that's not—" Another barista came out from a black door behind the counter, and I saw an opening to escape. I wanted to make sure Margaret was okay, but I couldn't risk the cops thinking I was to blame for a murder…at least not until I figured out where I was and what was going on.

The mass of limbs lunged for me, and I flipped over them, then dove across the counter.

"Get her!" the limbs said, and the barista who had called the police sprang toward me. I stepped away from her, narrowly avoiding the other barista while pushing open the door to the back room. Metal shelving lined the walls, stuffed with coffee beans and filters and flour and sugar. If I weren't so horrified and scared, I would have liked to taste some of their heavenly brews, but I had other things to worry about, like staying alive.

The sirens were right on top of the store now, and the mass of limbs smashed through the door after me. I snaked through the shelving until I reached a metal door leading out of the storeroom. It let me out into a pungent alley that smelled the furthest from coffee possible—rotten meat and old fruit stewing in the garbage behind the cafe.

Guilt ran through my body as I took off. I only hoped they could save Margaret and that I could find her later when all this was sorted. Doctors were in a better position to fix her than I was, and part of me was suddenly relieved at the crazy turn of events that had just taken place. I doubted I could have saved her in that basement, even with Kimberly's help.

Kimberly. Where was she? Had she been teleported with me? Would I ever see her again? But before I could ruminate on those answers, the back door opened and two officers dressed in dark black uniforms rushed after me. I sprinted forward and disappeared into the crowded street.

***

Where was I? It had to be somewhere they spoke English as their primary language. India? No, that didn't seem right. Maybe Australia? I'd heard a bunch of super British accents, hadn't I? But I heard American accents, too. Maybe I was in St. Louis, or Kansas City, or Chicago. I could be in Canada, I guess. It didn't feel cold enough for Canada in the winter, though. In fact, it was kind of nice outside, so, yeah…Australia. It would be summer down there, right? It sounded right. Maybe New Zealand? Tasmania, possibly.

Enough speculating, Anjelica. I needed to find a newspaper. One thing that was not in doubt—I was in a city, somewhere. The buildings rose high above me so that I would have to crane my neck to see their spires. Having grown up in big cities, I knew better than to do that. It made you a target for pickpockets.

What time was it? It must have been morning because everybody was out, briskly walking with pointed purpose. Men dressed in business suits and women in long dresses swam through the densely packed streets, failing to pay even the littlest bit of attention to the girl with blood on her hands and clothes.

Speaking of, I needed to get to a bathroom, too, and soon. There was a glass-walled building up ahead, and inside looked like all the trappings of a convenience store. Perhaps I could handle both things at once.

I stepped into the store to see a mustachioed man with salt and pepper hair behind the counter, wearing a wrinkled short-sleeved baby blue polo shirt. "Excuse me. Do you have a bathroom?"

"Customers only," he growled.

"I'm going to buy a paper, but I'd rather wash my hands before I pay you, so I don't give you cooties."

He grunted then pointed to the back of the store. "I do not know this cooties, but okay. First door on the right." He leaned forward. "You better not use the toilet. I'll know."

"Yes, sir," I replied, hiding my hands in my pockets as I headed toward the bathroom. The blood had crusted on my skin, somehow both sticky and hard at the same time, like toffee, and it took forever to wash it off my fingers. Eventually, I was satisfied that nobody would think I was a killer at first blush. I scrubbed at the blood under my fingernails when I noticed that there was more speckled on my jeans, but that was a secondary concern. The blood on my jeans looked more like paint anyway, or maybe ketchup.

The man eyed me as I returned, and I made my way across the store to the magazine rack. I had never heard of any of the magazines they sold there, which confirmed that I wasn't in America, and I probably wasn't in Britain either, as I would expect to at least see *Vogue* on the newsstands. I made my way to the end of the rack, where a stack of papers sat in a metal holder. I picked one up and unfolded it. The main headline read, "Thriean troops attack Berzol. Prince Yimnit urges optimism; constraint."

I read the headline three more times before the man behind the counter sighed. "We aren't a library!"

"Right." I walked over and placed the newspaper down on the counter. "Hey, this is going to sound weird, but…where are we?"

He waved his hand at me dismissively. "I don't have time for your games, girl. Can't you see I'm busy?"

He was certainly not very busy, what with not having left the stool he sat on since I entered, but I wasn't going to argue. "Please, just humor me."

He sneered. "Lambzen, of course."

"And is that in North America, Europe…or—"

He leaned forward, giving me the stink eye. "Are you taking a piss?"

I shook my head. "Absolutely not. You told me NOT to use your toilet, so I didn't, and I certainly wouldn't do that on your floor."

That made him crack a smile as he sat back. "Lambzen, Forche province, Onmiri. Is that enough? I can name our planet, solar system, and galaxy, too, if it helps."

"Honestly," I replied, "I don't know what will help." It was then that I pulled a dollar out of my pocket and realized he probably wouldn't accept US currency. Still, you only learn things by doing, so I placed it on the counter.

He looked at it and cocked his head. "Now I know you're taking a piss. What is this? Play money?"

"No, it's—" And that's when I bolted out of the store, with the man shouting after me. On my way out, I grabbed a travel map from a little kiosk by the door and disappeared back into the crowd. I hadn't asked him for change or taken my paper, so it was more than a fair trade.

CHAPTER 19

Okay, so I was on a different planet for sure, possibly in a different reality, and improbably in another plane of existence. Cool. That's cool. *Don't freak out, Anjelica.* Just breathe. Breathe. In—and out. In—and out. In—*holy crap, I'm on another planet.* I need to get home. *How?* Probably something with magic, yeah? I mean, this sounds like the kind of thing that magic could do for you.

How do you find magic? Maybe there was, like, an occult store that I could find and then petition. Maybe magic wasn't so underground here. What if there isn't any magic here? No, that didn't make sense. Why wo—

My palms started to sweat as my eyes tracked across the street and settled on a police officer moving through the crowd. She was tall, blonde, and broad—broader than I thought possible for a woman, honestly, and the crowd parted as she stepped through, like an ocean liner leaving the harbor, partially because she was humongous, but also because she swung her baton at her side as she strolled. She hadn't seen me, but it was just a matter of time if I didn't make a hard move soon.

I sat down on a bench in a small park off the main street, pulling out my map to cover the bloodstains on my pants, and waited for her to pass. I studied the map to find out where I was, but the city looked completely foreign to me. I wasn't a great traveler to begin with. Any time I found myself in a new place, I relied on other people to know where we were going. I looked up and found the name of the park. "Thirgal the Third Memorial Park" a plaque said in the middle of the rocky walking path.

This might be another planet, but these people still had to get places, which meant they needed maps. Like math, maps should be universal. Sure enough, the map worked just like the ones on my Earth, and I traced my hand until I found the park at the bottom of the map.

"That's a start, Anjelica. Now, you walked what, five blocks south and three blocks east since you left that coffee shop?" I traced my finger up. "Or was that six blocks south and five east?" *Why was I so bad with directions?*

A wave of frustration washed over me, and I crumpled up the map in my hands. "What does it matter? None of this helps me get home!" I slumped back on the bench and started to cry. Full-body heaves jerked me from my core. They seemed like they would never stop.

"Are you okay?" I heard a soft voice ask. A shadow cast over me, and I looked up to see the blonde policewoman, baton now stowed in her belt holster, looking at me. "It's too nice a day to be so sad."

The tears stopped immediately, and fear replaced my frustration. My mind clouded, and when my mouth opened, I only managed a small squeak. I tried again, with the same result.

The police officer gestured to the bench. "You mind if I sit down?"

I shook my head. I didn't know what else to do, and when she sat next to me, every muscle in my body tensed. I made sure the map covered my blood-splattered pants.

"Tourist?" she asked, gesturing towards the map. When I nodded, she smiled. "I can always spot a tourist. Get lost from your family or something? This city is not the easiest to navigate."

"Y-y-yes. I lost them."

"Do you remember where you were when you last saw them?"

I shook my head. "I turned around, and they were gone. I've been walking everywhere trying to find them."

"All right, let's try to envision where you were. Close your eyes, okay?" I really didn't want to, but I also didn't want to act suspicious. The more I cooperated, the faster she would be out of my life. "Good. Now, try to recall anything from where you were when you lost them."

Nothing came for a second, but I really did want to find out where I had come from, and so I tried. "There was a coffee shop."

"We've got about a thousand of those. Anything else?"

I squeezed my eyes tightly, trying to imagine anything that I missed. And then I remembered something. A really ugly sculpture. "Yes, there was a bird, a big, ugly, blue metallic one."

The officer laughed. There was a carefree energy to her, and I had to fight against loosening my inhibitions around her. "Yeah, that's the Bragimis Building. The owner has the worst taste in art in the history of the world."

The world…but not my world.

She traced her hand on the nap. "Wow, you walked a far way."

Her radio crackled to life. "We have a suspect description from the stabbing at 321 North Filsteen. Suspect has bright red hair, blue jeans, and a puffy, pink coat. Please be advised she is armed, dangerous, and suspected as being a witch."

She stood up and pulled a gun out of its holster. It looked like the kind we had on Earth, except it was golden, and the barrel was swirled like a soft-serve ice cream cone.

"I'm going to need you to drop the map and put your hands up, ma'am."

Dammit. I did what she asked and revealed the bloodstains on my pants. "It's not what you th—"

"Don't say another word." She reached to her belt again, this time pulling out a pair of golden handcuffs. "You need to come with me. You're under arrest."

***

I tried to convince the police officer that I was innocent, but it didn't matter. She was a beat cop. She couldn't let me go even if she wanted to, and she certainly didn't want to. It was amazing how fast her face hardened when it was time to arrest me. Gone was the gentleness in her voice and the softness in her face. Her grip was vicelike when she pulled me up, and she nearly pulled my arm out of my socket when she spun me around to put on the cuffs, even though I was cooperating.

She didn't have a cruiser, so we walked down the streets of Lambzen, my head hung low so that everyone passing could see that I was a criminal—except I wasn't a criminal. It was all a misunderstanding.

When we got to the station, she threw me in a cell and slammed it closed behind me. I was happy to be out of the tight cuffs that chafed my wrists, but I couldn't help feeling like I was in a worse spot now that I couldn't even see the sun.

"What are you in for?" a middle-aged man with a long beard asked. He was sitting on the floor, head resting against the back of the cage.

"They think I stabbed two people."

"Did ya? No shame in it," he replied. "I stabbed a man once. Sometimes, you got no choice."

"Did you have a choice?" I asked.

"Shoot, yeah, I did. Could've died instead." He collected himself. "It was him or me, and I got too much spite in me to die before I get some manner of vengeance."

"Spite is as good a motivator to stay alive as anything, I suppose."

"You got that right, sister," the man said. He turned and eyed me. "You look a right bit too pretty to be a killer, though."

"Only one of them died…I think," I said. "And you don't know me. If you did, you'd know under this innocent exterior, I am a demon."

"Me too, sister."

"Metaphorically…or really?" I asked. "Because I'm serious."

He furrowed his brow. "I wouldn't go around telling too many people that, especially here. Humans don't take kindly to magic folks around here, especially ones they deem evil."

"Noted. Are you magic, then?"

He shook his head. "No, but I have a fondness for magic folk. Might have a magic kid or two out there somewhere. Maybe I'll meet them one day when I need a kidney or something."

"People don't talk about magic where I'm from. Unless they're crazy."

He leaned in and gave a devilish smirk. "Who's to say I'm not crazy?"

Before I could answer, a tall man with a trim goatee and trimmer frame walked into the room with a manila folder.

He looked through the bars, then snapped his fingers and pointed at me. "You. Come with me."

A slight woman opened the door to the cell, and I walked outside. Before I followed him down the hall, I turned to the bearded man in the cage. "It was nice to meet you."

"It was a pleasure to meet you. Keep your head down, girl. It'll all be okay. Worst case, you die, and then, at least it will all be over…and my, won't that be sweet."

The man with a goatee led me down a long hallway into a small room with a metal desk and two awfully uncomfortable chairs on either side.

"Sit," he said, motioning to the far chair. He slapped the folder down on the table. "I'm Detective Wharez, and who are you? I'm sorry for asking such a simple question upfront. Usually, I have all sorts of information on my subjects, but with you…well, you don't seem to have a past, which is troubling…as is the nature of your crimes."

"I didn't commit any crimes," I replied. "I didn't stab that man. I didn't hurt my friend…I'm not even supposed to be here."

He scratched his eyebrow with his finger as he shook his head. "Oh, I believe that."

"How is she? Margaret?"

He looked up at me. "She's a little worse for wear, as can be expected. The other gentleman—well, this is where things get interesting because we have information on him, and we figured out about Margaret pretty quickly. But there's literally nothing on you like you appeared out of thin air, and since you did appear out of thin air, I have to ask…where are you from? Cuz it sure ain't here."

I scratched my head. "I don't know how to answer that question."

"The truth would be a good start."

"I'm afraid you're going to think I'm crazy."

"Right now, I think you're a murderer, so crazy would be an improvement."

"Good point…okay, so I'm from a place called Missouri, in a country called the United States…on a planet called Earth."

"Hm. So you're really not from around here."

I had just unloaded a heaping bowl of crazy onto this police officer, and yet, he hadn't even blinked to what even I, the person saying them, thought sounded like absolutely bonkers claims. If I hadn't lived it, I never would have believed me, and yet, he seemed to do so without question.

"I have to say, you're taking this pretty well, considering," I said.

He leaned forward. "Would you believe this is not my first rodeo? I've been walking this beat for a long time, and I've seen a lot of things, intergalactic visitors being one of them. I've been doing this awhile, and I figure this wouldn't be a big deal…except…"

"Except what?"

"Except you came here with a dead man…and the princess of this here country."

"What?" I gasped. "Margaret…a princess? But how?"

"That's a good question, and I'm sure the king will want to hear all about it when you meet with him."

"The king? I'm meeting with a king?"

Wharez stood up and nodded. "Of course. The king insists on meeting with everyone before he executes them."

Oh, nerds. This was not good. I was very attached to my head and my life. "Execute me for what?"

"Kidnapping, murder, witchcraft." The detective stepped back from the table. "You have to understand. This is a monarchy, and the king has complete control here. So, you better come up with better answers for him than you have for me, because if he doesn't like your response…you'll lose your head before noon tomorrow."

CHAPTER 20

To say I had a fitful night's sleep was an understatement, even though after my interrogation, they moved me into better quarters that reminded me of a quaint bed and breakfast, filled with doilies, lace trim, and a gigantic bed. The king, apparently, insisted that people be well-rested before they were executed, and well-fed before they were presented to him for judgment. I was asked what kind of food I liked, but since I had no idea what kind of food they had, I simply asked for one of everything and was quite surprised when they accommodated me.

Much of the food I recognized, though I didn't know its name in this strange new place. I ate lobster, shrimp, shawarma, and some sushi, along with three types of cheesecake and a souffle before I was stuffed. I'd barely made a dent in what they'd brought. It amazed me that even in this brand-new place, so much was the same. On some level, it made sense that people would need maps and newspapers and guns, but that we could evolve in parallel tracks and still end up in roughly the same place was mind-boggling.

I could have ended up anywhere. Everyone could have been squid monsters, or frog people, or giant insects, but instead, they were humans who spoke a similar form of English. What were the odds?

Probably as slim as me lasting through the next twenty-four hours. It seemed that everyone who passed through my bed chambers had already decided I would be hanged, and I had a feeling that everyone who made it into the lace-frilled, luxury room as I had wasn't long for this world. Still, I refused to ask to confirm my suspicions, figuring that in this instance, ignorance truly was bliss.

I had little choice but to hope for some sort of miracle, but nobody knew I was here, except for Margaret, who was in some hospital somewhere, recovering…*had somebody told her she was a princess yet?* I wondered if anyone would tell her I died when I was gone. The only other person with any hope of helping me was Kimberly, but I hadn't seen her when I entered this strange land and, in all likelihood, she was still on Earth—our version of it.

When the sun shone through the bars onto my bed, the door to my room opened, and a large woman wearing a bright, multicolored dress and powdered purple wig sashayed in.

"Good morning, good morning, good morning." She looked at me and frowned. "Oh, no, no, no, no, no, this simply won't do." She lifted me onto my feet and dragged me toward a vanity on the side of the room.

I hadn't bothered to look in a mirror since I came to this place. The heavy bags under my eyes made me look ten years older than I was, and my frazzled hair stood up on end, leaving me looking like quite a horrific sight.

"When was the last time you showered, girl?" she asked.

"I don't—Who are you?"

She stood up straight. "I'm Madam Fantasmo, here to make you presentable to the king. You can't possibly be seen in court looking like—like you look right now." She shook her head fervently. "This is going to take some work. Yes, yes, yes."

She shuffled toward a door inset in the wall. When she opened it, a curtain rack shot out, lined with dozens of dresses and accessories as fine as any I had ever seen.

"Why do I need to look good to see the king? Isn't he just going to order my execution?"

"Well, with an attitude like that, yes, he will." Madam Fantasmo looked over at me. "You look like an—yes, here is one." She pulled out a shiny green dress with a ruffled collar. "My job is to make sure you don't die today, and I am very good at my job."

"Like a defense attorney?"

"God, no. Nothing as untoward as that. I am a royal stylist. The absolute best in the realm." She hung her finger in the air. "If you look the part of a noble, and you can speak like one, then you can be saved, yes you can. Tell me, dear, how is your diction?"

"Ummm…fine…I guess?"

She sighed and pointed to a door behind her. "Go. Shower and wash your hair. We have very little time and much to do."

I slowly walked around Madam Fantasmo and into the bathroom behind her. The moment I stepped into the shower, my desire to live increased ten-fold. The water was delightful on my bare back, and I let out a sigh of relief that seemed to rinse the weight of the last weeks away.

By the time I was done, three more women had joined Madam Fantasmo's entourage, each more glamourous than the last. They shepherded me from the shower over to the vanity and wrapped my hair with curlers. Once they were done, they covered my hair with a plastic hair cover and began to work on my make-up.

"Is this necessary?" I asked. "I'm not much of a make-up person."

"Of course it is, dear!" Madam Fantasmo bellowed. "This isn't about you, it's about the king, and he insists on perfection. My job is to deliver it to him so that he pities your pathetic plight and takes mercy on you."

The women worked on my face, plucking my eyebrows, curling my lashes, reddening my lips, and powdering my cheeks. When they were done, I looked like a right clown. If this were the day I died, I would be dreadfully embarrassed to lose my head looking like a circus performer. However, the lot of them looked pleased, and they knew more about this world than I did, so I allowed them to do their work, hoping it would help me survive this absurdity. I had put my life in weirder hands before, after all.

With the make-up completed, they loosened my hair, and relaxed curls fell from them onto my shoulders. The women spent a good half hour teasing my hair until it was as thick and luxurious as they could make it—which wasn't much in the end—and Madam Fantasmo slipped a corset over my midsection.

"This is going to hurt, honey," she said. "But all good things do."

She pulled tight, and the corset squeezed against my ribs, knocking the air out of my lungs with its tight grip. When she was done lacing it up, two of her helpers walked me to the green dress they had picked out for me.

"Yes, yes," Madam Fantasmo said when she was done. "You look almost passable, child. Truly one of my best works." She clapped for herself, and the three others joined in. "A masterpiece."

I slipped into a pair of sparkly green high heels—walking in them was a skill I never mastered—and my ankles buckled with every step.

"No, that won't work," Madam Fantasmo said. "You look like a silly goose, and that will not do at all." She pulled the shoes off my feet and slipped on a pair of green slippers instead. "Well, you don't look as regal, but you can move in those, so they'll have to do. Luckily, your dress is low enough to cover your feet." She pulled open the door to my room. "Now, come."

She stepped out into the hallway before me, and when I walked out, she nearly choked. "No, no. That is not how we walk. When we walk, we glide across the room, like you're floating on air."

I tried a couple more steps, much to Madam Fantasmo's chagrin. "I don't know how to do that. I only know how to walk like a human."

"And look where that got you." She pursed her lips. "It's all in the hips, girl. You have to roll them forward and take short, fast steps to make it seem like you are an ethereal angel from the great beyond." She moved behind me and grabbed me by the puffiness of my dress. "Move."

As I did, she pressed her hands and moved my hips to do what she wanted. "Like this?"

"Exactly, my dear." She stood upright. "Now, just master that in the next five minutes before we get to court."

I tried, I really did, to walk like she told me, but every time I shifted, her grimace deepened. Still, I wasn't giving up. If this was the way to win the king's heart, then I would do it, no matter how stupid it made me look.

At the end of the hallway was a long, enclosed walking bridge that led far off across a busy highway into the distance. Windows looked out onto the city below us every few feet, and the red carpet on the bridge was plush, plumped perfection. Fantasmo waved her hand over the black wall, and it lit with a green arrow. The floor began to move beneath my feet, and that was when Madam Fantasmo turned to me.

"King Ulthar is a demanding king, but he is the greatest we have ever known. Under his reign, we have conquered half the known world and even some of the unknown one. He has brought riches to us that were unimaginable even a generation ago. It might not seem it now but look out on the city below you." It looked like a city to me, every bit New York or London, neither of which I had been to, but both of which I had seen pictures of in books. A large building in the distance consumed a whole city block, dwarfing everything around as it rose high into the air.

"All of this came about because of King Ulthar's vision and guidance. Because of his leadership, we have become the envy of the world." She turned to me. "The king is the loveliest man to those he likes, and the harshest man alive to his enemies, and that's what this—" she gestured to my dress— "is all about. Proving you are a friend to the great king, so he bestows his mercy on you instead of his vengeance."

"According to the detective I spoke to last night, I'm accused of kidnapping his daughter. I don't think there's much coming back from that."

"Nonsense!" Madam Fantasmo said. "The way I see it, you have traveled across the cosmos to bring her home. You are a hero and should be rewarded as such." She took a step closer to me. "I have my choice of cases, you know, and I personally requested to be on this one because I think you are a winner, my love. Do you think every accused gets such treatment?"

"I—yes?"

"Absolutely not. Yes, they are all treated well the night before they are to be brought before the king, as per the law, but these frivolities? They are because I have taken a special interest in your case, girl from beyond the stars."

"So, you don't think I'm a murderous witch."

She smirked at me. "No, but if you were…I would like to be on your good side." We arrived at a black door on the other end of the long corridor. "Now, make me proud."

CHAPTER 21

The door opened, and we stepped into the scent of roses—or floated if I had learned anything from Madam Fantasmo—in the opulent hall, lined with golden candle sconces and massive paintings of the poshest people I could imagine. A crystal chandelier hung twenty feet above us, with hundreds of candle lights in each of its gilded arms.

Madam Fantasmo motioned me forward down the purple hallway, where we passed several suits of polished armor and small marble tables holding weaponry of all types.

"These are some of our most treasured valuables in the whole kingdom," she explained. "Each weapon represents a country that has surrendered to us, and the suits of armor represent one of our generals fallen in combat for the glorious cause of building our nation."

"It's beautiful," I replied. "I'm truly overwhelmed."

Madam Fantasmo smiled. "Good. Keep your sentences full of reverence, just like that, when it comes to the king, and deferential. Anything you can do to pay him a compliment will greatly help your case." She sighed. "I should tell you before we enter that your fears about being hanged are not unfounded. Many earworms in the court want you to be used as an example of the king's great power, to show that even a powerful witch is nothing to him." She squeezed my hand. "You must be extra charming and incredibly cunning if you wish to survive. Do you understand?"

I nodded. "I do, but I'm neither of those things. I'm just a girl from Los Angeles who ended up in Missouri."

"I don't know what any of that means, but, girl from Los Angeles, today you must be grander than you have ever known and braver than you ever believed. Can you do that?"

"I—don't know." I squeezed her hand back. "But I will try. I really don't want to die."

"That's a good start." We stopped in front of a two-story-high golden door. She tipped my chin high into the air with her index finger. "Keep your chin up, curtsey, and bow low, but never lose eye contact with his highness, and whatever you do, don't trip."

Why did people say that? Don't trip. It was the kiss of death. Now, all I was thinking about was how my feet moved, and to keep them—*breathe Anjelica. Breathe.* The doors opened, and violin music filled my ears. Hundreds of eyes looked at us as we walked down the purple carpet into the next room.

Courtiers, dozens of them, all dressed in the most idiotic and over-the-top costumes I had ever seen, lined both sides of the carpet. The men had the same powdered faces and frilly frocks as the women, and their wigs were just as high as Madam Fantasmo's. All of them looked at me with contempt. I had never had so much scorn leveled at me at once, and I had been a cheerleader for years, enduring hatred from opposing teams and fans for a long time. This was way worse.

The music changed from a violin to a piano, and Madam Fantasmo stepped in time with the tune. I let her lead the way. The people muttered to each other on our way to the golden throne, sitting high above the rest of the room. Purple drapes hung on either side, one inlaid with a dragon and the other with a tiger, and between them, on the throne, was a bearded man, grey-haired and wrinkled, but still handsome, wearing a rose gold crown encrusted with emeralds and amethyst around its base, and clasping a scepter in his hand with a globe of crystals sitting atop of it.

His skin was darker than the others in court, and he was the only one who wore no make-up. His black eyes dug into me like coal burning through my defenses. On either side of him, garish soldiers wearing checkered shirts of every color and newsboy hats held their lances high in the air. As we approached, they lowered their lances to form a cross in front of the king.

"My good King Ulthar," Madam Fantasmo said, curtseying and bowing in the exact manner she'd instructed me. "May I present to you, the traveler, Anjelica Caldwell." *That wasn't my last name.* "She humbly prostrates herself before you, for your judgment."

King Ulthar cleared his throat, and all chatter stopped. "I must admit, Madam Fantasmo, that you taking an interest in this case gives me pause. You have always been a great friend to this court, yet this girl has been cast as a devious fiend. I was ready to order her execution on sight, and many in this court have wished as much of me. However, you do not. Why do you support this girl and risk your standing in the court?"

Risk her standing? Why would she do that for me?

Madam Fantasmo pursed her lips. "Of all your amazing qualities, my liege, the one I have always respected the most is your desire for justice to everyone in your kingdom. Your justice is swift and final, but I believe you have always delivered it to friends and enemies alike. It is in that spirit that I gravitated toward this young girl—and that is what she is, nothing but a young girl—who would still be in school had she grown up in our kingdom. I heard the outcries for her head from others in court, and they fell sour on my ears. That is not justice, my king." She swallowed. "And you are a just lord. I throw my support behind her because I know that it carries weight when I do so, and power is nothing if not wielded for justice." She bowed to the king again. "I would ask that you listen to her with an open heart and an open mind, but I know you will do so anyway because you are a good king."

"Well spoken," King Ulthar said, beckoning me forward. "Very well, girl, come forward."

I stepped forward slowly, trying desperately not to trip. I bowed low, careful never to break eye contact with him, and then I stood. "Thank you, King Ulthar. Madam Fantasmo speaks very highly of you."

"And I of her. I must be honest, though, that I believe she has chosen wrong in this case. Many in this court have already made their mind up about you. So, tell me, witch, why are they wrong?"

I swallowed. "First, I am not a witch. I don't know what brings me to your shores, but it is not witchcraft. At least, not any performed by me."

"Then what brings you here, girl?"

"Friendship." I looked down at the floor, trying to regain my courage, and then back up at the king. "I did not have to save your daughter, my king. I did so because I care about her. I did so because she showed kindness to me and because she was in trouble. That I am accused of witchcraft, that I would be sentenced to death because of a good deed, is not justice. You would not have your daughter back if I had not stepped in, and she would be dead at the hand of the same villain you found murdered in that coffee shop."

"Was this murder carried out by your hand?"

"No," I replied.

"Do you condone it?"

I will not lie. "Yes, I do. He threatened me, and he threatened my friend."

A flurry of noise erupted in the court, and while I couldn't discern every word, those that I did were not things one should say in polite company.

The king ignored the commotion, staring intently at me. "The person whose murder you callously condoned was my first cavalier and brother, who has been lost to us for as long as my daughter. He was her champion, and if you tell me that my own blood would try to kill my flesh, I do not believe it."

"Well, you don't have to believe it for it to be the truth."

"In this kingdom," the king grumbled, "what I believe is the truth." His lips went up in a sneer. "I sentence you to death for your crimes against the crown. May your death be a lesson to those who fight against my will." He turned to Madam Fantasmo. "And you will join her for conspiring against me."

"My king, that—" But before she could say anything, guards flooded into the room and grabbed us both, dragging us out of the room to the great cries of joy from the assembled crowd.

"My king!" Madam Fantasmo screamed, kicking and squirming in her struggle against the guards. "Please! This isn't justice!"

We were to be put to death, just as I feared, and I would look a fool doing it. I hoped they at least let me change my clothes before they lopped off my head.

CHAPTER 22

Well, that didn't go well. Not only did I get myself sentenced to death, but I was also responsible for the death of Madam Fantasmo and her three helpers as well. This day was not going as planned, and it might have been the worst of all the ones I'd had in recent memory, including the time I was kidnapped.

"I'm so sorry," I said as I sat in a small cell in the basement of the prison with Madam Fantasmo and her helpers. They had been stripped of their big hair and their garish outfits, and now, like me, they wore little more than a thin, brown dress. They were so much smaller than I had realized. Gone was all of their confidence; their shoulders caved into their chests, and their heads hung low. "I didn't mean for this to happen. I didn't want any of this to happen."

"It's okay," one of the women said. "We knew the risks."

"Did we?" another piped up. "Did we really? Cuz I sure did not think this was gonna happen." Her thick, posh accent had vanished since our last meeting, and she now sounded high-pitched and nasally. "I never should have left Bisyl."

"I'm sorry," I said again. "I feel I should know your name before we die together, especially since you're going to die helping me."

"Kim," she replied. "It's short for Vorkim."

"I know a Kim back home, though hers is short for Kimberly."

"That's a dumb name," Vorkim grumbled.

"I like your name."

She sighed. "Not gonna matter soon."

The girl next to her smirked and held out her hand. "I'm Quince. It's not short for anything. Some people try to call me Quincent, but I hate it."

"Some people, right?"

"Totally."

The third girl stayed silent, and when my eyes met hers, she turned from me. I didn't push the issue. I turned to Madam Fantasmo.

"Is Madam Fantasmo your real name?"

"Gods, I wish," she replied. "I'm Grimble. Born to a humble miner family in one of the Free States, back when they were really free. That's my dead name now, though, which is ironic, given that I'm going to die with my new name, too."

I smiled at her. "I like Madam Fantasmo better. You made the right choice."

"Shut up, honey. I know it." She smiled at me. "I don't want you to feel bad. This is just what happens here. We who speak on behalf of the accused…we share their fate."

"Then why did you speak for me?"

"Your picture," Madam Fantasmo said. "You were—are—so young, and your eyes. I saw the terror on your face." She turned to her girls. "I asked them all, despite what they say."

"Hey!" the quiet girl who refused to introduce herself said. "I never thought you would lose. You've never lost before. Excuse me for trusting you."

"That's my fault. I got cocky." She looked at each of the girls. "I regret involving you in this, I do." She turned to me. "I don't regret sticking up for you, though. I still think you're innocent, even if the king's word is the only truth."

"I appreciate that. I mean, I would appreciate it more if we weren't going to die, but I appreciate it all the same." And then I did something I didn't expect. I started to laugh—at the pure absurdity of it all. It took control of me, and by the time I stopped, everyone in the cell stared at me. "Sorry, it's just…so ridiculous. If you only knew what I've been through this past month."

Before I could explain further, the door opened, and two men walked in, both wearing black silk hoods to match their black suits. They beckoned us forward, and I wondered if we would fight, but Madam Fantasmo simply stood and walked out of the cage. Suddenly, a rage bubbled up in me. Seeing them, seeing her…knowing what would happen.

"No!" I screamed. "This is stupid! I'm not doing it, and if you want me to go with you, you'll have to force me."

"Don't," Madam Fantasmo said. "If you fight, they take it out on your family."

"I don't have family," I replied. "At least not wherever the hell this is."

Quince stood up. "Well, I do, and they'll take it out on mine if you resist. It's over, anyway. Might as well make it quick."

The silent girl followed her, and finally Volkim, who looked at me with a sad smile. "Hey, at least we don't have to worry about tomorrow anymore."

The four of them stood outside, sad and pitiful. I wanted to fight. I wanted to rail, but what good would it do in the end? I was just one girl. Besides, I didn't want anyone else to be hurt. It was bad enough the four of them were going to die because of me, and I didn't want their families to be hurt as well.

One of the black suits led us out of the room. I dragged my feet. The sounds of a crowd swelled as we walked toward a pinprick of light. The light washed over us when we reached the cobblestone square outside of the palace.

If hundreds of eyes looking at me filled me with fear, then thousands, jeering and screaming at me, should have filled me with terror. Instead, I felt a sudden calm rush through my body as we walked through the crowd. They threw rotten tomatoes and old garbage at us. They taunted us and screamed obscenities. Some exclamations I understood, while others were foreign to me.

In the middle of the square, a hangman's platform had been erected, with five nooses hanging from it. When I saw it, tears started falling down my face. My chest heaved as the truth of what was happening fully dawned on me. Before, it had all been academic. I knew I was going to die, intellectually, but now that I saw it, it hit me deep in my core. Now, it was really the end.

I turned to run, but the mass of limbs from the crowd grabbed me and pushed me back into a guard, who kicked me back to my place in line.

"No, no, no, no, no. I can't—this can't be the end—I won't—this won't—I have to—" I muttered under my breath, and I felt a hand on my shoulder. It was Madam Fantasmo, and her steadfast resoluteness made my heart stop racing so fast, and her smile stopped my chest from heaving.

"It's going to be okay," she said. "Believe that."

But I didn't. I couldn't. I was about to frigging die. Yesterday I was complaining about being stuck in a house with people who loved me, and now I was in a different dimension or something, about to die. So, no, I couldn't believe that everything would be okay. Nothing would be okay. And there was nothing I could do to prevent it.

My feet kept stepping forward even though I didn't want them to, even though everything in my body screamed to run. I knew it was useless. I plodded up the creaky, wooden steps and stood with the damned in front of a squad of guards holding machine guns, one for each of us in case we wanted to run. The lead black suit pulled a piece of parchment from his pocket and walked forward.

"These five have been convicted by our just King Ulthar of crimes against the kingdom. Of kidnapping, of murder, of sedition, of treason, and of heresy! They are to be hung by the neck until dead for their crimes, as an example to all that any crime against any in our kingdom is a crime against the king himself and will be punished as such."

The guards pushed their guns into our backs, leaving us no option but to walk forward.

"Please," I muttered back. "You don't want to do this. I'm not a bad person. I'm not bad. I'm not—"

Metal connected with my nose as the guard slammed the butt of his gun into my face. I stumbled forward, and the guard pulled me by the hair with one hand and tied the noose around my throat with the other.

"No, no, no. Please." I choked on my tears as the noose tightened around my neck. "Please, please, please."

The others were weeping as well, but it was hard to make them out over the cheers from the crowd begging for our heads.

"By decree of King Ulthar…you are condemned to death for crimes against the crown." The black suit said. "May the gods have mercy on your treacherous souls. Let this b—"

I looked over at the black suit to see blood seeping out of his chest. He let out a gurgling sound and fell to the ground, dead…and that's when all hell broke loose.

CHAPTER 23

Moments after the executioner fell with a bloody thud, gunfire exploded behind me, and the cadre of soldiers prodding us into the nooses fell down with a painful, collective moan.

"Finally," Madam Fantasmo said, loosening the noose and grabbing a knife from the belt of a fallen soldier. With one fell swoop, she sliced the noose from my neck before turning her attention to Quince and the others. "Grab a gun. We're not out of this yet."

I pulled the remaining fibers of the noose off my neck. "What are you talking about? What's happening?"

When she'd finished cutting her helpers free, she turned to me with a big smile. "The rebellion has announced itself this day. Now, grab a gun."

The guard behind me stared at me with dead eyes when I pulled the gun from his clutched hand. I didn't know what Madam Fantasmo expected me to do with it, but I had it. "Now what?"

Guards gathered on both sides of the stand, ready to attack us. From the edge of the crowd, an explosion rocked the ground, and then another from across the square. A ring of blasts erupted, and the crowd scattered, trampling the guards as they ran for safety.

"Shouldn't we be doing something?" I asked.

Madam Fantasmo clutched onto the frame of the wooden structure. "Yes, hang on tight."

No sooner had I grasped onto the frame of the hangman's stand when four explosions erupted from each of its corners. The ground below us buckled, and the whole stand collapsed down with a loud crash. Before the dust settled, Madam Fantasmo hopped down into the slushy sewers below. I followed her without asking any questions as the crowd screamed above us. We were halfway down the tunnel when the guards opened fire on the stand.

"Care to tell me what is going on?" I asked after fifteen minutes fumbling through the sewers. I could no longer hear the police.

"I'm sorry, love," Madam Fantasmo said. "We didn't expect it to get this far. This was sort of a last-ditch effort to keep you safe." She stopped. "Ah, yes. Here we are."

I walked forward to see a ladder that led up into the city above us. Quince and Volkim scurried up the grimy rungs, and Madam Fantasmo pushed me to follow. Light flooded over us when Quince loosened the manhole cover. I exited the sewer into a garden surrounded by buildings on all four sides. The wordless helper exited next, and finally, Madam Fantasmo after her.

"Oh, thank the stars. They made me memorize the map, and I swore I would get it wrong." Madam Fantasmo walked toward a brick house on our right. She reached into a potted plant to pull out an antique key, which she used to open the door and disappear inside. "Come on."

I followed the others through the ground floor of the house, simple but clean. It smelled like lemon and vinegar, which clashed with the wet dog smell wafting off of us. In the living room, a svelte, older man wearing tuxedo tails stood next to a collection of cleaning equipment.

"This is Enger," Quince said. "Strip to your underwear and leave your clothes for him. There are four showers upstairs and a change of clothes for each of you." She turned to me, then pointed to the nameless girl. "Sindra will come to help dye your hair once we're all clean and dressed."

"My hair?" I said.

She nodded. "We'll all have to go through modifications to make us look different if we want to avoid detection from the street cameras." She grabbed her chin and yanked, and a hunk of plaster came off, revealing a softer, rounder face underneath it. Meanwhile, Sindra removed a pair of blue contacts, revealing her purple eyes.

"It will be easier for some of us than others." Madam Fantasmo's voice dropped half an octave. "I haven't spoken like this in a long time. I hate it." She started to cry.

Volkim, who had taken off her wig to reveal a bald head underneath, reached over and rubbed Madam Fantasmo's back. "Hey, hey. Nobody can tell you who you are, and when this is over—"

"I know. It's stupid. It's just—No, it's okay. You're right. We all have to hide for a short time." She looked down at the wig. "Soon, my love, we'll be together again, and we'll never have to hide again."

She tossed the suit into a pile forming in the center of the room, discarding the remnants of a past life. We all stripped down and put on flip-flops before heading up the stairs. I looked over my shoulder and watched as Enger grabbed a handful of our discarded clothes, then opened a small door to what must have been the basement.

"What are you going to do to them?" I asked.

"Burn them, of course," Enger said, and disappeared into the basement. Moments later, an acrid smell filled the air, the result of burning hair and rubber.

***

Even after a thirty-minute shower and scrubbing myself red with the luffa Enger provided, the stink of the sewer was still on me. Worse, when I closed my eyes to wash off the soap, the guard's dead eyes haunted my memory. Too many dead people haunted my memories.

"Are you decent?" Sindra asked. Her voice was lovely, melodic, and calming, and she smiled brightly as I wrapped myself in a towel. "We need to get started on your hair."

I sat on the toilet and let her rub Vaseline along the base of my neck and the edges of my forehead. "What are you doing that for?"

"It prevents staining," Sindra said. "Haven't you ever colored your hair before?"

"No," I replied. "I kind of love my hair. It's the only thing about me that I like, honestly."

"It's beautiful," she said, pulling my hair into four sections and clipping them. "It's a shame to change it, but one day it will grow back, as long as you stay alive."

"I don't get it," I said as she began to paint the roots of my hair with a brush. "Why would you do all this for me?"

Sindra chuckled. "We didn't do it for you. You are a catalyst—a symbol. The rebellion loves their symbols."

"How am I a symbol? I'm just a girl."

"I'm just a hair stylist, Anjelica," Sindra said, crimping my hair with aluminum foil. "That's way above my pay grade." When she was done, she placed a plastic shower cap over my head. "We'll let that set for an hour, and you should be good to go."

She turned to walk away, and I reached out to stop her. "You have a really pretty voice. Why did you decide to stay silent with me?"

Sindra chuckled. "I'm terrible at keeping secrets. The only way I could stay hidden was to keep my mouth shut. You gotta do what you gotta do to survive, right?"

I nodded. "Absolutely."

"I need to change and shower again to rinse this junk off of me, but I'll see you around, okay? Don't touch your hair, no matter how much it itches."

I walked across the hall to a room where Enger had written my name on a piece of paper hanging on the door. Inside was a small bed, where he had laid a black skirt, dark gray shirt, and white sneakers. Alongside, there was a note, written in the same handwriting he used on the door.

I guessed at your size, but I am a very good guesser. If these don't fit, let me know.

"He tailored them himself," I heard Volkim at the door and turned to see her wearing a black skater dress and black boots. Her hair had been chopped into a pixie cut and dyed the same color as her dress. She placed her hands in her pockets and gave a spin. "Mine has pockets."

"Genius," I replied. "All dresses should have pockets."

"Agreed," she said, then took a long silence. "It's not all garbage, you know?"

"What isn't?"

"This planet. I know you've only seen the terrible stuff, but it's not all bad. There are some things worth fighting for."

"I'm sure there are. My planet also kind of sucks, but it's also sort of beautiful." I sighed. "Do you think I'll ever see it again?"

Volkim shrugged, her hands still in her pockets. "I don't know. But if there was a way to get you here, there's got to be a way to get you back, right? Anyway, I'll let you change. I just wanted to let you know that I'm sorry everything's been so terrible since you got here."

I smiled. "This moment's been kind of nice."

She nodded. "I agree wholeheartedly."

An hour later, Sindra came to get me. Her hair was now a dark brown, and a pair of brown contacts hid her vibrant, purple eyes. Her face looked slimmer than the last time I saw her, and when I told her, she laughed.

"You can make your face look like just about anything if you have the right make-up." She removed the foil protecting my hair and led me into the bathroom, where she washed out the excess color, then rubbed it quickly with a towel. "What do you think?"

I flipped my hair back and looked at myself in the mirror. It was like I was a completely different person. My hair was jet black, with none of the shimmering highlights of my natural color. "I hate it." I looked over at Sindra, whose face turned down. "It's not your fault. You did a great job; I just…I hate it so much. I hate all of this so much."

"I get it," Sindra said. "I'm sending in Quince to give you a cut."

I opened my mouth to protest but stopped myself. It wasn't a suggestion. I was going to get my hair cut.

Quince came in with a pair of scissors a couple of minutes later and got right to work. "You're lucky. I had to have Volkim cut my hair. You have me, and I'm way better."

My hair was down past my shoulders, near the middle of my back. Though Quince didn't give me a pixie cut like

Volkim's, she cut over six inches off so that my hair rested an inch above my shoulders.

"Shower, and then I'll style it," Quince said. Again, it wasn't a suggestion. I stepped into the shower as she swept the hair from the chair and floor.

There was no joy in that last shower, just rote memories, and painful thoughts as I washed off the snipped hair and any residual dye. When I was done, Quince styled my hair to make me look like a 1970s TV star, and Volkim used make-up to contour my face until I was nearly unrecognizable, finishing it off with a thick eyeliner that made me seem like a punk rock goddess. It was a look I never thought I could pull off, and when they were done, even I didn't recognize myself.

When I finally made my way downstairs, the others were waiting for me around a table. Madam Fantasmo stood up. She was as unrecognizable as I was, wearing smart khakis and a white collared shirt popping out of an argyle sweater. Her hair was cropped tight, and she wore brown loafers. All the joy was gone from her face, replaced with a resigned dignity.

"Enger made sandwiches for us. They're good." She sounded like a monotone, boring, blasé bank manager as she spoke.

The smell of burnt rubber had been replaced by warm sandwiches, and it looked as if we had never even come into the house from a dirty sewer. In fact, we didn't even look like ourselves. We looked like a happy family that belonged in this weird, little house, eating delicious cucumber sandwiches.

However, I knew it couldn't last long. The truth was, we were fugitives, and we would have to move soon or risk getting caught. Still, the sandwiches were delicious.

CHAPTER 24

Enger cleared our dishes as we finished them, and when we were done with our food, it was like we had never even eaten. In fact, it was like we never even stepped foot in the house at all.

"I must say, Enger," I said, turning to the kitchen. "You are the more fastidiou—"

Madam Fantasmo clasped her hand over my mouth as a key jingled in the door. Enger caught her eyes and nodded. He scooted across the hallway and opened the basement door. Madam Fantasmo made a circle with her hand, and the other girls stood silently. She nodded at me, and I nodded back to indicate I understood and followed them to the door. Enger slid behind us and pushed our chairs in, scooping the last of the crumbs up into his hand and stuffing them into his pocket. Then, he pushed the basement door closed just as the front one opened.

"Good afternoon, Master Sern," Enger said through the door. "You're home early."

There was the sound of footsteps entering the room. "They closed the consulate after the bombing."

"Bombing?" Enger said, aghast. "My word. What is this world coming to?"

A woman at the door laughed. "You really do not keep up on the events of the day. I love that about you." Two more feet stepped inside the house. "I believe Captain Temble is hungry. Could you fix him up a spot of lunch?"

"Of course, mum," Enger replied.

"I do so love your cucumber sandwiches, old boy," a gruff voice said, and more feet made their way across the floor toward the dining room where just moments ago we had sat, enjoying those exact same finger sandwiches.

"Meanwhile, I'm going upstairs to change," the woman said. I heard footsteps lope on the stairs above me, and Madam Fantasmo pulled me down to the bottom of the stairs.

"This is bad. This is very bad. Mistress Revil was supposed to be at the consulate until five, giving us plenty of time to get out of this house and meet up with the others."

"What are we going to do now?" Quince asked, nearly hysterical. "If the captain is here, that means there are at least four Jackboots outside."

"We wait them out," Madam Fantasmo said. "The mistress never comes down here, and as long as there's nothing suspicious in the house, which there isn't, then we should be fine. Let's cross our fingers they'll be gone soon."

I took a deep breath, trying to steady my beating heart. I had almost died too many times in my young life, and I had learned from those experiences that calm heads generally prevail.

"I'll go up and listen," I said. "That way, in case—you know—stuff goes down, we'll be ready." I crawled up the stairs just as Enger set a plate on the table.

"Marvelous, good boy," the captain tutted between bites of sandwich. "Just marvelous."

Loud footsteps skittered down the stairs. "Enger! What do you make of this? I found a pair of pink underwear in my bedroom, and it's quite too small to be mine."

"I don't know, ma'am. Maybe one of your—"

"Don't lie to me, Enger," Mistress Revil spat. "Is somebody in this house? Are you using my room as your own little sex dungeon?"

"No, ma'am, nothing untoward as that."

"Then what?"

There was a long silence, and my hands began to shake. Then, the sounds of a chair pushing out, and the captain cleared his throat. "No worries. I'm sure Enger isn't hiding anything, but if it will make you feel any better, I'll have my men do a sweep of the premises."

"Yes, Captain. I think that would be best."

Enger stepped forward. "I'm afraid I can't do that, ma'am."

Oh no. I ran down the stairs. "We have to go. They're going to search the place. It's all going to pot."

"By the gods," Madam Fantasmo grumbled. "We need to—"

A gunshot rang out, and we all rushed up the stairs and pushed open the door to see Enger standing over the captain, who had a knife in his throat. A smoking hole from a gunshot had been made in the ceiling, and blood pooled under Mistress Revil where she lay on the floor, a serving fork buried in her eye.

"I'm sorry, ma'am," Enger said, locking the door to the house as the guards slammed against it. "I tried to keep this quiet. Out the back. I will fend them off for as long as I can."

"Thank you, but—"

Enger pulled out one of our machine guns from behind the counter. "No buts. I believe goodbyes are in order."

Madam Fantasmo nodded sadly. "Goodbye, Enger."

"We live as one." He pounded his chest.

"We die as one." Madam Fantasmo pounded her chest and then rushed to the back of the house. We followed behind. Behind me, I heard the front door break open, and four gunshots fire in succession.

"Come on," Madam Fantasmo whispered as we crossed the quad. She squeezed into a narrow alley on the opposite side, and we all did the same. "Hurry."

I disappeared into the alley just as one of the Jackboots threw open the back door of the house. I thought I was silent, but the guard must have heard something. He looked in our direction. "Guards! It's them!"

"Well, shit," Madam Fantasmo said. "Split up. Volkim, Sindra, take Anjelica left. Quince and I will go right and try to guide them away. Meet where we said, and if we don't—"

She pointed to her chest twice, and so did the others. I didn't know what it meant, but I did it as well. Then, Volkim and Sindra each took one of my hands and pulled me along.

"What is she doing?" I said as we rushed away.

"She's going to cause a distraction, I hope," Volkim answered.

I watched Madam Fantasmo and Quince disappear one way down the street and then quickly take off in the other direction, two Jackboots rushing behind them. Meanwhile, Sindra, Volkim, and I reached the corner and began to cross. From the end of the street, another Jackboot ran toward us. Up close, I could see they were dressed much like the black suits, except with thick black metal helmets and black balaclavas to cover their mouths, along with goggles. The one following me pulled a long rifle up toward us.

"Stop!" he shouted.

The hairs on my head stood on end as a shot of blue electricity crackled past my head. A scream erupted from my body against my will, but we kept charging forward through a park where two men picnicked and a couple walked their dog.

The ruckus caused more Jackboots to descend on the park. These were different from the police officer we'd just met, and they were quite a bit more deadly, pulling their weapons before even screaming for us to stop.

"This goes without saying but DO NOT STOP!" Sindra called to me. We sprinted through the park and through an intersection where cars blared their horns at us. More electrical charges fired from behind, crackling through the cars as we slid behind them.

"There!" Volkim pointed at a man getting into a small, red convertible. As he turned the ignition, she kicked him in the face and threw him out of the car. I didn't even think; I slid into the back seat as Sindra jumped into the front, and Volkim took off into the road.

"That was a whole lot of effort on our wardrobes for nothing!" Sindra said. She was still shouting. "They'll have our faces everywhere now!"

"I know! I know!" Volkim didn't take her eyes off the road. "Just let me think."

"Think about what? How screwed we are?" I asked.

Sindra looked back at the Jackboots, who were busy helping the man off the ground. "They'll be in the system in a minute and shut this car down."

Volkim scanned the road. "There!" She skidded to a stop in front of a bike rack and leaped out, leaving the idling car in the middle of the street. She kicked the bikes off the rack and pushed one to me. "You know how to ride?"

I nodded. "Of course."

We pedaled through the throngs of pedestrians. At least with our new faces, we weren't recognizable to the average person. We weaved through the city for three blocks and then spun left and went for another two before Volkim came to a stop and kicked the bike to the ground.

"We go the rest of the way on foot."

Sindra nodded. "If you think that's best."

"Be inconspicuous." Volkim placed the bike against the side of the building and shoved through the crowd. She reached into her pocket and pulled out three face masks. I had seen a few other people wearing them before, and she handed them back to us. "If anyone asks, you're sick."

I put on my face mask, a black one to match my skirt, and we disappeared into an alley. We turned left when we were through and continued through another crowded intersection. We crossed another street and passed a tall steepled building with a full moon at the top. Volkim stopped.

"Please, please, please," she whispered. Several seconds later, a bell rung and a throng of students began to stream out of the building, all dressed in the same dark colors and holding school bags. They cut in every which way, and we moved through them. Volkim mocked their gait as she rushed forward, knocking into one and taking their red bag.

Sindra did the same with a girl who had a brown leather satchel. They moved too quickly for the girls to find them, but I knew what to look for. We followed a different group of schoolchildren for a few blocks, then stole into a big building with gold-trimmed glass doors. We didn't stay inside long, just enough to use it as a thoroughfare to get from one side to the other, and when we came out again, a city bus pulled up. Volkim got on, handing the driver enough money for all of us.

We sat down in the middle of the bus, and Sindra's shoulders slumped down. Volkim let out a sigh of relief as the bus pulled away. "Next stop, Incarta."

CHAPTER 25

"Where are they?" Sindra said, pacing back and forth in the lobby of a condemned diner. Rats skittered on the rotting floorboards where Volkim sat on a tattered stool.

"They'll be here," Volkim replied. "You have to trust them."

Sindra glared at the wall and said, "I don't trust anyone. Not after what just happened."

"Honestly," I butted in. "That's probably a good instinct."

"Hey!" Volkim said. "We're only alive because of Madam Fantasmo. Show a little respect."

"That's the truth," Sindra said. "But in fairness, I was about to be put to death because of her, too, so best-case scenario, it's a net neutral."

"We'll give it ten minutes, and then we'll go."

"And what if Madam Fantasmo was captured? What if they tortured her, and she told them where to find us?"

Volkim stood and walked menacingly toward Sindra. "Then we have way bigger problems."

"Hey," I said, shooting up from my place at a derelict booth. "I think that's a fair compromise. Ten minutes, and then we go. Meanwhile, you can tell me all about the rebellion and why you guys are part of it."

"That sounds cheery," Volkim said. "Pass."

"At least tell me what banging your chest twice means."

"It means our hearts beat as one. In the rebellion, we live as one, and we die as one, for the freedom of Onmiri.

For the freedom of us all." Volkim scowled. "That's all you'll get out of me."

"Fine, be that way." I turned to Sindra. "How about you?"

"I'm not supposed to talk about it," she said. "Then again, I've been doing a bunch of stuff I'm not supposed to do recently, so fine."

"Sindra!" Volkim hissed. "No."

"Oh, please. We all almost died to save her. Do you think she doesn't have the right to know why?"

"It's not our place," Volkim said, shooting me a glance. "No offense."

"I'm not offe—"

"None of this is anybody's place," Sindra growled. "We're all just trying to do the best we can, so unless you are physically going to stop me, I'm telling her." Volkim didn't make a move, so Sindra sat closer to me. "What do you want to know?"

"Everything…but I think that's probably not going to happen, so how about anything—literally anything as to what just happened."

"Do you have kings where you are from?" Sindra asked.

I nodded. "Some, but they don't have a lot of power anymore, far as I understand."

"Well, ours does. In fact, he has all the power and the most dominant army in the world. Formidable enough to steamroll over nations. Strong enough to flatten anybody who speaks an ill word about him. That's too much power for one person, any one person, but our king, Ulthar, is— well, he's a real dickhole."

"It's not all his fault," Volkim said. "All that power—it would corrupt anyone."

I shook my head. "I don't believe that. We have a saying that absolute power corrupts, but I don't think that's true. I think absolute power reveals. It reveals the true nature of people, so if the king is a massive dick, it's because he's a massive dick."

Sindra laughed. "We are always trying to equivocate, even in the rebellion, to say it's not all the king's fault, but I agree. It is his fault. He is the one wielding this power, which is where the rebellion comes in. We are working to bring down the monarchy and restore balance to the world."

"And you guys were like spies?"

"We played our part," Sindra said sadly. "You'd have to ask Madam Fantasmo about all the history stuff. I'm not good with details, but the rebellion's been around for as long as the king has. As the king has grown in power, so has the resistance, always in the shadows—always, until today."

"Why now, though? Why me? Do either of you have any idea?"

Volkim shook her head. "I just know it has something to do with you and with Margaret."

"Margaret? What does she have to do with anything?" *Maybe this was part of the prophecy.*

There was a rustling in the back of the building, and we all jumped to attention. When the shadow revealed itself, it was Madam Fantasmo, far worse for wear, stopping to lean against an exposed wooden beam. "It has everything to do with everything."

"Madam!" Volkim called out, rushing to her with Sindra close behind. They wrapped her up in a big hug, and she squeezed them tightly. "It's so good to see you."

"It's good to see you, too, girls." She smiled at me. "Do you want some of this, sugar?"

"I don't want to impose," I said. "This is a moment for the three of you."

Volkim beckoned me forward. "You're one of us now, if you want to be."

I smiled and took a hesitant step forward. "I'm with you, if you'll have me."

Sindra and Volkim wrapped their arms around me, and I wrapped mine around them, and we all wrapped Madam Fantasmo tightly and thanked our lucky stars we had each other.

"What about Quince?" Sindra asked, stuffed snugly into Madam Fantasmo's shoulder.

"She didn't make it." Madam Fantasmo pounded her chest. "We live as one."

Volkim and Sindra pounded their chest. I did so too, but a second behind them. "We die as one."

***

"Hurry, girls," Madam Fantasmo bellowed as she led us into the back of a bank warehouse. "I don't know if they know about this place yet, but they'll be here soon enough."

She flicked on the lights, and there were dresses and wigs for as far as the eye could see, on dozens of shelves and racks. I picked up a rainbow sequined gown that shimmered in a dozen different colors.

"What is this place?"

"It's where I store my old costumes, those that have been worn and are yet to be discarded or repurposed."

"They seem brand-new," I said, appreciating the glimmer on the collar.

"Of course, they are, darling. They've only been worn once."

"The whole warehouse is filled with clothes you only wore once?" My voice cracked at the sheer audacity of the thought.

"Of course, my love," she said. "You can't possibly be seen in court with the same clothes twice." She picked up a blue evening dress, bedazzled from collar to hem. "And gods forbid you are seen in the same clothes as somebody else. I remember the scandal when Countess Guile wore a similar dress to this one six months after me. She was run out of court and now lives in exile on the Juniter Islands."

"They sound nice at least," I said, picking up a purple wig.

"They aren't," she replied. "Mud farmers and dirt merchants are all that come from there." She tossed the blue dress to the ground and clapped her hands. "All right, ladies, find the least gaudy clothing and accessories you can. The goal is to blend in, which is a string of words I never thought I'd say in this place. We leave in fifteen minutes."

I searched through the racks of clothes and pulled out a pair of simple black pants, paired with a purple feathered coat and labeled *Hallentown 2014*. I mixed in a gray shirt that must have been the undergarment to a wolf outfit. I put on a gray wig and then a blue bowler hat and threw on a pair of silver sunglasses that were comically large for my face. When I was done, I couldn't help feeling a bit like Annie Hall and Audrey Hepburn's lovechild.

From the back of the warehouse, a whistle crackled through the building, and we all lined up in front of Madam Fantasmo, who was wearing a pair of blue leggings and a frilly beige blouse. Her large-brimmed hat flopped up and down while she looked me over and nodded her approval. Volkim and Sindra wore bland clothing like me, with Sindra in a gray dress with two holes in the back where she had ripped off a pair of angel wings, and Volkim in a burgundy jumper with a crop top underneath. Before Madam Fantasmo opened the door, Sindra put on a jean jacket bedazzled with fabulous lavender rhinestones, and we walked out into the street like we were the chorus to a very off-off-Broadway musical.

Madam Fantasmo walked with none of her garish brilliance, her arms swaying like a regular schlub, just trying to fit in, and we snaked around the buildings of the city. She used a small fan to cover her face from the cameras while Volkim and Sindra hid theirs with the scarves around their necks.

Once we had walked four blocks, Madam Fantasmo hopped onto a bus, which we took across the city to the end of the line, a quaint neighborhood that could have been confused with Greenwich Village, if that existed in this place.

"How much further?" I asked Volkim for the tenth time after we'd gotten off the bus. She answered with another roll of her eyes.

Madam Fantasmo hopped up the stairs of a simple brick building with no awnings, lattices, or balconies, just sad little windows separated by too far a distance and red brick all the way up. A metal overhang protected the glass door, and inside, Madam Fantasmo scratched her cheek while studying a bank of buzzers in a dusty call box.

"Do you remember the combination, my love?" she asked Sindra.

Sindra pushed one of several dozen buttons, initiating a harsh buzz. She thought for a second and pressed another pattern, which returned silence. She smiled and gave a slight nod, then initiated a half dozen more button presses in what felt like random order. A few seconds later, another harsh buzz preceded the unlocking of the door, and Volkim beelined for the elevator, where she hit the button for the basement.

"Most of these rooms are simply shells," Madam Fantasmo said to me. The others looked completely uninterested in the proceedings. "Offices and perches for us to see out into the world and designed so nobody can see us."

"And who is us, again?" I asked.

The door opened with a ding, and we walked out onto a catwalk overlooking a huge room much wider than the above building indicated. Corridors spidered off in every direction, with dozens of people sitting in front of computer banks.

"The rebellion, my love."

"Wow," I said. "I expected…I don't know what I expected, but…wow."

"Yes, I suppose it is impressive in its way." She waved me forward. "Come, I have to introduce you to the director." Over her shoulder, she spoke to Sindra and Volkim. "Debrief is in twenty. Meanwhile, get some food. You both look terrible." She glanced at me. "You look terrible, too, but you'll have to wait. We have business to attend to."

CHAPTER 26

Madam Fantasmo led me down the iron stairs to the ground floor of the base, her back straight, and shoulders thrown back. With each step, her chin lifted higher. By the time she reached the bottom, the fierce woman she'd been when I met her had returned.

"Welcome to the rebellion," she said, then winked. "Close your mouth. You're letting in flies."

I tapped my chin with my hand and realized my mouth was agape. "I'm sorry. It's just—you said rebellion, and I figured—well, in the movies where I'm from the rebellion are usually a bunch of scrappy upstarts with no means and no technology, except in Star Wars, but they're still underfunded compared to the empire—but this—this is incredible."

"Well, honey, of course, it's incredible. You think we can throw over the monarchy with sticks and spears?" She spun around, arms open. "And make no mistake, we will bring down the monarchy."

"It's good to see you alive."

I turned to see who had spoken. It was a woman in a gray pantsuit, her brown hair arranged in a smart mod cut. She walked toward us with her arms crossed and a stern look on her face. Madam Fantasmo squealed in delight and ran to her, lifting the woman up in her arms until they were both laughing and wrapped in a big hug.

The woman's smile transformed her voice. "It's so good to see you. I thought you were dead for sure."

"I had faith in you," Madam Fantasmo whispered, setting the woman back on her feet. "Maybe if you told me that, I wouldn't have, though. Criminy, did you really think you weren't going to get me out?" She pressed her hand on her heart. "I don't know how I feel about that."

"You know how hard that was to pull off? How many things had to go right? Shooting the executioner from half a mile away was the simplest part of the plan. We had to lay depth charges, make sure not to hurt innocents, and clear a path of workers, so they didn't report you across half the city." She pointed up into the air, and I followed her gaze to TV screens twenty feet high that showed our faces, all four of us. "This whole thing has been a nightmare. Jasper is going to kill you."

"Please, if he wanted us dead, then he could have just not done anything." I cleared my throat, and Madam Fantasmo seemed to realize I existed again. "Oh! Director Higley Frente, this is Anjelica, last name redacted."

"It's Arnold, or Campbell," I said, smiling and shaking her hand. "Anjelica Arnold-Campbell, I guess."

"It's a pleasure to meet you. We have been following your exploits all day. To say you've caused a commotion since you've arrived here is an understatement." She gestured in front of her. "If you'll follow me to my office. I think we have some things to discuss." She turned to Madam Fantasmo. "Thank you for your service. It won't go unnoticed."

"Um, I'm coming too." They stared at each other for a second, and as their contest continued, Madam Fantasmo's eyes narrowed. "That girl is my responsibility, and if you think I'm going to let her out of my sight, yo—"

"Fine," Director Frente replied. "It's not like I'm going to do anything untoward or lie to the poor girl."

"No, but you might conveniently forget to mention something to her, and as her counsel—"

"In the royal court."

"—In all courts, and with all people, as her counsel—it is my responsibility to make sure nobody takes advantage of her. Nobody but me, at least." She winked at me again. "Kidding! Lead the way, Director."

The heels on the director's shoes clacked loudly on the black marble as she led us down a sleek, white hallway. People shuffling past gave us a wide berth, their eyes filled with a combination of fear and awe. Halfway down the hallway, she turned into a conference room. A pitcher of water sat on the obsidian table, and I suddenly realized that I was desperately thirsty. I caught a whiff of sugar and carbs and watched as the director reached into a small shelving unit under a television monitor and pulled out a red box filled with donuts and other sweets.

"I'm sorry it's not a better spread. Frankly, we thought you would be here by now, and—well, some of the men got overzealous. I was able to scavenge this for you from the carcass of your welcome feast." She slid the box over and then dropped into a high-backed chair at one end of the table, while Madam Fantasmo and I took our seats on the other. I jammed a few of the cookies into my mouth.

"I wanted to start by saying that not everyone in this world is as backward as the king, and we welcome you, witch, to our dimension."

I smiled. "Thank you. I'm not a witch, though, and frankly, I don't know if this is a different dimension or just a different planet." Then I realized something. "Holy crap. You're aliens. I literally discovered aliens—either aliens or parallel worlds, and nobody will ever believe me."

"I hate to burst your bubble, but you are not the first travelers we've had visit our humble planet. In fact, previous travelers are precisely why the king dislikes you so much." She wrinkled her nose like she smelled something unpleasant.

"Honestly, I'm not surprised by the reaction. I've been thinking about it, and I doubt that if you came to Earth, you would get a better reception—" I ripped into a bear claw. "But yeah, why does the king dislike travelers so much?"

"Are you a religious person, Anjelica?"

Well, I just learned I was a demon, so I was coming around to it. I figured it probably wasn't the time to be telling them I wasn't just an alien but a demon to boot. "Not historically, but I'm warming to the idea."

The director leaned forward. "In our world, we believe that the gods abandoned us to explore the universe when the world was young, leaving us with nothing to worship but their knowledge." She stood up and paused as if carefully debating her next words. "We also believe that one day they will return and send a harbinger of their homecoming." She stepped closer to me. "The king sits on a fragile grasp of power, based upon one simple fact—"

Suddenly, it connected. "He's a traveler from another world."

"Yes. The people worship him like a god, and he has worked relentlessly to uphold that charade. He is obsessed with maintaining the idea his right to rule is absolute." The director stood before the window. Outside, hundreds of people bustled around. "We have laid in wait for so long, waiting for a chance to strike, and you have given that to us."

"I see what you're getting at, but I'm not a god, and I'm not a leader. I'm just a kid from Los Angeles, or Missouri, or whatever stupid place I'm from. All I want to do is go home." I bit my lip. "You said the king is killing off other travelers…does that mean no one has found a way home yet?"

"I don't know," Director Frente replied. "Many have simply vanished. Whether they are dead or gone back to their homes, we don't know." She turned to me. "I know this is not your fight, but you could help usher in a new era for us. An era of peace. The king—he is cruel and brutal—he terrorizes the whole world and warps their beliefs." She squeezed her fists together. "Even if you do not want to help our cause, doing so is the practical choice."

"How?" I asked. "It seems like it's going to get me killed."

She stared daggers at me. "If you could pick just one person in the world—who do you think would have the most information about getting you home?"

I looked over at Madam Fantasmo, who had been sitting quietly this whole time. "It's not a trick question, girl."

"The king," I said.

Director Frente slammed her fist on the table. "Exactly. He's obsessed with other worlds. If anyone knows how to get you home, it's him." She cleared her throat. "I will be plain with you. The king is a bad, bad man, worse than any I have ever met. Any time I think his cruelty has reached its zenith, he finds a way to top himself." She winced. "I am a woman of science, and yet even I cannot deny that you coming here is kismet."

"How?" I asked.

"He draws power from the idea that being a traveler makes him divine. Given that, there are only two people in the world that can usurp that claim."

"Margaret and I."

She nodded. "And we have you. If we had Margaret, too, then we could lay a legitimate claim to the throne and oust King Ulthar from power."

"It's not as simple as that," Madam Fantasmo said. "Powerful men do not relinquish power willingly. You would be damning the country…half the world…into a civil war."

"And in the end, we would have the path forward."

"If we win!" Madam Fantasmo shouted, shooting up from her chair. "Meanwhile, if we lose—"

"We won't lose!" Director Frente shouted. "We can't lose!"

"Wait!" I yelled, popping up between them. "Just so I'm clear, I'm supposed to stay here, on this planet, and help instigate a civil war. To what end? Become the queen of this country when it's over?"

"No," Director Frente said. "To relinquish power. To restore balance to the world. To let us form a republic from the ashes of the monarchy. I know that it's asking a lot of you—too much of you—but your best chance of getting home rests with the king. By helping us, you are helping yourself, too."

"This is nuts…absolutely nuts." I grumbled and took a few steps toward the door. "I need to think about all of this." I looked back at them. "Don't follow me."

CHAPTER 27

I didn't know where I was going. *Where could I even go?* I didn't know the area, and even if I did, every guard and police officer in the city was surely looking for me. If I was as dangerous to King Ulthar as Director Frente said, then I might be the most wanted person in the whole world.

Still, the thought of staying in that basement filled me with dread. I had to get out. The elevator door was surrounded by dozens of guards and agents, so I rushed to the other side of the office, where I found a set of stairs. I eventually made it to the lobby, and despite the heavy metal door's best effort to stay closed, it eventually swung open. Sindra was standing in front of the glass doors leading out into the street, waving and smiling like she wasn't part of a secret organization.

"Can't let you go out that way," Sindra said.

"What are you going to do. Kill me?"

"Oh god, no." She pulled a gun from the back waist of her pants. "I mean, I do have this gun and everything, but no, I wouldn't kill you." She pointed the gun at my foot. "My orders were to lightly maim, with extreme discretion. I'm pretty sure I could blow off a toe or shoot you in the leg, though that could make you bleed out if I nicked a major vein." She raised the gun to my shoulder. "Or, I could shoot you in the shoulder. Not a lot of important veins there." She dropped the gun to my stomach. "It takes a long time to bleed out from a gunshot to the stomach. There are so many ways to interpret 'lightly graze.'"

"Congratulations," I said, the air burning my lungs. "You have successfully intimidated me. You win."

She dropped the gun to her side. "Oh good. I mean, I take no pleasure in intimidating you, but we are taking a big chance sharing this information with a civilian, and since literally every single person in the country is after you right now, and you stick out like a big, red nose, they'll definitely find you, and without training, you will for sure turn on us with even the lightest torture."

"I will not!" I screamed.

"Really? I just threatened to lightly maim you, and you gave up on getting outside without even a fight."

"Fair point," I grumbled. "So, what now?"

"Let's go upstairs. There's a really terrible café on the top floor which has a very mediocre view of an ugly part of the city."

I smirked. She was charming for someone who had just threatened to shoot me. "Lead the way."

She pushed the button to the top floor, and we took the elevator to a small mess hall, not unlike the ones back in school, with long benches for eating and sneeze guards over a pathetic assortment of salad and sad-looking meat.

"You don't want any of that." She approached a meek, older woman wearing thick glasses that stuck out from her thin face and ratty black hair. "Two kirzes, please." The woman produced two paper cups from under the counter while Sindra paid, and the woman gave her two steaming yellow drinks, which she brought to the table nearest the window.

"You were right," I said, taking the cup. "This is a very average view." I tasted what was in the cup, and it tasted like hot sweet corn. It was actually quite good. "What is this stuff? It's great."

"This isn't even really good kirzes," Sindra said. "My mom makes the best." She swished her mouth from one side to the other as tears welled in her eyes. "She made the best kirzes fresh from alope from the garden."

I placed my hand on her. "I'm sorry for your loss."

"Thank you." She took a sip. "King Ulthar took everything from me when his men raided our village, part of a campaign—" She started to cry. "I lost everything, and they don't even teach it in school. They don't even talk about it." She looked up into the sky. "It wasn't even a strategic position. He just took it because he could."

"Is that when you joined the rebellion?"

Sindra shook her head. "I always wanted to design dresses—since I was a little kid. Mom taught me to sew, and Madam Fantasmo, she recruited me out of school. She has a knack for finding broken, little things and making them shine. I started helping her mend things in her workshop, and then, little by little, she trusted me more…when she offered me a job in the palace, I said yes, but not because of the rebellion. I wanted to kill the king myself, and she was a means to an end—she figured it out, though." Sindra wiped her eyes with a paper napkin. "She found a poisoned sewing needle in my bustle one day. I thought she was going to have me killed. Instead, she told me the truth and offered me two choices—death at the hands of the king or helping bring him down. I wasn't sure I'd made the right choice until I met you."

"Please, I'm nothing. I'm nobody."

"Exactly!" she shouted. When everyone in the café turned to her, she held up her hand in apology. "You are a nothing. That's exactly what we need. Somebody who doesn't think sunshine glows out of their butt for a change."

"I don't want a war, Sindra. I just want to go home."

Tears glistened in her eyes again. "Me too, but two things I learned when I was much younger than I am today, are that some things are worth fighting for, and you can never go home again. I'm not saying you should cooperate and help the rebellion, but I do want you to look me in the eyes and tell me it won't haunt you every day of your life if you don't at least try." She lightly touched my hand. "You're a good person, Anjelica. And that's the thing about being a good person. You have to do the right thing, or it eats away at you."

She was right. I took another sip and said, "Can we just sit up here and drink this corn thing for a minute and not talk about how I'm about to throw my life away?"

Sindra turned to the window and didn't say anything. My stomach churned as her words worked their way deeper. By the time we finished, I knew I was going to end up joining their foolhardy cause…

…but I wouldn't do it without a price.

***

"Can I tell you a secret?" Sindra said as we made our way back down to the basement. We hadn't talked much since the café, and even when we agreed to leave, it was all in a nod of the head and a tacit agreement by both parties. It was nice to hear her voice over the whirl of the elevator. "And promise you won't get mad at me."

"That's two questions, and while yes, you can tell me, I can't promise I won't get mad about it. That's a metaphysical reaction based on instinct."

"Can you just say it, though?"

"No way. We just met. I'm not gonna start lying to you already." I smirked. "I need to know somebody six to eight weeks minimum before I start lying to them all cavalier like that."

"I'm gonna tell you anyway," Sindra said, pulling out the gun. "This thing isn't loaded. I've never shot one in my life."

I laughed. "That's pretty funny. I'm not mad at that at all. You stopped me from making a dumb mistake. Maybe you should have been an actor."

She shook her head. "All I ever wanted to do was make clothes. If this is ever over, and if we win, I'm gonna make the most beautiful dress for you."

"No offense," I said. "But I hope I'm not around here long enough to wear it."

The door to the basement opened, and we walked out into the catwalk. With the ding of the elevator, the whole of the basement turned to see me.

"Come on," Sindra said, heading down the stairs. "Let's get you to the director."

I followed her through the sinewy passages of the basement until we arrived at a door when Director Frente written on it in golden letters. Sindra knocked but didn't wait for an answer before she walked in.

"Sorry, Director," she said, pointing to me. "But I thought you would like an update."

I peeked my head in the door to see Director Frente behind a wooden desk. Madam Fantasmo and an older man with white hair and a salt and pepper beard looked at me. When our eyes met, Madam Fantasmo leaped up and grabbed me into a bear hug.

"You're back!" she shouted. "I knew you would come back."

"You literally had somebody meet me with a gun in the lobby, and she said she'd kill me if I left."

"And it worked!" Madam Fantasmo dropped me gently and rustled Sindra's hair. "That's my girl."

I sat down in the chair that Madam Fantasmo had vacated. She left it quite warm. "I'm in a difficult position, as you can expect. I'm in a new land with no immediate way home, and the whole of the government is trying to find me. Meanwhile, you offer me a lifeline and a purpose. I am inclined to accept it, but only if you meet my conditions."

"I don't think you're in much of a place to make demands—" The Director looked around the room. The bearded man was nodding, but both Madam Fantasmo and Sindra stared angrily at her. "But you also have me in a difficult position because while I can be replaced, you can't, at least not unless another traveler from another world falls from the sky today."

"And I'm going to bet that's doubtful."

She nodded. "I can't predict the future, but it's doubtful."

"Number one, I want to go home. That one should be obvious. I'm not spending the rest of my life in this world."

"That's not easy since we have no idea how to send you home or even where you come from."

"I want somebody here working on it, night and day. When you figure it out, I'm the first to know."

"Fine," she replied. "Anything else?"

I nodded. "This one is the big one. Before we take down the king, we find Margaret and save her."

She smiled. "Well, that's a happy coincidence. We were talking about how to save your friend just now."

"Lovely." I leaned back in my chair. "Don't let me stop you. I'm all ears."

CHAPTER 28

Margaret had been released from the hospital earlier that day and was now recovering from her injuries. The manor where she was staying was an hour outside the city, on a ten-acre estate surrounded by a high stone wall with electrified barbed wire on top of it. Security cameras monitored every entrance, and more cameras were positioned as lookouts.

"That's the biggest weakness of King Ulthar's people," Director Frente said as she explained the plan to me. "They are over-reliant on technology and have a nearly godlike reverence for it. We've been inside their back end for months now, and they have no idea. We'll have two teams." A picture of the castle was projected onto a screen in the conference room we'd moved into. She slammed a pointer into the northern corner of the wall. "One will infiltrate here and make their way across the grounds on foot to provide tactical support. Their job will be to take control of this building." She indicated a small house offset from the main building by a hundred yards. "This is the guard house, which manages the security of the house and surrounding facilities. If we control that building, they won't be able to call for help while we infiltrate."

She gestured to a bespectacled man controlling the projector, and he flipped to a picture of a delivery truck. "Every afternoon at three pm, a food truck enters the facility to stock it with enough supplies to feed a small army. Tomorrow, that food truck will have an unfortunate accident and will be replaced by one of ours. A small team will enter the facility, make their way through the house, and recover the asset."

"And where do I fit into this?" I asked. "I'm not a soldier."

"That's true," she said. "However, we need the asset to come willingly. It's essential that you are there to show the asset we're not kidnapping it; we're liberating it."

"Can we call her Margaret, please? She has a name."

Director Frente stared at me coldly. Then, her gaze softened. "Of course. You're right. I know this seems like a lot of tactical mumbo jumbo, Anjelica, but it's important that we're all on the same page. We only get one shot at this. If we don't get her out, they'll move her into a more fortified facility, and we'll lose our chance."

"Can't we wait until she's better recovered, though? I mean, she just left the hospital this morning."

"Again, no. She's only in this manor house to recover. Once she's at full strength, she'll be moved to the palace, and we'll lose our shot to get her. This is a small window, but we know what we're doing." She closed the pointer. "I'm asking you to trust us. Can you do that?"

I nodded. "I think so, but I don't have much choice in the matter, do I?"

"We always have choices, Anjelica. They just might not be good ones."

"If I don't go along with it, are you still going to move ahead with your plan anyway?"

Director Frente looked around the room, then nodded. "Yes, we believe it's our only option and that Margaret is a valuable enough asset that we will risk a whole heck of a lot to recover her."

"Then I'm in if only to make sure you don't hurt her."

"We're not the monsters here, Anjelica," the director said. "We're the good guys."

"I know," I said, then blinked when someone flicked on the lights. *Or at least I know you say that.*

The director clapped her hands. "All right, we have one day to finish preparing and get in position." She pointed at the bearded man I'd seen in her office before. "Jasper, you organize your best people for this; we can't afford any muck-ups."

"Of course, ma'am," he said with a nod and walked out of the room briskly.

The meeting was disbursed, and soon it was just Madam Fantasmo and I sitting across from each other. She smiled at me, but I could not return the sentiment. "You should be happy, Anjelica. This time tomorrow, you'll have your friend back, and we have the best doctors in the city to look after her. I promise you that."

"I believe you," I replied with a sigh. "There's just something that feels off about all of this. I mean, you're talking about starting a war with the king."

"We've been at war with the king for some time. We're just making it public."

"And after this…that's when I make my statement?" I asked.

She nodded. "Yes, once we have Margaret, then we'll issue a statement, and you'll deliver your remarks. We'll have them for you in an hour so you can practice."

I pumped my fingers into my palm, trying to prevent them from shaking. "I've never been good at public speaking, and this is about the most public speech you can give, ay?"

"Think of it this way…with any luck, we'll find a way to get you home soon, and you can get back to your life."

"Yeah, but your lives will never be the same."

She placed her hand on mine. "That's exactly what we want. We don't want things to be the same, Anjelica."

I stood up. "This is just a lot to take in. Like, a few weeks ago I was a cheerleader in Los Angeles, and now, well, every time I think things can't get more intense, they do. First, I was kidnapped, then I was forced to move to a small town, then I fell through a portal, and now I'm being asked to be the face of a rebellion." I swallowed. "On top of that, I'm supposed to join a group of people who are assaulting a military compound. This is absolutely banana sauce, and I'm not doing okay when I try to process it."

Madam Fantasmo stood and wrapped me in a hug. "I don't think I'm the right person to comfort you on this, and I'm sorry this came to you, but it did. The gods never give you more than you can handle."

I pushed away from her. "That's garbage. They always give you more than you can handle. The gods are constantly upping the ante and then upping it some more, like boiling frogs. You turn the heat up little by little, and the little buggers don't feel they're getting boiled alive, and then, they die." I took a deep breath. "I feel like those frogs."

"That's silly, dear. You know the heat is being turned up on you. You're nothing like those frogs."

"We have one thing in common. We're both being boiled alive."

***

"I don't think you should do it," Volkim said as she and I flipped through bulletproof vests in the armory, trying to find one in my size. "This is suicide."

"I agree. I shouldn't do it."

"Then why are you?"

"Because I don't have a choice," I said, pulling one of the smaller vests off the rack and throwing it over my shoulders. "I would love to have the choice, but I am the only one who can do it." The vest wouldn't clip in the front. "This one is too small."

"That's garbage, and you know it. We all want to believe that we're the only person who stands between the world descending into chaos, but that's just not true, not for any of us. We're all replaceable." She pulled another vest off the rack and handed it to me. "Try this one."

"Easy for you to say." This time the vest snapped together perfectly. "You're not the one who fell into an alternate dimension, or whatever. You're not the one who's a dem—" I cringed and pulled back before I could say the word demon. There were some things you just don't talk about, at all, especially with non-magical people. "There's a lot on my head."

"That doesn't mean you should go jumping into a buzzsaw, though," she said. "If I were the only one who could do what you 'have to do,' I would walk away."

"Then I would never get home," I said to her.

"Would that be so bad? How great could your life be? You already told me that you were being hunted back on your planet, so would it be so bad to stay here?"

"I don't know how to say yes without insulting you. It's pretty frigging amazing that you can understand as much as you do about what I say, but this isn't my planet, and I want to go home." I handed her the vest back, and she placed it into a little cubby with the rest of the gear we pulled out. "Besides, I'm being hunted here, too. It's not like I could lead a normal life here."

"Just be careful, okay?"

"I'm literally about to go on a super dangerous mission. I don't think careful is something I can promise you." I smiled at her. "I promise that I want to be safe, though. I have no interest in dying out there; gods know where from home, okay?"

"I guess that's better than nothing." Footsteps clomped from down the hall, and a jacked woman with a square jaw and short, blonde hair walked into the armory. She was already dressed in full battle regalia like a Jackboot, dark black pants, long black shirt, bulletproof vest, and two guns holstered on her hip. She was only missing the black helmet.

"Recruit," she said harshly, walking forward. "Which one of you is Anjelica?"

I raised my hand as Volkim slid past her out of the room. "Me."

"I'm Commander Bivnol. Have you ever worked a gun before, soldier?"

I shook my head. "No, I've only held one before. Once."

She turned and beckoned me to follow her. She walked briskly with pounding steps until she pushed open a door into a shooting range. Several other officers stood in their booths, firing at targets on the far end of the room. Commander Bivnol reached into a cabinet, pulling out a pair of orange headphones and handing them to me before donning her own pair.

I wanted to protest. I had no interest in firing a gun.

As if she could read my thoughts, Commander Bivnol screamed over the earphones. "Our goal is to make it so that you don't have to fire this weapon, but you need to know the basics." She marched to an empty booth, pulled out one of her pistols, and handed it to me. "Hold the handle of the gun with your dominant hand. Brace it with your other hand. Feet hip-distance apart, take a breath, and fire, closing one eye to aim down the barrel when you do. Don't close your eyes. And watch the kickback—nobody is ever prepared for the kickback their first time."

My shaky right hand closed around the butt of the pistol, and I pointed it toward the target at the end of the gallery. The gun was heavier than I thought it would be, though I didn't know why that surprised me. After all, it was basically pure metal I was holding in my hands that protected me against a miniature explosion. I closed one eye and leveled my sight on the target.

"Legs!" the commander screamed, and I spread my feet apart to get a stronger footing. "Good! Fire!"

I took a deep breath and squeezed the trigger. It was harder than I thought. The trigger did not want to give, and I wasn't particularly interested in forcing the issue, but I knew the only way out of this situation was to fire, so I clasped my hand tighter until a huge explosion burst from the end of the barrel. My hands flung high in the air as the gun recoiled.

"First one's the hardest!" the commander shouted. "Again!"

I pulled the trigger again, and she was right. I could pull the trigger with—well, not with ease, but without the massive fear and trepidation that filled me before.

When I was done, I placed the gun on the ledge, and Commander Bivnol pulled the target close to reveal that I had hit over half the bullets inside the main target. Where the others landed, I had no idea.

"This is good," she said, looking over the target. "This is what we consider center mass." She pointed to the top of her chest and bottom of her stomach. "Aim here, and do what you just did, and you should stop anything running toward you."

"I really don't want to do that," I replied, watching the commander holster the gun. "Like, really, really, really."

"Nobody wants to kill people, recruit. Okay, that's not true, some people do. That's not our focus. We're moving into hostile enemy territory, so just stick with me, do as I say, and we'll get through it, okay?"

"Okay." My voice squeaked. I didn't believe the words coming out of her mouth, that it would be okay. Nothing would be okay. Not until I got home again.

Getting Margaret back, though, saving her from her sadistic father, that was a good start.

CHAPTER 29

I thought it would be hard for me to sleep the night before the big raid. After barely resting for the past two weeks, I fell asleep without issue on the cold cot provided me by the rebellion. It was staying asleep that was the problem. A familiar disembodied hand kept finding me and trying to drag me down into the darkness. I thought that maybe I had banished the hand in my old Earth, and I would get peace from it, but time after time, when I closed my eyes, it found me.

Every time it happened, I would wake up, splash water on my face, use the bathroom, and then try again to drift off to sleep. This repeated until the next morning when Madam Fantasmo came to call on me.

"Wakey wakey, eggs and bakey," she said, dressed in a black camo suit like the one I would be wearing in the near future. "Although I wouldn't get your hopes up. The café can find a way to ruin even eggs."

I rolled to the edge of my bed and set my feet down, the cold concrete sending shivers down my spine. "Please tell me you aren't coming with us."

"Oh gods no, child. I just wanted to show some camaraderie."

I followed her up the elevator and downed runny eggs with burnt toast. She was right about the eggs. When my belly was full, though not satiated, Madam Fantasmo brought me back to the armory where Commander Bivnol was suiting up, surrounded by a small team of men and women, none of whom I recognized.

"Morning, recruit," she said. "Meet the rest of the team." She pointed to a tall man with broad shoulders and a scruffy face. "Lieutenant Tarborniv. He's leading the other assault team to take down the guard tower." She pointed to three more people in the small room, a young woman with glasses, an older man with several teeth missing, and a Black woman who refused to look in my direction. "Otis, Grounir, and Shangil. Their success is your success, and their failure is our failure." She smacked her chest. "We live as one."

They all punched their chests. "We die as one."

"That's really a horrifying thought. Which team are you on, ma'am?" I asked.

"I'll be coordinating in central command." Commander Bivnol reached into her pocket and pulled out a small headset. "Put this in your ear, and you'll hear everything we have to say." She stormed out of the room. "Follow."

I hurried to catch up with her as she walked toward a bakery truck that said "Chitrer's Bakery" on the side. The people loading weren't dressed in the mercenary gear but in simple off-white jumpsuits with logos on the back that matched the side of the truck.

"Corporal," she growled as she marched toward them. "How are you doing?"

A baby-faced woman with a bright smile turned and saluted. "Good, ma'am. We'll be ready in five minutes."

"Excellent. Corporal Mercer, this is Anjelica. She'll be on your team, as we discussed. I leave her in your capable hands." Commander Bivnol turned to me and saluted. "It's a great honor to be working with you on this project. Thank you for your service to the rebellion."

I returned the salute, and she left. "She's a bit intense, right?"

Corporal Mercer laughed. "She's just trying to look out for us, but yeah, over the top is an apt definition. She's a dynamite training officer, though. More than once, something she taught me saved my life in the field." Corporal Mercer waved me forward. "Come on, I'll introduce you to the rest of the team."

She picked up a wooden box filled with baguettes and walked toward the truck. A dark-skinned man with piercing brown eyes hopped out as she slid the box into the back. "This is Thole. He's an infiltration expert, one of the best we have."

"One of? Please." He shook my hand. "I'm the best. Half of this plan was my idea, and the other half was cribbed from my past missions."

"He's not modest, either." She pointed to the front, where a portly man with a long, ratty beard waved toward me. "That's Inyss, our driver. If things get hairy, he's the one who'll get us out of a tough jam."

"I am also an excellent parallel parker," Inyss replied with a gruff voice.

"That's it?" I said. "Just the four of us?"

"We have to make it look like we're delivering baked goods, and even four is pushing it." She grabbed me by the shoulders. "That's why you're so important. You are here to convince Margaret to come with us willingly. We don't want it to get dicey in there."

"No pressure."

She dug through the back of the truck and handed me a jumpsuit. "Here, put this on."

"Oh." I took it. "I thought I was going to be wearing the camo and vest. I kind of picked one out already."

The three of them looked at each other, and Corporal Mercer spoke, "That is conspicuous as hell. No, we have to play the part. You get the jumpsuit. Once we unload, we'll give you a gun just in case it all goes to pot, but this is a simple in and out job."

I regretted not being on the other team. I'll bet they had bulletproof vests. Still, all of this hinged on me doing my part, so I dutifully shed my camo and put on the jumpsuit, then rejoined the team. By the time I finished, they were already packed up, and both teams were loaded into the truck.

"We'll drop Alpha team off first," Corporal Mercer said, helping me into the back of the truck. "And then we'll continue once they have breached. Sound good?"

No, it didn't. I didn't know what a breach was, but it didn't sound good at all. I didn't say any of that. "Sounds great."

***

It took an hour to reach the estate, taking it easy on the windy country roads, what with the added weight of seven people in the back of the truck, along with various assorted breads and cheeses to make us look legit. It was cramped and smelly, but the rumbling of the road under my feet lulled me into a sort of trance and made me forget how tired and scared I was…until the estate expanded out in front of us, and it all came rushing back to me.

Inyss swerved around the country roads until he reached the edge of the wall. When he stopped, Alpha team was ready. They leaped out in less than ten seconds, and Mercer closed the door behind them.

"So, you have an easy job right now," Mercer said. "All you have to do is not say anything. Here." She handed me a badge with my name on it, surrounded by green. "If anyone asks, you're new, and you have no idea what is happening. You're a last-minute fill-in. Say it back to me."

"I'm a last-minute fill-in. I have no idea what's going on." I gave a wry smile. "Well, that should be easy to remember because it's true."

The truck made it around to the front gate, and Inyss pulled up to the guard shack.

"Badge," a man's voice grumbled. Inyss pulled out his badge and showed it to the guard. "Open the back."

"It's already unlocked."

Footsteps crackled on gravel, and then the back door opened. I smiled at the tall gentleman staring at us. He didn't say anything. He just eyed us for several seconds and then closed the door again. My heart leapt into my chest, expecting the worst to happen, and when the gate opened a few seconds later, I felt all the air in my lungs escape at once. I hadn't realized I was holding my breath.

"Step one is down," Mercer said to me with a smile. I liked her. I really hoped she didn't die.

We pulled up to the back of the house, and Mercer opened the door, helping me down to the ground and then handing me a wooden crate.

The radio in my ear crackled. "We're in position. Next shift comes down in ten minutes."

"That's the go sign," Mercer said. "We have ten minutes before they find our guys. We need to be out of here in five. Inyss and Thole will make the trip to unload the supplies while you and I find the girl. Got it?"

"Got it."

Mercer picked up a crate and walked toward the castle. I had only ever seen castles in the movies, and this one was grand. A tower rose from each corner of the building, with high walls connecting them. As we passed through the stone archway into the building, a cool, stiff breeze hit me. If we hadn't been busy with a kidnapping, I would have loved to walk around the property and get a tour.

Inside the ancient walls stood a modern kitchen, complete with stainless steel appliances and marble countertops, every bit befitting a king's family. Mercer laid the crate down on the large island in the middle of the room and pulled a gun from inside the crate. She handed it to me before recovering a second one and putting it into the back waistband of her jumpsuit, motioning for me to do the same.

"Let's go," she said. She looked at Thole and pounded her chest. "We live as one."

He pounded his chest. "We die as one."

We stepped quietly but quickly through the hallway. A TV blared, and we passed a room where three Jackboot guards sat, enrapt in whatever sport they were playing on the screen. We turned the corner and ducked into a small inlet as two more guards walked down the hallway toward us. When they passed, we continued down to the end of the hall and took the circular stairs up two flights.

I could see why they needed Margaret to come willingly. It would have been impossible to drag somebody down the way we came without causing a ruckus. I wasn't sure how they got her upstairs with her wheelchair, but the Jackboots were all strong and strapping, so I had no doubt they could carry a little girl up two flights of stairs.

"This way," Mercer said, leading us forward. This level was considerably quieter and quainter than the first floor, which seemed more industrial and utilitarian. There were paintings on the walls here and plush carpeting.

Mercer rushed over to a wooden door with a brass knocker. "This is it. You have three minutes. Are you ready?"

No. "Yes."

Mercer knocked on the door and then pushed it open without waiting for an answer. I slid into the room, which was awash in purples and pinks. All sorts of beautiful dolls lined the shelves, interspersed with books and other knickknacks, but my eyes were drawn to the large canopy bed in the center of the room, where a heart monitor beeped wildly. When I pushed the mesh around the bed back, I saw her, Margaret, staring back at me, smiling.

"Anjelica!" she shouted, wrapping her hands around my neck. "You're alive!"

I wrapped her in a hug. "It's good to see you, too. I'm so glad you're safe." I pulled back from her. "Now, come on, we have to get out of here."

She cocked her head. "Why would I do that? I have everything I ever wanted right here."

CHAPTER 30

"What do you mean you don't wanna go?" I asked in amazement at Margaret's response.

"Look around, Anjelica," she replied. "I'm a frigging princess. A princess! Last week I was in hiding in a tiny house, and now I'm frigging Cinderella!" She cocked her head at me then, realizing something she had not put together until that moment. "Wait, how did you get in here? And why are you wearing a jumpsuit?" She looked past me to Corporal Mercer. "And who is that?" Her eyes darted back and forth between us. "What is going on here?"

"We're here to get you out of here," Corporal Mercer replied. "You're not safe, ma'am."

"You're—kidnapping me?" Margaret looked wounded, her face scrunched up in terror. "You're frigging kidnapping me after everything—how could you?"

I held up my hands. "Whoa, we're not trying to kidnap you. We want you to come with us, so we can keep you safe."

"Wait," Margaret said slowly. I watched the wheels churning in her brain. "Anjelica, are you in the rebellion?"

"I'm not—okay, yes, technically, but it's complicated."

"How could you be working with them? They're not the good guys, Anjelica." She scooted back from me. "My dad says they're trying to kill my whole family. He told me they were the ones who kidnapped me in the first place."

"That's not true," Corporal Mercer said. "I don't know who told you that bu—"

I held up my hand. "Please, let me handle this." I turned to Margaret. "Your father is a bad person. He's waging wars against the whole world. He's making things just…so bad. For everyone. He's not a good—"

"He's my family," Margaret said, nearly out of breath. "Do you know that my 'mother' never said two nice words to me…and now she's dead. You're trying to take away the only family I have left."

I shook my head. "No, I'm not. I'm trying to get you away from a dangerous situation."

"Oh yeah, real dangerous." She threw her arms in the air, gesturing at the luxurious room. "This is real dangerous. The only danger to me here is you. Get out, or I'll call the guards." Her hand glowed blue as she held it toward us. "Or worse, I'll deal with you myself."

"Please," I said. "If you stay here, there's nothing I can do to protect you."

"I don't need your protection. I don't need anyone's protection." Her face hardened. "GUARDS!!!"

"Shit!" Corporal Mercer said as Margaret slammed her hand down on a button. I hadn't seen it on the wall behind her bed. A siren screeched through the air. "We have to go. Now!"

"I'm not going without her!" I yelled, pulling away from Corporal Mercer's grasp. "I can't!"

"She's gonna get us all killed," she shouted, seizing my hand. "Come with me now! That's an order!"

"I'm not one of your soldiers!"

"GET OUT OF HERE!" Margaret said. She held her hands out. "*Vi dis*!"

A quake shot from her arms and threw me backward against the door. I moaned, trying to gather myself. There was a flash of pink light and a puff of purple smoke, and when the dust cleared, Kimberly stood in front of me, as glorious and amazing as the first time I saw her. There was no joy in her eyes when she saw me.

"You really stepped into it this time," she grumbled.

"Who are you?" Mercer said, pulling out her gun.

"Kimberly!" I said. "You're a sight for sore eyes."

"I wish I could say the same for you," she said. "Take my hand."

I grabbed her hand, and she took hold of Margaret's foot with her free hand. Then, Kimberly turned to Mercer. "If you want to live, I suggest you come here right now."

"Not until you tell me who you are."

Footsteps echoed down the halls from what had to be a whole squad of guards converging on our room. "You have ten seconds before that door slams open, and I won't be here when it does."

"Come on, Mercer," I pleaded. "This mission is a bust, but we can still save you."

"Get off me!" Margaret said, swiping her arms helplessly at us.

"NOW!" Kimberly screamed.

Mercer looked over to the door and then back to Kimberly, stored her gun, and leaped forward into my outstretched hand. The moment she did, the door flew open.

"Show me where I'm going!" Kimberly shouted. I closed my eyes and imagined the main floor of the rebellion base. As I did, an explosion rang out, and I felt a cold wetness wash over me as we vanished into the ether.

We saved Margaret. Wait—have I been shot?

***

I rematerialized in the rebellion base to the sounds of shouting as dozens of people reacted to seeing the four of us appear out of nowhere in a puff of purple smoke. Chairs swished out, and feet clamored toward us, but I could only concentrate on the damp wetness oozing from me. My legs gave out from under me, and I fell to the ground.

Mercer's voice rang out. "Get a medic!"

"Ow…" I whispered as I fell into unconsciousness.

***

My eyes fluttered open and focused on the stucco ceiling. The overhead fluorescent light washed out everything and made me blink uncomfortably. The next thing that came into focus was my ears and the sound of a heart monitor beeping…but not just one; there was a second one on the other side of me.

Margaret was in a bed next to mine, sleeping soundly. We had made it. I tried to push myself up, but my stomach burned in pain. When I pressed my hand against it, I felt the IV needle digging into the back of my left hand.

"Don't move so fast," I heard from the other side of me and turned to see Sindra. "You lost a lot of blood. You're going to be lightheaded for a while."

"Where—where is Kimberly?"

"She's in the brig," Sindra said, almost embarrassed.

"What?" I shouted, but the exertion of energy zapped what little strength I had left, and I fell back onto the bed. "She saved us."

"I know. I think we all know that, but you have to understand. She just…appeared in front of us. We've never seen that kind of technology before. It freaked us out, and Commander Bivnol thought it was the best move until we figured everything out."

I couldn't help but laugh. "That's funny. A cell can't hold Kimberly if she wants to leave."

"Well, we just checked on her, and she's still in there, so whatever we're doing must be working."

I listlessly shook my head from one side to the other. "She's only here because she wants to be."

Sindra brushed the hair out of my face. "We can talk about it later, but right now, you need to sleep."

"Maybe you're—"

And then I was out, falling into the inky blackness of my dreams. I was in a pool of black tar, and every time I tried to take a stroke to swim to safety, I was held back in its sticky ooze.

"Ah," a sound came from the edge of the liquid. A hooded figure stood over me. "You finally decided to join me." He barked at the abyss. "Get her."

Two hands shot out of the darkness, and I recognized them from previous dreams. They flew like they were shot out of cannons and grabbed my shoulders, lifting me out of the inky darkness with great effort. Once I was free, they carried me to the feet of the hooded figure, who held up his wrists. The disembodied hands snapped into place at the end of his arms.

"There," the being said in a deep, haunting whisper. "Isn't that better?"

"This isn't real," I said. "None of this is real. It's a nightmare. Any moment I'll wake up."

"Oh, my dear, just because it's a nightmare doesn't make it any less real." The figure snapped his bony fingers, and the muck binding me vanished. I could move again.

I pushed myself up. "Who are you?"

"A friend of your mother's," the figure said. "She asked me to check in on you when you left without a trace. I lost track of you for a while, but luckily time and space are of little consequence to me."

"My mother?"

The figure snapped its fingers again and sat down at the table and chairs that appeared. It pulled back its cloak to reveal fleshless eye sockets where orange orbs of light glowed.

"Please sit. Just because this is a nightmare doesn't mean we can't be civil to each other."

I wasn't about to insult a glowing-eyed skeleton, so I did what I was asked and took a seat. "Are you my father?"

The skeleton chuckled a whispered laugh. "No, child. I have not sired children in a long time, and I can assure you even in the gravest circumstances, your mother would not be so bold as to conjure your father."

"Then who are you?"

"Before your mother worshipped the Devil, she worshipped me. I have had many names, but perhaps the one I like best is Araphel, the divine darkness."

"Are you a god, then?"

"I find labels crass, but yes, if that helps your human brain, then I am a god."

"The god of darkness?"

"*A* god of darkness. My mother, Nyx, is the source of all darkness. I, as her offspring, work in and with the shadows, shepherding the dead to their final rest, which I have done since the exile of my brother eons ago."

I took all this in. *Wait, shepherding who?*

"I'm not dead, am I?"

"No, you are not dead, but your…injuries…awakened you to me and brought me here."

Relief rushed over me. I took a deep breath then looked around. "Can you tell me where I am then? Is this another dimension?"

"Nothing like that. You are simply on another planet created by the gods. Gods have ways of transporting between worlds, and it seems you found a way to slip into them, which…has serious consequences."

"I didn't do it on purpose!"

"Of course you didn't, my dear. I would never imply as such. We seem to be in a position to help each other, as it were. I am loathe to help humanity, as you can imagine, which puts me in a predicament you are uniquely qualified to ameliorate."

I frowned, not sure I followed. "What do you want?"

"There is a strong energy on this planet you currently inhabit, a dark, malevolent force that aims to take the power of the gods for themselves. They are smart enough to hide their face from me, but I can tell they are close. I want you to find the person who is trying to steal our power and stop them. If you do this, I will return you home to your planet across the cosmos."

I thought for a few moments. "Well, I'm new here, but I think it might be the king of this country who's messing around with things…and we're already trying to stop him."

"Oh goodie. This should be easy for you, then."
Araphel scratched his chin. "You should know your mother
loves you enough to offer her soul for your return to her."

"No!" I cried out. "You can't take it."

"Why should I not take something offered willingly and
out of love?"

"It's wrong. She doesn't know what she's doing."

"Trust me, your mother has always known what she is
doing, and everything she has done is for your benefit, even
this." Araphel held up his hand. "However, if you right this
wrong for the gods, I will forgive her debt, but you must go
see her and tell her what happened to you. She is very
worried."

"Is that your price for helping me return to my planet?"

Araphel stood. "No, just an observation."

"If I help you, then I want you to help my friends return
as well. Margaret and Kimberly."

"If they wish to leave, I will help them as well. You
have my word." All the heat left the room as Araphel took
a breath, and when he released it, the monitor beeped
loudly in my ear once more. "Be warned. You will have to
use every ounce of your ability to defeat this foe—do not
deny your demonic heritage."

Before I could answer, my eyes shot open, and the
fluorescent overhead lights stung them. I took a gasp of air
and thanked the gods I was still alive.

"Oh good," Madam Fantasmo said, rising from the
chair at my bedside. "You're up. You need to see this."

CHAPTER 31

Madam Fantasmo helped me into a wheelchair and rolled me past Margaret, who glared at me. Her hands were bound in leather straps. Above the restraints, she wore a thin scarf tied around each wrist.

"What are you doing to her?" I asked. "Why is she chained up like a prisoner?"

"She tried to escape, twice," Madam Fantasmo said. "She's a danger to herself right now, and until you can talk some sense into her, we think it best for her to be restrained."

"So, you lock Kimberly in a cage, and Margaret is chained to her bed. I'm starting to think you might not be the good guys after all. How are you any different than King Ulthar?"

"Here's why," she said as she pushed me into the main command center.

On the screens high above, and on every monitor around the bullpen, was an image of King Ulthar atop his throne. In front of him knelt six blindfolded men and women. I recognized their faces and clothing. It was the two teams from the extraction. Two of them wore their bakery disguises, while the other four were in black camo. All of them shivered in fear, sweat dripping down their faces, as Jackboots pointed automatic rifles at their heads.

King Ulthar's smirking image jittered on the screen. When Director Frente saw me, she nodded at Jasper. "Play it."

Jasper pressed his keyboard, and the message played.

"My loyal subjects," the king started, his voice full of the kind of pathos I wasn't sure he was capable of naturally. "Earlier today, a gang of rebellion thugs broke into my castle and kidnapped my beloved daughter right from under my nose." He choked back fake tears. "She is not well, still recovering from her injuries, and yet, with no regard for her safety, they stole her in broad daylight." He took a deep, growling breath. "This will not stand. I have always said that any aggression against any of my subjects is an aggression against me, and likewise, an aggression against me is an aggression against the entire kingdom, against each of you.

"Therefore, as penance for the actions of these brazen few, these six captured conspirators will be executed at high noon tomorrow on live television, across every channel. I compel every citizen to watch, to see what happens when you attack any one of us and that any hostility to the crown is intolerable."

He slammed his fist on the edge of his throne, then took another breath. "However, I am not without my familial instincts. I offer these criminals one chance to rectify their insurrection against us. An exchange. These six for one girl, my little girl." His lip quivered just a bit, and then his face hardened. "If you choose to keep my child from me, then the blood of these men and women is on your hands. Let it not be said I am not a merciful ruler."

The video cut out, and Director Frente turned to me. "This message went out on every station two hours ago, and since then, our men have been trying desperately to come up with a plan to recover our people. As of yet, we don't have any viable strategies."

"What do you want from me?" I looked at the director with a hard face. "You've already got everything I care about in the world—no, pretty much the whole universe—trapped down here."

The director stepped forward. "Margaret is a great asset, but only if she cooperates. Otherwise, she is not worth six of our men. So, you have four hours to convince her to join us willingly, or we're going to feed her back to the wolves."

I wanted to fight, to lash out, to do what Araphel said and embrace my demonic instincts, but Director Frente held all the cards. Not only did she have Margaret, but she also had Madam Fantasmo, Sindra, and Volkim. And there was Kimberly locked in a cell. I wasn't in a very good negotiating position.

"If you send her back there, she'll be in danger. You'll be condemning her to—"

"I know!" the Director said. "Your job is to convince her. My job is to do what's best for the rebellion. I'm not going to let six of my best men die to save one loyalist toady."

I spun my chair around and started to wheel away. "I need to talk to Kimberly before I go back to Margaret. If you've so much as touched one hair on her head, I swear to god I'm done with you all."

***

The brig was cold and dark. The walls were black and absorbed any light the soft bulbs gave off. When Madam Fantasmo closed the door, all sounds from the outside were drowned out by an oppressive silence. There were only three cells inside the room, and the two on the ends were empty.

Kimberly looked calm and serene. They had stripped her of the knives and pixie dust that had been her iconic look, and her hair was matted down to the top of her head.

When she saw me, she stood up from her cot and walked over to the bars of the cell.

"Thank the gods," Kimberly said. "I'm so glad you're okay." She looked down at my wheelchair. "You're okay, right?"

I nodded. "That's what they tell me. I'm still weak, but I can walk. The chair is just a precaution, I think." I wheeled toward her and placed my hand on hers, where it clutched the bars. "How are you doing?"

"I'm fine. Catching up on my meditation. I'm about ten years behind at this point."

"I'm so glad to see you, Kimberly," I said, tears welling in my eyes. "I thought you were dead—or back on Earth, our Earth."

"No," she replied. "I wish."

"What happened when you—how did you—where did you end up?"

"I flashed into the back room of that same coffee shop you did, but you got all the attention. I knew things wouldn't be good if I went out there, especially since I had no idea where we were, so I—I ran out the back—gods help me, I did." Now she was crying, too. "I was such a chicken."

"No," I said. "You saved us. You saved me."

She shook her head. "You never would have been in that position if it wasn't for me. After the coffee shop, I lost you. I didn't lose Margaret, though, so I turned my attention to keeping her safe. I went to see her in the hospital—let's just say that didn't go well. She doesn't want to go home."

"Worse. She thinks this is home."

"Well, in a way, it is, isn't it?" Kimberly said. "I mean, she is of royal blood, right?"

I laughed. "Oh, you are going to love this. The king isn't from here, either. I don't know if he's from our Earth, but he's definitely not from this planet. He's a traveler, like us."

"Well, I'll be," she said. "So, she doesn't belong here any more than the rest of us."

"Nope," I replied. "I don't think she'll believe me, though."

"She definitely won't. I already snuck in to see her. They can't keep me in here, and they can't keep Margaret, either. I tried to talk sense into her, and when I couldn't, I bound her so she couldn't use her magic."

"Is that what the scarves around her arms are?"

Kimberly nodded. "Never leave home without them. You have to understand, Anjelica. Back home, she's a nothing. Here, she's a princess. Who would want to leave?"

"Back home, I'm a nothing, and here I'm some sort of savior type human, and I want to go home so bad. Some of us would do anything to be nothing burgers."

Kimberly smiled. "That's why you're one of the good ones. One of the only people I've met who are worth dying for."

I squeezed her hand. "There's a good person inside Margaret. I've seen it, but she's being corrupted by money and power, just like her father." I stopped for a moment. "They want to give her back to him in exchange for the men they captured. They say if I can't convince her to come willingly, they're going to give her back."

Kimberly smiled. "I actually have an idea if you can't convince her. But I have faith in you."

"Thanks, at least one of us does."

***

Madam Fantasmo wheeled me back to my room. "Would you mind waiting outside?" I asked.

"Of course," she said. "If you need me, holler."

"I will."

I wheeled myself into the room. Margaret was sitting up in her bed, and she sneered at me when I made my way over.

"Wheelchairs suck," I said, hopping back into bed.

"That's not funny," she snapped.

"I'm not the enemy here," I said, sitting up on my elbow, facing her. "I'm trying to look out for you."

"Yeah, by kidnapping me." She glared at me. "You're just like the others. You think because I'm some poor little girl in a wheelchair, I need you to make my decisions for me. Well, I'm sick of it."

"That's not what I think," I said. "And I'm not trying to help you because I pity you. I'm helping you because you're my friend. King Ulthar is a bad man. He's destroying the whole world, and he's using the fact that he's a traveler to—"

"What did you say?"

"He's not from this planet." I shrugged. "Just like us, and he's manipulating the people to think he's a god because of it. They worship people like us, or at least some of them do."

"So, you want me to go from being a princess, living in a castle, who's worshipped like a god, to what? Some nobody from Missouri whose mom is dead, and who people look at with pity, who'll be lucky to be on disability for the rest of her life? Listen to yourself. I'm sorry to say that's not even an option."

"Come on, Margaret. That's not you."

"How do you know? You barely know me. We only hung out twice. One of those times ended with me in the hospital, and the other with me almost being captured by a bunch of scary agents. You don't know anything about me, so quit imprinting your version of reality on me."

"There's nothing I can say to make you believe me, is there?"

Her eyes narrowed. "I hate you. Don't you get that yet? Now, leave me alone. I never want to see you again."

CHAPTER 32

I tried. I really tried. I tried to make her see the light, but she was right. I didn't really know her at all. I risked all of this, my life, Kimberly's life, heck, even my mother's soul, on a person I barely knew. Maybe she was right, maybe I did take pity on her because she was in a wheelchair. Or maybe I liked her because she took pity on me. She was the first person who showed real kindness to me when I got to Missouri, and that alone made me think we were friends.

Either way, later that night, we loaded up several vans and made our way to the drop location that the king gave us, where we would meet Prince Yimnit and exchange their prisoners for Margaret. Maybe she was a prisoner, after all. What else would you call somebody that you held against her will?

I wasn't feeling up to travel, but the king insisted I be there for the exchange, along with Director Frente and Commander Bivnol, and so the four of us made our way to the drop site with another van for the hostages, where Kimberly waited just in case.

"I'm sorry I dragged you into this," I said to Margaret as we pulled through a pair of metal gates. We were within the walls of a hulking cathedral to Juno and Jupiter. A golden fountain spewed water from a naked satyr in the center of the great marble square. "I was just trying to protect you."

"You did save my life at the start of all this," Margaret said. "I still hate you, but I wouldn't be here if it weren't for you. Since I hope this is the last time I ever see you, I can at least thank you for that."

"You're welcome."

The van came to a stop, and Commander Bivnol opened the back seat, flipped open Margaret's chair, and helped her into it. I decided not to take the chair offered to me, even though I stood on wobbly legs.

I leaned against Margaret's wheelchair as I pushed it around the fountain to the entrance of the grand cathedral. All around us, stained glass windows shone down with reliefs of the gods mosaiced into them. They looked strikingly similar to the gods I knew. At the other side of the courtyard, a stone steeple rose high into the air, with a bell tower at the top of it, and capped with the image of an eclipse.

"We didn't think you would have the courage to show," a man said. Prince Yimnit. I recognized him from pictures. He had short black hair and dark skin and wore a thick fur cape. He was a thin but tall man who stood even taller with his perfect posture. He couldn't have been more than twenty. Back on my Earth, he would be in college. Maybe in another world, he could be my friend, but here, the corruption consumed him.

"My father didn't think you were dumb enough. I knew you would be."

"We have Margaret," Director Frente said. "Where are our men?"

Prince Yimnit snapped his fingers, and the doors to the cathedral swung open. Six Jackboots stormed outside, each pushing one of the hostages with the tip of an automatic rifle, like they had once done to me.

"We are men of our word, which is more than I can say for the likes of you."

"Tell your men to put their weapons down," Commander Bivnol said, going for her service revolver.

"Or what? You'll kill an unarmed girl? Please, even you are not that heartless."

"Heartless!" I shouted. "You're the heartless one!"

Prince Yimnit scoffed. "And you must be the wandering girl. The traveler that they have brainwashed to believe their cause is a righteous one. You should come with us, too. You will be showered with riches beyond imagination and lauded with adulation like you were a god. You will want for nothing, and every day until your last will be filled with joy. It is the greatest thing to actually being immortal." He stepped closer. "We know your part in this was coerced, and we will make that case to the people if you join with us now. However, if you choose to remain our enemy, you will be treated as such."

It was a tempting offer, hearing it in person, and I could see why it was so appealing to Margaret. There was nothing appealing about the life I had to go back to, but it was my life—the life I'd built, and I wasn't done with it.

"Your words are sweet, prince," I said. "If your riches weren't tainted with the blood of others, I might even take you up on it, but I could never live with myself knowing what you have done, knowing that all of your gains have been ill-gotten."

"I'm sorry to hear you say that." He closed his fist. "I think we're done here."

His hand dropped, and each man fired a bullet into the head of a captive, and they all dropped to the ground, dead. Before the echoes ceased in the courtyard, a dozen soldiers revealed themselves on the roofs above us.

As they did, Commander Bivnol played her only card left. She pulled out her gun and aimed it at Margaret. "I'll kill her."

"Go ahead."

"Brother!" Margaret shouted. "Please!"

He stepped closer. "I have no affection for you, sister." He sneered. "Look at you, a cripple. Father could never love you. He could never show you in public without shame on his face." He took another step forward. "Any value you have to us is far surpassed by your deformity."

"Then why do you want me back so bad?"

"You have but one purpose. To die at the right time. However, if you must die now, that is a risk we are willing to take."

He took one more step, and I drew my gun. Just like Commander Bivnol showed me, I aimed it at the prince's heart. I pushed my legs apart and closed one eye to aim down the barrel. "Say one more word or take one more step, and I will kill you."

"You don't have the resolve to pull that trigger, girl." He was right. When he stepped closer, I hesitated. "Taking down targets in a shooting gallery is one thing. Doing it in person, with a live being, knowing you will take the life from them, is something different." He took another step.

A puff of smoke appeared in front of us, and Kimberly drove a dagger into Prince Yimnit's shoulder. "Maybe she can't kill you, but I don't have any of her reservations."

Prince Yimnit stumbled backward and fell to the ground. "What are you waiting for? Kill them!"

Kimberly turned and grabbed each of us into a tight circle. "Time to go."

She didn't need my help to find the rebellion base this time. She vanished of her own accord, and when we rematerialized back at the base, there was little reaction. It was old hat to see Kimberly phase in and out. In fact, it was her plan to help us if she needed to, and she executed it flawlessly. Well, not flawlessly; we did end up with six dead men.

Commander Bivnol tapped her chest. "We live as one."

"We die as one," the director said in chorus, pounding her chest.

When the dust settled, I turned to Margaret, who was weeping. I leaned down to hug her. "I'm so so sorry."

She couldn't do anything but wrap her arms around mine and sob.

***

Prince Yimnit put out his propaganda across the airwaves: We ambushed them, and they had no choice but to kill the hostages; we were the villains. We knew that wasn't true. We just had to make sure that other people knew it, too.

"Are you ready for this?" I asked, hobbling into Margaret's room with a cane.

She was dressed in a blue dress with a red scarf and white buttons, and she smiled when she saw me. "Not at all. This is completely crazy."

We made our way to the elevator. I had proven myself loyal enough to get a key to the elevator. They were still on the fence about Margaret and Kimberly, but I expressed to the director and commander that we weren't in the business of keeping people prisoner, and they agreed to release them from their bonds…eventually, with lots of goading and convincing. They got there in the end and provided all three of us with our own rooms on the upper floors.

When we arrived in the basement, Madam Fantasmo took Margaret and brought her down a newly constructed metal ramp to the floor of the facility. She was dressed in a big, pink, sequin dress with thick make-up and a teased, blonde wig that easily doubled her head size.

"Do you have it memorized?" she asked the both of us.

I nodded. "I do, but mostly I'm just going to be standing behind Margaret and smiling, right?"

"No smiling," she replied. "This is deadly serious, and smiling is a sign of weakness in some animals. We don't want anyone to think we're weak."

We entered a TV studio, complete with three cameras, massive lights, and a stage with a picture of the city as the backdrop. Madam Fantasmo wheeled Margaret onto the stage and spent a minute futzing with her clothing until it was "perfect."

Then she turned to me, smiled, and nodded. "You'll do great."

She scooted down the stairs and out the door, closing it behind her. I looked around at the dozens of people in the room staring up at us and found Sindra in the crowd. She was counting down from ten with her hands. When she went to three, a red light popped up on the cameras, and then, at one, I opened my mouth and started.

"My name is Anjelica. This is Margaret. One week ago, we arrived on your planet. Since then, we have been threatened, convicted of crimes we didn't commit, assaulted, and had our lives threatened in innumerable ways."

"Then," Margaret said after I finished. "After all of this, we were slandered. The king lied to you, his people. What happened in the courtyard of that cathedral wasn't an attack by the rebellion, it was a coordinated ambush by the prince. He tried to take my life, and the life of my friend, to end a rebellion before it had a chance to get started."

Margaret swallowed loudly. "But it has started, and I am here to tell you, as the daughter of the king, that he is in the wrong. He is an evil man, and we know his secrets. We are not here to hurt you, citizens. We are here to liberate you, to bring you freedom."

"It's hard to even understand freedom," I said. "True freedom, until you have felt it, but I promise you, once you have felt it, there is nothing like it. Things are about to get very bad, very quickly. We are trying to remove a cancer from this planet."

"And when it is gone," Margaret said. "When he is gone, you will realize how unhealthy you have been all these years and how much better freedom feels. As my mother would say, 'I am doing this for your own good.' I never understood those words until now."

We both clasped our hands to our chests. "For freedom. For justice. For Onmiri. For Earth!"

I pounded my chest twice. "We live as one."

"We die as one," Margaret said in chorus, holding her hand to her chest.

Then, the lights went out, and my lungs tightened. We had just declared war on the king, and there was no turning back now. God, I hoped we were doing the right thing.

BOOK 3

CHAPTER 33

"So, let me get this straight," Director Frente said as she leaned into her desk, ping-ponging her eyeballs between Kimberly, Margaret, and me. Then, finally, with much consternation, she pointed to Kimberly. "You're a fairy." She turned her finger to Margaret. "You're a witch." Finally, her finger landed on me. "And you're a demon."

"I'm a pixie, actually," Kimberly said. "There's a difference."

"And I'm technically only half a demon," I added. "The other half is human, I think. I never really got confirmation on that."

"But you've got me pegged," Margaret said with a smile, snapping her fingers to produce a little flame. "Though I'm not very powerful…yet."

Director Frente leaned back and scratched her head. "I have to admit, this is the strangest thing I've ever heard."

"Really?" Kimberly said. "I mean, you have travelers popping up from other planets, and this is the strangest thing?"

"Well, yeah." The director stood up and began to pace. "That's just science, I think."

I laughed. "It's not science. These travelers have stumbled into the secret passages built by the gods that allow them to slip between worlds."

She pressed her fingers to the bridge of her nose. "Gods? Now you're saying there are gods?"

"Duh," Kimberly said. "You have demons, for one, which means you need angels, and then gods, and—it's a whole intricate system. You can't believe in one without the other."

"I even know an angel," I added. "Kimberly and I both do. Though I guess she's also a demon. I don't know. Cross breeding gets tricky."

"This is giving me a headache." The director pulled out a bottle of pills and downed several without water. "Is there a plan in all of this?"

"Aren't plans kind of your thing?" Margaret said. "We're just giving you the information. I can tell you, though, that if I'm a witch, then there's a good chance that the members of the royal family are witches, too."

"Wonderful."

"I think this is good news," I said. "I mean, you've been trying to fight fire with fire, but if the king and his family are witches, then you're not even playing the same sport."

"She's right, even if she's mixing metaphors," Kimberly said. "We need to make contact with the magical creatures on this planet. Maybe they can help us neutralize the king's powers."

"This planet doesn't have magical creatures," the director scoffed. "If it did, I would know."

"I met a guy in a jail cell that seemed to think there were," I said.

"Oh great, so I'm supposed to take my advice from a drunk in a jail cell."

"He wasn't drunk." I paused. "At least, I don't think he was."

"Ma'am," Kimberly replied, standing to her full height, "what you don't know can just about fill the Grand Canyon." She stepped forward. "You might not understand that reference, but I guarantee there are monsters in this world."

"I can't plan a rebellion on the possibility of magic—not without proof. That would be lunacy."

Kimberly disappeared in a puff of smoke and reappeared across the room moments later. "Hello, I am all sorts of magical."

Margaret snapped her fingers, and fire burned from the palm of her hand. "Same."

"Put that away," the director grumbled. "I'm not saying you're not magical. I'm saying there's no magic on this planet."

"There's magic on this planet. I'm sure of it." Kimberly furrowed her brow. "Go ahead and plan your little war. I'm going to find the magical folk in this city. You'll need them if you want to win."

"I want to go with you," I said, hopping up from my seat.

"It's too dangerous," Kimberly said. "You're one of the most recognizable people on the planet right now. Besides, if anyone outside of this room found out I was looking for magic to help the cause, the rebellion would turn into a laughingstock." She lifted her chin toward Director Frente. "The director proved that."

"I'm not going to be stuck here in this place while the whole world keeps spinning outside of these walls," I shouted.

"You won't be stuck here. I need you and Margaret for something else, anyway," Director Frente said. "We have a meeting with the president of Risyl, a nation that has been at war with King Ulthar for years. If we can gain their resources, it will go a long way to legitimizing our cause."

"Then we both have our missions, it would seem," Kimberly said.

* * *

"President Achel is a wise and noble leader," Director Frente said after we had landed in the small airport where we would meet our Risylian envoys. "Pragmatic and compassionate."

The door to the private jet opened, and we walked out onto the tarmac, where three long black limos were parked. Two dozen men and women in dark sunglasses and black suits stood outside the limos, staring at us intently.

One of the agents opened the door to the last limo in line, and a woman, wearing a bright blue fur coat, stepped out. Her white hair was done up in a 1950s beehive, and her lips were black as the night. Her eyes were ice blue but not cold, and when she saw Director Frente walk toward her, her deep scowl broke into a bright smile.

"Relonia!" she said with a light wave of her white-gloved hand. "It's so wonderful to see you again. It's been too long." She kissed Director Frente on both cheeks and then pulled her in for a quick hug before turning to us. "The two of you need no introduction. Your speech is all anyone can talk about. It takes a lot to surprise me, and even I was taken aback." She shook my outstretched arm with both of her hands and did the same with Margaret.

"It's very nice to meet you as well, ma'am," Margaret said.

"Please, call me Ynez. All my friends do, and I do hope we can be friends." She stepped back and admired all of us. "Well, shall we get started? I've prepared a room in my private hangar. I know this spycraft is a bit gauche, but if King Ulthar found out we were talking, especially before I had a chance to speak with my allies, it would not be a good thing. I hope you understand."

"Of course," Director Frente said. I didn't understand, not at all, but then I wasn't an expert in international diplomacy, so I just nodded my head and pushed Margaret's wheelchair toward a hangar that was surrounded by a cadre of guards.

One of the guards at the vanguard walked forward and opened the door, while another ducked in to secure it. When she came out and nodded, President Achel walked inside, and we followed. Next to the black jet docked in the space, there was a large conference table covered in food and drink. I had been eating nothing but café food for days, and the sight of sandwiches and chips—that hadn't been made the night before and left out to rot—nearly brought a tear to my eye.

"Please sit," President Achel said, and the three of us followed her to our seats. "Now, what can I do for you, Relonia? Your call was unexpected, to say the least. Though, much of the past week has been unforeseen."

Director Frente took a sip of water. "Once, long ago, you took a meeting with me…after I left my former post…and told me that while you were with my cause in spirit, your support must be private until such time as we had the means to make our move. I believe that time has come.

"I have spent the last several years building the infrastructure, and we now have hundreds of agents throughout the capital, and thousands more all over the country." She turned to the two of us. "And now, these ladies have helped turn public support to our favor. We believe we put enough pressure on the capital to force its implosion, but we are still small and need allies to push from the outside. More importantly, we need those who will acknowledge our new government when the king surrenders."

President Achel listened with growing consternation on her face, and when Director Frente finished, she thought for a moment before speaking. "Relonia, how long ago did you leave the service of the king?"

The question caught me like a punch to the jaw. *Director Frente worked for the king? How could she—*

"Seven years ago," Director Frente replied. There was a heavy sadness to her words, and when I tried to catch her eye, she avoided me.

President Achel took a sip of water. "You were his minister of war if I remember correctly."

"Undersecretary, Madam President."

"How many times did you sit across the table from me, a table just like this, and demand my surrender?"

"I—it wasn't—I'm not sure."

"Twelve," the president said sternly. "You sat across from me and demanded my surrender a dozen times, and every time I told you no. I told you that we would defeat your king and that he would regret waging war against the free states of Risyl. For those seven years, I have stood by those words, but I must admit that our will is faltering. Bread rations are meager already, and the king just took Tyim, our third biggest port. I don't know how much longer we can hold him off without help. So, I am inclined to assist you. However, I should tell you that the king's son, Prince Yimnit, has come to negotiate the terms of our surrender, just like you did so many years ago, and I am seriously considering taking him up on his offer."

Director Frente didn't seem surprised by this. She simply nodded. "I know why he is here, and while I need your help destroying the monarchy, I came to ask your permission in something more personal. I need your consent to kidnap the prince while he is on your soil as a bargaining chip for the king's surrender."

"You wish to poke the bear. His retribution will be swift and brutal."

"You can withstand his assault. The king has always had an air of invincibility to him. Margaret cracked that veneer, and losing his son will crack it further. The king rules by divine right, and until now, that has never been questioned. I'm saying we should question it. The best part is that you will not be implicated. This will be a rebellion operation, and when we are successful, you can condemn it all you want, though I would prefer if you used it as a chance to throw your support behind us and helped us bring more allies to the cause."

"You were always a cunning chess player," President Achel said. She turned to me. "The director puts a lot of her faith in you, and you haven't said anything, either of you. Tell me, why should we believe in you?"

I looked over at the director, who gave me a slight nod. "I'm not sure you should, frankly. There is certainly nothing in my history that shows I'm qualified to be a symbol for a whole movement—" If the director was upset with me for telling the truth, she wasn't showing it. "—but that's the position we find ourselves in. If I have learned anything in these past weeks, it's that you have to play the cards you are dealt. I don't know much about your world, but I know things have been the same for a long time. What we—Margaret and I—represent, well it's a catalyst, isn't it? Something that disrupts the status quo and allows for the system to change. The catalyst isn't a change in and of itself. It's just an agent of change, and for better or worse, that catalyst is us. I've seen things change already in my short time on your planet, and I know enough to know that if you don't take advantage of that catalyst and strike quickly, then you'll lose that spark, and you'll have to wait for the next one, and who knows when that will be?"

"It sucks," Margaret added when I stopped to take a breath. "It sucks that you have to rely on us, but it sounds like you are in a bad way. I doubt my father will be kind to you if you should surrender, especially since you have defied him for so long. Your back is against the wall, and here we come, two stupid kids who should definitely not be symbols for any kind of resistance. We're offering you something to rally behind, an out, and maybe, just maybe, a chance to change the solution that's been stagnant for so many years."

President Achel thought for a moment, stroking her chin. "Well, that was quite an eloquent speech. I can see why you have inspired your people."

"They are not my people," I said. "My people are back on my Earth. But there are good people here, and they need our help, both yours and mine."

She nodded. "I will talk to the Triumvirate and try to see what we can do. We have all been beaten back to the brink. Maybe we have enough for one last charge." President Achel eyed Director Frente narrowly. "I hope you know what you're doing."

CHAPTER 34

It was silent as we traversed the streets of Hjitew, Risyl, in the car that President Achel provided for us. It wasn't as fancy as a limo, and we had to drive ourselves, but it was a small kindness. Director Frente booked us a hotel on the outskirts of town in the eventuality that her plan would be acceptable to the president.

Anger bubbled up in my stomach as we drove. It started as mild irritation at the director's involvement with the king, but in the hour after our meeting, that irritation increased to ire, and that ire grew to anger, anger that surfaced after she had finished her phone call with Jasper to confirm the extraction.

"We'll have a team in place by tomorrow morning," she said with a smile as she hung up the phone, unaware of my festering rage. "Jasper has been laying out the logistics. It seems like—"

"How could you work with him?" I growled. "How could you say you're for freedom but then spend time working with that horrible, horrible man?"

She sighed. "I was hoping you would just let that go."

"Even if she did," Margaret said, "I wouldn't. What kind of rebellion leader fought for the enemy? You helped him conquer cities. You are at least partially responsible for this whole thing."

I broke in again, "Sindra—Volkim—they are from the outlying cities…did you help conquer their towns? Did you raze their cities?"

"I don't know, okay?" Director Frente took a breath to calm down. "I don't know. You have to understand—there is a powerful magnetism around the king, around the royal family. While I was coming up, we were all hypnotized by him." Her eyes dipped to the floor. "I'm not proud of it, but I desperately wanted to bring peace to the world…and that's what he said we were doing—spreading peace. He said we were prosperous and that other countries deserved as much. We were a shining example for the world. I thought we were doing good…for so long, I thought we were doing good. I joined the military after school and rose up the ranks."

She bit her lip. "I'm a very good tactician. The best, maybe, that they had. I planned a lot of their most successful battles…plans they probably still use today. It wasn't until years later that I realized—the places we conquered—they weren't getting any better. Then, I grasped the truth: we were stealing their resources to feed our prosperity. We weren't bringing them freedom. We were making them slaves."

She looked over at me. "You have to believe that I didn't want any of that. None of us wanted that—my friend and I—well, he went to confront the king…and his head ended up on a pike outside the castle. When they came for me, I was able to escape into the underground, and I have been spending every day since repenting for what I've done." She started crying. "I have only told that story a few times before, but you deserve to know the truth."

"Goddamn it," I said. "I really wanna be mad at you, but I guess you are trying to redeem yourself, aren't you?"

"I really am," she said with a smile. "Life is really hard, girls. I know you already know that, but it just gets harder over time, and every one of your mistakes compounds on the others. I don't think I'll ever be able to make up for the pain I caused, but if I can pull out the weed, root, and branch, that will be a start."

"That's a hell of a penance," Margaret said.

"Yeah." Director Frente wiped the tears from her eyes. "Hey, don't tell anyone you saw me cry, okay? I have a reputation to maintain."

"My lips are sealed," I said.

"Mine, too," Margaret added.

"Good, good." She smiled at me. "Hey, who wants ice cream? We have a big day tomorrow. Least we can do is gorge on sugar to prepare."

***

We ordered massive sundaes and ate while watching cheesy movies on television. It felt so much like home it was weird. Kimberly said that the gods only really know how to create things one way, but even given that, this planet was so much like my Earth that it was eerie. Maybe it was because they put so much stock in travelers, and it seemed, at least, like the king was from Earth, and maybe even America, and the ideas he brought with him permeated across the globe as he took city after country.

Eventually, my eyes grew heavy, and I fell into the inky blackness of sleep. This time, however, before I could fall into the lake of ooze, two hands caught me and dragged me to land, where Araphel sat waiting for me with a pot of tea. He poured some for me in a flowery cup and some for himself.

"Welcome again," he said.

I slid into the seat. "So, am I going to keep falling into this stupid pit for the rest of my life, or are you just stalking me for a little while?"

"Stalking? That's not a concept I understand. I have come to deliver a message." He cleared his throat. "Your plan will fail unless you embrace your true nature."

"Yes, you told me that before."

"I did?" The light in his eyes dimmed slightly. "Oh dear, I must have forgotten. I have so many things on my mind these days."

"I know that feeling." I took a sip of tea. "Since you are here, though, you can expound on that bit. Do you mean I should be torturing people or cheating them out of their soul, cuz I'm not really into either of those things?"

If I didn't know a skeleton couldn't smile, I would have sworn a slight one grew on Araphel's face. "That is not demon nature. That is a thing they do. Demons are impulse. They are fire. They are…hot-headed." He pointed to where his stomach would be. "The inferno in their gut is where they get their power." He pointed to his heart. "Angels get theirs from the heart." He looked up. "Oh, my. It seems like our time is up. I do wish we had more time."

He snapped his fingers, and my eyes fluttered open to the light of the morning creeping in. I heard the shower running, and Margaret was busy eating breakfast on the small table by the TV. A few moments later, Director Frente stepped out of the shower.

"Shower's free, ladies. Hurry up. We have a timetable."

We showered and ate a quick breakfast, then took the car across town, where we parked in an underground garage. When we exited the car, Commander Bivnol, Jasper, and seven other commandos dressed in black gear and carrying heavy guns stepped out from the shadows.

"Good to see you, commander," Director Frente said. "Are we ready to go?"

"Yes, ma'am," Commander Bivnol replied. "The consulate got word this morning of the prince's route. He'll be down this road in five minutes. We have a truck across the street that will box him in on either side, and then we'll extract him in the panic. Four more snipers on the roof of each building and the van stationed a block away will bring us to the airport, where the plane is fueled and ready to go."

"Wonderful," she said. Then, she gestured at us. "Come, girls. We're going to get a bird's eye view."

"Aren't we going to stay down here?" I said.

"Are you kidding?" Jasper said with a snort. "This is way too dangerous. Stay with the director. She'll keep you safe."

"Hey!" Margaret said. "Don't treat us like kids. We've seen stuff, okay? We've been in multiple firefights and just negotiated—"

"That's enough!" Commander Bivnol's shout echoed through the garage. "Take this key and wait for our signal. That's an order."

Director Frente nodded at Commander Bivnol and took the key. "Thank you."

I pressed Margaret's wheelchair forward and leaned in to whisper to her. "Don't worry about them, Margaret. We're totally badass, whether they know it or not."

***

Director Frente took us up the ramp to the hotel above the parking garage. We took the elevator up to the third floor and entered a room with a perfect view of the street. I had to admit; I was happy not to be down on the ground floor. I had gone up against Prince Yimnit before and had no interest in doing it again. Knowing that he might be able to use magic made him all the more dangerous in my eyes, and he was already one of the most dangerous men I had ever met, below only his vicious father.

"They do realize we have magic, right?" Margaret said.

"All I know is that I'm perfectly happy not being in that firefight. And you should be, too."

I stared out the window, watching as a string of black limos with diplomatic plates turned up the street. As they neared the hotel, a big truck pulled back into the street from a loading dock on the other side of it. The limo parade stopped, and two Jackboot officers emerged, stomping up to the truck. Moments later, gunfire exploded from the truck, and the Jackboots fell. The limos tried to turn back, but another truck pulled up the side of the street and blocked their way out. Commander Bivnol's troops rushed out of the parking garage and surrounded the cars as the doors opened and both sides opened fire.

"On second thought, you're right. I'm really glad we're not down there," Margaret said.

"Duh," I replied, peering out the window. "Oh, I think they got him."

Sure enough, Commander Bivnol rushed through the downed officers and pulled Prince Yimnit out of the car, his big fur coat flowing behind him as he screamed at the extraction team.

"We did it—" Director Frente started, but then a shockwave exploded the windows all around us and shook the building, sending us backward to the floor.

I recovered and pushed myself to my feet, rushing back to the window to see the prince surrounded by a ball of blue fire. The extraction team was either lying on the ground or stumbling in retreat. There was no doubt now. Prince Yimnit was a magic user.

"We have to help them!" I shouted. The words Araphel said to me echoed through my head. *Your plan will fail unless you embrace your true nature.*

What did that mean? He told me to trust my gut, but that couldn't have been right because my gut was saying to leap out of the window and take on the prince one on one. That would be suicide, even if I could survive the fall.

Two of Commander Bivnol's soldiers rushed forward to engage, and Prince Yimnit threw a torrent of blue fire at them, evaporating them where they stood.

"NO!" I screamed.

Instinct. Rely on instinct. Or we would fail. My instinct was telling me I needed to get down there…fast.

I took a step back and then leaped into the air when I reached the broken window, pulling myself into a tight ball to avoid the shards of glass along its edges. And then I fell. I fell and I fell until I landed with a crash into the ground between Commander Bivnol and Prince Yimnit with a crater cracked into the ground where the road absorbed my impact.

I stood, and to my great shock, I felt…fine. Absolutely fine. In fact, I felt better than fine. A fire burned in my belly and flowed through my legs and arms, giving me a jolt of energy.

"The traveler," Prince Yimnit growled. "I'm not surprised you have powers, little one, but I have been dealing with your kind for years."

He circled around me, and I countered his movements. "Oh, you have never met anyone like me. I'm sure of that."

"What are you, elf, dragon-born, halfling, sorcerer?"

"I'm afraid you'll have to beat me to find out," I said with a smile. *Where had all this confidence come from?* Moments ago, I was terrified, and now I brimmed over with unearned bravado.

"Gladly," he said with a grin, and he unleashed another torrent of blue fire. I didn't think. I didn't second guess myself. I acted on instinct. Holding my hand out in front of me, I pulled the fire toward me. It swirled around my body, warming my face. I took my other hand and clasped them together.

The fire swirling around me shot forward toward Prince Yimnit, detonating around him and sending him flying backward into the wall of the hotel. He fell to the ground and slumped over as his fire dissipated into nothing.

Commander Bivnol rose to her feet and stared at me, wide-eyed. "What just happened?"

Sirens screeched in the distance.

"We can talk about it later. Right now, we have to get out of here if we don't want to get arrested."

I could see her processing everything—the fire that nearly killed her, me leaping out of a building, the sirens coming—and finally, she nodded and ran toward Prince Yimnit's unconscious body. "Let's go, everybody!"

Director Frente and Margaret rushed out of the building toward the parking garage. "That means us, too."

A frantic rush ensued as the remaining members of the extraction team grabbed Prince Yimnit and carried him toward the getaway van. We leaped into the car, bolting down the street and turning the corner just as multiple police cars arrived on the scene.

We had made it out by the hair of our chinny chin chins, and I finally exhaled. I was the only one who felt any sense of relief, though. The other eyes in the car were filled with tense fear as to the power they had just witnessed. A small part of me—a very small part—fed on that fear and loved it.

CHAPTER 35

The trip back to base was filled with quiet bewilderment as we reflected on what we had just been through capturing Prince Yimnit. The eyes of the others fell on me often, and when I felt their gaze, I returned it…only to see them turn hastily away from me. I wasn't a mind reader, but it didn't take one to know what they were thinking. They had watched me take down an overpowered magic user without breaking a sweat, and the fear in their eyes was palpable. Even Prince Yimnit wasn't without dread when his eyes caught mine.

The only person who didn't have a problem with my powerful display was Margaret, and she peppered me with questions all the way to the airport about how I was able to channel Yimnit's energy. However, when I replied to her questions with nothing more than "I don't know," she eventually fell silent, too, more from disappointment than the concern that gripped the rest of our party.

How did I channel the energy Prince Yimnit shot at me on that street? It felt like I had always known how to control the flame, deep down in my bones, and I just needed something to unlock it within me. However, even now that I had done it, I wasn't sure how it happened, and I didn't know if I could repeat it. It was like Araphel said…it was instinct, an instinct I never knew I had and wasn't sure I wanted. An instinct that proved I wasn't human, no matter how much I looked like one.

When we finally reached the base, Sindra wrapped me in a big hug. It was the first true kindness I had received since my battle with Prince Yimnit.

"We heard you got him!" Sindra said excitedly. "That's awesome. We finally have a win."

"Did you hear…how it happened?" I asked, hoping against hope that maybe she was just cooler than everyone else and didn't care that I was a freak.

Sadly, she simply shook her head. "They don't tell me that kind of stuff, but we're all really happy that Prince Yimnit is under our control now."

I cracked a smile. "Have you seen Kimberly?"

Sindra pointed to the brig. "She's been doing something in the prison all day."

Just a few days ago, the base was a maze to me, and now I navigated it with ease. I entered the brig and saw Kimberly drawing runes on the walls with a black marker, muttering to herself.

"Good," she said when I approached. "You're back. Prince Yimnit didn't give you any trouble?"

I shook my head. "He's been unconscious most of the ride, and we bound him like you told us."

Kimberly looked up at her handiwork with pride. "Nice. Well, I'm almost done here."

"What is all of this?"

"Runes to prevent Prince Yimnit from using magic, just like the ones hidden in Junebug and Carl's house. I'm hoping that the rules of magic are the same here as on our planet. There's no reason they wouldn't be, given that pretty much every other rule about the universe holds true from gravity to physics to even how the grass grows."

Director Frente walked into the room. "Are you ready?"

Kimberly nodded and stood up. "Yes, ma'am. This should hold the prince."

Director Frente poked her head into the hall. "Bring him in!"

She moved out of the way, and Commander Bivnol pushed Prince Yimnit into the cell in the middle of the room, the same one that once held Kimberly, and pulled off the cloth that bound his hands together before removing the shackles from his hands and kicking him into the cell.

"You will pay for this." Prince Yimnit held up his hands as if he was trying to cast a spell, but nothing happened. He tried again, and a second time, he failed. "What is—" Finally, he looked around the room and saw the runes all along the walls, ceiling, and floor. "I see. Who of you knows of the old ways?"

"That would be me," Kimberly said. "This isn't my first time dealing with sorcerers. You'll find your magic quite ineffective here. Even I can't cast within these walls."

"So, you use magic like your friend?"

"Who?" Kimberly asked. "Anjelica? Not quite. The magic I have is different from hers but equally powerful."

Prince Yimnit thought for a moment and then sat back on the cot against the back wall of the room. "Very well. It matters not. By now, my father will know I have been captured, and soon enough your friends will bend the knee and tell us where you are…or be destroyed in the process."

"And how will he destroy an entire country?" Director Frente said. "Because as I see it, for the first time in forever, we have the upper hand."

"For now, but wheels are in motion which will allow us to enact our final battle, and then we will be unstoppable. All will bow before us or be obliterated from existence."

Commander Bivnol stepped forward. "We'll see about that. For now, we'll let you stew in your cage. When you see that all hope for rescue is lost, then perhaps you'll talk willingly. If not, well, I certainly look forward to making you talk—unwillingly." She cracked the knuckles on her thumbs. "I have been looking forward to it for a long time."

Prince Yimnit smiled at her. "Interesting, because I haven't thought of you, not for one moment, until today. That is the advantage of being royalty. The thoughts of commoners don't concern you."

Commander Bivnol tensed, but a soft hand from Director Frente calmed her, at least for a moment. "You'll get your chance. For now, let him rest and contemplate his fate."

***

"Torture never works," Kimberly said when we had all regrouped in Director Frente's office.

"Says you," Commander Bivnol replied. "Sounds like the mutterings of a civilian who doesn't have the guts to do what needs to be done."

"Hey!" Kimberly shouted. "I've been at this long enough—I've killed enough demons—I've seen things that would make you quake in your boots. I've found that it's a lot easier to get somebody to tell you the truth through trickery and sympathy than torture. People will say anything to stop torture."

"Exactly what I'm sa—"

"They'll beg, borrow, steal, and lie." Kimberly continued through Commander Bivnol's interruption. "And every time they lie, we have to track that lie down. If Prince Yimnit is to be believed, that his father is close to developing a weapon that forces countries to surrender…"

"That's an empty threat."

Kimberly shook her head. "He doesn't seem like the kind to threaten or be threatened. We have to get him to tell the truth willingly."

"And how do you propose we do that?" Director Frente asked. "I'm all ears."

Kimberly turned to me. "Send Anjelica to talk with him."

"What?" I shouted. "You can't be serious."

"I am. You bested him in combat. Even if he doesn't want to, he respects that, and he might even fear it. With the backing of the rebellion and the fact that you bested him in combat, you're the most likely one he'd talk to. Plus, you have one other thing going for you."

"What's that?" I said.

"You are a young, cute girl. Powerful men always underestimate people like you. He will assume your victory was a fluke or that you cheated, and you can use all of those power dynamics to your advantage." Kimberly turned to the director. "And if that fails, then you can torture the prick until he screams bloody murder."

"I like that last part the best," Commander Bivnol said. "I say we just skip to that."

"What do you think, Anjelica?" Director Frente asked.

I shook my head. "I can't—I mean, I'm just—" My eyes met Kimberly's. "You're asking too much of me."

"That doesn't change the fact that it's still our best plan." She slapped her hand on my shoulder. "I know this has been the worst month of your whole life, Anjelica, and I sincerely hope it is the worst month you ever experience for the next eighty years. But the world doesn't stop turning just because you think the pressure is too much to handle.

You have the whole of this rebellion on your shoulders now. You can do this. I believe in you."

"I wish you weren't so good at speeches. Now I'm all riled up and ready to go." I took a deep breath. "This really has been the worst month of my whole life."

"Good news is that after this, you'll be prepared for anything."

"If I live through it," I said. "Let's just get this over with."

***

I was about to interrogate a prince. How was this my life? If I ever got home, who would ever believe any of this? Silly, Anjelica. *When will you get it through your head that you aren't going home?* Never. I will never get that through my head. All I have to do is destroy a royal line and free an entire world, and the gods will bring me back to my mother. That sounded so stupid. *I really was a naïve little thing.*

Well, if I wanted to bring down a king, then I had to get the prince to talk—the same prince that had tried to kill me multiple times. *This should be easy.*

I stood outside the door to the brig for a long time, gathering my nerve. Nobody dared come down the hall near me. Word of what I'd done in Risyl spread through the rebellion in whispered conversations, carried like a virus on the air, and now there were few kind eyes left for me.

That hostility propelled me into the brig and toward Prince Yimnit's cell. When he saw me, his face hardened. There was a hint of fear in his eyes that he covered with anger. "I was wondering who they would send. I thought the director, or the commander…to send a child is an insult to my position."

There was a long pause as he scowled at me. "I beat you," I finally said. "This child beat you."

"Hrm," he said. "So, you did. A surprising turn of events, to be sure, but not completely so. Almost all travelers end up being magic users or are sent by magic users. However, none have bested me before. What makes you different?"

"Perhaps you have gotten slow…or perhaps it's because I am a demon."

"A demon?" Prince Yimnit laughed. "Of course. I wondered why I smelled sulfur coming off you. I will remember to use water on you next time."

I took a step closer. "There will be no next time…because you'll never get out of this cell unless you help us, and I already know there is no chance of that."

"Using reverse psychology on me won't work."

I shrugged. "I don't know what that is, but I'm not trying to use anything on you. As you mentioned before, I am a child. That would have been an insult to me even a month ago, but if I've learned nothing in the past weeks, it's that I am a child, naïve in many things." I leaned against the bars. "But at least I'm smart enough to know how naïve I am and that you will never part with anything you are not willing to give." I sighed. "Commander Bivnol wants to torture you. Frankly, I want her to torture you, not because I think that it will make you tell us anything, but because you deserve pain after what you have done."

"You really are the most terrible negotiator I've ever met."

"That's not even the hundredth worst insult I've heard recently. It's not even an insult. It's the truth." I turned away. "I will tell everyone that you wouldn't give me anything and that they should torture you. Commander Bivnol will be so pleased."

"Wait," Prince Yimnit said. "You didn't even try! Aren't you supposed to make me an offer or something? Tell me what you want before you subject me to torture?"

There was fear in his voice when he talked about torture. "Fine. You're right. I'll make you an offer, though you'll never take it." I spun back to him. "Tell us what your father is planning and how to take him down, and we'll let you keep your pretty, little fingers."

He smirked. "That's better. This is how diplomacy is done, my dear. You make me an offer, and I make a counteroffer."

"I'm not interested."

"Well, I will give it to you anyway." He stepped to the edge of the cell. "I will help you, and in return—when my father is deposed—you will name me the rightful king. I will withdraw our troops from those countries we have taken and end this accursed war of attrition once and for all."

"You want the war to end?"

He nodded. "That's why my father won't step down from the throne. He will never step down, not until he dies—and trust me, he will not die for a very long time. Not given the magic afforded to him and what he plans." He took a long breath. "I alone know the way through the tunnels under the city which lead into the castle, and only the royal family knows what my father is truly planning."

"And what is he planning?" I growled, glaring at him.

Prince Yimnit smiled. "To capture a god."

CHAPTER 36

I relayed the information Prince Yimnit gave me to Director Frente, Commander Bivnol, Kimberly, and Margaret. They all listened in rapt silence as I spoke, and when I was done, a pall fell over them.

"We can't agree to that," Director Frente said. "First of all, our goal is to blow up the monarchy and salt the earth so nothing like the royal family can ever take power again, and two, the simple idea that there are gods, and that somebody could capture them, is so insane that I couldn't possibly sanction following up on it without becoming a buffoon on the international stage."

Kimberly leaned forward. "There are gods, director, and saving one from capture wouldn't make you a fool. It would make you indebted to a god, which is a good place to be."

"And," I added, "there might be a way to give Prince Yimnit everything he wants…without giving him anything that he wants."

"Explain," Commander Bivnol said.

"Well, in our world, there are things called constitutional monarchies. There is a queen, for instance, in Great Britain, but they have almost no power, except ceremonial power. All the real power is controlled by the Parliament. If we can get Prince Yimnit to agree to something like that, then we all might be able to make this work."

Director Frente looked down into her lap. "I don't know."

"Think about it, Director," Margaret said, after a long bout of silence. "There are lots of people who love the monarchy, aren't there?"

"I know I saw a lot of people who loved the king on my time walking through the city," Kimberly said. "A lot, a lot. Way more than I thought possible."

"And if we just depose the king, cut off his head, and start something new, then we won't have backing from all of those people that support the king," Margaret said. "But if we can instill a king who believes in the rights of the people, and he gives us the power of democracy, then it's likely we can get even more support than if we just assassinated the king in a coup."

Director Frente stood and paced behind her desk. "How can we trust Prince Yimnit, though?"

"Exactly," Commander Bivnol echoed. "He's a snake who has tried to kill us multiple times."

"Ah," Kimberly said. "But a snake will leave you alone if you don't disturb him. Giving him the perception of power without any responsibility to rule might be the exact solution both sides need."

"I have to think about this and discuss it with—others," the director said. "Meanwhile, how do we figure out if there really is a weapon that can destroy a city and capture a god?"

"If you can capture a god, you can harness its power." Kimberly scratched her head. "The question is whether we can build such a device. I believe I have a beat on some magical creatures in this city. However, they are not friendly to fairies." She turned to me. "You need to come with me. I think I've found demons, and you have a better chance at communicating with them than me."

"I thought we agreed that I wasn't going anywhere looking like this," I said, pointing to my face.

"Let's just hope Madam Fantasmo can do her work and make you look like a new person because I can't do this without you."

I shot up. "That so many of your plans—" I pointed between Director Frente, Commander Bivnol, and Kimberly— "rely on somebody so unqualified for them to work doesn't make me feel very good about this organization."

"I don't disagree," Margaret said. "But Anjelica, for some reason, this whole thing keeps circling around us. It's like fate is guiding us along. We can either lean into the skid and go with it and maybe live or fight against it and most definitely die."

I laughed. "I can't believe you think there's any way we live through this. I love your optimism." I stood up and brushed my hands together. "All right, let's go see Madam Fantasmo so I can be a pawn in your stupid plan."

***

"There," Madam Fantasmo said when she finished with the contour brush on my cheeks. "Have a look."

She moved away from the mirror, and I didn't recognize the woman looking back at me. This one had much darker skin than me and high cheekbones and dark eyes. I looked like royalty.

"How—" I asked, stunned speechless.

"You can literally make anyone look like anything," Volkim said from the other side of me as she pulled my hair back into a tight bun. "If men knew that, they would never trust us again."

"I'm pretty sure they don't trust us already," I said.

"With good reason," Volkim said with a wicked smile. "Look at what we can do."

"You look simply fabulous," Madam Fantasmo said. "Just gorgeous. Of course, I liked you the other way, too, but now, you wear a masterpiece on your face. Try not to smudge it."

I stared at myself in the mirror. "This feels like an insane risk."

"All of this seems insane," Sindra said, walking into the room. She wore a black dress and combat boots. "I mean, you're a demon. Is that right? Are we really styling a monster?"

I looked at my hands. "I…don't know. I don't feel like a Hellspawn or anything, but then, I guess I don't know what being a human feels like, either." I met her eyes. "I didn't know how you would feel about me when you found out." I turned to the others. "Any of you."

"Please," Madam Fantasmo said. "We've styled dukes and queens, and they are truly demonic. If we can get through them without batting an eye, we're certainly not going to get hung up on you, girl. Seriously, win one fight with a prince, and it all goes to your head." She laughed loudly at her own joke.

I smiled back at her, and my eyes welled with tears. Volkim rushed over to me with a tissue. "Don't you dare go crying and ruin Madam's work." She dabbed at my eyes. "You can cry all you want when you get back."

I nodded. "You got it."

Sindra put a hand on my shoulder. "We understand that you're emotional and everything, but seriously, it's for your own good if you can just, like, not cry for a little bit of time. From what I hear, demons aren't really comfortable with emotions."

She was right. That was the intel Kimberly gave us, anyway. These demons we were meeting were mean and ornery cusses that didn't care for any that weren't their kind. I had to keep it under control.

I said my goodbyes to the girls and went downstairs to find Kimberly in a simple pair of khaki slacks and a black jacket. Her hair was matted down, and her face had none of the lush make-up she usually wore. She walked me outside to the car waiting for us and slid inside. When I joined her, the car jutted forward.

After a few minutes, Kimberly looked over at me. "How are you holding up?"

"Terrible," I replied without hesitation. "This sucks, maybe worse than being kidnapped by demons. You do remember that the last time I interacted with demons, they were kidnapping me, right?"

She nodded. "I know, and I already admitted this situation sucks, but you are no longer an antichrist, and so there is no reason for them to kidnap you again."

"How about just because it's fun? Don't demons do things like kill people, rip their arms off, and kidnap them for fun?"

Kimberly furrowed her brow. "Some of them. Some of them do worse, others better. These ones didn't seem like the 'evil for the sake of evil' type."

"What type did they seem?"

She scrunched her face from one side to the other. "They seemed like the sowing chaos type and then letting humanity hang its own noose." She must have realized that I had been hung by a noose just a few short days ago because her face contorted in shame. "Sorry. It's just a turn of phrase."

"Aren't they all," I replied, rubbing my neck. "It's okay. So, what are we trying to get from these demons again?"

"It's pretty simple. We need to know if the king has a device to trap a god, if they helped him build it, and how we can destroy it if they did."

"And if they didn't?"

"If I know demons at all, they did. It takes an incredible amount of power to create something like that. Fairies could do it, maybe, but the only beings who could possibly have any idea how to capture a god are demons…or angels, and the heavens help us if they've turned on the gods."

CHAPTER 37

Forty minutes later, sitting in bumper-to-bumper traffic for most of that time, Kimberly tapped the driver's headrest. "It's just up ahead. We'll walk from here. There's a lot around the corner. Make a left. Third floor. Wait for us."

The driver nodded, and Kimberly pulled me out of the car. We passed two dingy bars, which seemed to be the perfect place for demons to hide, but we didn't stop at either of them. Instead, we walked toward a garden center on the corner. Inside, it smelled of roses and begonias, tulips and peonies. Rows of flowers were set up in the middle of the room, and bags of manure and mulch were stacked high along the walls, as well as equipment and machinery.

"Welcome," a short woman with a lazy eye waved at us as we walked in. When she got a good look at Kimberly's face, she growled. "What are you doing here?"

"I'm here to see the manager," Kimberly replied. "I bought some flowers the other day, and they died when I threw them off a balcony. I don't know what I've done wrong."

"Not everyone has a green thumb." The woman's voice was now two octaves lower than it had been just moments ago. "We have a no refund policy, though, so you're out of luck there."

"Oh, I'm not here for me. I'm here because my friend has business with your boss." She yanked me forward, and I slammed hard into the counter. "You told me to come back with one of your kind, and well, here you go."

The woman sniffed the air. She spent a long time glaring at me, slowly moving her eyes down my body. It wasn't sensual, and it wasn't kind. She eyed me like a cow bound for slaughter. When she finished, she reached under her desk and pushed a button. A buzzer squawked at us, and the door to the back opened.

"It's your funeral," the woman said. "We won't let you off so easy this time."

"What happened last time?" I asked as we walked toward the back.

"Have you ever heard the term 'pound of flesh'?" Kimberly asked.

"Of course," I replied.

She pulled up her sleeve to reveal a gash in her arm. "They didn't quite take that much."

"That looks awful," I said, stopping in my tracks. "We should go."

Kimberly shook her head. "No. It's fine. They just caught me off guard. I won't let it happen again."

In the hazy fog of the back room, four different demons stomped toward us from the long rows of plants. Their hideousness caught me off guard. I had only seen a handful of demons in my life, and these were mangled and deformed in ways the ones on Earth hadn't been, as if they were an early prototype to a botched experiment.

"I thought I told you to leave and never come back!" a big, brown demon with huge teeth screamed. "Or wasn't the price we forced you to pay enough?"

Kimberly held up her hands. "You told me not to come back without one of your kind to vouch for me." She turned to me. "Gui'el'dek, meet Anjelica, my friend, who I really hope will vouch for me."

Gui'el'dek moved close to me, sniffing. Without asking, he grabbed me on either side of my body and lifted me in the air.

"I think that's more than enough," I said. "Please put me down."

The other three demons laughed, but Gui'el'dek set me back on the ground. "I'm sorry, but you must understand that many try to trick us into helping them, and we have become…more cautious over time."

"I get it," I replied, smoothing out my clothes and trying to appear calm. "Maybe ask before you get that close next time, though. It's common courtesy."

"My apologies," Gui'el'dek growled. "You must think me a cad. No matter, is it true that you vouch for this pixie, my sister?"

I nodded. "I vouch for her. She's saved my life many times."

Gui'el'dek turned to Kimberly. "Then I offer you my thanks. It is not often that a pixie protects our kind. They prefer to stick to the skies, while we prefer direct contact with our enemy."

"And you think humanity is your enemy?" I asked.

"We only think everything is our enemy," Gui'el'dek growled. "That is how we few are still alive. There are not many of my kind left on this planet. In fact, these are all the demons left on this planet, along with my sister out front and the handful of imps who are out on deliveries right now."

"What about other magical creatures?" Kimberly asked. "You mentioned pixies. Are there fairy folk, too?"

Gui'el'dek grimaced. "I do not like being addressed by something so below me, but I will answer for our sister's benefit. Magic is sparse on this planet, and that which does exist has been harvested by the king for his own means."

"That's what we're here about," I said. "The king. We have been told he has a weapon that can summon and trap a god and then harness their power to destroy his enemies."

All of the demons grumbled and hissed before Gui'el'dek spoke again. "It's true. For the past fifty years, the king has scoured the world for magic. When he came to us, it was for a favor, to help him channel the energy into one single device, for exactly the purpose you mentioned. We are gardeners, you must understand. When we left the underworld, we just wanted to make an honest way in the world, but the king was insistent." Gui'el'dek touched his face. "He is so powerful, and we agreed to help him in return for him sparing us."

"Sparing you?"

Gui'el'dek choked back a gasp. "Our job was to chase down what magic there was so that he might make his machine more powerful, and in return, he would not destroy our clan. We are not proud of the thing we did, but we do not regret it."

"Wow," I said. "I thought you were all powerful, fearsome demons, but here you are, just a bunch of wusses."

"What did you say to me?" The demon's face grew stern. "I let none talk to me that way, sister."

"I have spent the last month trying to fight against the king, only to find out my own kin have helped him, and they did so because they were scared. Pathetic."

Gui'el'dek lumbered forward. "I will give you one chance to apologize before I rip out your throat where you stand."

Kimberly swung a dagger from the back of her pants and held it to his throat. "Try it, and I will end you."

Gui'el'dek took a swing at Kimberly, who ducked easily to avoid it, and the other three demons were on us at once.

"I don't want to fight," Kimberly said, breaking free of the mayhem. "But you won't catch me unprepared like last time, and trust me, I am very capable of taking out four exiled demons at once. Please, just stop. I don't think anyone wants the king to capture a god."

"And why not?" Gui'el'dek spat the words. "Pan abandoned us. Baron Samedi discarded us. Why should we care if this place burns?"

"Hello!" I shouted. "Because you live here…and…so do plants?"

Gui'el'dek cocked his head in question.

"Yeah, I mean, you wouldn't want plants to burn, would you?"

He thought for a moment before letting out a low chuckle. "Fair point, little one. You are wiser than you look."

"I get that a lot. Now, believe me when I say that if the king gets this weapon functioning, then everything, including plants, will burn. Help us stop it, and we will save everyone…and everything…in this world."

Gui'el'dek stepped back and held up his hands. There was a tiny trickle of blue blood from where Kimberly had pressed the knife against him, but it didn't seem to faze him in the slightest. "I am only a part in this, you understand. However, I once delivered some items to a woman who claimed to be the architect of the device. I will give you the address, sister, if you promise to end this."

I nodded. "I promise to do my best. I am only one person, though."

"I have learned that one person can destroy the world. Maybe one person can save it, too."

"I hope so."

CHAPTER 38

Dr. Jortensur worked at a high-tech laboratory outside of the city. Its exterior was sleek and white, shiny enough that the sun glistened off the polished surface. The lobby was a massive place, sparsely decorated save for a few white couches and a futuristic-looking reception desk in front of glass panes that reflected the light streaming in from outside.

The receptionist was dressed in white from her turtleneck down to her boots. Honestly, she looked like a James Bond henchman, complete with a white headband pulling back her brown hair. When she smiled, her teeth gleamed in the light, just like the rest of the lobby. I hated her because no matter how hard I looked, she didn't seem to have a single flaw.

"Good afternoon, welcome to Fleranox." She fluttered her big blue eyes as she spoke. For all her perfection, there was nothing behind her eyes—no hope, no joy, no love, but also no hatred or pain. Just vacant blankness. "How may we help you?"

"Yes," Kimberly started, looking as out of place as I had ever seen her. "We're looking for Doctor Jortensur."

"Is she expecting you?" the receptionist asked, her voice chipper yet monotone.

"Not exactly. We have a package to deliver for her."

The receptionist held out her hands. "I can take it."

I shook my head. "I'm sorry. We have strict orders to deliver it to the doctor personally."

The receptionist's face twitched slightly before she smiled again. "I can assure you that leaving it with me is like leaving it with her."

Kimberly's eyes narrowed. "We have orders."

The receptionist cocked her head, first left and then right. "And where is your package?"

"Excuse me?" I said.

She pointed to our hands. "You have four hands between the two of you, and none of them have a package in it."

Kimberly patted her jacket. "That's because I have it in my pocket. It's fairly small but quite important."

The woman blinked, trying to process our lies. Then, she smiled again. "Very well. I will phone the doctor and ask if she is available. However, I will warn you that I haven't seen her today."

"Thank you for trying."

"Yes," the receptionist said into the phone after a moment. "Is the doctor available for a package delivery—yes, I know—they insist—I see. I will let you know." She placed the phone down. "I'm sorry, but the doctor is not in today. Now, if you will please—"

"When was the last time she checked in?" Kimberly asked.

"I can't give you that information."

"Fine. When was the last time you saw her, personally, with your own eyes?"

The receptionist scrunched up her face. "I believe she left for lunch three days ago, and I have not seen her since. It's not uncommon for me not to see her for several days. She tends to stay in her office while working on a project."

Her face returned to the neutral expression she'd had for most of our conversation, and she held out her hand. "Now, the package."

"But she's not in her office," I said. "When was the last time you remember her missing a day of work?"

She laughed. "She has never missed a day of work in all the time I've known her, though she was working on a project for the ki—an outside contractor. Perhaps that's where she's gone." Her eyes narrowed. "These are very odd questions for a pair of delivery drivers."

"We're nosey," Kimberly said, pulling a notepad from the inside of her pocket and pressing it down on the table. "Make sure she gets this, okay?"

"Will do."

The receptionist placed the pad behind the desk with a look of bewilderment and confusion. When we were outside, Kimberly turned to me. "Do you think your people can find out where the good doctor lived?"

"I think so, but they're not just my people, they're our people, right?"

She looked at me. "I'm forced to work with them right now, but my only people are fairy kind, not humanity. This will be bad for both of us, so it just so happens that at this moment, our goals are aligned."

"And what if our goals diverge?"

"Let's hope it doesn't come to that. Now, let's find a phone and call the director to get that address."

***

Director Frente gave us an encrypted emergency line we could use to make immediate contact with the base, and when we called, they patched us through to a tech team that found the good doctor's address in a matter of minutes.

Dr. Jortensur lived in an elegant area of the city, close to the palace, which made sense if she worked directly for the king. The beautifully maintained row houses on her street reminded me of the one Madam Fantasmo brought us to after we'd escaped our execution. The car pulled up in front of her townhouse, and it stood out from the ones on either side of it, both for its size and the fact that it was the only black house on the block. It was like the inverse negative of the office and walking up the steps to her house, I already liked her better, simply for the fact that her taste was odd.

"Be careful," Kimberly said. "If she works for the king, she's not to be trusted."

I nodded, and she knocked on the door. After several seconds, she knocked again, more loudly. When there was no response, Kimberly tried the door. There was a time that I wouldn't have walked into somebody's house without their permission, but those days were long gone.

Kimberly jiggled the handle, and it popped open for us. The smell of rancid meat kicked me in the face before we even entered. I gagged and nearly threw up, but Kimberly didn't seem phased.

"I need a bucket or a toilet," I said, heaving.

"Do not throw up here," she said. "You don't want to leave your DNA at the scene of a crime."

"What crime? I mean, besides our breaking and entering?"

But she didn't answer. She walked up the stairs, where the stench grew worse, toward the sounds of somebody talking. She held up her hand as she neared the top. Her blue wings appeared out of her back, and she lifted herself into the air. Her hands went for her daggers as she disappeared into the hallway.

There were a few moments of silence, and then she reappeared. "It's okay. Well, it's not okay, but—just come up here."

I entered the upstairs room, where the dead body of an older woman was on the bed. She had died watching the TV, which explained the sounds we heard downstairs.

Bile backwashed into my throat, and I choked it down as Kimberly went to the body. She picked up a glass of water next to the bed and smelled it. I don't know how she could have smelled anything over the stench of the woman.

Dr. Jortensur looked at me with her dead eyes. I turned toward the television. The news was on, the crawl saying, "King vows swift retribution on Risyl for abduction of son."

The image flashed to one of King Ulthar in front of his throne, holding a golden scepter in his hand. "Yesterday," he said in his grandest voice, "the government of Risyl conspired with the rebellious contingent of our people to abduct my son from a peaceful, diplomatic motorcade. We are working diligently to find the rebellious scum, but we must make clear that any aid given to enemies of the crown is an act against all of us. I have worked for years to bring a peaceful end to our war, but President Achel's actions have made it clear that there can be no peace. Tomorrow, as the sun rises on our great nation, we will demonstrate our full power using Risyl as an example. Once Risyl falls, the other nations will bend the knee or face the same fate."

The king's glare softened. "I tell you this to give you time, citizens of Risyl, to find safety and to beg your government to return Prince Yimnit before it is too late. If they surrender before daybreak tomorrow and return my son, then all will be forgiven. If not—well, I am a kind and merciful king to those that adore me and a cruel one to those that oppose me."

The television faded to black, and when I turned back around, Kimberly held a remote control in her hand. "She was poisoned. I'm sure of it. No doubt to prevent her from telling anyone how to stop this machine."

"What do we do now?" I asked. "We can't let him fire that weapon."

"We won't. Dr. Jortensur wasn't working alone. Whoever it was, we have to find them and get them to help us shut down this device before sunrise tomorrow…or a whole country's blood will be on our hands."

CHAPTER 39

The rebellion hackers were able to break into Fleranox's human resources system and find the names of Dr. Jortensur's team, though any record of their projects had already been erased from the system. My gut said the king was trying to erase everything about the project they were working on, starting with the records and ending with anyone who might know how to stop it.

There were three assistants on the project's core team, along with Dr. Jortensur. She was already dead. I hoped we could get to at least one of the others before the king finished the job. The first person on the list, Giudal Tery, lived on the third floor of an apartment complex close to the center of the city. Fire trucks were already at the scene, shooting water into a charred black hole on the third floor of the building. We didn't even get out of the car to examine it further. We knew Giudal's place was the one ablaze.

The second assistant was a grad student named Sysyn Nilt. She worked mostly from her office in the king's university. Our driver let us out as close to her dorm as he could get, but we had to hoof it the final hundred yards. By the time we arrived, a small crowd was disbursing as an EMT crew loaded Sysyn's dead, lifeless body onto a stretcher.

"Shit!" I screamed. "They've gotten all of them. Every single one."

"Hey!" Kimberly said. "Calm down. We still have one assistant left, okay? Think positive. We're going to figure this out, and if we can't, then we'll figure out something else."

I didn't have any of her optimism. The last months had stripped it from me, flaying me until there was no hope left inside of me, just a bitter husk left who didn't much believe that good things would happen anymore.

Maybe I was cursed. If I went away, perhaps Kimberly would have better luck on her own. I could open the door and leave right now, just tuck and roll away and give her a fighting chance. I grabbed onto the metal door handle and tried to convince myself to open it, but as I gathered my nerve to leap, the car jerked to a stop in front of a little ranch house that must have belonged to Ingyr Borsti, the last of Dr. Jortensur's assistants.

"Think good thoughts," Kimberly said, not knowing that was an impossibility for me at the moment. *Maybe ever again.*

I got out of the car anyway and followed Kimberly to the door. It was already cracked open. Not a good sign. The smell of rotten eggs followed us through the house as we snaked our way to the kitchen, where we found the body of Ingyr Borsti, head in the oven. Kimberly turned off the gas.

"Well, crap."

"What was that you were saying about positive mental thoughts?" I asked. "Can I spiral yet?"

"Yeah," she said, kicking the wall. "Spiral away."

That was quite enough adventure for one day. I could never see another dead body for the rest of my life, and I would be perfectly happy, thank you very much.

***

We arrived back to the base into a pandemonium, people skittering anxiously and heavy with panic. When I stepped onto the main floor, Volkim turned a corner so fast that she barreled into me, knocking papers into the air as we fell to the floor.

"Oh shit, I'm sorry," she said, gathering the papers from around her. Kimberly and I helped her. "It's been a little bit hectic around here since—well, all day, actually."

"I heard the king," I said once we'd successfully gathered the papers into a messy pile. "Is that what this is all about?"

"Pretty much." She pointed down the hall. "The director wanted to see you in her office ASAP. She's been locked in there most of the day on calls."

"Fabulous."

Kimberly and I made our way to the director's office, where she was stacked elbows to ankles with Margaret, Madam Fantasmo, Commander Bivnol, and a bunch of other suits and soldiers. A voice I barely recognized as President Achel squawked at them from the phone on the desk.

"I can't risk my country for one prisoner," President Achel said. "You can either return him to us by midnight, or you will have made an enemy of Risyl."

"No offense, Madam President," Commander Bivnol said. "But your threats didn't work two hours ago, and they aren't going to work now. We are working on a plan to end this tonight, and if we don't, then we'll move on to plan B."

"Wait," I shouted, crowding into the room. "You can't honestly be thinking of surrendering, are you?"

"Who is that? Is that somebody new?" President Achel said. "Whatever, it doesn't matter. I'm giving you an hour to start fixing this, or you leave us no choice. Time to think outside the box, people."

"Margaret is about to go on the air and deliver our response," Madam Fantasmo said. "It's going to be fantastic."

"It better be," President Achel snapped, and then the line disconnected.

Director Frente rubbed the bridge of her nose. "So nice of you to join us, Anjelica. Please tell me you have good news and that I haven't been getting chewed out all day for nothing."

I looked over at Kimberly, who nodded at me slightly. "Well, we have some good news…and some bad news."

"Well, that's better than us," Margaret said. "We only have bad news."

"Out with it," the director barked.

"We know who built the device for the king, but…she's dead."

"Poisoned," Kimberly added. "Along with her three assistants. And all their information has been wiped from their databases."

"We already knew that," Jasper said from the corner.

"Which means you have nothing," Commander Bivnol said. "Swell."

"It's okay," Margaret said. "We just fall back to Plan Moonbeam, then."

"What's that?" I said.

Margaret turned to me. "I offer an exchange. Me in place of the prince."

"That's crazy!" Kimberly shouted. "I mean, who would make that trade?"

She shrugged. "We don't have many cards left to play. If nothing else, it might cause a distraction and buy us some time."

"You can't!"

Director Frente slammed her hands on the desk. "She can, she will, and she is. Now, everyone out. Madam Fantasmo, bring Margaret to the studio and get her on the air in five minutes. Let's just hope this buys us some time." The group disbursed. "Anjelica, Kimberly. You stay here for a minute, please."

I didn't like the tone of her voice. I slipped through the stream of soldiers as they passed, giving Margaret's shoulder a squeeze before she left the room. When the last of them were gone, the door clicked closed.

"This isn't going to work," Director Frente said. "We're just hoping for a stall, so it looks like we're doing something, and hopefully, we can swing public opinion back to our side for a minute."

"The president can't possibly be thinking of surrender, can she?"

"I don't know. She's tough, and Risyl is strong, but this weapon he's designing…I have no idea how to stop it and no idea how powerful it is. If the king can really harness the power of a god, then he might just be able to destroy the world while barely lifting a finger. There's only one thing that brings me hope."

"And what is that?"

Director Frente pressed her hands into her desk as she leaned against it. "If he had the power to use the weapon, he would have already done it."

Kimberly nodded her head. "Which means either he doesn't have the weapon or—"

"Or he's waiting for something to perform the ritual," I said, finishing Kimberly's thought.

"Maybe not just something. Maybe he needs the timing to be right," Kimberly replied, stroking her chin. "Lots of magic is dependent on certain times of day, or times of the year, to work." She turned to Director Frente. "Is there anything significant about tonight?"

"Significant how?" She paused. "There's a full moon tonight if I remember right."

"That could be it," Kimberly said. "I can't believe I am saying this, but I think there's a ritual he has to perform tonight to finalize the weapon, which gives us one more night to save the world before King Ulthar is unstoppable."

"Then we have to attack tonight," Director Frente said. "Prince Yimnit and I have agreed to terms. He will lead our team into the tunnels tonight."

"And if he's leading you into a trap?"

"Then it's still the best chance we have."

I had an idea. It was a daft idea, but maybe there was still a way to communicate with the dead. After all, I kind of had an in with Death.

I turned to Kimberly. "Can you get me some sleeping pills?"

***

After Director Frente released us, I stepped into the booth of the studio and watched Margaret psych herself up on the stage.

"I don't like this," I said to nobody specifically. A handful of other people in the room, including Madam Fantasmo, turned to me.

"None of us do, hon," Madam Fantasmo said. "This is war, and in war, there are rarely good choices, just ones that stink less than others. Risking one person to save a country is a terrible trade, but it's the best one we have."

"We're live in five," a balding man in front of a bank of video monitors said into an earpiece. "Four, three, two, one…and we're live."

Red lights blinked on in the stage, and Margaret rolled herself forward. "Two days ago, we captured Prince Yimnit from the Capitol of Risyl. We worked alone with no help from President Achel or her people. It was a secret mission, and our men barely escaped with their lives. I know this to be true because I was on a diplomatic trip to Risyl, trying to get their support. They refused, despite the dire situation. However, we thought the reward was great enough that we decided to carry out our operation anyway—even without President Achel giving us the authority."

She took a breath. She was a natural at this. Calm and cool on stage, even with the fate of the world on her shoulders. "One of the advantages of working outside of the law is that we do not have to abide by international treaties to fulfill our aims. I beg the king to understand that even though this abduction happened on foreign soil, it was conducted by our people and ours alone. However, we do have your son. And we will not give him up."

She dipped her head for a moment, and I wondered if it was a natural move or rehearsed. "I'd like to offer you an exchange. The rebellion will retain Prince Yimnit, and you, in turn, will receive a hostage—me—as a promise we will not hurt him. You may do with me what you will, for you say you are a just and merciful king. I am willing to take you at your word and hope your words are truthful."

The red lights turned off, and I realized I had been holding my breath since she started talking. I exhaled loudly just as the door to the studio opened. Kimberly held up a bottle of pills.

It was time to meet an old friend in the darkness and see if I could locate a soul in the abyss.

CHAPTER 40

This time I was ready for the darkness and my meeting with Araphel. More than prepared, I welcomed it—no, I needed it. I washed the sleeping pills down with some warm milk and settled down in my bed, closing my eyes.

I woke up in a place I recognized. It was my home, my childhood bedroom in Los Angeles. I was snuggled in bed as the alarm rang on my bedside table. I slammed off the alarm and pulled the covers back over my head. The smell of pancakes wafted in, followed not far behind by the aroma of bacon. An irresistible combo. I threw the covers off and slid on my slippers. Even in the heart of Los Angeles, the wood floor was cold in the winter.

I made my way down the hallway, stopping to admire a picture of my mother with me on her lap. I was a baby, and she was little more than a child, a few years older than I was now. Her blonde hair plumed wildly, and her smile was infectious. I smiled along with her—a smile which faded as I remembered the heavy weight of my task.

"Breakfast is ready!" a deep voice called out, and a few seconds later, Araphel appeared from behind the counter and placed a plate of bacon on the table. "There you are. Come, eat."

I stepped over the peeling linoleum and took a seat. The wooden table had golden metal legs and wicker chairs stained too dark for them to be reasonably considered the same set. The wicker crinkled to greet me. I grabbed a piece of bacon and chomped on it. Even though this was a dream, it didn't mean I wasn't dying for a homecooked meal.

"Nice spread," I said as I shoveled a pair of pancakes onto my plate and slathered them with syrup.

"I thought you might be homesick, so I whipped this up for you. Being a dream, you can eat as much as you want and not gain an ounce."

"And I will," I replied. "It's a nice gesture."

"Something weighs on you," he said, watching me. "You have a question for me."

I finished my bite of pancakes and put down my fork. "You told me once that you work with the dead. Is that true?"

"It's true. I shepherd them to the end. Why?"

"The ruler, the one you want me to kill. He is planning something really bad right now, and he killed the only people who know how to stop it. I figured, since you work with the dead, maybe you could…" I tried to stretch my words so that he would finish my sentence.

"Yes, I see." He stuck a long, bony finger in his coffee. "What I do, no mortal should see. I have honestly already told you too much. If my mother ever found out…"

"I get it, you're a mama's boy."

Araphel chuckled. "You do not know my mother. She is more powerful than you can ever imagine."

"And how would she feel if the king captured a god and used it to destroy everything?"

"She would take over, and there would be quite a bit more bloodshed than if you handled it yourself." Araphel sighed and looked at me with his glowing eyes. "I see what you are doing. Death is not something to be taken lightly. Should you come with me…the things you will see, you cannot unsee."

"Then, I don't want to come with you. Can't you just go and bring them back?"

"I'm afraid not. I know who you want to speak with, the four I've shepherded along already. Three have been processed, but there is one—just one—whose fate is in dispute. We must find him before Baron Samedi makes his decision, or we'll have to bargain with the Devil, and you do not want that." He held out his hand. "Do you have the will to see into the other side of the veil?"

I hesitated, then put my hand in his. "I'm ready. Let's go."

"I wish you the gods' fortitude," and then he snapped his fingers, and we disappeared, with the taste of whipped cream on my tongue.

***

When we blinked back into existence, we were not in the inky blackness nor my house, but the edge of a large cave on the tip of an enormous mountain. Below us was a layer of black haze that stretched beyond where my eyes could see. Black ash and soot fell from the sky like rain, even though there were no clouds above us.

I turned to Araphel. "Where are we?"

"This is Yrowet, the home world of Death." He must have noticed my face contort in fear because he held out his hand to calm me. "It's not so bad. People have the wrong impression of death. It is as much a part of the natural order as life." He waved me along. "Now, come."

I wasn't thrilled about tunneling further into a mountain on the home world of Death, but unless I wanted to swan dive—or cannonball maybe—into the black haze below, I had little choice in the matter.

The cave was oppressively dark, with only the occasional light from Araphel's eyes to guide me. I held my hands out in front of me and walked slowly to avoid the jagged rocks protruding all around me. Every few hundred feet, Araphel would realize I couldn't see in the dark, apologize, and then move back toward me. Each time, he would forget as quickly as he remembered, leaving me alone in the stifling black as often as he walked by my side.

"What is it about you and darkness?" I asked, scraping through a tight crevice.

"The light is too bright, and the creatures of the darkness give me comfort. Most fear what they don't understand, but there is little to fear from the darkness if you embrace it."

"That's…not very comforting, actually."

I followed him through the caves until a pinprick of light appeared. Eventually, it broke into a massive cavern, with hundreds of crooked columns rising from the ground.

"You cannot fly, correct?" Araphel asked.

"Not that I know of," I replied. "I did learn recently that I can control fire, though."

"Impressive, but not helpful in this specific instance. Give me your hand."

We lifted off the ground together. As we passed into the canyon, a gust of wind rushed through me—not into me, but straight through me—and I remembered that I was still asleep, lost in hallucination.

"These columns used to house hundreds of reapers and thousands of imps who kept the whole of the universe moving toward the beautiful dance of death."

As we neared one of the columns, I saw that they were offices, cubicles really, stacked on top of each other. Most of them were empty and, if their level of disrepair was any indication, they had been for some time. Mixed with the dark, though, lights speckled the columns occasionally, and in every lit room, a reaper in a long black robe wrote with an ancient quill and pen on a piece of parchment.

"So, death is just an ancient bureaucracy?"

"We were the model around which all other bureaucracies formed. Major governments all over the universe owe their existence to this cavern." He sighed deeply. "Of course, we are long past our peak."

He grew quiet, which was fine by me. I was happy to feel the air flow through my body and watch the crooked towers as they passed. After several minutes of floating, I realized we were heading to a large, tall tower built on top of a colossal stalagmite directly in the center of the cavern. Unlike the other buildings, which were uniform in structure, plain and mundane as the next, this tower was intricately carved with gargoyles and demons guarding the outside in stone relief.

Araphel stepped down onto the cold rock and walked toward the wooden door. He grabbed the metal door knocker depicting a screaming demon and slammed it down. After a moment, the door creaked open, and Araphel led us both inside. He walked up to a large round desk piled with books both on top of and behind it.

"This is my mother's private archive. It houses her personal collection, along with the name of every dead soul in the universe." An ancient demon, gray rather than the red or orange I had grown to expect, hobbled forward on a cane. He focused his coke-bottle glasses at Araphel as he stroked a long, gray beard.

"What ho, Hjilin?" Araphel asked.

"It is the same as it was and the same as it will be. What can I do with you, Master Araphel?"

"I am looking for records on a dead soul. A Mister Giudal Tery, from Earth 39429. I need a requisition form to speak with the fellow. I believe that's FMJ-2201, if I'm not mistaken." He turned to me and leaned close. "I am not mistaken."

"Very well, Master Araphel." The old demon walked away. "It shouldn't take more than a hundred years or so to process this request."

"A hundred years!" I shouted. "We don't have that kind of time."

"Young lady, will you please be quiet…this is a library."

"The girl is right, Hjilin, though she's gone about it in a very impolite manner. Perhaps you could tell me the reaper who covers that quadrant, and I could speak to them about expediting my request."

Hjilin tsked. "Very unorthodox. Very unorthodox indeed. Master Thanatos would never—"

Araphel slammed his hands on the table. "My brother is not here!" He cleared his throat and cracked a crooked smile. "He hasn't been here in a long time, and it's time you got used to the new order."

"Rudeness is another thing he would never tolerate. However, since this request will no doubt get you out of my hair, I'll give you the name."

"And I will gladly go," Araphel grumbled with the kind of seething anger that only came from having a long history with somebody. "Gladly."

CHAPTER 41

"That was…contentious," I said as we flew away from the tower toward the cubicles in the furthest edge of the cavern.

"I'm sorry to make you uncomfortable."

"It's okay. I'm a big girl. Are you okay, though?"

"I am an immortal being. It takes a lot to hurt my feelings. I have done my best in my brother's absence, but I am not equipped to lead this place. That much has been thoroughly communicated to me."

"Where did he go?" I asked, even though Araphel clearly didn't want to talk about it.

"A long time ago, my brother, along with three others, stood against the gods with the titan Surt. When Surt was defeated, my brother was banished, leaving the universe in turmoil. I have tried, along with my brethren, to fill his shoes, but we can only do so much. The reapers…they do not answer to me. Souls refuse our commands. Recruitment is in the toilet. It's been…awful. We soldier on, as we all must, even in the face of terrible challenges."

There was only one light on in the last tower in the cavern. The building had cracked at the bottom and now leaned against the rock for support. When we landed there, the entire structure felt like it would teeter under the lightest pressure.

"Are you Zekeliot?" Araphel asked a hooded figure scribbling behind a desk.

I was surprised to see that the face under the hood belonged to a young woman with dark amber eyes and full red lips. She pulled back her hood to reveal a thick mane of red hair, just like my natural color, that fell to her shoulders in thin curls.

"That's me," she said with a huff. "Don't get many visitors back here. How can I help you?"

"Yes," Araphel said. "You cover Earth 39429, do you not?"

"I do," she said. "Along with about a thousand others."

"There is a soul there that waits for judgment. His fate sits on the head of a pin. I'm hoping you can help me notarize form FMJ-2201 so I can intercede on this woman's behalf to get some answers from him before his fate is finalized."

"That's Baron Samedi's planet. He's a real peach, and if you can't tell, that's sarcasm. He's the worst. Yeah, as long as it doesn't get back to me, I'll authorize your stupid form." She smirked. "He's gonna eat you alive."

Araphel pulled a piece of parchment out of his jacket and pushed it over to her. "I've dealt with the baron before. We have an understanding. As long as I bring the proper paperwork, he's polite enough, assuming you don't have to barter with him."

She looked up into Araphel's eyes. "Well, you're a guy, so that makes sense. He's a sexist prick." She turned to me. "You better be prepared. He's gonna try to bargain for your soul. It's one of his favorite pastimes." She sniffed the air. "Oh yeah, a fresh one like you, oozing with magic. He'll do anything he can to make sure you never leave the underworld." She signed the paper and pushed it back. "Good luck to you. I don't think any of us reapers have been lucky in a long time. Maybe today will be the day, though."

***

Araphel grabbed a torch from one of the offices, which made the return trip through the caves much easier. Back at the top of the mountain, he grabbed my hand and snapped us away. It was funny, even though it had been hours since breakfast, I still tasted whipped cream on my tongue when we vanished into the ether.

We rematerialized on the edge of another great chasm. While the one on Yrowet was dull and pale, this one was filled with bright oranges and reds lighting up every part of the cave in an overwhelming glaze that mixed painfully with the pained screams and gurgling cries of thousands of humans echoing off every wall. A gust of hot air and the smell of charred flesh stung my nose.

"Oh good," Araphel said. "We made it without incident. I was worried form FMJ-2201 wouldn't be enough to grant me access to this plane."

"Are we...in Hell?" I said.

Araphel narrowed his eyes. "For the sake of argument, I'm going to say yes, though your planet's concept of the underworld is flawed. Still, there are things here that even a half demon should never have to see." He took a step toward me. "With your permission, I would like to blindfold you, lest you have nightmares the rest of your natural life."

"Actually, that sounds nice. Not the nightmare part, the blindfold part. Go for it."

He snapped his fingers, and a black blindfold appeared. He grabbed it and wrapped it around my eyes. "Would you like earphones as well?"

"Kind of."

I heard him snap again, and then a pair of earphones covered my ears, and the sounds of the damned fell away. I could still hear them in the muffled silence, but they felt far away. Finally, Araphel grabbed my hand and lifted me into the air.

Even with my ears and eyes covered, I was shaking with fear. It was as if my soul knew we were in an unnatural place. The smell of charred flesh mixed with sweat and blood which drove me to gag, and even the touch of the air felt tinged with suffering.

I felt solid ground under my feet again, and Araphel removed my blindfold to reveal a tall building. It was a dead ringer for the DMV by my house in Los Angeles. He pushed through the door to reveal the familiar sight of a line that snaked back and forth a dozen times before it disappeared through another door.

I pulled off my earphones. "Please tell me we don't have to stand in that line?"

"Gods no," Araphel said. "One of the advantages of being one of us is that you have a skip-the-line pass, everywhere."

He dragged me past the line filled with demons, orcs, zombies, trolls, changelings, gorgons, and every manner of beast I had only ever read about in books. He pushed through a cadre of imps, and another of sidhe, before finally arriving at the desk of a plump satyr sitting behind a sign that read "GODS ONLY."

The satyr didn't look up when he spoke. "What can I do for you today?"

"Hello, good friend," Araphel said, slapping his paper on the counter between them. "I believe you'll see that everything is in order."

The satyr took the paper slowly and stared at it. "This is form FMJ-2201."

"Exactly. Request for an audience with a soul before it is condemned."

The satyr typed into a primitive version of a computer. Really, it was little more than a stone tablet surrounded by tree bark. "This soul was condemned twenty minutes ago to pit seven. You'll need form JYR-4120, in triplicate, signed by Baron Samedi, if you wish to see this processed through."

"Dagnabit," Araphel grumbled, turning to me. "I'm afraid that while I love it, bureaucracy can sometimes move too slowly. I wish I could do more, but I—"

"Oh no, don't even start that with me," I said. "I have been through too much in this dream state to stop now. Do you understand the amount of shit that we'll be in if King Ulthar succeeds with his plan?"

He held up his hands. "I'm sorry, but there's nothing I can do without seeing the baron, and frankly…he frightens even me."

I spun around. "Fine, I'll do it myself."

I stormed toward the door until Araphel's bony hand grabbed me and turned me around. "You don't want to talk to the baron. Trust me. He will mess with your mind and destroy your soul, and he'll have fun doing it."

"Then you talk to him," I said.

"I—I—"

"That's what I thought." I shook myself free. "Thanks for the help, but I'll take it from here."

CHAPTER 42

I flung open the door to the building, and every sound that Araphel's earphones had masked crashed into me at once and sent me collapsing to the ground. The unholy cries and unearthly shrieks bombarded my ears so viciously all I could do was let out a piteous wail as I writhed on the ground.

Several seconds later, Araphel placed a hand on my back, and the sounds fell away—not completely, but enough that I could think again, even if every cell in my body wanted to burst into flame.

"That was stupid," Araphel said. "I can't decide if it was brave, too, but it was certainly stupid." He helped me to my feet and brushed me off before he spoke again. "Yes, I do know how bad it will be if King Ulthar completes his device, which is the only reason I have gone this far. If you are determined to go further, then I will go with you." He pressed the earphones into my hand. "Wear these. They really help."

I put the earphones in my ears and looped my hand in Araphel's elbow as we walked down the street. I was surprised at how banal it was in the underworld once you got past the smells and the sounds. Demons and monsters walked down streets lined with stores and restaurants, just like humans did back home. It didn't seem to have electricity, as gas lamps lit every block and bicycles whizzed past, along with carriages and monsters on horseback. It would have been beautiful if it hadn't been so horrible.

"So, where is the baron's castle?" I asked after we had walked for several minutes.

"Oh, he's not so aristocratic as all that." Araphel patted my hand. I could hear him perfectly through my earphones, though they drowned out everything else. "The underworld takes on the personality of the god, and Baron Samedi truly loves being among his subjects, singing the songs, watching the plays—" He stopped in front of a small bar. "—and drinking the drinks."

He pointed through the window to a Black man in a red tailored suit and top hat. Half of the man's face was painted white, and it was out of that side of his mouth that he hung a long cigar. A long boa constrictor coiled around his neck, and it caught my eyes before the baron did. When the man finally saw me, the white on the side of his face moved into a skull that overlaid his eyes and nose.

"Well, well, well," he said as we walked in. "If this isn't a surprise, Araphel. You aren't usually so kind as to deliver souls to me personally. I am quite obliged."

Baron Samedi slid out of his stool at the bar and reached toward me, but Araphel slapped his hand away. "It isn't this girl's time. She simply needs a favor from you."

"A favor?" Baron Samedi said, eyebrows raised. "From moi? That is very, very interesting indeed. You know how much I love a tit for tat." He emphasized "tit" and "tat," then bit at the air when he was done. "I'm sure you have told her, though, that no favor comes free."

"I'm right here," I said, removing my earphones. Luckily, from where we were standing, the sound from the underworld was little more than a low din. "And he told me how much you like to play games."

"Oooh, a feisty one," Baron Samedi growled. "So much fun to break."

"Better men than you have tried to break me."

He winked at me, as did the snake on his shoulder. "I am no man, despite my appearance. Now, what is this favor you need from me?"

I looked over at Araphel, who nodded hesitantly at me to continue. "I need to speak to a soul who is condemned here. They can help me stop an evil man from destroying the world and possibly disrupting the universe."

"It's true, Baron. This man—"

But Baron Samedi didn't want to hear it. He flicked his wrist at Araphel and went back to his drink, sucking it down with one sip. "Everyone thinks they are righteous, and their enemies are evil. It is so rarely so." After he was done with his drink, he turned back to me. "Your favor isn't a small one, you understand. There are processes in place here. Disturbing them is like throwing a wrench into an engine. On top of that, you come with another god to sully my kingdom. I don't like any of this." When Baron Samedi went to his drink again, it had been filled for him, and he took a long sip. "What do you think, pet?" He stared into the snake's eyes for several seconds and then nodded. "Is it true you are a demon, girl?"

"Half demon," I replied. "Half human, I think."

Baron Samedi scratched his chin for a long time before finally saying, "Then I will help you if I have your service after your death."

"I hate to tell you this," I said. "But the Earth I'm from is a long way from here."

He shrugged. "No matter. Your life will be long." He squinted, studying me. "And filled with such wonders as I can't even begin to enrapture you with. You will be a fearsome addition to my stable of warriors and lovers until the end of time."

"How dare you!" I shouted. "I am nobody's whore."

He held up his hand. "You misunderstand me. Nobody is forced to do anything in my stable. They come because they agree to and for no other reason. But I am all ears if you have a compromise worth the baron's time."

"I will bring you a king. If you send me back with the information I need, I will send you one king—an arrogant one, blood-hungry and strong-willed." I took a step closer and lowered my voice. "You must know the one. He has sent so many to you."

"Yes, yes. He has been very good for business, but perhaps he has outlived his usefulness." The baron thought for a moment. "And you guarantee me this king?"

I nodded. "Before the sun rises. If I don't give him to you, then I will agree to bind my service to you for all of time."

"That," he said with a smile, "is a big promise, darling. I love your fire." He held out his hand. "Very well. I agree."

As he shook my hand, he snapped his fingers with his other hand. Out of the ether, a charred body appeared in one of the seats in the back of the bar, screaming bloody murder.

"One Giudal Tery, as you requested."

"But I didn't even tell you—"

Baron Samedi spun on his stool back to the bar. "In my realm, I know all, my dear. I look forward to your service when you fail, and I promise you will fail."

"We'll see about that."

***

"I don't think you quite understand what you just did," Araphel said as we approached the screaming man at the back of the bar.

"No, I don't, but I'm so sick of talking. You gods love your talking. We're in the middle of a crisis, and in a crisis, you have to be willing to give up a lot to get a little better chance of winning. If we can get this information, maybe we can improve our odds from 'not a chance in hell' to 'the slimmest of odds.' If I have to give up eternity for it, then so be it."

"You are quite a human," Araphel said.

"Except I'm not a human. Not entirely at least." I turned to Giudal, whose mouth was open, shrieking. "Giudal. We need your help."

He didn't listen to me. He faced forward, his features contorted in pain like he was still being tortured. Araphel held out his hands and touched the man, who visibly flinched, and then, after a moment, calmed down. He blinked, and then finally, he looked at me.

"Who…where am I?" He looked down at his charred hands. "Oh my god. It's true. It's all true, I'm—in—"

"Enough, Giudal," I said. "Yes, you're in Hell. If you want to know why, part of it might be because you helped King Ulthar build a weapon to destroy whole countries at his whim."

"No—" he said. "I'm a good person. I'm—"

"Maybe," I said, sliding in across from him. "Or you might kick puppies and burn ants for fun. I don't know. I don't care. What I do know is that right now, the king is readying a weapon that he says will destroy all of Risyl in an instant. Is that something he can do?" The man's eyes were blank as they looked at me. "Giudal? Giudal!"

"I was a good person," he whispered. "Wasn't I a good person?"

"If you were a good person, then you'll help me now and answer my question."

Focus returned to his eyes, and they suddenly looked at me instead of through me. "The weapon? Yes, if we built it correctly, then it can destroy a city. Oh god, is that why I'm here? I thought…I thought…it was science…"

"How do we stop it?" I asked. "There has to be a kill switch somewhere."

Giudal nodded. "There is…but…the doctor is the only person who knew about the kill switch. She insisted on it. She thought that if we didn't know how to destroy the weapon, we would be safe." He looked down at his hands. "I guess she was wrong."

"Well, that sucks," I said, pushing myself to stand. I walked over to Baron Samedi. "He doesn't know. We need to see Doctor Jortensur."

The baron finished his purple concoction and turned to me. "My, my, my, another favor. I don't know what you could possibly have that I want anymore, my dear. I already have your eternity."

I shook my head. "This is the same favor."

"I'm afraid not." He smiled smugly. "You said that if I brought old Giudal to you, then you would bring me a king or your eternal soul."

"No, I said if you send me back to Earth with the information that I need, I would do those things. Giudal over there doesn't have the information I need, so no deal. If you want my soul, bring me the doctor."

"She's right," Araphel said, gliding toward us. "And more importantly, you know she's right." Baron Samedi's face turned into a snarl, and the snake lunged at me. Araphel caught the snake in midair. "Don't take it out on her because you're a sore loser."

Baron Samedi snapped his fingers, and Giudal Tery disintegrated. "Fine."

In Giudal's place, a calm and collected woman sat in the booth. She didn't scream or whine. She just sat, stone-faced, as if she'd expected this eventuality.

"Ah," she said. "Barkeep, can I get a Thungin' Slammer?"

Baron Samedi growled at her. "Get it yourself."

Doctor Jortensur stood up. "Don't mind if I do." She slid behind the bar and started pulling alcohol off the glass shelves, pouring what she needed into a cocktail glass and topping off the drink with an olive. When she finished and took a sip, she moaned.

"Ah yes, that's the stuff." Her eyes narrowed at us. "Now, which of you summoned me?" She pointed at the baron. "I think it was you."

"Very good. You are taking this very well, your death," Araphel said. "I have rarely seen one handle it better."

She took another sip. "After being convinced that the gods existed, I made some rational leaps that the underworld existed as well, and that the stories I read as a child were probably more historical than mythological. I had hoped to earn my freedom from the goddess we captured, but clearly, the king had other plans." She took a longer sip, finished the glass, and mixed another. "I assume it was the king that killed me?"

I nodded. "We're not sure, but yes, I would assume the same. Giudal said there was a kill switch that only you knew how to work. Is that true?"

Doctor Jortensur downed her drink in one sip and started on a third. "This is probably the last drink I will ever have for a long time. I want to make the most of it. Now, Giudal, you say. The poor dear, how is he holding up?"

"Not well," Baron Samedi said. "Which is to be expected."

"Poor chap. He was sweet but not very strong of will." She snapped her fingers after tasting the drink. "Bitters. That's what we're missing." She grabbed a small bottle and poured some of its contents into her drink, then took another sip. "Much better."

"I'm glad you're having a pleasant time," I said, growing impatient. "We're in a bit of a rush with the whole end of the world and everything."

She nodded. "Oh yes, I know."

I slammed my hands on the bar. "And you don't even care, do you? The world is going to end, and it doesn't even bother you. How can I care about your planet more than you do?"

She gave me a level look. "Because you are a child, and you haven't seen the world. Now, I am very sure that I've overstayed my welcome. I know I have talked you into circles, but I was just trying to prolong my stay. Torture isn't my bag." She turned to Baron Samedi. "Before I go, I must ask, do you need a brilliant scientist for any purpose in this dank, dark place?"

Baron Samedi thought for a moment and consulted with his snake. "You do have a certain flare to you, don't you? There might be a position for you, but only if the world doesn't end. If this world ends, then I'm off to the next one, and there is nothing for you there."

"Fair enough." She turned to me. "When you get to the device, there is a circular base, which binds the god into place. Search the control panel for a button called 'unberiler,' a word I made up. Lift the panel. Inside the chassis, there are three wires. Cut the blue, then the yellow, then the black. Once you cut them in that order, slam the unberiler button, and the entire thing will fizzle and die." She finished her drink. "I can't wait to see what a god will do to that heathen of a king."

"Thank you," I said.

"Don't mention it." She waved her arm before turning to Baron Samedi. "Now, let's talk about a team. I happen to have a great one already put together. Best in the world."

"My, my," Baron Samedi said with a chuckle. "You really are a cheeky little devil."

I couldn't listen to any more of her prattle. I gave Araphel a pleading look.

"It is time you get back," he said. "I do hope you win."

"Me too."

A rush of wind filled my lungs, and I opened my eyes in my room in the rebellion base. I caught my breath, trying to put everything I saw out of my mind because right now, I only had one mission: *Save the world.*

CHAPTER 43

Director Frente stared at me blankly as I relayed to her my experience with Araphel and what I learned from the undead soul of Doctor Jortensur. When I was done, she let out a long sigh, and then she placed her fingers on the bridge of her nose like I had seen her do in frustration so many times before.

"So, let me get this straight. You expect me to build our entire plan on a fevered dream you had after taking sleeping pills?"

"That's right."

"This…is…absolutely insane."

"More insane than me being a demon, or Kimberly being a pixie?" I asked.

"Oh, very much yes. So much more insane than any of that, which is saying something. Your dreams could literally mean anything. I had a dream last night that I ate a giant fart sandwich. Dreams are nonsense."

"One, that's gross, and two, my dreams have always meant something, especially lately. Araphel tells me things, he tells me things that come true. He's the reason I was able to stop Prince Yimnit. I believe in him."

"I believed in a lot of crazy things when I was younger. I can't ask my people to fight and die for some weird dream."

I stood up from my seat and leaned across her desk. "What's your grand plan then? What are you willing to bet your life on and the lives of your people?"

"We're going to give Margaret to King Ulthar and use that as a diversion to sneak under the castle using the maps that Prince Yimnit provided us. When we get to the device, we'll blow it into the Great Abyss."

"Fine," I said. "Then let me go with the team. If I'm wrong, you can blow the whole thing to kingdom come. If I'm right, though…"

She shook her head. "I'm sorry." She bit her lip, reluctant to tell me something. "They demanded something else besides Margaret." She looked at me, and the guilt in her eyes told me the truth before she said it. "They demanded you, and we agreed."

"Excuse me?" I shouted, flailing my arms in the air. "How many times do I have to be a sacrificial pawn to you?"

"One more time," she said, her voice brimming with false determination. "If we don't succeed tonight, then nothing else will matter."

I slumped back into my chair. "You're sending us to our deaths."

"We'll figure something out. Nobody is going to die tonight."

I chuckled. "Well, I sure hope the king does, or else I have quite a debt to pay." I opened the door to her office, then stopped on my way out. "Oh, right. I forgot you don't believe in that type of thing. You only believe in the things that are convenient to you."

***

After everything I had done for the rebellion, how close we had gotten to victory, Director Frente still thought of me as nothing more than a child with wild fantasies. If she didn't trust me, then I would come up with my own plan, one that got me close enough to the king to slaughter him and rid the world of his evil.

As I barreled through the halls of the base, I heard light footsteps behind me and turned to see Sindra walking toward me. When I turned to her, she stopped, confused, and just a little bit off-put.

"What?" I said.

"It's just that—well, I was going to run up behind you and turn you around in dramatic fashion before wrapping you in a big hug. You kind of ruined that, didn't you?"

"Oh." I was taken aback by her eagerness, and it made me smile. "I mean, I can turn around and run away again..."

"No, no. The moment is ruined." She sighed. "Madam Fantasmo told me they're using you as bait again. That sucks."

"It really does. It sucks. I'm not surprised, but it sucks."

"This whole place is on edge," she said. "Everyone thinks we're doomed. The advance teams are preparing like they're going to their deaths." She looked me deep in the eyes. "Do you think what we're doing is hopeless?"

"Yeah, I do. I think we're all probably going to die." I grabbed her hands and squeezed them tight. "This whole thing is crazy. We're talking about storming a castle with directions provided by our sworn enemy. There's zero chance this isn't a trap."

Her eyes dropped to the ground. "So…it really is as hopeless as they say."

"Hey," I said with a soft smile. "I've been in hopeless situations before, and one thing I know is that when all hope is lost, that's when you have to hope the hardest."

Sindra chuckled, tears falling down her face. "That's stupid."

"This is all stupid, Sindra. Life is stupid. Look at us. We're fighting over nothing. This land, it's not mine, and it's not yours. When we're long gone, the Earth will still be rotating, and yet here we are, fighting over who has the right to pretend to control it for a time. And me? I'm fighting to leave this planet and return to my own."

"I don't want you to go," she blurted out.

I took a deep breath. "I'm going to kill the king tonight, Sindra. I don't know how, but I'm going to stop this, and when it's over, we'll look over the ashes together and decide how to move forward."

"What if you don't come back?"

"Listen to me very carefully." I placed my hands on her shoulders. "I'm an actual, real-life, frigging demon. I'm coming back."

I had no idea if it was true, and Sindra's quivering lip told me she didn't either, but I had to believe enough for the both of us, for all of us. I pulled her close to me and squeezed her tight as the tears came.

"I'm going to come home."

It was the first time I had called this planet home.

I kind of liked it.

***

Any path to success involved Kimberly. I searched for her a long time before I found her in the shooting range. She wasn't firing a gun. Instead, she flung throwing knives, embedding them in the wall on the other end of the gallery. Since nobody else was there, she had no problem walking downrange to pluck the daggers out of the wall.

"I was wondering if you would find me before you left," she said, holding up a target with three holes ripped in its center mass. "I'm pretty good, it turns out."

"What dumb thing does Director Frente have you doing tonight?" I asked.

She shook her head. "She hasn't said anything to me for a while. Not since she told me you were going to be offered to the king, and I threatened to cut her throat open on the spot."

"I'm glad you didn't."

"Are you? So, you're okay with them using you like a pawn over and over again?"

"Well, no. I don't much like that either, but—I don't know, man. This is all so screwed, and if it's how I can be most helpful, then whatever."

"Did Araphel help you find a way to destroy the machine?"

I nodded. "He did. The director laughed at me when I told her about it, though. She clearly only believes in magic when it's convenient for her."

"I assume you have a plan—to avoid dying, I mean."

"Kind of. Remember when you asked me to imagine where I wanted you to travel, and then we disappeared there—well, here?"

"I do. I was with you."

"Well, you haven't been to the castle, but Prince Yimnit has. I figure we can force him to let you see into his mind to get a sense of where you can hide. You can hang out there until the time is right and then come save me. From there, we can kill the king together."

She didn't have to think long before she agreed. "I like it. Are you intending to tell Director Frente any of this?"

"The fewer people who know, the better. I'm not even telling Margaret." I swallowed as much fear as I could, stuffing it deep down into my gut. "I'm putting all my faith in you, Kimberly. My life is literally in your hands. If you can't save me, the king will kill me."

"I won't let that happen," Kimberly said. "I have been through too much shit saving you to watch you die now."

I chuckled. "Yeah, I guess I have been a pretty big pain in the ass, huh?"

"The literal biggest of my whole life." She patted me on the shoulder. "Now, let's go save the world."

CHAPTER 44

Prince Yimnit was under heavy guard. Two soldiers stood outside the brig, and two more were directly in front of his cell. Luckily, we were known members of the director's inner circle, so the worst we got was an icy glance from the guards as we entered the room.

"We need to see Prince Yimnit," Kimberly said to one of them. "Alone."

They looked at each other, nodded, and stepped out of the room, shutting the door behind them.

For our plan to work, we had to get Prince Yimnit out of his cell and somewhere that magic worked. Kimberly had done a good job warding up the brig. So good, in fact, that even her magic didn't work there.

"Nice trick," Prince Yimnit said. "It's lovely to have power, isn't it?"

"Only if you use it to help the powerless," I spat back.

"That's what you think you are doing? Helping the powerless?" His sarcasm dripped over each syllable and made me want to punch him.

"Absolutely," I said. "Helping them get rid of you and achieve freedom."

Prince Yimnit laughed. "Do you think people want freedom?"

"Of course," I said.

"What a dumb question," Kimberly added.

He smiled with one corner of his mouth. "Tell me, on the planet where you are from, do they have freedom?"

I nodded. "Of course."

"And are they any happier than the people you have seen here? The everyday people—the ones who sell your paper or make your food—do you think they are happier on your planet than they are here?"

"I…do?" I said, confused. "Is that a trick question?"

Prince Yimnit shook his head. "It's not, but it proves you are naïve. People do not want freedom. They want justice. They want safety. They want a good job for themselves and their family. People care less about freedom than you believe when you weigh it against those things."

"We have both in America."

He let out a laugh. "I'm sure you believe that. I've seen democracy in action in Risyl. Their government is at a standstill while their people die in the streets. We have no such barriers to our justice. My father says the word, and his word is the law."

"And yet…you're working with us to build a democracy. Why?"

Prince Yimnit was quiet for a few moments before he responded. "Heavy is the head that wears the crown. Every word my father says is dissected; every dictum analyzed. He takes all the blame and receives very little glory for it. I have no wish to lead my father's life. With this rebellion, I see a way out. Give the people freedom—as you like to call it—while achieving freedom for myself. All the glamour of royalty with none of the trappings."

"I don't believe you," Kimberly said. "I want you to know that. I think you're walking them all into a trap."

"Prove it," the prince growled.

"I don't have the time." Kimberly pulled one of her runed strips of cloth from her pocket. "Hold out your hands." He did, and Kimberly moved into the cell to wrap his wrists in them before clipping a pair of shackles above the cloth. "Guards, open this door."

One of the guards reentered the room and looked at the scene. "I'm sorry, ma'am. I can't do that. The director was quite explicit that we aren't to move the prisoner."

Kimberly extended her wings behind her and walked toward the guard. "This man has information in his brain vital to the survival of this mission. Do you want to be the one who made us fail tonight's mission, killing so many of our men and women because you were just following orders?"

"I—I—I—I can't, ma'am."

Kimberly pointed to the key ring on the man's belt. "Are those the keys?" He didn't say another word. "Then you don't have to help me. Just don't stop me." Kimberly reached forward and grabbed the keys without breaking eye contact with the guard. "We're not going far, just out into the hallway. Prepare your men. If he moves a muscle, shoot him."

"Y—yes, ma'am," he saluted and turned away, scooting out the door like a frightened child.

"I thought for sure he wasn't going to let me have the keys," she said with a smile. She opened the door and pulled Prince Yimnit out of the cell. "This can go one of two ways. You can show me what you know about the layout of the castle—rooms, hallways, nooks, secret passages, anywhere I could hide easily from your guards—or I can take the information by force and leave you a muttering husk of a person. You'll be alive, but you will wish for death."

"You wouldn't dare disturb the tenuous peace my father has brokered."

"Wouldn't we?" I said. "We're not from here, and our number one priority is finding a way home. The rest of this is just a bonus."

Kimberly pushed Prince Yimnit out into the hall and forced him down on his knees. She beckoned the guards close, and they all took positions around the prisoner, guns drawn, ready to fire at the smallest sign of distress.

Kimberly placed her hands firmly on Prince Yimnit's head. "Now, show me every room of the castle. Make it as vivid as you can, down to the last detail."

There was nothing for a moment, and then Kimberly's head jerked back violently. The guards raised their weapons.

"Wait!" I shouted and held my breath. A moment later, Kimberly's head jerked again, and then a third time, before Prince Yimnit opened his eyes.

"That's everything I know," he grumbled.

"Perfect," Kimberly said. She patted her hair back into place. "Guards, take this man back to his cell. Maybe give him an extra dessert for being so helpful."

Director Frente stood at the entrance to the hall, hands on her hips. "What the hell is happening here?" Before we could answer, she threw her arms up in the air. "You know what, I don't want to know. Just tell me you didn't hurt him."

Kimberly shrugged. "He's fine."

Director Frente shook her head slowly. "Just…come on. We're about to get started."

***

The director led us back into the main room with all the computers and screens, where it looked like the entire base, save for those guarding Prince Yimnit, had gathered.

She indicated a spot in the back near Margaret, where she wanted us to stand. Meanwhile, she stalked to the front of the room and stood before the bank of monitors, where tactical plans were being projected.

"This is it," Director Frente started. "This is the pinnacle of everything we've built with this organization over the past—forever. The entirety of this rebellion comes down to tonight's strike on the palace. If we succeed, we can bring freedom to this entire planet. If we fail, we doom Risyl and the rest of the planet to servitude. I don't want to put too fine a point on it but rest assured: The future rests on our shoulders."

Director Frente cleared her throat. "Alpha team will infiltrate the tunnels beneath the castle from the east." As she spoke, the monitors flipped to blueprints of the castle, marked with red lines. "According to Prince Yimnit, these will lead into the main chambers. Infrared scans of the palace confirm the tunnels exist." She snapped her fingers, and a blue line appeared, crosscutting the red line. "Beta team will come from the west, making their way to the throne room."

A third image, this one of an orange dot placed behind what appeared to be the throne room. "Our intel shows that the hottest signature is coming from here, which we presume is where the device is located." She snapped her fingers again, and an orange line overlaid atop the blue line and a green line overlaid atop the red line. "Charlie and Delta teams will make their way from the north and south of the tunnel to meet up in the center, and all four teams make your way to the throne room. Each of you is outfitted with explosives, but that is a last resort."

She turned to Jasper. "We have the greatest technological minds in the world in this room, and all of them will be here to help with the safe disassembly of the device. However, if we cannot disarm it safely, then you will be tasked with blowing it up."

"Wait!" one of the men said. "That much energy could destroy five city blocks."

Director Frente gulped. "That is the price of freedom. I pray it does not come to that, though." She pointed to her chest. "We live as one."

Everyone else pounded their chests. "We die as o—"

A sudden quake rattled the whole base and sent us all falling to the floor, including the director. She righted herself first and barked at the men and women around her. "What was that?"

"I don't—"

Before anyone else could say anything, the monitors turned on. It was the king. He stood in front of a long, cylindrical device that glowed white and pulsated like a heartbeat. The light gave the power-hungry king an eerie pall.

"My people," he said. "Moments ago, we made a metalogical breakthrough for the ages." He swept his arm toward the cylinder. "Behold, for we have captured a GOD!" The white light dissipated as worried mumbles flew through the room. As the being behind the glass returned to normal, I recognized the face of Baron Samedi. He screamed at the glass and pounded on it fruitlessly.

The king turned back to the camera. "Yes, my children, gods are real, and we have captured one. Now, we will show you what it means to go against my chosen people!"

The image changed, showing the outside of the castle. A white light exploded out of one of the many spires of the palace and shot high into the air. The screen went black for a moment.

My heart dropped because I knew what was coming next. When the screen came up again, it showed the capital of Risyl. One moment, it stood untouched, and in the next instant, a white light washed over it. The camera shook on the image of an explosion and then cut to black.

"Oh my god!" Director Frente said. "Somebody try the president. Find out what just happened."

"It's—we're getting nothing—" one of the techs said. "It's like…they all vanished—the whole country."

"A massive heat signature just appeared on the ground in Risyl right now," another called out. "It matches the one coming from the palace. I'm afraid—it looks they have leveled the capital…oh my god…what kind of power could do that?"

A moment later, the king appeared on the screen again. "It brings me no joy to destroy Risyl. They were a great foe, proud and noble. Let this be a warning to those who oppose us. Surrender, and you will be embraced with warmth. Otherwise, come morning, you will be destroyed. You have twelve hours to make your decision."

The king paused, tapping his lips with the tip of his scepter. "Oh, yes…and Madam President, if you are relying on the rebellion to save you, rest assured that while it was difficult to track them down…we have found them now."

An explosion rang out from the brig, and when we turned, Prince Yimnit rushed out of the smoke-filled hallway, hands unbound, and the four guards tasked with restraining him now pointed guns at us. The lights turned out, replaced by the red emergency backups, and the sprinklers rained down. A scream rang out, and the elevators all opened at once. Jackboots stormed into the base like a raging river, firing on everyone in their wake.

CHAPTER 45

Gunshots sprayed over me as I dropped down to the floor. Kimberly screamed. The monitors blew up in a shower of sparks.

"We have to get out of here!" Kimberly said, grabbing my hand.

"No," I yelled. "Take Margaret. I have to find the director. Get as many people as you can to safety, and then come back to me!"

"Like hell, I will!"

I was already gone, ducking under a desk in my rush toward the back of the room where the director stood just moments ago. There was a flash of pink and purple smoke as Kimberly disappeared.

"Spare no one," Prince Yimnit called out, "except my brat of a sister! She should be easy to spot in her wheelchair!"

Bodies fell to the left and right of me as I crawled through the desks. The group of Jackboots walked slowly, methodically spraying bullets across the ground.

"Anj—Angie—" a voice gasped. I turned to see Madam Fantasmo bleeding out of her chest, face white as a sheet. Her hand flopped toward me. "Save—"

"No, no, no, no, no," I said as I wrapped her in my arms. "Don't die. It's going to be okay. Kimberly is coming back for you. Just hang on. Please, please hang on."

"—them." It was the last word she said before she shuddered in my arms and fell limp. My tears fell as I placed her back on the floor. Behind her, Volkim looked at me with dead eyes, a pool of blood under her. "No, god no."

My hands shook with fear and rage as I looked at my two friends, the ones who had saved me from execution and led me through this world. Dead at the hands of the Jackboots.

"Sindra!" I shouted. "Sindra!"

It was a bad idea to draw attention to my position. I barely ducked away from a hail of bullets. If Sindra was dead—no, I couldn't think like that. Out of the corner of my eye, I saw a puff of pink smoke, and then, in an instant, it vanished again. It followed me through the room, popping in and out every few seconds.

"Anjelica," the director whispered when I reached her. She was bleeding from her stomach and leg. "Get out of here. You can't—my gods—I really thought we stood a chance."

"We still do," I replied, sliding down next to her. "I'm going to finish this. I swear to you that the king and his prick son will pay for what they've done here tonight." I squeezed her arm. "Don't you dare die. You're going to live to see the end of this."

She winced as she touched her stomach. "That would be my penance, huh? To be stuck remembering everyone I let down. Everyone that I sent to their deaths."

The puff of smoke appeared in front of me; Kimberly took my hand. "I got everyone I could." She turned to the director. "Now, let's get you out of here."

We faded into the ether. Somehow, in the chaos, I slipped from Kimberly's grip. I fell from her, into the darkness below, until I disappeared into the nothingness and bounced back into a folding chair surrounded in blackness.

"This is not going well," Araphel said from the other side of the table. "Honestly, it's hard to imagine how it could go any worse."

"I can still fix this," I said, panting. "I can still save everyone."

"Ah yes, there it is," he said.

"There what is?"

"The optimism. The assurance. The belief that you can't be defeated, that even when all hope is lost, you must hope harder. It's at the heart of every great hero."

"I don't know if I'm a hero, but I'm all this planet has right now," I replied, sucking in a deep breath. "Will you make sure they are taken care of, the dead?"

He nodded. "I will see to it personally."

"And will you tell them, Volkim—Sindra—Madam Fantasmo—" I choked back my tears. "Tell them that I love them—and that I'm sorry."

"I will," he said.

Out of the darkness, white lights began to shine. Hundreds of them appeared from the nothing, and I recognized them. They were my friends and colleagues from the rebellion, staring out, looking down at their glowing hands, trying to come to terms with their fates.

"Can I—can I talk to them?"

Araphel shook his head. "They wouldn't be able to understand you. This is better. I promised to take good care of them, and I stand by that."

"Thank you." I pounded my chest twice. "We live as one. We die as one."

Araphel snapped his fingers, and I whizzed through the darkness, crashing through the abyss, and back into Kimberly's arms. We fell to the ground together.

"Shit," she said. "I thought I lost you."

"So did I."

Sindra stood next to me, crying. She dropped to her knees and embraced both of us, and there for a time, we cried for those that we'd lost.

***

Nineteen of us was all that remained of the rebellion. Sindra, Kimberly, Margaret, Director Frente, four SWAT members, three intelligence officers, two maintenance workers, and six support staff. A television glowed in the back of a veterinary clinic where we took Director Frente to tend to her injuries. Risyl had been wiped off the face of the map, leaving only a crater. Millions of citizens vaporized in a single instant, giving King Ulthar ultimate power in the world.

"It's over," Director Frente grabbed her rib as a medical tech moved her to clean her wounds. "Everything we worked for, over."

I shook my head. "No, it's not. I will not accept that Madam Fantasmo, Commander Bivnol, Volkim, and everyone else died in vain. There has to be something we can do."

"The Jackboots are combing through our files right now. Even if they can't beat our encryption, it would have taken every member of our organization to carry out that plan. In case you haven't noticed, we're at about two percent capacity right now."

"We were working on a plan," Kimberly said, rubbing her face with her hands. "A covert plan to save Anjelica in case you all failed. I think we can adapt it to kill the king instead, or in addition to what we had already planned. If we add in your troops as a diversion, then maybe Anjelica and I could get inside and execute him once and for all."

"You want me to risk everything we have left for a daft plan concocted by two teenagers that has almost no chance of succeeding?"

Kimberly nodded. "Yes, that's exactly what I want, actually. I'm glad that came across. I know it's an imperfect plan, but we have no allies left. We don't have enough support to do this right. The king thinks he's won, which will make him cocky."

"Well, cockier," Margaret added.

Director Frente looked around at her remaining troops. "I can't ask them to risk their lives for this."

"They risked their lives just being part of this rebellion," I said. "If tonight taught us anything, it's that. If we don't stop the king, they'll be running for the rest of their lives. We have this one chance to make a final stand, this one night before the rest of the world capitulates."

"And if they won't follow? If this is too far a bridge for them?"

"Then we'll do this without them," Margaret said. "I won't sit back and watch my father win. Not while I still draw breath."

Director Frente's eyes ping-ponged between the three of us. "You realize you're all going to die, right?"

"I've met Death," I said. "He's pretty nice."

"And I've been to Hell," Kimberly added. "I do not fear death."

"I do," Margaret said. "But I'm doing it anyway."

Director Frente nodded. "I'll ask the remaining agents for their help, but if they refuse, I can't force them, even if I wanted to."

CHAPTER 46

Director Frente went from table to table, asking for help from the remaining members of the rebellion. She didn't receive a single no, but some of them insisted on tweaking the plan, so it was less of a suicide mission. We ended up with something that wasn't completely insane, just mostly crazy.

Step one of the plan involved recording a final video to the king, wherein Margaret and I would offer our lives in exchange for the lives of those in the rebellion that still lived. In step two, a team would deliver us to the palace, where we would prostrate ourselves on live TV for the amusement of the king. Kimberly would jump the remaining soldiers into the palace to sit and wait for her sign—that was step three. In step four, Kimberly would use the information she'd gotten from Prince Yimnit to sneak through the palace into the throne room. In the final step, the remaining members of the rebellion would cause a distraction, leaving us alone with the king. That's when Kimberly would strike the king down and free us so that we could destroy the device.

"I feel like a fool asking you to believe in magic," Director Frente said to her people before she set us upon our final course. "But you have seen it first-hand. You only live now because of magic. It is our only hope for a better future. So, I ask that you believe in it as I do, and with the help of Kimberly, Margaret, and Anjelica, three magic users from beyond the stars, we will succeed."

We relocated several miles outside the city, where Director Frente had a small cache of weapons and equipment in a storage locker.

"I have this here in case of emergencies," she told us as we rode up to a non-descript building. "I kept it off the books, just in case I would ever need it for any reason. Better safe than sorry, I guess. I never thought I would need it."

She slid open the storage unit, and we all filed in to load up the equipment into vans she procured for us. It wasn't just weapons and armor. There were also computers and other technology that we could use to rebuild a temporary base of operations. With the gear in tow, she brought us to a small, abandoned house in the nearby woods. Had I not known better, I would have thought it condemned, and yet, several cables ran into the house from the road several miles away.

"None of this is up to code," Director Frente said without us asking. "I had this built as the final safehouse we would ever need. I called it Plan Z."

An hour or so later, we were set up inside the house with a makeshift studio built in front of a roaring fire. Director Frente stood next to the camera while one of the techs fiddled with some final checks.

"We'll only have thirty seconds of access before they find us and shut us down," the tech said. "They closed down all our other nodes of access. Once I lose this one, it's all over, so make it count."

"No pressure," Margaret said with a smile.

"You'll do great." I squeezed her shoulder. "Let's do this."

Director Frente nodded and pointed to us as the camera began to roll.

I took a deep breath. "You have won, King Ulthar. The rebellion is effectively dead. Those of us left have scattered to the wind. We do not wish to hide from you. We are still willing to turn ourselves in. However, we demand the safety of our remaining freedom fighters in return— seventeen lives, for the two of ours. If you agree, call the encrypted line embedded in this file in five minutes. Please, we don't want any more bloodshed."

The tech drew a line across his neck and the line cut out. "We're out."

Margaret exhaled. "Now, we wait."

We didn't have to wait for long. A minute later, the phone rang. Director Frente beckoned me over and held up the phone to my ear. A familiar voice growled on the other line. "Your terms are acceptable. Come alone, or I swear we will destroy your rebellion on live television, and if they so much as poke their head up for the rest of their lives…we will end them."

The line cut and I placed the phone back on the hook. Margaret tugged on my arm. "Well, what did he say?"

"We're on." I looked over at Director Frente. "They are definitely tracking our location now."

"Good thing we won't be here long." She tossed me the keys to the van. "You take this. We'll get the others to Kimberly's rendezvous location. Once you're inside, we have no way of communicating with you."

"You have Kimberly, and that's all you need. Trust in her like I trust in her."

"That is a lot of pressure," Kimberly said, then broke into a smile. "Luckily, I thrive under pressure."

***

"We're probably going to die," I pulled onto the main road toward the palace. I was surprisingly calm. "Definitely."

"Yeah, this is not how I thought I would be spending my teenage years."

"Do you forgive her?" I asked.

"Who?"

"Your mother. She was overbearing, yes, but she also tried to protect you from this."

"She should have told me." Margaret gritted her teeth. "I'm not a child. If she had just told me, I wouldn't have hated her so much—I'll never forgive her for making me hate her." She was crying hard, her back heaving as she tried to calm herself. "The day—I yelled at her when she locked me in my room—now, I see it as the panic of a frightened woman, someone desperate to make sure I was safe. She should have told me. I could have helped her."

"Yeah, parents are always saying they know more than you, and they know how to help you as if you're a baby for your whole life. In the past month, I've fought demons and kings, saved myself and been saved, been fired upon by guns and literal fire, and been in mortal peril more times than I can count. I'm stronger than my mother thought when she was trying to shield me from everything." I bit my cheek. "Still, I wish I had told her I loved her because now I'm probably never going to see her again—I wish I could talk to her one more time."

"I moved a lot in my life, often in the dead of night, and one thing I can tell you for sure is that you always want one more conversation with the people you miss, no matter what. Even if you had a wonderful last conversation—even if you have a perfect day, you will never not want to talk to them again." Margaret turned to the window. "Maybe it's a blessing my mom's dead because I know I can never see her again. It hurts. It really hurts, but there's a finality to it."

I knew better. Death was not the end. Araphel taught me that. He showed me that death was only the beginning—that we have torture and pain to look forward to—or at least people like Margaret did. For me, it was an eternity of servitude if I didn't kill King Ulthar in the next couple of hours.

***

My chest tightened with every turn of the tires, and I fought my hand's natural instincts to turn the other way and escape. My rational brain kept trying to remind my gut that we had a plan, and we couldn't give up now, but my instincts didn't want to hear it. My whole body screamed to flee my destiny. Even if it meant the death of everyone else, at least I would be alive.

I felt like a coward thinking something so horrible when so many people depended on me to be strong and brave. Then again, maybe brave was doing the stupid thing even when your body burned with the urge to be a coward and save yourself.

"Are we really going to do this?" Margaret asked as we neared the palace gates.

"There's no turning back now," I replied.

"That's not true. We can absolutely turn back. We can go underground. We can save ourselves."

"What kind of life would we live? You've already lived a life full of hiding and fleeing. Is that what you want to go back to? Not me. That's not living. And after this, I want to live."

"But you said it yourself. We're probably—definitely—going to die."

I gripped the steering wheel. "There are worse things than death."

Were there? Or was I just trying to convince myself? Baron Samedi was the god of the underworld after all. Perhaps, when King Ulthar captured him, it sent the underworld into chaos. Perhaps if we died and he stayed captured, I would not be forced into servitude.

Last chance, Anjelica, I said to myself as I passed the final checkpoint for the palace. *No, I am doing this, even if I die in the process.*

I spun the wheel toward the gate at the entrance to the castle and stopped in front of two intimidating Jackboots. The one on my side of the van stepped forward as I rolled down my window.

"Business?" she growled, her dead eyes staring at me menacingly.

"Do you recognize me? I'm Anjelica, and this is Margaret." I pointed to the passenger seat. "We have a meeting with the king. He should be expecting me."

The Jackboot pressed a button on the edge of the gate. It swung open, and she walked toward me again. "Go to the entrance. Leave your van with the valet, and the king's butler will come to escort you inside. On a personal note, I just want to say that I hope you burn in Hell for all eternity for what you have done."

My eyes narrowed. "Same to you."

Burn in Hell. Ever since I came here, all I had done was try to defend myself. Yes, some people had died, but the king she defended had destroyed an entire country. She's telling *me* to burn in Hell? *Breathe, Anjelica. Breathe.* People hate what they don't understand.

I stepped out of the van and grabbed the wheelchair from the back before lowering Margaret into it and pushing her toward the palace, which was, admittedly, spectacular.

Blood money built it, but it was still magnificent. Behind us, a large stone wall blocked us from the streets, and high white stone buildings rose from the other three sides, higher even than the walls, with hundreds of windows glaring down. Every window had a stone gable etched with intricate flowers and angels, and the motif continued to the porticos and columns that buttressed the awning over the door. A familiar face appeared when the door opened. It was no butler that came to collect us. It was Prince Yimnit, pushing a golden wheelchair. He looked at us and smiled.

"You have a terrible habit of staying alive, did you know that?" He wheeled the chair down the ramp on the edge of the stairs. "I'm sure you realize we can't let anything into the palace, but not to worry, we have provided this wheelchair for you."

Margaret didn't argue. It didn't matter which wheelchair she used. That wasn't part of the plan. "So, are you going to kill me, brother?"

Prince Yimnit laughed, leaning into her. "How could I? You're the only way I will become king this night." He looked over at me. "Is that not so?"

I was shocked into silence for a moment, but I regained myself. "I don't know what you are talking about."

Prince Yimnit laughed. "Very well, keep your secrets. I will take you to see my father, who is simply giddy to see you again, sister."

CHAPTER 47

"Why is Margaret so important to you?" I asked Prince Yimnit as we walked through the foyer of the palace, which was as ostentatious, no, more so, than anything I had seen before. Long purple banners embroidered with large cursive U's fell from a high ceiling carved with angels, gods, flowers, and demons. Elegant tapestries hung from every wall, depicting King Ulthar, usually topless, as he fought bears and armies in equal measure. Somebody had an inferiority complex, that was for sure.

"Did you know that King Ulthar had two sons when he came to this world?" Prince Yimnit asked as if he was asking my favorite color. "Of course you didn't. Any information on my brother Clevin was expunged from the records. When I came here, I was four, just barely old enough to remember, and my brother, he had just been born, one of a set."

"Twins?" Margaret said.

"Yes," Prince Yimnit said. "Powerful magic in twins."

"What happened to him?" she asked.

Prince Yimnit bit his lip angrily. "My father—our father—was obsessed with returning home to my mother. He found an ancient spell that would allow him to travel on the paths of the gods again, but it required a sacrifice from his own world to light the way."

"Oh no," I said, slowing. "He didn't."

He nodded. "He killed my brother to open the path, but when it opened, I got scared and ran away. The bridge was unstable, and my father had to make a choice, my life or you and mother's. He charged my uncle, his cavalier, with finding your mother and bringing you back home while he stayed back with me. A slight he has never allowed me to forget."

Margaret sighed. "My mother…she's dead…"

"I see," Prince Yimnit said. "How?"

"In battle with your uncle," I said. "They came for Margaret, for both of them, and I guess she died in the crossfire."

"Horrible." Prince Yimnit thought for a moment. "Our uncle was supposed to use you as a sacrifice, just like the king used Clevin years earlier, to return my mother to him. I don't think anyone thought it would take so long to find you. Mother must have been a powerful witch."

Margaret nodded. "She was."

Prince Yimnit sighed. "After my brother's sacrifice, my father set about making a life here and found that he had the power to charm the royals of this place. Eventually, he set about building an empire." Prince Yimnit turned to Margaret. "With your blood, he will return to Earth and claim what he believes is his birthright, the complete domination of two worlds."

"He's awful," I said. "We have to stop him."

Prince Yimnit continued with us down the hall. "And so you shall. I have done unspeakable things in his name, and tonight that all ends, by your hand."

"Why couldn't you kill him?" I asked, following next to him.

"I am not strong enough to go against my own father. It is my great shame."

"I don't trust you," I grumbled.

"Nor should you. And yet, it seems to be your only choice."

"No," I whispered to him. From the corner of my eye, a pink cloud of smoke flashed. It was Kimberly, bringing Director Frente's troops. "I could kill you both, father and son."

Prince Yimnit laughed. "And how would your puny rebellion quell the unrest in the city? You are twenty left, if that. We still have an army. No, you need me if you hope to have peace." He stopped in front of the doors to the throne room. "Let us get through this one thing and then deal with the next."

He clapped his hands, and two Jackboots opened the golden doors. We walked into the hall, which felt much bigger without a thousand different nobles inside staring at us. The last time I was in this room, with Madam Fantasmo, the gods rest her soul, it felt small and claustrophobic. Now, it seemed as though a football field could squeeze inside of it, or at least a small basketball court.

The doors that I hadn't noticed my first time in the throne room were open now, and I could see the glowing cylinder in the next room, tended by a squad of Jackboots. We approached the throne, where King Ulthar sat, clutching the massive scepter.

"I have brought them to you, Father," Prince Yimnit said.

The king's eyes were stone cold, narrowing into little beads. "These are the children that have caused so much trouble." He stood. "Look at them. They are puny and wretched. It is an insult that they have been able to do so much to thwart our efforts." He walked down toward us. "Still, you have done little more than irritate, like a pebble in the shoe of a giant." He spun around me. "Your deaths will show there is nowhere that is not under our watchful eye, and no one can contend with my reign, even if they come from beyond the stars." Turning to Margaret, he said. "And you will return me to the world I once knew, this time as a conquering hero."

Gunshots rang out from the hallway, and the Jackboots clattered through the hall, trying to defend against our ambush. The lights to the room fell, though the light from the cylinder still burned brightly.

"What is happening?" the king shouted.

"The rebellion must be mounting a final assault!" Prince Yimnit said.

The king screamed to the Jackboots. "Take them down! Leave none alive!" As the Jackboots filed out of the room, King Ulthar smiled at me. "I only knew you should try something so foolis—"

A flash of pink light exploded behind him, and blood fell down his royal purple robe. Kimberly pulled the dagger out of the king's back and wiped it on her coat. Then, she held it up again toward Prince Yimnit.

"That was so very satisfying." She lunged for the prince. "And now, for you."

"Wait!" I shouted, holding her back for an instant. "We might need him for the transition."

"No," Kimberly growled. "We need to kill him now before his evil spreads. We have this one chance to—"

Prince Yimnit clapped his hands, and a shockwave shot out, knocking Margaret and me back toward the throne. "Fools. Do you really think this was about a silly throne?"

"Yes," Margaret replied. "You're saying it's not?"

"My father thought so small." Prince Yimnit advanced on us. "He wanted to use the power of the gods, but I found that with the right weapon, you can *become* a god!"

"A weapon?" Margaret said.

"Yes, little sister." He reached down and pried the scepter from his dead father's hands. "What is bound inside this scepter can bend the will of a god." He gazed at it and then, in one swift motion, smashed it into the ground until it shattered. From inside of the scepter, he pulled out a long two-handed sword. Prince Yimnit gripped its hilt. "With this weapon, I will become a god."

"I can't let you do that!" I screamed, rushing toward him.

Prince Yimnit raised his hand and ice shot from it. "I have learned new tricks since last we met!"

I fell back toward Kimberly. The moment I touched her, she flashed us to the other side of the room, where she grabbed me and flung me toward Prince Yimnit. I curled into a ball and hit him in the stomach with all the force I could muster. He fell backward, and Margaret pushed out her hands to cast a fireball. It didn't have to kill him. It just had to be a distraction. I ran toward the cylinder, and as I passed Kimberly, I screamed, "Keep him busy!"

I sprinted toward the device in the next room. It had only been moments since the king died, and the Jackboots were making their way back toward me. *Unberiler,* I said under my breath, searching the console until I found it.

"Hey!" The Jackboots raised their guns. "Stop there!"

I ignored them. I ran around the device until I found it, in big letters. *Unberiler.* I flipped up the panel below and found three wires—yellow, blue, and black. What was the order? *Think, Anjelica.* The shouts were getting louder and mixing with gunfire. I drowned them all out, every one of them, and thought back to the underworld and the words of Doctor Jortensur. The answer entered my brain from the ether: *Blue, yellow, black.* I cut the wires in that order. When I was done, I pressed the panel down again and slammed the button. The whole room went white.

I barely felt the light against my cheek as my shirt filled with wet, sticky blood. I counted three bullets before I fell to the ground, gasping and wheezing, and then there was darkness.

CHAPTER 48

I splashed into an inky black pool of tar. Gasping, I swam to the surface. As I did, two disembodied hands pulled me from the ooze and brought me to shore, where I dripped like a wet dog. I sucked in air, even though I knew I was not in need of it, not anymore.

I looked up to see Araphel seated on a bench, patting for me to sit next to him. "I'm dead, aren't I?"

"Right now, you are in the between." Araphel looked straight ahead. "I am concentrating on your aura, trying to buy your friends additional seconds to save you."

"Did we win?"

"It would seem so. You saved Baron Samedi, who turned the battle in your favor. Of course, having a god on your side has a tendency to do that. It took them ninety seconds to find you after the carnage stopped." He looked over at me. "If you didn't have demon blood inside of you, there would have been nothing I could have done for you."

"It seems to be all sorts of helpful, doesn't it?"

"And you won your soul, too, in the end." Araphel nodded at no one in particular. "Oh, good. It looks like you are going home after all."

I looked down at my hands. They were fading out. "Is this a good thing?"

"Only if you like being alive."

"I really do." I faded from the darkness. "Corny as that might be."

My eyes blinked open, and I was inside the throne room. I sat up gasping for air, for real this time. Baron

Samedi knelt next to me while Margaret and Kimberly stood behind him.

"You are very lucky," Baron Samedi said. "Lucky that I am a benevolent deity and that I was in a magnanimous mood."

My chest burned, but when I looked for the bullet holes, they had healed. "What a load of crap. We saved you! It only makes sense that you would return the favor."

He helped me to my feet. "That would be human rationality. The gods do not keep the same logic."

"Then…thank you, I guess."

"And thank you, little one. I did not think you would be able to deliver me this king of yours. He is even more terrible than you described."

"What about the prince?" I said, looking around suddenly. He was dead on the floor. "Good riddance."

"Looks like you were wrong," Margaret said. "We didn't probably definitely die."

"Speak for yourself." I coughed as if hot lead still filled my lungs.

***

It took several weeks for the dust to settle. The capital royals all sided with the king, but it didn't take much convincing to bring in our own reinforcements once other countries learned that the king had been deposed. Within a month, the political situation had been attenuated to a seething unrest.

Director Frente decided that a constitutional monarchy in the way I'd described it was a good course of action, at least for the short-term stability of the realm. When it came to appointing a leader, there was nobody better qualified than Margaret, who agreed to be coronated and then oversee turning the monarchy into a republic.

"This is quite a way for your prophecy to come true," I said with a smile.

"Oh yeah." Margaret said as we stood in the throne room where just days ago, we had killed a king. "I forgot about that. I guess it did come true, didn't it? Man, that's weird."

"Are you sure? About staying here, I mean." The coronation, though it was broadcast on national television, had been a small, quiet affair. We still had no idea who in the royal court we could trust.

"I am," she replied. "I will need a counsel, you know? And the new country will need a prime minister. I think you would be great for either role."

I laughed. "So, you want me to sit behind a desk all day? No thanks."

"I didn't think so," Margaret said. "But can I ask you a favor, in my capacity as queen?"

"Of course, your majesty." I bowed. "I still can't believe I'm calling you that, but of course."

"Our standing is low in the world, and as we're rebuilding our reputation and giving the other countries back their lands, I would like for you to stay and help with that effort, at least until we are stable."

"How long will that be?" I asked.

She smiled. "Not long. One or two lifetimes, max."

I squeezed her hands. "This is not my home."

"Home is where our heart is. There is nothing for you back on Earth. Here, you can have everything and be part of something important."

I nodded. "This is a big choice. Can I think about it?"

"Yes, but not long. We need to get started immediately."

***

I waited in my dreams for Araphel's hands to pull me down into the darkness, but they didn't come, not for weeks after the siege of King Ulthar's castle. Then, one day, I felt a familiar tug on my leg, and I smiled as it dragged me away.

Araphel materialized at the kitchen table of my house and slid a pile of pancakes in front of me. He sat in a chair next to me, while the chair across from me, piled high with another stack of pancakes, rested empty.

"Where were you?" I asked. "I waited for you."

"You had a big decision to make, and I didn't want to come until you made it."

"Then you know," I said.

He nodded. "It was a difficult decision, I'm sure, but I think the best for all parties involved."

"You will still take Kimberly back, won't you?"

"Of course. She has much work to do on her planet, though not as much as you have on this one."

I looked down at the pancakes. "Did I make the right choice?"

"For you."

I shook my head. "I don't mean just about staying here. I mean…did I make the right choice, helping to bring down the king?"

"That was the only choice. Despots and autocrats destroy the natural order. They yearn for power, and if left to their own devices, they can upset the balance of the universe. Only the gods were meant to wield such power, and we have had an eternity to learn how to wield it properly."

"And you still get it wrong sometimes."

"Yes, that too." He sighed. "I have brought someone to say goodbye to you. Think of it as a parting gift for saving the world."

He snapped his fingers, and my mother was there, smiling. The wrinkles on the edges of her eyes and creases in her cheeks had grown deeper since I'd last seen her, and her blonde hair was mostly white with age and worry.

"Hi, kiddo," she said. "It's good to see you're safe."

"Safe is an operative word." I turned to Araphel. "Is this…real?"

He nodded. "Of course. It might be a dream, but it is also very real."

I smiled my own broad smile. "Hi, Mom. I'm so sorry that I left."

She clasped her hands in front of her chest. "It took time to understand, but Araphel helped me appreciate what it means for you to stay and how much danger you are in on Earth. God, I really mucked it up, kiddo. I should be the one apologizing to you."

"Maybe we should just both say we're sorry for the little hells we put each other through."

She started to cry, and then I did too. We stood and wrapped our arms around each other and stayed there for a long while, listening to each other breathe, hearing our hearts beat against the other's chest. We had never been closer, even a universe away.

It would be okay. Even if it all went belly up, it would be okay. I believed that deep down in the bowels of my soul. I had to. It was the only way to have any hope in this crazy universe.

***

You have just finished *Evil,* but there is so much Godsverse left to go. Keep reading after the author's note to get a sneak preview of *Time*, starring Anjelica's adopted sister Lizzie in a brand-new solo adventure.

AUTHOR'S NOTE

I rewatched all *The Hunger Games* movies and started rereading the series while I wrote this book. Can you tell? I've written a couple of dystopian books in my day, *The Vessel* and *The Marked Ones* among them. I suppose you could make a claim that a couple of the Godsverse stories are dystopian, but not in that *The Hunger Games* kind of way.

Most of the heroines of the Godsverse are fully powered, capable women, so having a naïve and frightened main character, a fresh-faced teenager without any idea how to control her powers, was interesting to me. I love how Anjelica grew from her start in *Magic* to leading her own book.

One of the most important parts of having a "new" heroine who hasn't had time to get hardened is that Anjelica isn't callused over yet. She cries, a lot. I don't think the other characters in the Godsverse cried more than a handful of times in all the other books in this universe. However, Anjelica cries all the time. Her strength comes from being scared, or being wounded, and continuing anyway.

Kimberly talked about this with her at the end of the first part of this story, where she says that to do the work of being a hero, you need to be hard, otherwise life will beat you down. Anjelica proved that theory wrong time and time again throughout this story, being both heroic and vulnerable at the same time.

Because this story is so different from any other story in the Godsverse, I was nervous writing it. When Anjelica gets sucked through the portal and ends up in a new world,

I asked myself, "what am I doing?" Traveling to other worlds is a staple of the Godsverse, but never so far into the story. I had just established her new life, for jeepers creepers, only to rip her away from it. I did that for a reason, though. It was important to show who Anjelica was and what she was giving up before tearing it all away from her. All of that meant that it took a bit longer for everything to coalesce.

This was more of a slow burn, while *Magic,* for instance, literally started in the middle of everything. It's important for me to make all the books in the Godsverse "feel" like they are written in the same style, in the same universe, but also feel like their own thing. It's not easy to do, especially when you have so many books, all overlapping with new characters smashing into each other. I've been writing this series since 2017, and I've changed a lot since then, so falling back into my old rhythms is always a challenge. It was really hard not to devolve this into a straight dystopian sci-fi book, and I had to work against those instincts to keep infusing it with fantasy elements.

Having different worlds that all kind of look the same, but are at different stages of development, is a big part of the Godsverse, and while I've touched on it in other stories, it's never been quite so apparent as in this story. Even Rebecca only touches on the other worlds in *Doom,* and none of the other books deal with it very much at all.

So, having this story was important for me, and an important addition to the Godsverse mythos. You also get the inclusion of Caribbean mythology with Baron Samedi, one of my favorites of all the gods in any pantheon. In every book, I try to introduce more gods from different pantheons.

If you're reading this as the second book in the series, you might be really confused right now, but this is the **_ninth_** Godsverse book that I've written, even though it's only the second in the series order. The first book I wrote in the series is *Deathr.* It continues from there, wraps around to *Magic,* and then this book.

Because this is both the second and ninth book in this series, it was important to introduce you to some of the high concepts of the Godsverse while also making it accessible to new readers. The later books in the Godsverse are excellent, but they are not easily accessible for new readers, which was the whole reason I took this project on in the first place. I decided that to get people into those later books, I needed to have a better introduction to the series, which is really weird. I don't know if I've ever seen an author just completely blow up their series and write multiple new entries at the beginning. My intention is that there will be four novels before *Death.* I've seen people write one new book to begin a series, but four? Nope.

I hope it shows you just how much I love the Godsverse to write so many additional books to give people a better entry point into the universe. I know if you get to the later books, you'll love them. People told me for years that as much as they loved the Godsverse, it was hard to bring somebody into the universe. I hope these first two books in the series help do that in a fun and exciting way for new and existing readers alike.

I hope you loved it. If you did, then you should check out *Heaven*, where Anjelica plays a pivotal role, along with Kimberly, who pops up all over the universe. If you haven't read *Magic* yet, make sure to check out the origin of Anjelica's adventure in the pages of Ollie's book, where there's another cameo from Kimberly as well.

***

Now, here is a sneak peek of *Time*.

TIME

Book 3 of The Godsverse Chronicles

By
Russell Nohelty

Edited by:
Leah Lederman

Proofread by:
Katrina Roets

Cover by:
Psycat Covers

Planet chart and timeline design by:
Andrea Rosales

CHAPTER 1

In the ashes of her past, she will rise, and her death will save us all.

My mom thought getting a psychic reading would be a good birthday present. After all, I was constantly worried about the future ever since my adopted sister disappeared through a portal into another world and never returned. Even though the pixie Kimberly came back and told me that Anjelica was just fine on whatever planet she'd ended up on, that didn't make me feel much better. I mean, I was happy she wasn't dead but—well, I didn't even know being whisked across the universe was a possible future for somebody. I was only twelve and hyper-impressionable, so I became rather obsessed with the idea that something I couldn't even fathom would come out of left field and suck out my soul, or vaporize me, or turn me into a toadstool for the rest of my life.

No matter how many times my mom, Junebug, told me, "Lizzie, you're being a drama queen," I had one irrefutable piece of evidence that proved my worries were warranted. After all, it happened to my sister, or at least the closest thing to a sister I ever had. We weren't blood, and I only knew her for a week, but Junebug and Carl adopted her all the same, just like they had me, and that made us family. They never made that mistake again, unfortunately, which made me an only child, at least on this planet, what with Angelica living her life somewhere across the galaxy.

The town we lived in—Bronard, Missouri—had a lot of weird people in it. Some might even call them monsters. I don't know what drew so much fairy folk and monsters to our little piece of America, but Mom liked to boast that we had the most fairy folk per capita anywhere in the contiguous United States. I didn't know if that was true. It's one of those unverifiable pieces of Americana, like the world's biggest ball of wax or the biggest ham sandwich. Sure, maybe even Guinness would back us, but there's no saying somebody didn't make a bigger sandwich just for laughs. It was a big sandwich we had in Bronard though, and fairy folk were the meat inside of it, that much I knew. We weren't cannibals or anything, I'm just bad at metaphors.

One of the most unique of all the fairy folk that lived in Bronard was the Oracle, just like the ones that used to reside in Delphi. They said this one was a descendant of theirs, but that was just hearsay—little towns ran on gossip, and Bronard was no different. Nobody really knew the truth about the Oracle for sure. Most people kept clear of her since she rarely gave good news. The best you could hope was that her prophecy had nothing useful in it at all and just said you were gonna be a boring sod plowing sod for the rest of your life. That's what I was hoping for, at least, when I'd gotten my reading.

Mom had thought it would be a good idea to get me one, even with all the warning signs, if for no other reason than to prove that I was destined to live a simple, old life, helping her with the bakery and helping Dad with the farm. Might seem like a boring life to some people, but that's all I wanted. I didn't need to become a space pope. I just wanted a little piece of Earth and a little peace of mind.

That's not how things worked out, though.

I remembered every moment, every aching syllable, of our interaction. It stuck to me like a wet shirt.

Mom brought me to Starr Wolfsong—what a name for an Oracle— a couple of days after my sixteenth birthday in 1990, back before cell phones or AOL, when we still had to play phone tag to catch somebody instead of checking their away message. It was a simpler time, though maybe it was just simpler for me.

The Oracle lived in a trailer park, in a double-wide that sunk as we stepped up to it, creaking at us to stay away. We didn't listen. It was double for Mom to sit and listen to the fortune, and when she asked if I wanted her to stay, I shook my head. I was a brave girl. I could handle it, or so I thought.

"Would you like half my grilled cheese?" Starr asked with a hoarse voice, her gray-skinned hand wobbling as she held out her bony arm to me.

"No, thanks," I said.

Starr looked unhealthily gaunt, skin hanging off little more than bones as if the muscles underneath had melted away. She lit a cigarette and took a deep inhale, and then blew it out the open window next to her. The whole of the trailer reeked of smoke and misery which, even without the woman looking like she would keel over any moment, was enough to make me lose my appetite.

"I sense apprehension in you," she said through her thin lips. "If I may offer you a piece of advice. You will not like what you hear, so I suggest you leave now."

"How do you know?"

She ran her bony fingers through strands of thinning hair. "I have lived too many years and performed too many readings. Were I a charlatan, I could pretend that I don't see the death of every soul that walks through my trailer. If I were a better showman, I might be able to imbue my prophesies with an ounce of hope." She coughed a wet cough into her hand for a long moment before catching my eyes again. "People do not want the truth. If they did, I would be as rich as Miss Cleo or any of them who prey on the insecure. People pay for comforting lies, not harsh truths."

"My mother seems to think it will help me."

Starr flicked the cigarette out of her hand, and it landed in a puddle of muddy water. She turned to me, setting her hands face up in the middle of the table. "Place your hands in mine, and your fate will be known—though I warn you: None get out of this world alive."

"Are you saying you will see my death?"

She took a shallow breath, wheezing as she let it out. "I do not know what I will see. That is the nature of my power. I am a slave to it."

I nodded and slowly, gingerly placed my hands inside hers. The moment I did, a shock jolted through my body as if my fingers were touching an electrical wire. I opened my mouth, trying to scream, but before I could, the sensation passed, and my body relaxed.

Starr was still, her eyeballs rolled back into her head so that only the bloodshot whites were visible. She muttered under her breath for a long moment, her voice barely audible. With every loop of her circuitous words, I made them more clearly until they filled my soul with dread.

"In the ashes of her past, she will rise, and her death will save us all," the Oracle gurgled like her mouth was filled with water. "In the ashes of her past, she will rise, and her death will save us all."

She continued in that manner until her words boomed against the walls, echoing off every surface. I tried to pull my hands from her clutches, but her weak arms held me tightly, no matter how hard I pulled back.

"Stop!" I shouted. "STOP! MOM!"

The door slammed open, and my mother saw what horror she wrought on me as she heard Starr's screaming words. "In the ashes of her past, she will rise, and her death will save us all!"

Seeing the dread in my face, Mom reached forward to pry me free from the Oracle's fingers. When her hands weren't strong enough by themselves, she ran to the kitchen and pulled a butter knife out of the drawer. She wedged it under the woman's knuckles and wrenched me away, one finger at a time.

When I was finally free, Starr's shrieking stopped, and she fell onto the table, limp. She wasn't dead, but she had been knocked unconscious.

"Should we call an ambulance?" I asked.

"Don't bother." A woman stepped out from the hallway. She had big red hair like Reba McEntire and a gruff, gritty voice like she gargled with rocks. "Happens three times a week, and she couldn't afford the ambulance ride even if you did call." She brushed past me. "Just go. I'll take care of her." She turned back to me and narrowed her eyes. "I hope it was worth it."

It wasn't, but I didn't say that. Instead, I looked over at Mom, who made her way out of the trailer. There was a deep shame in her eyes like she'd known what would happen. Or maybe she knew what I would do next.

In the ashes of her past, she will rise, and her death will save us all.

I spent the next week thinking, ruminating over those words. I went back to the trailer park, looking for the Oracle, but she had packed up and left town. I was the straw that broke her back, apparently, and I didn't quite know how to feel about my prophecy causing such a reaction in her that she had no recourse but to flee town.

The only thing I knew for sure was that Carl and Junebug, my parents, were in trouble. They were my past and they were my present. I did not want them to turn to ash so that I could rise. I didn't want any of it, and I especially didn't want to be a savior.

I did the only thing that I could think of to save my parents. I ran away and didn't stop running. Maybe it was a rash decision, but it was the right one. I was sure of it. It was hard at first, moving from town to town the minute I caught feeling for something or someone, desperate not to have a past, so there would be nothing to burn.

Over the next ten years, it got easier, at least that's what I told myself. Nothing like a comforting lie to help you sleep at night.

CHAPTER 2

My latest home was a small town called Oakmont, California, far from the hustle and bustle of places like Los Angeles and San Francisco. Most people think that the Golden State is all glitz and glamour, full of coastal liberal elites, movie stars, and beaches. Really, most of California was farm country, filled with farmers, truckers, and people who worked with their hands.

Sure, Los Angeles had an outmoded influence in the state, but even at a million square miles, it was a fraction of the total land in the state. Oakmont rested above San Francisco and east of Napa Valley, up where the slanted coastline turned straight for Oregon. I had worked up in Oregon as a waitress for three months before somebody caught feelings for me, and I left.

There were a few keys to being able to leave a place in the dead of night at the drop of a hat. First, you needed a crappy job that paid you in cash at regular intervals. You couldn't spend two weeks waiting for that last paycheck. It also helped to have a job you hated. It was another bonus if they didn't ask questions about your work history. Any job that needed a resume was out. Waitressing fit all those things at once. Almost all my wages were made in tips that I pocketed at the end of the night, and it was terrible work that I absolutely hated.

Nothing against the profession. I knew there were people who liked waitressing and were much better at it than me. I didn't have the personality for it. Getting yelled at for getting an order wrong, standing on your feet for twelve hours, and smelling like greasy, sweaty, swamp ass after a long shift was not my idea of a good time, not to mention the pay was crap, even in bigger cities—though I almost never stopped in those since they were too expensive.

So that's the first and second key to life on the road, I guess. The third, final, and most important, was that you could never form an attachment to anyone, no matter what. My rule was that I couldn't stay in a place more than six months even if I liked it because just being around people enough made me like them and liking somebody was a good way to build a past with them, and I didn't want anyone to burn because of me.

I would never admit it to his face, but that's the reason I left the last town. I liked a boy too much. His name was Tom, and I liked him enough that I was already considering leaving before he admitted the attraction was mutual, and it pushed me over the edge. If I was honest with myself, I probably stayed too long even before Tom confessed his love for me, all because of a serious bout of lonely, and he was the treatment. A stout, gentle, country boy, who always said "please" and "thank you" after ordering, and called me ma'am, no matter how many times I told him to call me Lizzie.

There were Toms all over the country, ghosts of lives I might have had if I stayed in Bronard, if I'd had the simple future I wanted. It seemed like at least twice a year, I fell for somebody in one town or another along the road, and it was happening more frequently with each passing season. It was a lonely life, and I was still a warm-blooded woman at the end of the day. It was all I could do not to act on my impulses…but I never did. I hadn't even kissed anyone since my boyfriend, Pete, in high school.

He had been the hardest one to leave. We were together since middle school—since Anjelica taught me how to flirt so, I could get his attention. He would have graduated college already. I often wondered about what he was doing, but he was my past—a past I was trying to protect by being on the run. I wasn't doing him any favors by keeping him in my thoughts.

I was in Oakmont now, and the present was where I needed to focus my attention. I had been working at Murray's for four weeks since blowing into town and was just getting the hang of the regulars who came in for their morning breakfast before work and the ones that caught me on the way home after their shift.

It always amazed me how every town was the same. They all had their little diners, at least one that had the best pancakes in town and another that made its money by being open later than the others, even though their food was average.

Murray's was the former. I had worked in dozens, maybe hundreds at this point, and every one of them had their own little customer base, and they always tipped better if you remembered their orders by heart.

"Short stack, over easy, with a cup of joe?" I asked a bearded man with long, black hair and olive skin. His name was Jeff, and I appreciated that his order was simple and consistent. There were bigger orders than Jeff's, and bigger tippers, too, but Jeff was quiet and polite, with dark brown eyes that you could get lost in forever. Yes, I certainly had a type.

"That's right, ma'am," he said, and I bit the inside of my lip to stop from letting out a little moan. It got harder and harder to deny my body's needs. We were pack animals, after all, and forced celibacy was driving me nutty. "And could you bring some sugar and cream, too?"

"Of course, sugar," I said with a playful smile that oozed with unintentional flirtation. "Be right back."

I wrote down the order and slid it into the queue on the kitchen counter. A big, gruff bull named Oscar spun the orders around the belt until he grabbed it, grunted, and then went to work.

"What are you waiting for?" Victoria, one of the other waitresses, the nosey one who's always up in everyone's business—every workplace I've ever been at had one like her—said to me. "He is Heaven on a stick."

I shook my head. "He's not my type."

"Pardon my French," Victoria said. "But that's a load of bull. I see the way he looks at you, and I hear the lilt in your voice when you chat with him. Not to mention the bounce in your step when you walk away from his table."

"There is no bounce!" I replied, indignant.

"You're lying to yourself, kiddo." Victoria shook her head. "That's the worst kind of lying."

The bell rang behind me, and an order came up. "Comforting lies are all I have."

I grabbed the order and brought two plates to a couple of truckers in the corner that I didn't recognize. Since it was a small town, ninety percent or so of the customers were regulars, and if I didn't recognize them by now, it meant they were probably just passing through. The diner wasn't far from the freeway, which made it convenient for long haulers to stop off for a meal while they were on the road. Once I served the truckers, I went to fill up water glasses for a family of four on a road trip, and a woman eating alone, drinking coffee like it was going out of style.

The whole time, I kept the side of my eye on Jeff, thinking about what Victoria had said. Maybe it would be okay to have a one-night stand with—no, that's how it started. One night became ten, and before long, you had a past and a future, and then you were dead.

I spent a lot of time thinking about not risking anybody's life, but I would be lying if I didn't admit the biggest reason I was avoiding my prophecy was to prevent my own death. Yes, the past would burn, but when it did, I would die…and I didn't want to die.

"Order up!"

I picked up Jeff's order from the window and brought it over to him.

"Looks delicious," he replied with a smile. "Oscar's talents are lost in a place like this."

"Yeah, they're really lucky to have him, I guess." I turned around. "I'll be right back with your coffee."

I rushed behind the counter; my breath hurried with teenage adrenaline just from being near Jeff. I needed to calm down. This wasn't like me. I was cool, controlled, and focused. He was only a guy—one of a hundred guys I'd crushed on over the years, who vanished out of my brain the moment I was a hundred miles away.

I brought the coffee and set it down next to Jeff. He took it with a smile, and when I turned away, he cleared his throat.

"Yes?" I said, turning back to him but trying to avoid his fiery eyes.

"You forgot the sugar, sugar," he said with a carefree smile.

"Dang it! Right." I grabbed a handful of sugar packets from another table and brought them over to him. "Here you go."

When I set them down, he slid his hand over mine, just for a moment. A flash of electricity flowed through me. I turned to look into his eyes and saw my entire life flash between us. I saw a wedding and children, and happiness…but I also saw a fire, and finally, my death.

I yanked my hand away quickly. I gave him a small smile and turned, taking a big gulp of air. Well, this town was nice while it lasted, but it was time to move on before beautiful Jeff became a casualty of my prophecy, and then, inevitably, I did, too.

CHAPTER 3

I learned very early in my travels that if you wanted to leave at a moment's notice, you had to travel light. Over the years, I only accumulated enough stuff to fill my old purple Jansport from before I dropped out of high school, and a small rolling suitcase where I kept two pairs of jeans, a black pleated skirt, and a black dress, along with enough underwear to last a week, plus two pairs of heels that needed to be repaired or replaced, a pair of slippers, and an extra pair of tennis shoes, along with a puffy coat and a light jacket. In my backpack, I kept a lockpicking kit, toiletries, a small make-up kit, a CD player, whatever books I was reading at the time— I'd just finished Anne Rice's *Interview with a Vampire,* and now it was Dan Brown's *Angels and Demons*—and a first aid kit. For a while, I kept old aprons and nametags from all the places I worked, but I packed in a hurry some years ago and lost them somewhere around Nebraska.

It was for the best because they linked me to my past and the memories I made along the way. As it stood, I tried my best not to keep any clothing for more than a year if I could help it. The only thing I kept from my childhood was a black opal necklace that my mother once gave me for protection.

There was nothing else to bind me to the past, not even my name, which I made sure to change at least once a season whenever I could find a good counterfeiter. Usually, I worked with some high school or college kid who could connect me with somebody that made fake IDs, but they were of dubious quality. I needed them to fool even the police. In a pinch, I could make one, but good equipment wasn't cheap, and I rarely had extra money lying around.

After cleaning out my motel room, I walked to the front desk. There wasn't a fancy name for it or anything. It just said "motel" in big, neon letters that buzzed through the night. Bugz kept the place clean enough, and the price was right. Apropos of the owner's name, the place was littered with cockroaches, but they scattered when the lights were on. I almost always stayed in motels wherever I traveled. I didn't even want to commit to a month-to-month lease.

"Evening, Niobe," Bugz said to me, giving me a smile that showed all four of his chipped front teeth. "What can I do ya for?"

"Checking out, Bugz," I replied.

His face dropped, and he scratched the stubble on his chin. "That's a shame. You were a good tenant. Never made no trouble for me." He leaned in. "Not like some people who come here for all sorts of illicit activities."

"I've heard 'em here and there," I said. "I just try to keep my head down and stay out of trouble."

His face scrunched. "Seems like trouble found you, though, didn't it?"

He pointed past me to a shadow that stood next to my Civic hatchback. I recognized Kimberly's outline immediately, even in the dark. She had a way of standing out when she wanted to look tough, and she had tracked me down enough times that I knew the way she leaned against my car.

I grumbled to myself and put down a wad of money. "Looks that way. This should be enough since I paid up last Friday."

Bugz flipped quickly through the wad of fives and ones, and then nodded. "Seems like it's all there. Take care of yourself, Niobe, ya hear?"

I pushed open the glass door of the office. "I'm trying, but some people aren't making it easy."

I felt like stomping across the parking lot and having it out with Kimberly, but that's exactly what she wanted—to get under my skin—and I wasn't about to give her the satisfaction. Instead, I smiled brightly at her, putting on my best "aggrieved waitress trying desperately to stay sane face", and walked towards her.

"I thought I finally lost you," I said. "How did you find me? This town isn't even on the map."

Kimberly had bangs that cut across her face like Aaliyah, and her black hair was just as shiny. I had no idea how she fought when she could only see out of one eye, but she managed somehow because she was still alive. In her line of work, that meant something. It wasn't just anybody who could track down demons and slaughter them. I was deeply scared of Kimberly the first time she tracked me down but had since numbed to her incredible powers.

"You're getting sloppy," Kimberly said. "You used to drive for days, zig-zagging across the country before you stopped. This one was less than a day's drive, and it seems like you took the 5 all the way down here. You didn't even switch cars. That's amateur." She pushed off the car. "Plus, I got a look at the stash of IDs you keep in the glove box last time, and there are surprisingly few Niobe's in California."

I sighed. "Yeah, I knew I was going to have trouble with those weird names I bought last time. Then again, I figured you would just go away."

"It's been a decade, kiddo. When will you learn I'm never going away?"

"When will you appreciate what I'm trying to do here? Oh right, you don't fear death because you're immortal."

She held up her hands. "I am as the gods made me."

"As Thanatos made you if I remember correctly." I shook my head. "What do you want?"

She sighed. "Junebug is sick. Doctors don't think she's going to make it through the month. She wants to see you before the end."

My fists clenched. I felt my heart thump faster in my chest and the tears well in my eyes, but I did everything in my power to appear calm. "So?"

Kimberly's brow furrowed. "You've been trying to outrun your past—to decouple your emotions from everything you were for over a decade, and one mention of your mom sends you to tears. Maybe that's a good indication running isn't a good idea anymore."

"Goddamn it!" I threw my hands in the air. "I'm doing this to save them."

Kimberly had found me a dozen times before in a dozen cities around the country, and every time she did, she tried to convince me to return home to be with my parents—that I could have a normal life, even knowing what I knew. She tried to tell me that my past wouldn't burn and I wouldn't die. Every time, I sent her back to my parents empty-handed, but now with my mom dying…*how could I not go?*

"That's garbage!" Kimberly screamed. "You're doing this to save yourself. That's fine, honestly, but why don't you think of somebody other than yourself for a change and go see your mother before she dies?"

"All I do is think of other people!" I shouted back. Before the words even left my mouth, the tears began to fall. Big, heaping tears like I hadn't cried in years—like I don't know if I had ever cried, at least not in the past decade. It was as if every emotion I'd siphoned away flooded out of me at once. I collapsed on the ground, right there in that motel parking lot, and curled up in a ball.

"What's going on out here?" Bugz shouted as the door to the motel office flung open. "You okay, Niobe?"

I don't know what I said to him, but whatever I pushed out of my mouth seemed to be enough to satisfy him, and he went back into his office, though when my eyes found the window, I saw him watching me as Kimberly rubbed my back.

Eventually, the tears were gone, and there was nothing left to do but clean myself up. I walked back into the lobby and asked if I could use his bathroom. Graciously, Bugz gave me the key to my old room.

"You still technically have it 'til morning." He smiled at me as I left him.

I didn't notice that Kimberly had followed me inside until I came out of the bathroom and yelped in surprise at her standing there. I thought about saying something vicious but choked it back and sat on the bed, alone, as she sat on the chair across from me.

"What does she have?" I asked.

"Cancer," Kimberly replied.

"What kind?" I whispered, barely able to keep it together.

"One of the bad ones. Pancreas, or at least it metastasized there, and her lungs, and her—the last set of x-rays lit up like Rockefeller Center on Christmas, Lizzie. I think it would be easier to tell you where she doesn't have cancer right now."

"What about chemo? Radiation? Whatever other stuff they have to fight this stuff?"

"She's been sick for a long time," Kimberly said. "She swore me to secrecy. Didn't want me to guilt you into coming home. Now there's nothing left but to wait for the end."

"Why are you telling me?"

"Cuz I want you to see your mom before she dies. She's earned that much. Even if she doesn't want it, she needs it. I think now she's just holding on…she's just holding on to the hope that you'll come home—"

I had never seen Kimberly waver in all my years, but the tears came, even for her. I walked into the bathroom and brought her a roll of toilet paper. She took a few squares and dabbed her eyes, taking a moment.

"Junebug would kill me if she knew I told you this." Kimberly sighed. "Or she would if she wasn't bed— bedridden." She barely choked out the last words, and I felt for her. She was family to my mother, and vice versa.

"If waiting for me to come home is the only thing that's keeping her alive, then I can't go back. I can't be the reason she dies—I can't."

Kimberly nodded, more to herself than me. "I figured you would say that. I hoped maybe this time would be different, but deep down, I knew it wouldn't." She pushed herself off the chair. "You're the most selfish being I've ever met in my whole stupid existence…and I'm including demons into that equation."

"How am I selfish? I'm staying away to save her!"

"No," Kimberly replied. "You're staying away to save yourself. It's okay, like I said. I don't know why I expected this time to be any different."

She reached into a pouch on her belt and pulled out a pinch of pink powder. Without another word, she threw it on the ground and disappeared into a puff of pink smoke. With the lingering smell of burnt ember from Kimberly's smoke, I threw myself on the bed and began to cry again.

***

If you enjoyed that preview, make sure to pick up *Time* today.

ALSO BY RUSSELL NOHELTY

NOVELS
My Father Didn't Kill Himself
Sorry for Existing
Gumshoes: The Case of Madison's Father
Invasion
The Vessel
The Void Calls Us Home
Worst Thing in the Universe
Anna and the Dark Place
The Marked Ones
The Dragon Scourge
The Dragon Champion
The Dragon Goddess
The Obsidian Spindle Saga

COMICS and OTHER ILLUSTRATED WORK
The Little Bird and the Little Worm
Ichabod Jones: Monster Hunter
Gherkin Boy
How NOT to Invade Earth

www.russellnohelty.com

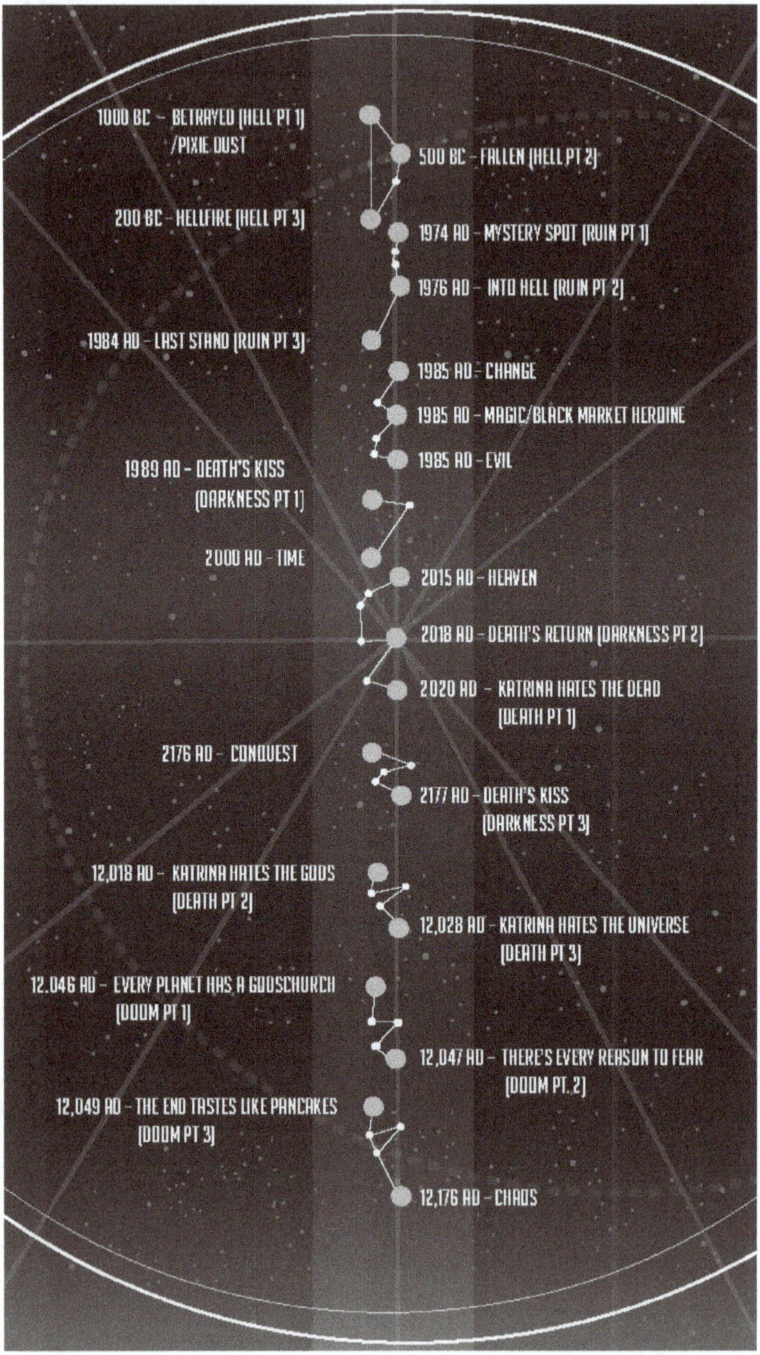

1000 BC – BETRAYED (HELL PT 1)
/PIXIE DUST
500 BC – FALLEN (HELL PT 2)
200 BC – HELLFIRE (HELL PT 3)
1974 AD – MYSTERY SPOT (RUIN PT 1)
1976 AD – INTO HELL (RUIN PT 2)
1984 AD – LAST STAND (RUIN PT 3)
1985 AD – CHANGE
1985 AD – MAGIC/BLACK MARKET HEROINE
1985 AD – EVIL
1989 AD – DEATH'S KISS
(DARKNESS PT 1)
2000 AD – TIME
2015 AD – HEAVEN
2018 AD – DEATH'S RETURN (DARKNESS PT 2)
2020 AD – KATRINA HATES THE DEAD
(DEATH PT 1)
2176 AD – CONQUEST
2177 AD – DEATH'S KISS
(DARKNESS PT 3)
12,018 AD – KATRINA HATES THE GODS
(DEATH PT 2)
12,028 AD – KATRINA HATES THE UNIVERSE
(DEATH PT 3)
12,046 AD – EVERY PLANET HAS A GODSCHURCH
(DOOM PT 1)
12,047 AD – THERE'S EVERY REASON TO FEAR
(DOOM PT. 2)
12,049 AD – THE END TASTES LIKE PANCAKES
(DOOM PT 3)
12,176 AD – CHAOS